D1020489

FURY

FURY

AARON ALLSTON

BALLANTINE BOOKS • NEW YORK

Star Wars: Legacy of the Force: Fury is a work of fiction. Names, places, and incidents either are products of the author's imagination or are used fictitiously.

A Del Rey Books Mass Market Original

Copyright © 2007 by Lucasfilm Ltd. & ® or ™ where indicated.
All Rights Reserved. Used under authorization.

Excerpt from *Star Wars: Legacy of the Force: Revelation* copyright © 2007 by Lucasfilm Ltd. & ® or ™ where indicated. All Rights Reserved. Used under authorization.

Published in the United States by Del Rey Books, an imprint of The Random House Publishing Group, a division of Random House, Inc., New York.

DEL REY is a registered trademark and the Del Rey colophon is a trademark of Random House, Inc.

This book contains an excerpt from the forthcoming book *Star Wars: Legacy of the Force: Revelation* by Karen Traviss. This excerpt has been set for this edition only and may not reflect the final content of the forthcoming edition.

ISBN 978-0-345-47756-9

Printed in the United States of America

www.starwars.com
www.legacyoftheforce.com
www.delreybooks.com

OPM   9 8 7 6 5 4 3

acknowledgments

Thanks go to:

Karen Traviss and Troy Denning, my partners in crime;

Shelly Shapiro, Sue Rostoni, Keith Clayton, and Leland Chee, for making things work right;

My Eagle-Eyes (Chris Cassidy, Kelly Frieders, Helen Keier, Beth Loubet, Bob Quinlan, Roxanne Quinlan, and Luray Richmond), for helping keep my errors down to a necessary minimum;

My agent, Russ Galen; and

Dr. James Dooner, without whose skill and generosity I might not have retained enough vision to finish this book.

THE **STAR WARS** NOVELS TIMELINE

1020 YEARS BEFORE *STAR WARS: A New Hope*

Darth Bane: Path of Destruction
Darth Bane: Rule of Two

33 YEARS BEFORE *STAR WARS: A New Hope*

Darth Maul: Saboteur*

32.5 *YEARS BEFORE STAR WARS: A New Hope*

Cloak of Deception
Darth Maul: Shadow Hunter

32 *YEARS BEFORE STAR WARS: A New Hope*

STAR WARS: EPISODE I THE PHANTOM MENACE

29 *YEARS BEFORE STAR WARS: A New Hope*

Rogue Planet

27 *YEARS BEFORE STAR WARS: A New Hope*

Outbound Flight

22.5 *YEARS BEFORE STAR WARS: A New Hope*

The Approaching Storm

22 *YEARS BEFORE STAR WARS: A New Hope*

STAR WARS: EPISODE II ATTACK OF THE CLONES

Republic Commando: Hard Contact

21.5 *YEARS BEFORE STAR WARS: A New Hope*

Shatterpoint

21 *YEARS BEFORE STAR WARS: A New Hope*

The Cestus Deception
The Hive*
Republic Commando: Triple Zero
Republic Commando: True Colors

20 *YEARS BEFORE STAR WARS: A New Hope*

MedStar I: Battle Surgeons
MedStar II: Jedi Healer

19.5 *YEARS BEFORE STAR WARS: A New Hope*

Jedi Trial
Yoda: Dark Rendezvous

19 *YEARS BEFORE STAR WARS: A New Hope*

Labyrinth of Evil

STAR WARS: EPISODE III REVENGE OF THE SITH

Dark Lord: The Rise of Darth Vader

10-0 *YEARS BEFORE STAR WARS: A New Hope*

The Han Solo Trilogy:
 The Paradise Snare
 The Hutt Gambit
 Rebel Dawn

5-2 *YEARS BEFORE STAR WARS: A New Hope*

The Adventures of Lando Calrissian

The Han Solo Adventures

STAR WARS: A New Hope YEAR 0

Death Star

STAR WARS: EPISODE IV A NEW HOPE

0-3 *YEARS AFTER STAR WARS: A New Hope*

Tales from the Mos Eisley Cantina
Allegiance
Galaxies: The Ruins of Dantooine
Splinter of the Mind's Eye

3 *YEARS AFTER STAR WARS: A New Hope*

STAR WARS: EPISODE V THE EMPIRE STRIKES BACK

Tales of the Bounty Hunters

3.5 *YEARS AFTER STAR WARS: A New Hope*

Shadows of the Empire

4 *YEARS AFTER STAR WARS: A New Hope*

STAR WARS: EPISODE VI RETURN OF THE JEDI

Tales from Jabba's Palace
Tales from the Empire
Tales from the New Republic

The Bounty Hunter Wars:
 The Mandalorian Armor
 Slave Ship
 Hard Merchandise

The Truce at Bakura

6.5-7.5 YEARS AFTER
STAR WARS: A New Hope

X-Wing:
Rogue Squadron
Wedge's Gamble
The Krytos Trap
The Bacta War
Wraith Squadron
Iron Fist
Solo Comman

8 YEARS AFTER STAR WARS: A New Hope

The Courtship of Princess Leia
A Forest Apart*
Tatooine Ghost

9 YEARS AFTER STAR WARS: A New Hope

The Thrawn Trilogy:
Heir to the Empire
Dark Force Rising
The Last Command

X-Wing: Isard's Revenge

11 YEARS AFTER STAR WARS: A New Hope

The Jedi Academy Trilogy:
Jedi Search
Dark Apprentice
Champions of the Force

I, Jedi

12-13 YEARS AFTER STAR WARS: A New Hope

Children of the Jedi
Darksaber
Planet of Twilight
X-Wing: Starfighters of Adumar

14 YEARS AFTER STAR WARS: A New Hope

The Crystal Star

16-17 YEARS AFTER STAR WARS: A New Hope

The Black Fleet Crisis Trilogy:
Before the Storm
Shield of Lies
Tyrant's Test

17 YEARS AFTER STAR WARS: A New Hope

The New Rebellion

18 YEARS AFTER STAR WARS: A New Hope

The Corellian Trilogy:
Ambush at Corellia
Assault at Selonia
Showdown at Centerpoint

19 YEARS AFTER STAR WARS: A New Hope

The Hand of Thrawn Duology:
Specter of the Past
Vision of the Future

22 YEARS AFTER STAR WARS: A New Hope

Fool's Bargin*
Survivor's Quest

25 YEARS AFTER
STAR WARS: A New Hope

Boba Fett: A Practical Man*

The New Jedi Order:
Vector Prime
Dark Tide I: Onslaught
Dark Tide II: Ruin
Agents of Chaos I: Hero's Trial
Agents of Chaos II: Jedi Eclipse
Balance Point
Recovery*
Edge of Victory I: Conquest
Edge of Victory II: Rebirth
Star by Star
Dark Journey
Enemy Lines I: Rebel Dream
Enemy Lines II: Rebel Stand
Traitor
Destiny's Way
Ylesia*
Force Heretic I: Remnant
Force Heretic II: Refugee
Force Heretic III: Reunion
The Final Prophecy
The Unifying Force

35 YEARS AFTER STAR WARS: A New Hope

The Dark Nest Trilogy:
The Joiner King
The Unseen Queen
The Swarm War

40 YEARS AFTER
STAR WARS: A New Hope

Legacy of the Force:
Betrayal
Bloodlines
Tempest
Exile
Sacrifice
Inferno
Fury
Revelation
Invincible

*An ebook novella

dramatis personae

Alema Rar; Jedi Knight (Twi'lek female)

Allana; Hapan princess (human female)

Ben Skywalker; Jedi apprentice (human male)

Denjax Teppler; Corellian Minister of Information (human male)

Genna Delpin; Supreme Commander of the Corellian armed forces (human female)

Han Solo; pilot and firefighter (human male)

Jacen Solo / Darth Caedus; Sith, joint Chief of State of the Galactic Alliance (human male)

Jagged Fel; pilot and hunter (human male)

Jaina Solo; Jedi Knight (human female)

Koyan Sadras; Corellian Five Worlds Prime Minister (human male)

Kyle Katarn; Jedi Master (human male)

Kyp Durron; Jedi Master (human male)

Leia Organa Solo; Jedi Knight (human female)

Luke Skywalker; Jedi Grand Master (human male)

Syal Antilles; pilot (human female)

Tenel Ka; Hapan Queen Mother (human female)

Toval Seyah; Galactic Alliance scientist-spy (human male)

Tycho Celchu; military analyst (human male)
Valin Horn; Jedi Knight (human male)
Wedge Antilles; pilot (human male)
Zekk; Jedi Knight (human male)

chapter one

ABOVE THE PLANET KASHYYYK, ABOARD THE **MILLENNIUM FALCON**

The *Falcon* banked over a vision of hell.

Directly below was a roiling surface of blacks and yellows, reds and oranges. Eastward, the carpet of fire gave way to doomed forest. The line between the two zones was an irregular and uncertain one, and even at the distance of a couple of kilometers Han Solo could see individual trees at the border burst into fire, some of them exploding from the heat.

Westward, superheated air rose in a column kilometers in diameter, hauling smoke high into the atmosphere, obscuring the afternoon sun. And it was the smoke column that showed the real danger of the maelstrom. As that column rose, it drew in air from all directions, constantly fanning the fire around it, feeding the voracious beast that burned out of control.

It had once been an unbroken vista of soaring wroshyr trees and other foliage. But a few days earlier, the Star Destroyer *Anakin Solo*, at the order of Jacen Solo, had directed its long-range turbolasers at the surface of Ka-shyyyk, concentrating fire to cause square-kilometer patches of forest to explode in flames. These strikes were intended to punish the Wookiees for harboring Jedi and for dragging their feet before committing their forces to Jacen's Galactic Alliance.

Punish they had. The fires had grown into firestorms raging out of control ever since.

The *Falcon* kicked as she glided over a thermal updraft. Han brought her back to smooth, level flight, cocking his head to hear any sound of a panel dislodge, a bolt kicked free by the unexpected motion, but no new noise was added to the catalog of thousands he knew by heart.

The communications board crackled with Leia's voice. "Sweep complete. I've planted the last beacon."

Han sent the disk-shaped freighter into a bank and descent toward their rendezvous point, about two kilometers outside the fire zone. "Any problems?"

"Nothing but. Had to make some quick repairs on one of the beacons. And I keep having to dodge streams of fleeing animals."

The *Falcon* bucked harder as a particularly ferocious thermal caught her, and then she was out over unburned forest. The ground was higher here, the trees far shorter—not one of them was over half a kilometer in height. Geological surveys showed that the soil here was too shallow to support full-grown wroshyrs—a subterranean ridge of stone, stunting the trees, would mark the fire's stopping point, in this area at least.

Han checked the comm board, looking for the signal being transmitted by Leia's last beacon, and homed in on it. "Waroo! Stand by on the winch."

There was an affirmative growl across the intercom. Han could also hear it, more faintly, echoing up the cockpit access corridor behind him. Waroo was standing by at the starboard docking ring, open to Kashyyyk's atmosphere, ready to retrieve Leia.

Han allowed himself a brief smile. It was good to have a Wookiee aboard the *Falcon* again. It reminded him of the old days, when he and Chewbacca were young and carefree—assuming that being hunted by bounty hunters and Imperial anti-smuggler forces didn't count as "cares."

And Waroo wasn't just any Wookiee. He was Chewbacca's son. A clever son, a good warrior.

If things had been very different, if Han's son Jacen had not turned out the way he had, perhaps the *Falcon* could have been Jacen's someday, with Waroo at his side, a continuation of Han's roguish legacy.

Instead Jacen had become something dark, something terrible, a self-appointed leader determined to impose rigid control over the galaxy. He had conspired, tortured, betrayed, murdered, all with a confidence in the rightness of his cause that was the match of any madman's.

And though Han tried to tell himself that Jacen was dead to him, nothing but a stranger wearing his son's face and name, each new outrage Jacen committed still gripped his heart in an iron fist and squeezed hard.

The communications board beeped to indicate that they were close to the beacon source. Han depressed the bow to give himself a better downward look. He heard a thump from the starboard side, followed by a growl of complaint, and grinned again. "Sorry. No more sudden maneuvers. I promise."

The wroshyrs were still tall enough here that the forest floor was a deeply gloomy and dangerous place. There was no clearing to set down in. But Leia was visible, her white robes starkly contrasted among all the greenery, standing on an upper branch as if loitering on a Coruscant pedwalk, unconcerned about winds or the potentially pesky force of gravity. She waved.

Han positioned the *Falcon* directly above her. "All right, Waroo. Bring her up." A moment later he heard the whirring sound of the winch lowering its line to Leia.

The crew of the *Millennium Falcon* was about to commit an act that, under other circumstances, would have been considered as horrible as Jacen's setting of fires . . . because the two acts were almost the same.

A Confederation cruiser in low planetary orbit would soon fire its turbolaser batteries down at the forests, setting portions of them ablaze. But this strike would be surgical, precisely following the kilometers-long line of beacons Leia had planted. Once that line was drawn, the turbolasers would broaden it toward the east . . . and the *Falcon*, other freighters carrying fire-snuffing foam, and Wookiee fire-fighting teams would control it along its western perimeter. The controlled burn, once extinguished, would leave only char for the advancing wildfire to meet—and that char would be too broad for windborne sparks to jump.

The fire would end here. And the *Falcon* and other ships would move on to create firebreaks elsewhere, eventually checking the wildfire everywhere. Finally, its food all consumed, the firestorm, the beast, would die of starvation.

Leaving behind millions of burned acres and a scarred, smoke-shrouded world.

Han heard the winch stop its whir then, moments later, resume it, bringing Leia up to him. He felt a wash of relief. He knew she could take care of herself. That didn't mean he didn't worry whenever she put herself in the path of danger.

He set the *Falcon* into a gentle eastward course, sending it away from the firebreak area, and checked to make sure his communications were still set to the Confederation frequency. "*Millennium Falcon* to *Lillibanca*. Beacons are in place. You can begin. At Number One, if you please, not Number Twenty."

He heard a chuckle before the voice of the cruiser's male communications officer replied, "Acknowledged, *Falcon*. And thanks."

Then there was a new voice—female, pitched low and seductive—from close behind Han. "Your feelings betray you."

Jolted by adrenaline, Han jerked around to look.

Standing in the entrance to the cockpit was a woman. She was robed nearly head-to-foot in dark garments. Only her face showed, and it was a beautiful face, blue-skinned, cheerful of expression.

Her name was Alema Rar, and she had come to kill him.

Han drew his blaster. As he did, Alema gestured, a flourish that swept her cloak away from her body, and reached out with her left hand as her right snatched her lightsaber from her belt. Han's pistol, barely clearing its holster, flew from his grip and into hers.

Han gaped at her. She should not have been able to do that. Her left arm was useless, had been ruined years earlier—but now it was fine.

She *tsk-tsked* at him. "We are a Jedi. We choose not to be shot. We have been shot before. It is not pleasant." She dropped the blaster. It rang as it hit the deck plates.

Han put bravado he didn't feel into his voice. "So? What are you going to do, talk me to death?" His mind flashed through the weapons and resources he had at hand. They included one hideaway vibroblade, which wasn't much use against a Jedi like Alema, and one very large weapon that had seldom let him down.

"We are going to wait until your piranha-beetle of a wife can see, and then we will shove our lightsaber through your heart. She can hold your corpse and cry. Won't that be nice?"

"Not really."

There were times when it was a wonderful thing that Han knew the *Falcon* as well as he did—that he knew her well enough to handle every control, every instrument even if blind or disoriented. Without taking his gaze off Alema, he reached forward and disengaged the freighter's inertial compensator and artificial gravity generator. In the same instant he hit the thrusters and hauled back on the control yoke.

He stood the *Falcon* on her tail and blasted off toward space. With the inertial compensator off, the sudden acceleration crushed him back into his seat. His head swam with unaccustomed dizziness.

Alema's expression changed from one of good humor to round-eyed surprise as she fell backward. Han heard her thump against the wall of the cockpit access corridor—she had to have hit where the corridor angled away toward port and stern. He heard his blaster pistol clattering along after her. Then there were more thumps and clatters as Alema and the blaster rolled down the slope the angle wall now constituted.

There was also laughter—peals of Alema's laughter.

Waroo, his golden-brown fur gleaming orange and red in the glow of fire visible through the docking ring, was just hauling Leia aboard when the *Falcon* bucked, her bow suddenly pointed straight toward the smoke-filled sky, and accelerated. Waroo and Leia were slammed into the aft bulkhead of the corridor just inside the starboard docking ring. Abruptly the bulkhead was floor, and the acceleration pressed them down like a big invisible hand.

Leia unbuckled herself from the winch harness and drew

in a breath to shout at Han. Could he have failed to notice that the *Falcon*'s artificial gravity wasn't functioning? Then she heard it, laughter echoing off the *Falcon*'s bulkheads and floor plates.

Waroo stood, his great strength making the move look easy despite the several gravities of acceleration hauling at him, and offered a confused-sounding rumble.

"Alema Rar. She's aboard." Leia drew on the Force to augment her physical strength. She stood shakily, took her lightsaber in hand, and ignited it. "Let's go."

Stiff-legged, she marched the several meters down the boarding ring corridor, the ramp that was the Solos' usual means of entering and leaving the *Falcon* now constituting a grimy wall to her right. She reached the hatchway leading to the freighter's main corridor, the curved passageway that offered access to all of the *Falcon*'s compartments.

But stepping into the main corridor would cause her to drop for a considerable distance. Then the curved corridor wall, acting as a steeply angled floor, would cause her to tumble painfully until she reached the gap accessing the freight lift. At that point, she'd fall several more meters and slam into the bulkhead separating internal compartments from the sublight engines. Her gymnastics ability and Force skills would allow her to handle those movements without injury under normal circumstances, but at several gravities she wasn't as sure.

The freight lift was probably where Alema was now. But Leia couldn't be sure of that, either. The laughter had ceased, and Leia could not find Alema in the Force.

Leia glanced over her shoulder at Waroo. "Get to the cockpit. That's where Alema is going to end up. Protect Han. Watch out for poison darts."

Waroo groaned an assent. He moved past Leia, crouched, and leapt across the main corridor, catching with both hands the corner where a side corridor led to the weapons turret access tubes. Even against the multiple gravities hauling at him, he clambered up until he stood on that side corridor wall, turned to face Leia, and leapt back toward her, this time grabbing the sides of the hatch opening well above her head—the opening that led to the cockpit access corridor.

Han's voice came over Leia's comlink. "Hang on, guys."

Wincing in anticipation, Leia grabbed both sides of the hatch access where she stood. She heard Waroo's grumble of complaint.

The *Falcon* snap-rolled, spinning axially and simultaneously changing direction. Straining to hold herself in place, Leia saw nothing change around her, but she heard the sounds of cargo containers, furnishings, and loose wall and floor plates ricocheting around the freighter's interior, and she felt disoriented.

Then she realized why. Above her, Waroo's legs were no longer hanging downward; they were splayed across what should have been the corridor's ceiling. That meant the *Falcon* was now upside down. As Leia watched, the Wookiee wriggled his way into the cockpit access corridor. He was out of her sight, but she could still hear him complain.

Leia rolled forward, an acrobatic tumble that propelled her into the main access corridor. She landed carefully so as not to crush any of the glow rods, sensors, or other items mounted on what should have been the ceiling but now served her as floor.

She had to find Alema—but that wouldn't be too difficult, for the mad Twi'lek's merry laughter reached her again, distinctly from the direction of the *Falcon*'s stern. Lightsaber lit, she carefully moved in that direction.

Ahead to the left, upside down to her current position, was the freighter's engineering station, its consoles permitting the monitoring of every system aboard ship. Ahead to the right, the curved wall gave way to the broad opening leading into the engineering bay, with its access to the freight lift, hyperdrives, sublight engines, and other critical systems.

From that direction, there was the sound of a lightsaber humming, but it was a constant tone—a weapon being held still, neither advancing nor maneuvering.

Leia reached out through the Force, looking again for her quarry. She detected first Waroo, then Han, then Waroo again—

Again? She opened her mouth to call a question over her comlink, but the lightsaber ahead of her began snapping and hissing as it contacted a metal surface. Leia swore under her breath and charged forward.

As she rounded the corner into the engineering bay, she spotted her quarry. On the far side of the freight lift, Alema Rar stood beside the broad circular housing of the hyperdrive. She held her lightsaber in two good, steady hands as she drove its point deep into the housing, sending up sparks that illuminated the bay brilliantly.

And she was standing on the floor—the true floor, her feet planted on the surface above Leia's head, as though gravity didn't matter.

She looked over as Leia entered. "Princess! Come help us destroy the hyperdrive. Then together we can cut the engines to pieces."

Wary, Leia advanced. "I'll cut you to pieces first. That will show me how to do it."

"You first—"

Alema's words were cut off as the *Falcon* suddenly spun axially, dropping the floor from beneath her feet and sending her crashing into the ceiling, throwing Leia shoulder-first into the starboard bulkhead.

* * *

A few moments before, Lumpawaroo had held the four corners of the cockpit doorway with both hands and both feet. He grumbled loudly at Han.

Han glared at the Wookiee over his shoulder. "I don't care what Leia said, get back there and help her."

Grumble.

"I'll shut the cockpit hatch. If Alema gets back up here, she'll have to cut through it, which will give the two of you plenty of time to get here."

Grumble.

"If it'll make you feel better, I'll look where I'm flying." Han turned to face forward. "Not that there's anything else up here! And the proximity alarms will let me know if—"

The proximity alarms shrieked an alert and the sky outside the cockpit viewports lit up so brightly that Han's vision washed away to whiteness. He believed he could feel an instant sunburn on his face and hands. Waroo howled.

Shutting his eyes, Han snap-rolled to starboard. Waroo's howl of complaint remained constant—the Wookiee hadn't been torn free from the cockpit opening.

What had he almost flown into? Then Han knew. *Lillibanca*, in orbit, had begun her firebreak bombardment, and Han's maneuvers had sent the *Falcon* straight toward the first blast.

But now which way could he go? He couldn't see, and any direction might send him straight toward—*into*—the second blast.

Any direction but two.

He continued his spin into the tightest rightward arc he could manage, bringing the *Falcon* around 360 degrees so swiftly that the freighter's struts and rivets groaned in complaint. Then, when only his pilot's experience told him he was again on his original course, he pulled the yoke back and sent the freighter straight up once more.

Flying that way, he couldn't move laterally far enough to hit the second beam. He was momentarily safe.

Waroo wasn't. The Wookiee's howl modulated from outrage to surprise. Han heard Waroo slam into the bulkhead of the cockpit access passage, then follow Alema's earlier, bumpy path as he rolled down the corridor.

There was a momentary silence. Han winced as he visualized Waroo being catapulted into the main access corridor. In an instant would come a big bang of Wookiee on metal—

The *Falcon*'s spin pinned Leia against the corridor for long moments. She drew on the Force to help her push away from it, resisting centrifugal effect, but it took all her concentration—that, and the need to keep an eye on Alema and an ear on all the items of cargo, machinery, personal gear, and, for all she knew, personnel ricocheting off bulkheads all over the ship.

Alema was not as encumbered by the *Falcon*'s movements. The spin had pinned her for a moment to the ceiling, but now she rose as if its gravity were proper and steady.

She rose on two good feet, despite the fact Leia knew she'd lost half of one foot. Her features were as youthful and unblemished as when Leia had first met her fifteen standard years before.

Leia forced herself to keep her voice low and calm. "Finally invested in some prosthetics, did you?" *And some vanity surgery to rid yourself of facial lines, sags, scars . . .*

"Nothing so crude. We are simply ageless and eternal now, as we have always deserved to be." Alema lifted her lightsaber in a traditional salute, a come-fight-me gesture.

The *Falcon* stood on her tail again. Leia, caught off-guard, hurtled toward the rear of the engineering bay—right past Alema, who didn't budge.

Leia spun her lightsaber in a defensive arc, an attempt to block the blow she knew must come, but it didn't. Alema merely danced aside. Leia crashed into the stern bulkhead, an impact that sent waves of shock through her back muscles, shoulder blades, spine . . .

For a brief second she was helpless, bent with pain. But Alema didn't whip out her blowgun to send a dart her way—she didn't even essay a lightning-quick leap followed by a maiming slash with her weapon. She advanced slowly, walking carefully down the ceiling toward Leia.

Recovering, Leia reached out, a flailing motion that sent a wash of Force energy toward her enemy. Alema merely rocked back on her heels and looked faintly amused. "Growing weaker? Perhaps it is the infirmity of age."

There was a dull rattling noise and Waroo, spinning like a child's toy, hurtled down at Leia from the main corridor.

Leia twisted aside and exerted herself upward through the Force, slowing Waroo's fall. The Wookiee crashed into the bulkhead beside her, but softly, not hard enough to impair a being of his size and strength.

Alema's smile broadened. In a movement that was curiously clumsy and unpracticed, she raised her lightsaber and charged to swing it down at Waroo.

Leia raised her own blade, catching Alema's seemingly unpracticed attack; their blades met, sizzled, sparked. Waroo rolled away from the two of them and sat up, swinging his bowcaster off his back and aiming it at Alema. The weapon, built tough to Wookiee standards, did not seem to be damaged.

"No!" Leia lashed out with her foot as Waroo fired. She connected first, kicking Alema backward, and angled her own lightsaber to catch the bowcaster bolt; it sizzled out of existence against the blade.

Puzzled, Waroo offered an offended growl. He rose to his feet and hastily recocked his bowcaster. Leia got her feet under her and leapt toward Alema, positioning herself between the Twi'lek and the Wookiee. She caught Alema's next strike, this one as suitably swift and ferocious as any Jedi's, before it could sever her right arm, but she did not press her attack. "Waroo, don't shoot. There's something wrong. *Trust me.*"

Waroo offered a little grumble of complaint. He aimed but did not fire.

Leia strained against Alema's blade, panting from pain and exertion. Their blades sparked and sizzled as they pressed against each other, slid along each other's lengths.

Alema tried to disengage and strike, but Leia simply followed her step for step, staying close, fighting purely defensively. Alema struck a second time and a third, all shots toward one of Leia's limbs, but Leia blocked two of the blows, dodged the third.

Alema's smile did not fade, but after another moment her strength seemed to. She sagged back as Leia continued to push. "Fine." Her tone was light, but there was a forced, brittle quality to it. "We will meet later."

She leapt up and backward, landing on the main corridor wall above, her motion so light and graceful that it seemed she could not possibly be affected by the *Falcon*'s constant upward acceleration. Then she turned and ran toward the hatchways to the circuitry bay and crew quarters.

Leia and Waroo leapt after her, an effort for both Jedi and Wookiee. But, though Alema had been out of sight for only a few moments, though she could not have made it as far as either hatchway, she was gone.

chapter two

The adviser's voice was like the droning of insects, and Darth Caedus knew what to do about insects—ignore them or step on them.

But in this case, he couldn't afford to ignore the drone. The adviser, whatever her failings as a speaker, was providing him with critical data. Nor could he raise a boot to crush the source of the drone, not with Admiral Cha Niathal, his partner in the coalition government running Coruscant and the Galactic Alliance, sitting on the other side of the table, not with aides hovering and holocam recorders running.

To make matters worse, the adviser would soon wrap up, and inevitably she would address him by the name he so disliked, the name he had been born with, the name he would soon abandon. And then he would once again feel, and have to resist, the urge to crush her.

She did it. The blue-skinned Omwati female, her feathery hair dyed a somber black and her naval uniform freshly pressed, looked up from her datapad. "In conclusion, Colonel Solo—"

Caedus gestured to interrupt her. "In conclusion, the withdrawal of the entire Hapan fleet from Alliance forces removes at least twenty percent of our naval strength and puts us into a game of withdrawal and entrenchment if we are to keep the Confederation from overrunning us. And the treachery of the Jedi in abandoning us at Kuat is further causing a loss of hope among the segments of the population who believe that their involvement means something."

"Yes, sir."

"Thank you. That will be all."

She rose, saluted, and left silently, her posture stiff. Caedus knew she feared him, that she had been struggling to maintain her composure all through the briefing, and he approved. Fear in subordinates meant instant compliance and extra effort on their part.

Usually. Sometimes it meant treachery.

Niathal addressed the other aides present. "We are done here. Thank you."

When the office door *whoosh*ed closed behind the last of them, Caedus turned to Niathal. The Mon Calamari, her white admiral's uniform almost gleaming, sat silently, regarding him. The stare from her bulbous eyes was no more forbidding than usual, but Caedus knew the message that they held: *You could fix this mess by resigning.*

Those were not her words, however. "You do not look well." Hers was the gravelly voice so common to her species, and in it there was none of the sympathy that Admiral Ackbar had been able to project. Niathal was not expressing concern for his health. She was suggesting he was not fit for duty.

And she was almost right. Caedus hurt everywhere. Mere days before, he had waged the most ferocious, most terrible lightsaber duel of his life. In a secret chamber aboard his Star Destroyer, the *Anakin Solo,* he had been torturing Ben Skywalker to harden the young man's spirit, to better prepare Ben for life as a Sith. But he had been caught by Ben's father, Luke Skywalker.

That fight . . . Caedus wished he had a holorecording of it. It had gone on for what had felt like forever. It had been brutal, with the advantage being held first by Luke, then by Caedus, in what he knew had been brilliant demonstrations of lightsaber technique, of raw power within the Force, of subtle Jedi and Sith skills. For all his pain, Caedus felt a swelling of pride—not just that he had survived that duel, but that he had waged it so well.

At the end, Caedus had lost a position of advantage— Luke had slipped free of the poison-injecting torture vines with which Caedus had been strangling him—when Ben had driven a vibroblade deep into Caedus's back, punching clean through a shoulder blade, nearly reaching his heart.

That had ended the fight. Caedus should have been killed immediately. For reasons he did not understand, Luke and Ben had spared his life and departed. It was a mistake that would cost Luke.

Bearing dozens of minor and major wounds, including the vibroblade puncture, a lightsaber-scored kidney, and a fierce scalp wound, Caedus had been treated and resumed command of the *Anakin Solo,* only to experience more injury—emotional injury, this time. In Kashyyyk space, his Fifth Fleet had been surrounded by Confederation forces. Late-arriving Hapan forces could have rescued him . . . but the Hapan Queen Mother, Tenel Ka, his comrade and lover, had betrayed him. Swayed by the treacherous persuasion of Caedus's own parents, Han and Leia Solo, she had demanded a price for her continued military support of the Alliance, and that price had been his surrender.

Of course he had refused. And, of course, he had battered his way out of the encirclement, leading the remnants of the Fifth Fleet back to the safety of Coruscant.

So when Niathal said he did not look well, she was correct. He keenly felt his worst injury. Not the vibroblade wound, not the scalp tear, not the kidney damage—all three were healing. All three were the kind of pain that strengthened him.

It was the wound to his heart that plagued him. Tenel Ka had turned on him. Tenel Ka, the love of his life, the mother of his daughter Allana, had forsaken him.

Niathal's severe expression didn't waver. *You could fix this mess by resigning.*

He gave her a tight smile. "Thank you for your concern, but I'm recovering quickly. And I have a plan. We'll need to follow the recommended protocol of a fighting retreat for the next few days . . . at which time the Hapans will come back into the war on our side. Our job today is to figure out how best to employ them when they return to the battlefield. Since the Confederation thinks they are staying on the fence, we can utilize the Hapans for one devastating surprise attack. We need to decide where that attack will take place."

"You are sure the Hapans will rejoin us."

"I guarantee it. I have an operation in motion that will ensure it."

"What resources do you need to carry it out?"

"Only those I already have."

"Have I seen details of your operation?"

Caedus shook his head. "If I don't forward a file, no one can intercept it. If I don't speak a word of detail, no one can overhear it. Too much is riding on getting the Hapans back for me to wreck things by divulging details too freely."

Niathal remained silent. A more incendiary personality would have taken offense at Caedus's implied questioning of her ability to handle secret matters. Niathal chose not to recognize it as an insult. She merely turned to the next matter on her agenda. "Speaking of secrets . . . Belindi Kalenda at Intelligence reports that Doctor Seyah has been pulled off the Centerpoint Station project. Seyah reported that he had come under suspicion of being a GA spy."

"Which, of course, he is. What's his new posting, and can he get us any useful information from there?"

Niathal shook her head in the slow, somber way of the Mon Cals. "Kalenda ordered him out. He is already back on Coruscant."

Caedus resisted the urge to break something. "She's an idiot. And Seyah is an idiot. He could have stayed, weathered whatever investigation they brought against him, and begun feeding us information again."

"Kalenda was certain that he would be arrested, investigated, and executed."

"Then he should have stayed in place until arrested! Who knows what his cowardice has cost us? Even reporting on ship and troop movements could provide us with the critical advantage in a battle." Caedus sighed and pulled out his datapad. Snapping it open, he typed a brief note to himself.

Niathal rose and leaned over so that her bulbous eyes could peer, upside down, at his screen. "What is this?"

"A note to myself to have Seyah arrested. He provided Kalenda with false information that led her to extract him from a danger zone, which is the equivalent of desertion under fire. He will confess. He will be executed."

"Ah." Niathal resumed her seat, but offered no protest.

Caedus appreciated that. Niathal was clearly growing to understand that Caedus's approach was best—it kept subordinates motivated, kept deadwood out of the ranks. "What next?"

"Bimmisaari and some of her allied worlds in the Halla sector just announced they were defecting to the Confederation."

Caedus shook his head dismissively. "Not a significant loss."

"No, but it's more unsettling as the possible first sign of a trend. Intelligence has detected more communications traffic between Corellia and the Imperial Remnant, and between Corellia and the worlds of the Corporate Sector, which may be nothing more than an increased recruitment effort by the Confederation. Or it may have been initiated by the other parties, a prelude to negotiations and more defections."

"Also irrelevant." Caedus felt a flash of irritation. Yes, these were matters that the joint Chiefs of State needed to address, but they would all be resolved when the Hapes Consortium came back into the fold. "Anything else?"

"No."

"Excellent."

When the meeting was done and Niathal had departed, Caedus remained in the office. He stared at the blank walls. They soothed him. He needed soothing.

Inside, he was ablaze with anger, resentment, a sense of betrayal—all the emotions that fueled a Sith.

In the days since his fight with Luke, he had come to the realization that he was all alone in the universe. It was like the plaintive wail of a five-year-old: *Nobody loves me.* He could manage a smile at just how self-pitying it sounded.

But it was true. Everyone who had once known love for him now hated him. His father and mother, his twin Jaina, Tenel Ka, Luke, Ben . . . Intellectually, as he had embraced the Sith path, he had known that it would happen. One by one, those who cared about him would be peeled away like the outer layers of his skin, leaving him a mass of bloody, agonized nerves.

He had known it . . . but experiencing it was another matter. His body might be healing, but his spirit was in greater pain every day.

Everyone he had loved now hated him . . . except Allana. And he would not allow Tenel Ka to turn his daughter against him. He would cut down anyone who stood between him and his child.

Anyone.

SANCTUARY MOON OF ENDOR, ABANDONED IMPERIAL OUTPOST

Years earlier, before Jacen Solo had been born—before, in fact, Luke and Leia knew they were siblings, before Leia had confessed even to herself that she was in love with Han—Yoda had told Luke that electrical shocks, applied at different intensities and at irregular but frequent intervals, would prevent a Jedi from concentrating, from channeling the Force. They could render a Jedi helpless.

But Yoda had never told Luke that emotional shocks could do the same thing.

They could. And just as no amount of self-control would allow a Jedi to ignore the effects of electrical shocks on his body, neither could self-control keep Luke safely out of his memories. Every few moments a memory, freshly applied like a current-bearing wire on his skin, would yank him out of the here and now and propel him into the recent past.

Boarding the *Anakin Solo*. Finding Jacen torturing— *torturing*—Luke's only child, his son Ben. The duel that followed, Luke against the nephew he'd once loved . . . the nephew who now commanded Master-level abilities in the Force, though he had not been, and never would be, elevated to the rank of Jedi Master.

And no pain Luke suffered in that fight was equal to Ben demanding the right to finish Jacen. That demand had brought Luke to where he was now, sitting cross-legged on the floor of an upper-story room of an abandoned Imperial outpost, staring through a wide transparisteel viewport at a lush Endor forest he was barely aware of, his body healing but his spirit sick and injured even after all these days.

Shocked almost beyond understanding by Ben's bloodthirst, Luke had prevented his son from executing a death blow against Jacen. Nor had Luke chosen to finish Jacen himself. He had led Ben in sudden flight from the *Anakin Solo*—a flight to prevent Ben from taking the next, possibly irreversible, step toward the dark side that Jacen had planned for the boy.

But was it the right decision? At that moment, it had seemed like the only possible choice. Ben's future, his decency, had teetered in the balance. Had either Skywalker killed Jacen, Ben would have fallen toward the dark.

Some people came back from the dark. Luke had. Others didn't. Ben becoming a lifelong agent of evil had not been a certainty.

What was certain was that Jacen was alive. And now, as Jacen furthered his plans for galactic conquest, more people would die. They would die by the thousands at least, probably by the tens or hundreds of thousands, perhaps by the millions.

And Luke would be responsible.

So had it been the right decision? Ben against thousands of lives?

Logic said no—no, *unless* in falling to the dark side, Ben became as great a force for evil as Jacen Solo was or their mutual grandfather, Anakin Skywalker, Darth Vader, had been.

Emotion said yes—yes, *unless* Ben interpreted Luke's refusal to kill as a sign of weakness, and that decision fostered contempt in him, contempt for Luke and the light side of the Force. That could push him along Jacen's path despite Luke's intent.

And either way, those thousands would die.

A translucent white rectangle, tall and very thin, appeared on the viewport ahead of Luke. It rapidly broadened, revealing itself as the reflection of a door opening in the wall behind him. Jedi Master Kyp Durron stood in the doorway, his brown robes rumpled, his long graying-brown hair damp with sweat and unkempt. His expression, normally one of mild amusement layered over what was usually interpreted as a trace of cockiness, was now more somber—neutrality concealing concern. "Grand Master?"

"Come in." Luke did not turn to face Kyp. The view of Endor's wilderness was soothing.

Kyp moved in and the door shut behind him, eliminating the illuminated rectangle from Luke's field of vision. "The door chimes do not appear to be working on this passageway, and you were not responding to your comlink . . ."

Luke frowned. "I didn't hear it. Maybe the battery is dead." He pulled his comlink from the tunic of his white Tatooine-style work suit. The ready light on the small cylindrical object was still lit. A quick examination showed that the device had been shut off. Puzzled, Luke turned it on again and tucked it away.

"Just a routine report. The StealthXs are spread, by wing pairs, across a broad area, under camouflage netting.

Many of the pilots found useful landing spots in areas where debris from the second Death Star came down and created burn zones. The younglings are packed into two large chambers, acting as dormitories, on this outpost, but a reconnaissance team of Jedi Knights has found a cavern system not too far away that will provide ample space for a training facility . . . and some defense against orbital sensors. The Jedi Knights are relocating a nest of rearing spiders there. Once they're certain the spiders and their eggs are all gone, we'll begin transferring the younglings."

"Good. But don't put too much effort into making those caverns livable. We'll be leaving Endor before many more weeks pass."

Kyp nodded. "Otherwise, we seem to be dealing well with the local Ewoks."

"Any we know?"

"No . . . Wicket's family group's territory is still limited to areas south of here. But your idea of bringing in See-Threepio as an interpreter is paying off. The local clan seems to like him."

"Good."

Kyp did not immediately reply, so Luke turned to give him a look. The younger Master seemed to be pondering his next words. Luke cocked an eyebrow at him. "Anything else?"

"There's been some question about our next action against Jacen."

"Ah, yes." Luke turned to look out the viewport again. "I don't know. Why don't you arrange that?"

There was a long silence, then: "Yes, Grand Master."

The rectangle of light reappeared. Kyp's reflection moved into it and it closed again, leaving Luke in silence and peace.

And confronted by the memory of Jacen, bloodied and battered almost beyond recognition, crawling away from him, Ben's vibroblade lodged in his back. Ben's face appeared before him, mouthing the words, *This kill is* mine.

Luke shivered.

chapter three

KASHYYYK, MAITELL BASE, HANGAR HOUSING
THE **MILLENNIUM FALCON**

There were still bright spots before Han's eyes, right at the center of his focus, from the brilliance of the turbolaser blast he had almost flown into. He had to scan, traverse his line of sight, in order to work around them.

Directly before him was an old sabacc table with a rusty rim and a grime-spotted felt surface; a brandy bottle and a set of tumblers rested upon it. Beyond was the *Millennium Falcon*, her boarding ramp down, with Wookiee utility vehicles and Confederation spacecraft parked beside her. The long hangar door the *Falcon* faced was open, showing riverbank, trees that were stunted and tiny by Kashyyyk standards, and skies filled with haze and smoke clouds dimming the sunlight. Other buildings were visible on the far side of the river, all remnants of a long-abandoned spaceport dating from the years of Imperial occupation.

The medics had said the bright spots would fade within a few hours. Not that this was much comfort. He wanted to be working on the *Falcon* now, at this instant. Grinning momentarily at his own childlike impatience, he lifted his tumbler and took another sip of the liquid within it. It burned a little as it went down, a smooth, flavorful heat.

"What is it?" Leia, seated in the spindly metal chair next to his, had seen his smile.

"I was thinking that if you're going to have to put up with enforced downtime, there are worse ways to do it than with a good brandy and your best girl."

In his peripheral vision, he caught Leia's smile, but her tone was slightly less agreeable. "So many things wrong with what you said. First, you don't mention *liquor* before your wife. Then there's the whole girl–woman issue, but that's not relevant because you clearly didn't mean it in a spirit of dismissiveness or disenfranchisement. But the phrase *best girl* implies there are other girls . . ."

"There are. There's one now." Han pointed.

Descending the *Falcon*'s boarding ramp was their daughter, Jaina. As diminutive as her mother, and as beautiful, though with narrower features, she had inherited her father's knack for mechanics, as suggested by her current form of dress—overalls spattered with spots of lubricant and hydraulic fluid. She had also inherited her mother's way with the Force, a fact attested to by the lightsaber hanging from her belt. As she descended, she wiped her hands on an oily blue rag, then noticed Han watching. "Dad! All fixed."

"You're kidding."

Jaina shook her head, then took a chair at his table. "Alema's attack did some damage, but she didn't have much time to root around in the hyperdrive before Mom interrupted her. I replaced a couple of parts, and it checks out in the green. You'll want to take her up and do a practice run or two, I expect."

"I expect. Thanks." He gave Leia a sidelong look. "I'm

getting more obsolete every day. I don't even have to patch up the *Falcon*'s battle damage anymore."

Leia gave him a smile tinged with malice. "You'll never be obsolete as long as some people prefer old-fashioned tactics and parts."

"It's such a shame you can't spank a Jedi."

There was a clattering of heels, and Han looked up to see Jagged Fel and Zekk coming down the boarding ramp.

Fel, son of one of the Empire's most celebrated fighter pilots, and nephew of one of the New Republic's, was a well-muscled man of middle height, his hair, neatly trimmed beard, and mustache black, a white lock at his hairline marking an old scalp wound. He wore a black flight suit; on a dark night, he would look like a face and hands floating in the air.

Zekk, Jaina's Jedi partner, was unusually tall, his long dark hair currently braided. Like Leia, he was dressed in ordinary Jedi robes.

Jag held a blaster pistol, his finger not in the trigger housing, and as he neared Han he reversed it, offering it butt-first. "Found it."

Han set down his drink. He took the pistol, twirled it experimentally, and holstered it. "Now I feel dressed again. Where was it?"

"During your acrobatics, a hatch over one of the escape pods must have popped open. Your blaster fell into it, and the hatch closed and locked the next time you were right-side up."

"Thanks." Han turned back to Leia. "Actually, I could get used to this. Have the youngsters do all the work, all the time. Hey, somebody get me a drink."

Zekk sat in the fourth and last chair, picked up Han's tumbler from where it rested, and moved it two centimeters closer to Han. "Your drink, sir."

"Well, some chores are easier than others."

"So." Leia fixed the three newcomers with a quick, serious look. "Anything? Any sign of Alema?"

Jag, still standing, shook his head. "None." His voice was thoughtful. "*Extra* none."

Leia frowned, puzzled. "What does that mean?"

Zekk cocked a thumb over his shoulder toward the *Falcon*. "Alema left behind no fingerprints. No threads from her robes. There weren't any skin cells on any of the bulkheads you said she hit."

Han scowled. "She had to have left fingerprints on my blaster. She pulled it to her with the Force, caught it in her hand."

"Her *left* hand, you said." Jag's voice was thoughtful.

"Yeah."

"She has to have finally accepted prosthetics," Jag considered. "Though the custom is to obtain prosthetics identical to your original limbs, down to every mole and fingerprint whorl, that's not because of some unbreakable law of cybernetics. She could have gotten replacements without identifying features."

Leia shook her head, clearly unhappy. "So there's nothing to prove Alema was ever there."

Han snorted. "Nothing but a damaged and repaired hyperdrive."

"Which still isn't proof." Zekk gave Leia an apologetic shrug. "We really don't have any forensic means to distinguish between the cuts of different lightsabers. But why do you need proof? We believe you."

"Because I'm not sure I believe myself at this point. I couldn't even feel her in the Force. Only Lumpy. I mean, Waroo." Leia looked around guiltily, caught in the act of using a childhood nickname abandoned by its owner. Fortunately, Waroo was not in the hangar. "I don't even know how she escaped."

"I have an idea." Jaina frowned, thoughtful. "But it's pretty weird."

"Let's go with weird. Much better than nothing." Han paused to refill his tumbler, then waved the bottle around, a want-one? gesture.

Jag nodded. "I'll have one."

Zekk looked at him, startled. "Colonel Clean Living accepts a brandy when he might have to fly later in the day?"

"Who is it who says I need to learn to unclench before I lock permanently into a full-body grimace? Seems to me it was a tall Jedi with too much hair." Jag accepted a tumbler from Han and gave the older man a nod of thanks before sipping.

Jaina gave Zekk and Jag an admonishing look. "Back to the subject. Instead of this attack of Alema's being some new tactic, a new piece of the puzzle, maybe it's actually an old one with a new coat of paint."

Leia leaned back in her chair, which gave off a metallic creak. "Let's hear it, sweetie."

"Remember when Jacen and Ben went to Brisha Syo's asteroid? Ben had a fight with an evil Mara phantom."

Han and Leia exchanged a glance. Han shrugged. "You're saying we just fought a phantom."

"A phantom wouldn't leave fingerprints, Dad. A phantom could vanish instantly from a sealed freighter."

Han shook his head. "But Brisha Syo is dead. Her mother, Lumiya, is dead."

"Right, Dad. But we're getting reports that Alema is now piloting a craft that resembles an ancient Sith meditation sphere."

Han stared accusingly at his daughter, then at the liquor

bottle. "Sacred brandy, you've failed me. My daughter is talking and I don't understand her anymore."

Jag smiled. "Like her father, she's prone to skipping steps when describing her reasoning." He gestured to quell any protest from Jaina. "She means, the only Sith we're aware of in all this mess is Lumiya, and we know Alema has been associating with her. Alema probably inherited the Sith ship from Lumiya. What *else* did she inherit? Perhaps some sort of weird Sith Force technique?" He swirled his tumbler and took another sip. "Plus, I'm not convinced there even *was* a Brisha Syo."

It was Zekk's turn to raise an eyebrow. "What do you mean?"

Jaina's voice was soft but insistent. "Stay on target, Jag."

"I'm on target. I'll discuss Brisha Syo later."

Leia considered. "So why was I seeing Alema but feeling Waroo?"

Her daughter shrugged. "I don't know. But I suspect that your instinct not to cut her down was a very good one."

"She's going to use this technique again. And she'll get better with practice." Jag set his empty tumbler on the table, shaking his head at Han's silent offer of a refill. "So our need to find her is more pressing than ever. Especially in light of the fact that she's the number one suspect in the murder of Mara Jade Skywalker. We don't want the Grand Master to devote more and more resources to hunting her down, not with the civil war becoming bloodier, more complicated. The Jedi are needed elsewhere."

Han nodded. "So you'll need . . . Colonel Solo's shuttle. The one he used on the trip to that asteroid."

Jag looked dubious. "Brisha Syo, or Lumiya, would never have let the shuttle leave with a correct plot of the asteroid's location."

Han grinned. "Just because you're young doesn't mean

you have to be stupid, Jag. Sure, she'd have fixed the coordinates in the shuttle's memory. But go deeper into the shuttle's records. Amount of fuel burned, to the milliliter, per burn. Duration in hyperspace for each jump. Amount of time after leaving hyperspace until the shuttle hypercomm receives traffic, to the millisecond, compared with when that traffic was originally dispatched."

Jag considered, and whistled again. "We'd need some high-end computing and decryption power to process that kind of data."

"We can get it, sonny. Talon Karrde or Booster Terrik will give it to us, if no one else. But first we'll have to get aboard . . ." Han tried to prevent himself from grimacing, but couldn't, not quite. "Aboard the *Anakin Solo*. Get a crack at the colonel's shuttle. Planning session?"

Jag nodded. "A couple of hours. You can comm around and get that computer time for us. We all need some downtime for our brains. Zekk and Jaina wanted to get in some lightsaber training for when we do run Alema down."

"Two hours." Han rose, bent to kiss his wife, and marched toward the *Falcon,* feeling slightly better than he had when the talk had started—better because things now made a little more sense, better because he now had a direction.

Then, vision still faulty, he stumbled over the bottom of the boarding ramp and was reminded that not everything was back to normal yet.

Jaina and Zekk left moments later. Leia debated going with them, getting in some additional training, but decided she'd had enough lightsaber work for one day.

Jag stared a moment at Han's chair, then sat in it. He glanced at Leia, his posture typically rigid. "Don't tell anybody I'm doing this."

"Doing what?"

Slowly, methodically, he leaned back in a typically Han Solo–esque slouch. Once his back was flush against the angled back of the aged chair, he put his elbow up on the table, propped his head against his hand.

Leia laughed at him. "How does it feel?"

"So wrong, I can barely describe it. How has your husband managed not to sustain spinal damage all these years?"

"Stubbornness."

"Jaina's certainly inherited it. Stubbornness, I mean. Not bad posture."

"She got her posture from my side of the family." Leia sobered. "What did you mean about not being convinced Brisha Syo actually existed?"

Jag took a deep breath before answering. "I can't say I have all the skills of a security investigator like Corran Horn. But I'm suspicious of anyone who seems to have only one purpose in life and then immediately dies." He looked off into the distance, past the *Falcon,* past the walls of the hangar, past the smoke clouds and the burning horizons of Kashyyyk. "Nobody had ever heard of her before she showed up on Lorrd. We've been able to trace a few of her movements and have a single garbled message that suggests she was Lumiya's daughter. She died—according to Jacen, who has never turned in a detailed report of what went on at the asteroid and is no longer available for debriefing. And the only consequence of her death seems to be that it provided motivation for Lumiya to be on Coruscant, breaking into Galactic Alliance Guard security and shadowing Ben, who may or may not have killed Brisha Syo—he certainly doesn't remember doing so. That's the sum total of her existence." He held out a cupped hand as though to catch a falling raindrop. "There's nothing there.

People tend to leave more traces, more memories. It seems more likely that she was a fiction. An agent of, or an alternate identity of, Lumiya herself."

Leia studied him. Focused on some distant place, Jag seemed unaware of her presence, and in his eyes Leia saw a bleakness, an emptiness she had not previously noticed.

"Jag, *you're* leaving memories."

Startled, he looked at her. "What?"

"You were comparing yourself to her, weren't you? To Brisha Syo. You have one purpose left to you, and when that's done you wonder if you're just going to vanish, leaving no trace behind."

Jag's expression darkened. He sat upright, his posture once again rigidly military. "Jedi mind tricks."

"I wasn't reading your mind, Jag. Just your face."

Jag rose. His voice became cordial but impersonal. "I need to see about commissioning the building of some specialized gear." He spun on his heel and strode from the hangar, boot heels clicking.

chapter four

SANCTUARY MOON OF ENDOR, JEDI OUTPOST

The flat top of the outpost had once been a landing pad for shuttles and TIE fighters, and now, some forty standard years later, relics of that era still littered the pad—a discarded wheel from a shuttle's landing gear, a rusty rolling cart that had once held tools, a scattering of corroded nuts and bolts that neither wind nor time had managed to scour from the surface.

They met there, Jedi Masters in exile: Luke Skywalker, Kyle Katarn, the Mon Cal healer Cilghal, Kyp Durron, Corran Horn, the fierce reptilian Saba Sebatyne, and Octa Ramis of Chandrila. Octa, trained by Kam and Tionne Solusar, both still recovering from their near-fatal wounds at the hands of Jacen Solo's soldiers, was more subdued than the rest, her stillness in the Force clearly a consequence of rigid self-control rather than inner peace.

Kyp caught Luke's attention. "I have something to bounce off you." With a flick of his wrist and an exertion through the Force, he sent the ancient wheel soaring through the air toward Luke.

Luke somersaulted to the right and the wheel flew harmlessly over him. He came to his feet, igniting his lightsaber, as the wheel dropped to the landing pad surface and rolled nearly to the far edge of the roof before toppling and lying still. "Funny." He advanced toward Kyp in mock menace. "Is this every Master for himself?"

Kyp shrugged and ignited his own lightsaber. "Might as well."

Luke heard *snap-hisses* as the other Masters lit their weapons. This friendly exercise would be horribly dangerous to anyone but a Jedi Master, but all of those present were so in tune with the Force and one another that the odds of a mishap were, as usual, almost nil.

Luke charged Kyp but then, well outside lightsaber strike range, skidded to an abrupt halt. Kyp's face had just enough time to register suspicion before Luke exerted himself through the Force, reaching upward to tree limbs that had grown out over the outpost. He yanked downward. A broad branch slapped down atop Kyp, bearing him to the landing pad surface and sending leaves swirling out all over the roof.

Kyp laughed and rolled free, coming up to his feet. "No fair."

"Tactical superiority is never *fair*."

"I mean, getting leaves and bugs in my hair."

Luke felt the approach of Cilghal from behind. He leapt up and backward, inverting as he flew, and blocked the Mon Cal Master's strike with his blade in passing. He landed behind her. A few meters away, Saba Sebatyne and Corran Horn dueled, each adopting a traditional, formalized lightsaber posture—Saba using a lightsaber in each hand, Corran with his own weapon adjusted to its second setting, its blade now three meters in length and a brilliant purple instead of its usual silver. Octa Ramis, who had supplied Saba with her second weapon, was content to stand off to one side, using the Force to hurl stones, plucked from the ground far below, through the tumult of practicing Masters. Kyle Katarn stood near her, watching all the others, practicing ritualized sword forms and waiting for an opponent to come open.

Kyp advanced against Luke again, striking at Luke's ankles while Cilghal engaged the Grand Master's blade. Luke danced over the low strike and put a foot into Cilghal's torso, more of a push than a kick, before landing again. The Mon Cal staggered back a few steps, offering a nod of appreciation.

Kyp threw a succession of fast blows at Luke's shoulders, occupying him while Cilghal recovered. "Actually, it's a plan for a mission against Jacen. A capture-or-neutralize," he said, his lightsaber flashing at Luke.

"*Neutralize.*" Luke frowned. He circled Kyp, trying to put him in the middle of their three-way exchange, but Cilghal paced him so that Luke remained in the center. "Meaning 'kill.' "

Kyp nodded, not repentant. "This isn't a mission of assassination, Luke. But if the capture isn't clean, if the choice is to run away and leave him in charge of the Alliance or finish him then and there . . ."

"Yeah." Luke felt Cilghal's approach behind him. He bent over backward, his lightsaber hand coming down on the landing pad surface to hold his upper body clear of it, and Cilghal's lightsaber passed through where his waist would have been. Luke instantly straightened, catching her hilt with his free hand, and stepped away, her lightsaber now in his grip. He twirled one blade at each Master. "Go on."

With an exasperated sigh, Cilghal stepped back and exerted herself toward Kyle. The man's lightsaber leapt free from his grip and flew to Cilghal's. Kyle offered no resistance. Cilghal caught it out of the air, called "Thank you," and dashed toward Corran.

Kyp looked dubiously at Luke's twin weapons and fell into a defensive posture. "The team will consist of one or two Masters, three or four Jedi Knights, and a native guide. They'll approach the Senate Building through the undercity." As Luke neared and began throwing probing attacks in quick succession, Kyp deflected them close to his body with equal speed and minimal movement. "When Jacen enters or leaves the building, they spring the trap. Coma gas and shock nets as the first wave, the Jedi making their direct assault immediately afterward." He stopped to stare intently at Luke.

Luke felt the attack—the Force, propelling numerous small objects at him. He jumped back and brought up both lightsabers as a shower of old nuts and bolts came at him with missile speed. It was like defending himself against Yuuzhan Vong thud bugs for the first time in years, but the old skill was undiminished—he calculated which objects had a chance of hitting him and incinerated only them with his blades, letting the others fly harmlessly past.

The trouble was, the ones that flew past soon curved around for another attack.

Meanwhile, Kyp continued, "We have a shuttle or other enclosed vehicle land for a quick extraction. But the trick is, it's an empty droid vehicle. Our group, with Jacen, their captive, actually reenters the undercity through a ground-side maintenance access hatch modified to serve as an exit. While the shuttle makes its escape run and draws off pursuit, our group goes back the way it came to the true departure point."

"Who's the team leader?"

Kyp shrugged. "Not determined yet."

Corran's and Kyle's voices rose simultaneously: "Me."

Luke, thoughtful, finished incinerating the last of the fly-ing bolts. He switched off Cilghal's lightsaber and tossed it over his shoulder. He heard it slap down into her big webbed hand. "What about your native guide? Someone to get you through the undercity, I'm guessing. Do you trust him?"

Kyp nodded.

"Not as far as I can throw her." That was Corran, his voice punctuated by zaps as Saba advanced on him, trying to bat his longer blade aside.

Kyp made a sour face. "Horn, you can't throw anybody any distance. With the Force, anyway. This calls your judg-ment into question."

"*Her.*" Luke switched off his lightsaber. "Maybe I should meet her."

Kyp deactivated his own weapon. "She's one level down. I can have her come up if you want to meet her now."

"Sure." Luke looked around for something to serve him as a chair—an impromptu throne of the Jedi Grand Mas-ter—and decided against the landing gear wheel as being just slightly below his dignity and preferred altitude. He chose the old tool rack and sat upon it. Its corroding wheels groaned under the weight; one of them, decayed past the point of functionality, slowly collapsed, tilting the rack slightly forward.

Meanwhile Kyp spoke into a comlink. The other Mas-ters left off their exercise, extinguished their lightsabers, and gathered around.

A section of roof slid aside and a metal plate rose to oc-cupy that space, lift-style. On it stood a teenage girl in Jedi robes. She was redheaded, and she nervously twirled one lock of hair in her fingers. At Kyp's gesture, she ap-proached.

Luke recognized her and frowned. "I know you. Seha, from the Temple."

She came to a stop in front of him and nodded. "Yes, Grand Master." Her voice was faint. Her face was so pale Luke thought she might be on the verge of fainting.

He tried to remember her record with the Jedi Order. She hadn't been with them long. An orphan since childhood, he recalled. She'd been sponsored to the Order by . . .

By Jacen. Ah. "There would seem to be some question as to your reliability."

Seha nodded, agitation making her motion fast, jerky. "Some people don't trust me."

"Why?"

"Because I'm a traitor to the Jedi Order."

Corran Horn's eyebrows rose. He looked faintly impressed. "Well, I'll give her points for honesty."

Luke ignored him. "Perhaps you'd better explain that."

Seha glanced around, as if looking for sympathetic faces, but returned her attention to Luke. "I was little when the Yuuzhan Vong came to Coruscant. When the Vongforming happened. Most of my family died. I don't remember them, except my father. We lived in the undercity, so deep and out of touch that the Yuuzhan Vong had been driven offworld for months before I even learned about it. My father was dead by then, stung by a Yuuzhan Vong insect he didn't see in time. I stayed there, with the other refugees and crazies and rejects, because they were the only people I knew.

"But I met Jacen. He'd come down from time to time—sometimes his visits were years apart—to visit his friend the World Brain. My home was close to the World Brain's lair. I thought it was a horrible, evil thing, but Jacen told me how it was just acting according to its nature, that what it looked like had nothing to do with what it was inside. Jacen figured out I was Force-sensitive and arranged for me to become an apprentice to the Order, even though I was old for an apprentice."

"I know what it's like to be old for an apprentice." Luke's voice was gentle, but now he let an edge creep into it. "So how did you betray the Order?"

"I did things for Jacen. Kept him updated on goings-on in the Temple. After he became the head of the Guard, he asked me to take things into and out of the Temple for him, like spare datapads and replacement electronic components." She took a deep breath before continuing. "When your son disappeared . . . I was the one who helped him get out of the Temple without being seen."

Luke stared at her for a long moment. "At Jacen's order."

"Yes."

Luke looked away from her as his emotions threatened to spin out of control. Ben's account of his solo mission had never included a confirmation that Jacen had sent him. Ben had never volunteered details of where he had gone or what he had done. Luke had known intellectually that only Jacen could have dispatched the boy. But now, at last, Luke had proof, a corroborating witness, and the confirmation hit him harder than he would have expected.

This girl had helped effect the plan—had endangered Ben. All out of a misguided loyalty to a very bad man.

Luke stared at her again. He tried to remain impassive, but she apparently saw something in his expression and took an involuntary half step backward.

Luke didn't bother trying to keep anger from his voice. "How were you found out?"

"She wasn't. She came forward." Cilghal put a comforting hand on Seha's shoulder.

"When we received word about the massacre on Ossus." Seha blinked, and tears came. "I don't know how he could do that, send in a crazy man to bargain with the young-lings' lives, to torture Kam Solusar and Tionne and kill all those others." Her tears flowed freely now, but she ignored them. "I betrayed the Order . . . but not like *that*. I'm not going to do *that*."

"You're no Jedi." Corran's voice was harsh. "Your emo-tions are all over the map. Even an apprentice knows that. So we can't trust you as a Jedi, we can't trust you to be a calm, collected operative, and now you've left the most dangerous man in the galaxy disappointed in you—" He gestured at Luke. "Plus, you've volunteered to go on a mis-sion to capture the *second*-most dangerous man, when all you had to do to retain everyone's trust was keep your mouth shut."

Seha glared at him. "Trust isn't worth anything when it's built on lies. Maybe I'm the stupidest girl you've ever met, but even I can figure that out."

No one answered her immediately. Even Corran's ex-pression was more evaluative than angry, and Luke knew, both from experience and from what he felt through the Force, that Corran had been goading the girl profession-ally, his own display of emotion simulated.

Finally Cilghal broke the silence. "In fairness, after the Order broke ranks with Jacen and the Alliance at Kuat, when the Guard moved against the Temple to seize it, Seha helped destroy the computers. She carried out a complete set of records and led two Jedi Knights to safety through the undercity."

Luke cleared his throat to catch Seha's attention. "You can stay in the Order without going on this mission."

A brief, uncertain smile flashed across Seha's lips. "I can?"

"You can. You should. Jacen is . . . extraordinarily dan-gerous. If he sees you, he might devote only a single, negligent attack to you. Such an attack would distract a Jedi Master, hurt a Jedi Knight . . . and kill you."

She swallowed. "Does anyone in the Order know the undercity approaches to Jacen's offices?"

"Zekk, perhaps."

She shook her head. "He doesn't know it since the Vongforming. Since the rebuilding after the war. I'd better stay with the mission."

"And keep your head down."

"And keep my head down."

Luke took a long breath, then looked around. "Will you all excuse me? Kyp, please escort Seha downstairs, then return to me in a few minutes."

They all bowed and, grave-faced, withdrew, descending via the lift plate by which Seha had arrived.

Alone, Luke stood away from the ill-balanced tool rack, closing his eyes, immersing himself in the Force . . . looking for guidance.

His heart should have been the only guide he needed, with the Force offering the occasional nudge when things were unclear. But his heart had been burned beyond recognition when Mara had died, and what was left was in pieces, each piece suggesting a different course of action. *Throw everything into the effort against Jacen. Hunt down Alema Rar and make her pay for killing Mara. The rot is too deep; the Jedi Order should withdraw and let the warring states fight their way to a finish; only then can rebuilding begin. This kill is mine. This kill is mine.*

And the Force was silent. It seemed like forever since it had shown him any guidance about the bigger picture. All it offered him these days was guidance for immediate problems, the here and now. It had been that way since—for how long? Since Mara's death at least. It could have begun before then.

Perhaps he could no longer read the Force. Perhaps it chose not to speak to him anymore.

And if that was true, he could not remain the Grand Master of the Order. He would lead the Jedi into ruin.

"Grand Master?"

Luke opened his eyes. Kyp stood before him. Luke had neither heard nor felt him coming.

Luke forced his thoughts back to the present. "You've been putting together the plan for this mission."

"Yes."

"Why is there some doubt as to who is going to lead it?"

Kyp hesitated a moment. "Masters Horn and Katarn have volunteered. I am also willing to lead it. But I haven't assigned a mission leader yet . . . because I think *you* should lead it."

"Absolutely not."

"Please hear me out. There's worry in the Order. It comes from not knowing where we're going. The Jedi need you to show them. They need you to lead. A mission like this shows them your goals, your heart."

If I lead this mission, I will strike at Jacen with hatred. One of us will die, and Ben will follow our mutual example and be lost to the dark side. Luke did not need the Force to show him the future to know that this was true.

He thought about it a long moment. "Here's my decision. Master Katarn will lead this mission."

Kyp's face fell. "Yes, Grand Master."

"I'll leave it to the two of you to finalize details." The conference done, Luke turned back to face the sunlit Endor forest and the momentary peace it offered him.

chapter five

HAPES, GALACTIC ALLIANCE SHUTTLE,
APPROACHING THE PALACE
OF THE QUEEN MOTHER

The engineering officer aboard the Galactic Alliance shuttle had a five-day growth of whiskers, a patch over his right eye with the edges of a blaster scar peeking from beneath at forehead and cheek, and a dress uniform whose tunic was pulled out from the waistband.

Anyone who had served a few years in any armed force would recognize the man—not by his name, not by his individual identity, but by what he was. Clearly, he was a lifelong military man, one who had risen to the highest rank noncommissioned personnel could attain. Indispensable in his role, he could flout regulations and authority with impunity. He was too valuable a resource to court-martial for anything less than a capital offense. New officers appointed over him would try in vain to make him shave, wear his uniform according to regulations, accept a prosthetic eye to replace the organic one he had obviously lost in a battle, and treat his officers with the respect their commissions warranted. He would ignore them for a year or two, and then they'd move on, to be replaced by other officers with equally futile agendas.

Military personnel would recognize this man, but they would be wrong. Under the synthskin appliances on his cheeks, under the pasted-on whiskers and cosmetic eye patch, was Darth Caedus. He sat quietly in the copilot's seat of the cockpit, monitoring vehicle system diagnostics, assisting the pilot with various checklists, and responding in monosyllables to attempts at conversation.

He did perk up, though not visibly to the pilot, when the shuttle, in its final descent into Hapan airspace, came within sight of the cliffside approach to the palace of the Queen Mother. The entire cliff, towering as high as an office building, had been carved in the likeness of some long-dead Hapan noblewoman, down to the too-perfect features and intricately detailed jewelry.

His visible eye was alert, taking in every detail, as the shuttle entered the visitors' hangar of the palace, incongruously through the mouth of the giant carving. Following space traffic controller directions, the pilot immediately turned to starboard, sending the shuttle along a series of bay spaces paralleling the giant queen's left cheek.

Caedus calculated numbers of Hapan shuttles, crescent-moon-shaped Miy'til fighters, airspeeders, speeder bikes. He noted with satisfaction the continued presence of a StealthX starfighter, the one flown here by Tahiri. It was still awaiting transport back to the Jedi or the Galactic Alliance—doubtless still waiting for Hapes's own allegiance to be resolved before it could be moved. The StealthX, with its odd, mottled fuselage covering—looking like a patch of starfield with illusory depth like a hologram—stood out, starkly dissimilar to the elegant and stylish Hapan vehicles.

Caedus's shuttle, on repulsorlifts, cruised past many

civilian workers and military personnel, the majority of them women. Then, directed by flickering landing lights, the shuttle maneuvered into a bay and set down.

The pilot, a white-furred Bothan male, turned to face Caedus. "Why don't you inform our passengers they may . . ." Then he stopped, scrutinizing Caedus's solemn, impassive expression and slovenly dress. His snout twitched. "Never mind. I'll do that." He rose and squeezed past Caedus into the main cabin.

Caedus half listened through the partially shut cockpit door as the pilot addressed the diplomat and aides who constituted all the passengers the pilot knew about. " . . . are cleared to leave the shuttle, but they do not confirm a meeting with the Queen Mother . . . be in for quite a wait . . ." Most of Caedus's concentration was elsewhere, as he searched in the Force for the distinctive trace of his child.

This was risky. Opening himself up to the Force tended to make him easier to detect by Jedi. If Tenel Ka, the only other Jedi-trained individual he knew to be in the region, detected him, things would go badly.

Almost immediately he found Allana, a bright, joyous flare in the Force, not far away as the hawk-bat flew. But between the two of them were countless warriors and security measures.

In addition, just finding her through the Force wasn't enough. He had to *see* her. He opened himself still further, hoping for a vision of his daughter.

He felt her presence grow stronger within his senses, and then he could see, as if through a long tube, her eyes and nose. He did not pour his strength of will into what he was doing—that Sithly impulse would not be helpful with this delicate task. He simply waited, became more still, focused on the image.

His point of view drew back and away. And there Allana was, all of her, seated on a chair in front of a broad table low enough for a child her size. Directly before her was a set of controls—a horizontal monitor screen divided into several subscreens, one showing a wire-frame image of something like a crude replica of a bantha, one subdivided into dozens of colors and textures. In the center of the table was a set of articulated tubes and spindly droid arms; the tubes exuded resins or blew hardening agents upon those resins, while the arms moved and reshaped them. It took Caedus a moment to realize that the controls allowed Allana to model a toy while the apparatus simultaneously fabricated it, instantly making it real.

I will buy her one, he thought, then pushed the notion away for the time being. He needed something else from this vision.

Allana's hair, her clothes—her dark red hair was at the moment a wave of ringlets that swayed as she moved, and she wore a knee-length blue play dress and white shoes that showed no signs of scuffing.

Caedus breathed a sigh of relief. He had seen her wear that dress before, and it was one of the seven styles he'd had replicated for this mission. He relaxed, letting the vision slip away but maintaining his awareness of Allana's location.

He was almost certain Allana was not with her mother. That was good. He didn't want to confront Tenel Ka. If he did, he would probably have to kill her. That would pain him, and it would be even worse if Allana witnessed her mother's death.

Caedus heard the main cabin's exterior hatch open, heard the passengers descend the boarding ramp, heard the hatch close again. Through the forward viewport, he watched as the diplomatic party moved away from the shuttle. It was greeted and scanned by a half squadron of Hapan security officers. As the knot of them then moved toward waiting turbolifts, he could feel no one aboard—no one but himself, the pilot, and one other.

Finally the pilot came forward again. "I hope you're a better card player than you are a talker." He resumed his seat in the pilot's chair. "We could be here for days or weeks."

Caedus nodded. He reached into a tunic pocket as if to withdraw a pack of cards. Instead, he took out a small, expensive hold-out blaster. As the Bothan's eyes began to widen, Caedus shot him in the chest.

The blaster was set to stun. The pilot's eyes rolled up in his head and he collapsed.

Caedus stood and stepped away from the seats. He pushed the pilot over so that the Bothan slumped between the seats, no longer visible from the outside by passersby at floor level. Though the blaster was highly rated for effectiveness, Caedus put another couple of stun bolts into the pilot's back to be sure he'd remain unconscious for hours. Then he pocketed the weapon again.

Yes, blasters *were* clumsy and random, to quote an oft-repeated saying Luke Skywalker had picked up from someone in ancient times, but they could be useful. For someone trying to avoid alerting a Jedi-trained opponent, stun bolts were far better than lethal attacks, lightsabers, or anything that manifested strongly in the Force.

He went aft, into the cargo area, and spent a few moments unloading baggage cases from atop a large polymer crate. He punched a number into the crate's security keypad. The light beside it changed from red to green, and he lifted the lid.

Inside, a solemn-faced little redheaded girl looked up at him. Her voice was high and piping, but unafraid. "Your beard is nasty."

"Isn't it?" He stooped to lift her out of the case. She seemed in good spirits despite the hours she'd had to remain lying down, but the ready supply of snacks and availability of a game-laden datapad had doubtless helped. "Were you afraid, Tika?"

"No. I really have to go to the refresher. Really *really*."

Caedus gestured forward, to the narrow door just on his side of the entry to the main compartment. "Go ahead. And when you're done, we're going to put you in a new dress and do your hair, then have some fun."

"Good. I want to *play*." She dashed to the refresher.

"You will."

Elsewhere in the palace, levels above and many meters away from the visitors' hangar, Queen Mother Tenel Ka stared into a mirror, seeing the worry in the gray eyes of her reflection.

A delicate chime sounded. Tenel Ka said, "Enter," freeing the security measures on the door. It slid to one side, admitting her father, Prince Isolder.

A mature man once counted among the most handsome in the galaxy, he had grayed with an inevitable grace and dignity that made him a target of envious anger by anyone who had not aged so well. Had he been a common man, he could have earned a lavish income promoting exercise regimens and health supplements. But the loose-fitting, flare-sleeved blue tunic he wore cost more than a year's such income.

He bent over Tenel Ka to kiss the top of her head. "You seemed to be anxious for privacy. As a good parent, of course I can't accede to your wishes."

She smiled despite her mood. "You're still a pirate at heart. Disobedient, conceited, cocksure . . ."

"A lovely compliment. Thank you." He moved to settle on a scarlet divan. "What has you so upset?"

She shrugged. "I think it's this meeting with the GA representatives. I can't seem to settle on the right amount of time to keep them waiting. It's a harder choice than usual. It's not just about queenly dignity or meeting the expectations of my court about royal prerogatives."

In the mirror, she saw her father nod. "You want to see them when they are at their most desperate. When they are most likely to agree to your demands to have Colonel Solo removed from power."

"Yes."

"And you're weighing that against the lives being lost every day in the war."

"Yes."

Isolder considered. Tenel Ka watched him. Normally she did not need or seek political advice. But her father offered a rare exception. He was not scheming to put himself or some other favorite on the throne. He had decades of political experience not only within the Hapes Consortium but also outside, in the galaxy at large. Political and—as she had reminded him—piratical, his decision making was grounded as much in the realm of bloody deck plates as in the rarefied air of Hapan noble maneuvering.

Finally he met her gaze again. "You've already made your demand of them. At Kuat."

"I did."

"Send these diplomats home. Today. Seeing them would only give them the opportunity to argue with you. Seeing them later gives them the hope that they can argue with you then. Ejecting them from Hapan space tells them that there will be no negotiation. That, more than anything, will increase their sense of desperation."

She cocked her head, considering. "You're right."

Another series of chiming musical notes filled the air. This was not a door signal, but a communication indicating that the security alert level within the palace had just eased up another notch.

This was not an unusual event. Alert levels rose and fell with the frequency, and usually meaninglessness, of corporate stock values on Coruscant. Still, Tenel Ka had known the reason for the last one, an hour ago—the arrival of the GA diplomatic shuttle, with the usual security disturbances such an intrusion demanded. This one did not relate to any change of condition she knew of.

She pressed a button on the edge of her vanity table. "Lady Aros?"

A moment later, her chamberlain entered through the same doorway Isolder had used. A woman of that broad span of years, from their midfifties to midseventies, when Hapans devoted more and more effort to disguising their ages, and did so with considerable success, she had green eyes, a long, aristocratic nose, and features made for twisting into expressions of disapproval—though she directed only a look of concern toward Tenel Ka. Her gown, layers of iridescent synthsilk in gold and brown tones, was appropriate to a Hapan noblewoman, and scarves in the same material and colors bound up and concealed her hair. "Queen Mother?"

"Why the last alert change?"

"I will find out, Queen Mother." Aros bowed and withdrew.

Isolder smiled, amused. "You *are* nervous today."

"Yes, I am. So I have to hope something is actually going

wrong. I don't want to pick up the reputation of being . . . unwell." She repressed a wince. Her mother, Teneniel Djo, had been unwell, sick in her mind, dissociated from reality, for a time before her death.

Teneniel Djo had not been able to stand up to the emotional shock of feeling, through the Force, the deaths of thousands of people slain by use of Centerpoint Station's main gun during the Yuuzhan Vong War. Tenel Ka could not afford for anyone to think her similarly weak. It would be an invitation to another attack, another assassination attempt.

Aros reentered the chamber. "It was an automated elevation of the alert status, Queen Mother. When enough random events occur that the security computers register them, the programs do what is known, I believe, as 'raising flags,' simply indicating—"

Tenel Ka gestured to cut off her explanation. "What random events?"

"Small static interruptions in security holocam feeds. But none has lasted more than a few seconds. Security says that during intrusions, holocam interruptions last for much longer periods, a minimum of half a minute or a minute—"

"They've checked to be sure that the holocam views, once they resume, are current images? Not recordings?"

"Yes, Queen Mother." Aros's voice was endlessly, unnecessarily patient.

Tenel Ka frowned, not convinced, and opened herself to the Force. First she sought out Allana and found her— nearby, calm, sleeping. Then she broadened her perceptions, looking for anything amiss.

She felt it almost immediately, a short, distinct pulse in the Force.

Her eyes snapped open. "There is a Force-user in the palace." She punched additional buttons on the keypad of her vanity, and her own image in the mirror suddenly faded, to be replaced by an overhead view of a child's playroom.

She breathed a sigh of relief. Allana was there, undisturbed, sitting at her modeling table, head down as she worked intently at the controls. Her hair spilled around her face, obscuring it. The bantha that had been her newest creation now had four giant bulbous feet.

Then Tenel Ka frowned. A moment earlier, an *instant* earlier, Allana had been asleep.

She keyed in another location and the view changed to that of the door outside her daugher's play chamber. It was closed, sealed, innocuous.

Except for the fact that the two guards who should have been on duty there were missing.

Coldness, hard as an ancient ice comet, froze her stomach. Tenel Ka stood fast enough to hurl her chair backward. It thumped down on the carpeted floor. She spun on Aros. "Alert security. Intruders in the palace. They're making an attempt on Allana—" From beneath her robes, suited to an afternoon's lounging beside an artificial waterfall, she pulled her lightsaber and dashed past Aros, her father behind her.

Security chimes were sounding as the two of them reached the main corridor accessing the secondary royal quarters. Rightward, it led toward Allana's playroom. Leftward, it led to security stations that in turn gave way to less secure areas. Security agents dashed in either direction as noblewomen, pursing their lips in disapproval of the confusion, stayed out of their way.

Tenel Ka paused and extended her senses into the Force

once more. It took only seconds—seconds that dragged on like hours—and then she felt her daughter again.

To the left, and down.

She spun in that direction and ran, allowing the Force to lend her speed, leaving her father far behind.

chapter six

It was as though an invisible thrill killer had been on a spree within her palace. Tenel Ka ran past a group of courtiers huddled around an open door; beyond was a uniformed guardswoman, her throat slit, blue eyes open and fixed, blood pooling beside her. A few meters past, in a nook frequented by lovers and conspirators, a musician held the curtain aside to reveal a male courtier lying on the floor, his neck at an unnatural angle.

Tenel Ka felt a ripple in the Force at the next nook beyond. She tossed the curtain aside. No scene of murder met her eyes, but there was a hole in the floor, roughly circular, a meter across, its edges smoking.

A security officer running in her wake panted, "Queen Mother, we must precede you!" Ignoring her, Tenel Ka dropped through the hole.

She fell ten meters. Drawing on the Force to soften the impact, she landed on the hard, uncarpeted flooring of a service corridor, a gray-walled, cheerless passageway she had never seen before. The plug that had been cut out of the ceiling above was beside her.

Up and down the corridor kitchen workers and food

servers, the subdued colors they wore indicating their lowly status, stood as if paralyzed by shock. There was no sign of the assassin's passage. But a serving boy of perhaps sixteen years, his eyes more alert than most of those around him, jerked a thumb back over his shoulder . . . then shielded his eyes from the sight of the Queen Mother racing past him.

Ahead, around a bend in the corridor, there were more workers circling and staring at the body of a cook.

A minute later Tenel Ka took another ten-meter drop, this time to the roof of a stopped turbolift. She stepped into the access hatch and fell two meters to the turbolift floor.

The lift doors were open; beyond was the visitors' hangar. Here, nothing as delicate as chimes indicated a security breach; shrill alarms screeched. Security and maintenance personnel ran toward her, away from her, some rushing to their alarm-situation duties, some just panicking.

At least two vehicles were active. Not far away, a shuttle painted in white, sporting the Galactic Alliance crest on its sides, had its repulsorlifts going. It was moving, but only to edge ever closer to the stone wall alongside its bay. A security team was in place behind stone and duracrete columns all around the shuttle; some were aiming at the vehicle with blaster rifles, while the leader, speaking into a field comlink strapped to her wrist, was doubtless broadcasting instructions to the pilot.

But Tenel Ka could not see a pilot through the shuttle's forward viewports. She reached out toward the vehicle with the Force and detected something aboard, but that presence felt inert, nearly lifeless.

A diversion. She broadened her perceptions again, looking with increasing desperation for Allana.

There. Forty meters past the tableau with the shuttle, another vehicle had its engines running. It, too, was surrounded by a security team holding positions behind columns.

Tenel Ka raced past the shuttle, ignoring a salute from a startled-looking guardswoman, and got a good view of the other active vehicle.

Tahiri's StealthX. The coldness in her gut intensified. She did not need to peer into the visor of the pilot's helmet to know who had her daughter. It could only be Jacen.

She was halfway to the StealthX when she realized that while its repulsorlifts were being used at full strength, filling the air with what sounded like an animal scream, the starfighter was not moving. Its shields were up, too, though no member of the security detail was firing—Tenel Ka heard one of the guard officers shout, barely audible over the repulsorlift howl, "Hold your fire! He has the girl with him!"

Another two steps, and Tenel Ka could now just see the top of Allana's head. Her daughter was in Jacen's lap, webbing holding her to her father. Her head was forward as though she were asleep or preparing for a crash landing.

Tenel Ka felt a little flicker in the Force—from behind her, not from Jacen's direction. She stopped and spun, igniting her lightsaber.

There was no attack coming from that direction, but the diplomatic shuttle was now flush against the hangar's stone wall. And Tenel Ka's sense of dread, of anticipated attack, grew.

"Get back!" Her words could not possibly carry to the security officers surrounding the shuttle, but she poured her anxiety and intent into the Force, broadcasting her command on an emotional level. "Get behind cover!"

Suiting action to words, she leapt behind one of the natural stone columns lining the hangar bay and put her back to it. She turned her head to glance toward Jacen.

He looked straight at her, offering a tight little smile, then held up a comlink. He pressed the button on it.

The universe went white and the column kicked against Tenel Ka's back . . .

Tenel Ka heard her daughter calling for her. But the Hapan queen stood in red mud up to her knees, with Allana nowhere in sight. Broken columns tilted at odd angles, and severed arms and legs the size of public transportation speeders protruded from the mud—as far as the horizon, in every direction.

"Mommy—"

Tenel Ka opened her eyes and sat up, looking around wildly for her child.

Her head hurt and her ears rang like someone playing a tympani on a gong. She recognized her surroundings, one of the numberless waiting rooms up at the royal residence level. This one, decorated in subtle variations of purples and off-whites, was adjacent to Allana's playroom. She must have been dreaming.

Tenel Ka sat on a morphing divan that had been adjusted to daybed dimensions. Isolder rose from where he'd been sitting on a chair opposite her. "Lie down. You're hurt." His words were dim, hard to hear over the ringing in her ears.

Instead, she stood, wobbling in sudden, passing dizziness. "Where's Allana?"

"Jacen Solo has her." Isolder's face was pale, as ashen as it had been the day his wife had died. "The shuttle blast, a shaped charge, was sufficient to blow a hole in the hangar's exterior wall large enough for his starfighter. He made orbit in his X-wing and escaped."

The coldness in Tenel Ka's gut spread to envelop her entire body. Her legs shook. Her father put his hands on her shoulders, steadying her. "Please, sit. We have battle cruisers and Battle Dragons strung along the routes between here and Coruscant. But it's likely that he will have picked an escape route we can't predict."

She let Isolder guide her back down to the divan's surface. "How long—"

"Two hours ago. The diplomatic party has been detained and is being interrogated." Isolder's voice was grim. "The shock they're expressing . . . I can only guess at this point, but I think it's genuine. It looks like they thought they were on an actual mission of negotiation, and that Solo used them only as a diversion."

"Has he communicated—has he sent terms for her return?"

Isolder's expression became even more sour. "He left a message. A datachip handed to me by the little girl who acted as Allana's double. I'll play it for you." He rose and moved to a table to activate the monitor upon it.

"Who is the girl?"

"A Coruscanti orphan named Tika. Solo promised that if she would do this one thing for him, he'd take her to a world where there were thousands of beautiful women, one of whom would become her new mommy."

Tenel Ka clapped her hand over her mouth. It was just one more horror, and the least of the ones she had endured in just a few waking minutes, but it somehow pointed more starkly to Jacen's inhumanity than all the murders he had perpetrated to seize Allana.

Isolder stepped away from the monitor. Jacen Solo

popped up on the display, somber, dressed in his Galactic Alliance Guard colonel's uniform.

"Greetings to the esteemed Queen Mother of the Hapes Consortium." His voice did not exactly drip with sarcasm, but the excessive formality he employed, treating Tenel Ka as some distant ruler, ignoring all that they had been to each other, was just as hurtful. "At Kuat, you put me into an untenable situation. Being abandoned to my enemies, abandoned by one for whom I once had considerable affection and respect, was like being murdered . . . and surviving.

"So I'm going to repay the favor. You have a choice to make, like the one you tried to force upon me. You will put all Hapan military forces under my command, with ships' senior officers to be supplied by the Galactic Alliance . . . or your daughter will die."

Jacen leaned forward so that his face more completely filled the monitor screen. His eyes were bright, inhuman in their intensity and focus. They even seemed lighter in color than usual. "By doing what you did to me, you changed me into someone capable of doing exactly what I have promised. This threat is not a bluff, and if it takes place, it will be your doing. Something to keep in mind the next time you play the Hapan cultural game of backstabbing and bloodletting."

The screen went dark.

Tenel Ka let out the breath she realized she'd been holding since Jacen first appeared on screen. Isolder said nothing.

Finally, she turned to him. She struggled to keep her voice even, but it wasn't easy; her breath wanted to come in pained gasps. "Prince Isolder. In your opinion, is he capable of carrying out his threat?"

"I don't know him nearly as well as you, Queen Mother.

But . . . yes." He glanced at the monitor. "I've watched the recording a dozen times, and each time I see a man whose humanity has been utterly extracted from him."

Tears came to Tenel Ka's eyes. "He was right, you know. It's like being murdered and surviving."

chapter seven

KASHYYYK, MAITELL BASE, HANGAR HOUSING
THE **MILLENNIUM FALCON**

Waroo set the oversized metal case down on the sabacc table. The Wookiee offered a mild growl of a question.

Han looked down at the case. It looked like the sort wealthy travelers used to transport delicate, expensive clothing. Outfitted with foam inserts, a case like this was also ideal for transporting weapons, and this one was large enough to hold several blaster rifles with folding stocks or a couple of squadrons' worth of blaster pistols.

Han, opposite the Wookiee, shook his head. "You got me, pal. You sure it's for me?"

Waroo nodded.

Leia looked closely at the case. "I don't feel any sense of menace from it. Did you do a routine scan?"

Waroo grunted an affirmative.

"Clean, huh. But no indication who sent it." Han gave the top seam locks another look. In the shadow cast by the case itself, the broad locking tabs glowed slightly. "That's not too comforting."

"It's a scanner." Jag, leading Jaina and Zekk, was walking in from deeper in the hangar, where their X-wings had their bays. Just back from a routine patrol, he had reported that the firebreak lines carved by *Lillibanca* with the help of the Solos and other pilots, including Lando Calrissian, were holding. "They read thumbprints."

"Huh." Experimentally, Han placed his thumbs over the tabs, but did not touch them. He glanced at Leia. "I assume you'll give me a push if this starts to blow up."

She affected disinterest. "Probably."

"Yeah." He placed his thumbs on the tabs.

They beeped, shrill little noises, then gave way under the pressure of his thumbs. He pressed harder and they clicked into place. Gingerly, Han lifted the case's lid.

The case did indeed have foam inserts, but it did not hold firearms. In the bottom was the front piece of a breast-plate, shaped in a stylized representation of a male human chest, well muscled. In the top of the case were two metal gauntlets, nearly elbow-length. All three items were made of a dull metal, something like brushed silver or burnished iron.

A piece of flimsi was tucked into the gap between one gauntlet and the foam insert that held it. Han pulled it free, unfolded it, and read aloud the words hand-printed on it: "With deepest sympathy."

Leia frowned. "Sympathy for what?"

A weight settled on Han's chest. He tried to ignore it. "These are crushgaunts. A Mandalorian weapon. Illegal for generations, plus very hard to make anyway, on account of the Mandalorian veins of *beskar* mostly ran out. That's what they're made of."

Jag shook his head, not recognizing the term. "*Beskar?*"

"Mandalorian iron. Tough, tough metal. Legend says armor made from the stuff can take a lightsaber hit and survive. Mechanisms in the gauntlet hands allow them to crush whatever they grip. Necks, heads, blaster rifles, just about anything. I saw a pair once, years ago. Another smuggler showed 'em off before delivering them to Jabba the Hutt."

Jaina looked puzzled. "Is this that pair?"

"No, sweetie. These are new. Unscarred."

The answer did not clear up Jaina's confusion. "So the armor is a Mandalorian breastplate?"

Han nodded. "Yeah. The back plate is probably under it." He lifted the front plate, revealing a matching piece of armor, its surface contoured more like a human back, lying there. The front plate was not heavy—it felt more like aluminum than iron. "Uh-huh."

Jaina shook her head. "I still don't get it."

"It's a present, Jaina. From Boba Fett."

Han heard Leia's intake of breath. He sat heavily in his usual chair. Not wanting to worsen Leia's pain or his own, but unable just to ignore Jaina's continued curiosity, he held up the piece of flimsi. "Get it? Sympathy for my loss of a son. Something he understands, since he lost a daughter. A daughter tortured to death *by* my son. He's saying, *So sad you lost your kid. Here's a little toy you can finish him off with.*"

Jaina's face became impassive. "Oh. Are you going to use it?"

"No."

"So he's wasted a lot of money for nothing."

Han nodded. "A *lot* of money. Even if the Mandalorians are mining *beskar* again, this is a lot of credits and effort for a snide joke." He looked at the case's contents again. "Except it's only half a joke. He'd like to help whoever it is kills the killer of his daughter. He'd probably like to do something for whoever takes Colonel Solo out of the equation. He may even feel real sympathy." He reached over to slam the case lid down. "His message is as complicated, as much of a mess, as Fett himself."

Jaina, clearly uninterested, shrugged and turned away. "Time for a sanisteam." She tugged at Zekk's sleeve. "Then more training."

He followed, protesting: "How about training first, then the sanisteam? That way we don't have a pointless sanisteam in the middle."

Jag remained behind, eyeing the case. "Han, at the risk of sounding insensitive . . ."

Han snorted. "If *you* think it's insensitive, whatever it is will probably take the paint off a Hutt's refresher."

Jag gave him a brief, apologetic smile. "You're really not going to use this gear?"

Han shook his head.

"Armor that stops a lightsaber, with Alema Rar our target . . ."

"You think it would be useful to you."

"Not as useful as something you said the other day, but yes. Very much so."

Han frowned, puzzled. "What did I say?"

"Something about Alema's tactics." But Jag did not elaborate.

"All right, kid. Take it, it's yours."

Leia broke in on Han's words: "On one condition."

Jag stopped in the act of picking up the case. "Of course. Name it."

"Tell me what's wrong with my daughter."

Jag hefted the case experimentally. It was apparently nowhere near as heavy as he had expected. "She is entirely focused on our target. Alema Rar."

"I know that. But even facing a dangerous enemy shouldn't make her so cold, impassive."

"Emotionless." Jag looked after the departing Jaina and Zekk. They were walking toward a tree-shaded glade they often used as a sparring site. "Well, it's the whole Sword of the Jedi thing. She thinks she's figured out what it is to be the Sword of the Jedi. Going after Alema Rar is just practice for her. She thinks she's going to have to face her brother. And that one of them's not going to come out of it alive."

Han sighed. He reached up to take his wife's hand. Leia's fingers gripped his hard. "Sure, kid. A lot of people are looking forward to a showdown with Colonel Solo."

"Jaina . . ." Jag hesitated, struggling for the words. "She thinks that any distraction now could be fatal to her then. That means enjoyment of any sort. Anything that would make her smile is the enemy. The thing is, she's really a lot *like* her brother, before his change, and I don't want her to cast off her humanity the way he has." He offered Leia a brief smile of apology for those words. "I'm trying to find a way to tell her that if you sharpen a sword all the time, even when it's not dull, by the time you need it there's no metal left. It will break. But she's not listening."

Leia's voice was low, concerned. "Have you used those exact words?"

"She doesn't learn from words, Jedi Solo. She only learns from success. And failure." Jag gave her a sympathetic look and walked out into the sunlight, metal case in hand.

chapter eight

CORUSCANT,
GALACTIC ALLIANCE GUARD BUILDING

Allana opened her eyes. In front of her was the corner of
the bed she was lying on—a plain bed, its mattress very soft
and comfortable but old-fashioned, not adjusting its shape
to her as she moved. Beyond it was a bare brown wall, its
simulated wood pattern hard to make out in the dim light
of half-shadowed glow rods.

She didn't know this place.

She rolled over to see the whole room, and there he
was—seated in a chair by the bed, tall and handsome,
wearing his black uniform, his eyes so bright and intent
they almost frightened her.

But she shouldn't be frightened of him. He was her
mother's friend.

She held out her arms. "Jacen."

His face twitched a little when she called his name, but
he came to her and held her. "Allana. You slept a long
time."

"Where am I?" Her voice was muffled against his shoulder.

He drew back to look at her again, and now his eyes were normal. "You're on Coruscant."

"Where's Mommy?"

"She's back on Hapes."

Allana fidgeted, and, reluctance on his face, Jacen released her. "Why is she there and not here?"

"You don't remember?"

She shook her head.

"Bad people came to your palace. They wanted to hurt you and your mother."

"Like before."

Jacen nodded. "They used coma gas, which puts people to sleep. Since you're little, it put you to sleep for a long time. I had just arrived there for a visit. Your mother thought you'd be safer if you came home with me. That way, the bad people won't know where you are."

"Oh." That made sense, but her mother had said that anyone Allana was going to be sent away with like that, even if there wasn't time for a good-bye, would know the special words. And Jacen hadn't said the special words yet. "Can I talk to Mommy on the holocomm?"

Jacen shook his head. "Not yet. The bad people could trace the transmission. Do you know what that means?"

Allana nodded. "Like following a trail of bread crumbs."

"Exactly. That would lead them right here, which would undo all the good your mommy and I have done. So we'll just have to stay hidden for a while. But I'm arranging to have all sorts of things brought here for you to play with. Toys and gadgets and musical instruments."

"And friends?"

"Not yet. Soon, I hope. I'll have a droid friend for you

tomorrow." He gave her another hug. "I've got to go, but I'll be watching through that holocam." He pointed straight up, but Allana could see nothing on the ceiling there. "So you'll always be safe. Just call for me if you need anything."

"All right." She watched him leave, then lay down again.

And she wondered how long it would be before Jacen remembered the special words, and what she should do if he never said them.

CORUSCANT,
BENEATH THE GALACTIC ALLIANCE
GOVERNMENT DISTRICT

There were five of them, Jedi all, ranging in experience from a teenage girl to a graying veteran who had first seen action as a stormtrooper serving Palpatine's Empire.

Valin Horn, son of Corran, breathed a sigh of relief that he was not at the low end of the age ranking. In his late twenties, he was, by a statistical accident that seemed to plague him, often paired with much older Jedi. Here Master Kyle Katarn was indeed his senior, by some forty-odd years. But the Falleen male, Thann Mithric, and the Bothan female, Kolir Hu'lya, were both his junior by several months. And the human girl leading them, Seha, was youngest of all.

Not that seniority mattered much on a mission like this. Valin was just pleased that he was getting old enough not to be at the bottom of every age sorting.

All five Jedi wore matte-black garments that covered them from neck to toes. The material, slick against abrasive surfaces like duracrete and metal drainage pipes, retained heat in cold surroundings like water but radiated it in warmer environments. The Jedi carried—and sometimes, as now, dragged or pushed—packs containing their lightsabers, robes that could be folded into very compact bundles, other weapons, and climbing equipment.

None of which was likely to help them at the moment, as they wriggled their way like worms along a damp, constricting waste-fluids pipe. Seha had said that it hadn't served its intended purpose in all the time she had been alive. But cracks all over the ancient city infrastructure allowed water from other pipelines to leak in, some of it foul smelling. And Seha had told them that during a fierce rain, pipes like this could be flooded and washed clean.

"Don't worry," she'd said. "If there's a flood, we'll have a few moments' warning. You just whip out your lightsabers and cut a hole in the pipe."

"Can you whip out your lightsaber, Kolir?" Valin made his whisper loud enough to carry to the ears of the Bothan, who crawled before him. All he could see of her were her black-clad feet and lower legs, barely discernible in the light from the glow rod tucked behind his ear.

Her voice, a low growl, floated back to him: "Quiet, you."

"Just asking. Polite conversation. You're not claustrophobic, are you?"

"No!"

"Because that would account for your irritability."

"So would hunger. And you're beginning to sound a lot like red meat."

"When we're done here, I'd be happy to treat you to dinner."

"Sons of famous fathers *do* have to try harder, to compensate."

Valin grinned. At least she could banter.

He heard a familiar buzzing noise from ahead and stopped to listen. Yes, it was a lightsaber, but not being used in haste. Kolir stopped, too. The buzz went on for nearly a minute, then ceased.

Kolir finally passed back the news. "Seha reached a new obstacle, a metal grate. She was using her lightsaber to cut through it."

"Her lightsaber, which I suppose she dropped, and now she needs to borrow one."

Very distantly, he heard Seha's voice: "I heard that." Then Kolir was crawling forward again, and Valin followed.

Moments later he wriggled out through the newly opened, still-warm end of the tube and dropped lightly to a duracrete floor two meters down. Here, too, there were no working glow rods, but at least he could stand upright. He stood aside to let Mithric drop beside him.

Valin glanced around. The others had smudges of grease and filth on their faces. Kolir's tan fur was matted and encrusted in places. Mithric's ponytail had a spherical, six-legged bug climbing through it. Valin assumed he himself looked equally unappetizing.

Seha, the least filthy of them, glanced around to get her bearings. "We're inside the second security zone, under the plaza approach to the Senate Building." She pointed in the general direction the pipe end faced. "That way is toward the Senate Building. If we keep going, we run into the innermost ring of security, the thickest concentration of sensors. It's not that they're especially hard to get past individually—just that there are so many, with overlapping coverages, that it's practically impossible to disable them all or get through them undetected. It could be done, but even someone with much better skills than mine would take weeks to do it."

Master Katarn nodded as if satisfied. "Staging from here

will be fine. Though it would be better if we had several lines of sight and firing positions."

Seha gestured forward and up, toward a dark vertical shaft accessed by durasteel rungs inset into the permacrete. "That's the closest one. There will be a sensor at the access hatch, but we can disable it. I can take you laterally to three or four similar spots, each with a view of the front entrance."

Katarn considered. "I need to have the position closest to Colonel Solo's usual approach to the building. We'll spread out among all the accesses. Seha, I want every one of us to be able to find our way back to this spot by touch. And this will be your station, too. Your job is to stay alive, stay here, and get us all out, regardless of whether the mission is a success or a catastrophic failure."

Seha nodded, clearly intimidated by the responsibility placed on her.

chapter nine

COMMENOR

At times like this, Lieutenant Caregg Oldathan wondered who creaked more—himself, or the aging K-wing assault starfighter he flew. Both of them had been recalled from honorable retirement to active duty when the civil war had begun, and both were in dire need of maintenance and rest.

Not that they were likely to get any today. Rising through high planetary orbit to the engagement zone, where Alliance ships were once again arriving to assault planetary defense forces, he shook his head and offered up a near-silent curse. The Alliance units being brought to bear against them were not enough to crack Commenor's defenses, but were sufficient to keep them from being deployed to other theaters of war. They were enough to wear those forces down over time, and Oldathan was certain they were doing their job.

"One minute to contact," he said. "Weapons check."

"Lasers in the green." That was the voice of Lieutenant Danen, his bombardier-gunner for this mission. He occupied the starboard cockpit of the vehicle's dual-cockpit arrangement. "Bangers report operable."

Bangers were, in Commenori military parlance, concussion missiles, and this K-wing's hardpoint attachments were laden with them. Oldathan would have preferred *boomers*, or proton torpedoes—his starfighter's primary mission was to prey on capital ships—but at this point in the conflict they were in short supply.

The next voice over the comm board was not Danen's but that of their flight controller, operating from a sensor station on the ground. "Grayfeather Squadron, report."

Oldathan frowned. "Grayfeather One here."

"Divert to heading one-eight-oh immediately. We're picking up an intermittent blip that suggests a vessel approaching on the night side, but we can't get a fix on it. Coordinates should be on your sensor board now."

Oldathan glanced at his sensor board and saw a broad green dot over equatorial Commenor a few thousand kilometers to the west, which marked the start of their new search zone. "Got it. Grayfeathers on the move. Out." He took a moment to retransmit the coordinates to the other four K-wings in what was left of his squadron, then led them westward.

In atmosphere, the trip would have taken hours, but a high ballistic trajectory like this, outside of atmosphere, would be done in a fraction of the time. Still, Oldathan was twitchy with impatience. The battle zone, where his comrades were fighting and dying, was behind him. This was like running away.

Unless, of course, the phantom blip was indeed some sort of Alliance attack, not just another malfunction of Commenor's overtaxed planetary defense sensor system.

When they reached the target zone, they found it empty of airborne traffic except for one ground-based courier shuttle sprinting off into space, its crew hoping to get clear of the planet's gravity well and enter hyperspace before Alliance forces detected and intercepted it. Nothing else showed up on sensors.

Oldathan shook his head, annoyed. "Another monkey-lizard chase. All right. Two and Three, head spinward a hundred clicks. Four and Five, anti-spinward. Begin spiral patterns outward. I'll stay here and do the same. Report all contacts instantly."

He received four confirmations and saw the two wing pairs peel off to head toward their respective start zones. He felt no undue worry. The shovel-headed, thick-winged starfighters were not particularly fast or elegant, but he knew they could take care of themselves—they were more heavily armed than just about any comparable vehicles the enemy was likely to field.

As he began his own spiral pattern, he tuned in to the general fleet frequency to listen to the battle's progress. Things weren't going badly. One enemy frigate had been destroyed, one enemy cruiser had sustained enough damage that it had withdrawn. Starfighter losses were about even between the two sides.

But there were disturbing little signs in the comm transmissions. One rescue shuttle pilot reported, "Have retrieved six friendly 'walkers.' " That meant six pilots who were extravehicular from having ejected before the destruction of their starfighters. But what were the odds that, randomly, the rescue pilot had run across only friendly pilots? Most rescue beacons were on common comm channels and unscrambled, with interplanetary rules of war dictating that forces of any side perform rescues. Had the shuttle pilot just ignored signals from enemy walkers? Had he fired upon enemy ejectees?

Oldathan didn't know. What he did know was that he'd

been hearing more and more of these communications in recent weeks. He knew that rumors of harsh treatment of enemy prisoners of war were increasing—both in GA camps and in Commenori camps. He knew that overtaxed Commenori personnel were, increasingly, channeling their anger and frustration into private activities: entertainments made specifically to cater to their changing tastes, such as underground bloodsports, or so rumor had it. This bothered Oldathan a lot. It was something his fellow pilots—sophisticated, educated men and women compared with many serving in the armed forces—had not done even at the height of the frustrations and terrors of the Yuuzhan Vong War.

The military leaders officially didn't see any of this. Unofficially, they approved. Fewer pilots were cracking up—that meant more experience was staying in the cockpits. That was all that mattered.

Danen's voice interrupted his musings. "I just saw a star disappear."

"Sure you did." Oldathan checked his sensor board again. He saw nothing but the five starfighters of his squadron. "If the Alliance can make whole stars disappear, we need to surrender *now*."

"No, really. In the Jeweled Lizard. Second star from the end of the tail."

Oldathan craned his neck to look upward, then brought the nose of the K-wing up so it would be easier for him to look. Sure enough, the tail of the familiar constellation had only four stars in it now, not five.

Then the missing star reappeared.

Almost holding his breath, Oldathan sent the K-wing into a spiraling climb toward that distant point in space, widening the pattern as he ascended. A moment later, the last star in the lizard's tail vanished, then reappeared a few seconds afterward.

And there was still nothing on his sensors.

"Grayfeather One to squadron, Grayfeather One to Starfighter Control. We have an anomaly here, spaceward from my position, distance unknown, size unknown. Suspect it may be a cloaked capital vessel." Starship cloaking mechanisms were rare due to the tremendous power drains they cost their host vehicles and, depending on the design, the usually fatal price of the vehicle controllers having no ability to detect anything outside their cloaking fields. But they *did* exist, and had been used within living memory.

"Grayfeather One, acknowledged."

Oldathan switched to squadron frequency. "Two through Five, maintain your current patterns, but scan visually along the line I'm about to transmit." He had Danen plot a missile-firing solution toward the anomaly zone and transmit it to the others. It appeared on the sensor boards as a line from his current position to the farthest reaches of the Commenor system, toward the end of the Jeweled Lizard's tail.

A few moments later Grayfeather Four reported in. "I have it, sir."

"Give me a plot."

Seconds passed, and then another red line appeared on the sensor board. Together with Oldathan's line, it formed two sides of a very long, narrow triangle. The third line, the triangle's base, had it been drawn, would have been much shorter than the other two, and would have spanned only a fraction of Commenor's diameter.

"Everybody, keep at it, update sightings on our sensor board. I'm heading up." Oldathan switched back to fleet frequency, then sent his K-wing on a rapid ascent straight toward the target. "Control, blip is definitely an inbound ship. We're triangulating to get its speed of approach."

"Understood, Grayfeather One. We'll have support your way within minutes."

Oldathan shook his head. Starfighter Control was not likely to divert vehicles already engaged in Commenor orbit, meaning that what he'd get would be some reserve squadrons—likely as not, some planetary defense TIE fighters so old that their solar array wings wobbled.

As Oldathan climbed away from Commenor, the other Grayfeathers continued to supply him data. More lines appeared on his sensor board. They didn't form a clean image; the triangle was shortening.

Danen muttered to himself as he ran mathematical calculations. "Best guess, it's now at about twenty thousand clicks. And moving at about forty thousand clicks per hour."

Oldathan grunted an acknowledgment. "It should begin decelerating pretty soon."

Under constant acceleration, Grayfeather One closed the distance to the target in short order. Oldathan decelerated and swung wide of the incoming vessel's approach path—not being able to see it or precisely calculate its speed made him twitchy, nervous about collision.

But now his target was easy to detect. Sensors still did not pick it up, nor could the naked eye, but there was a growing dark spot in space where stars just blanked out.

A *big* dark spot in space. "Danen, can you give me an estimated size?"

"Uhhh . . . Circle it, would you?"

Oldathan did, drawing ever closer as he maneuvered. His own estimates made his mouth go dry. "I hope your numbers are friendlier than my guesses."

"I don't think so. I'd hazard . . . thirty, forty kilometers across. At least."

"Grayfeather One to Control. Incoming blip is meteor-sized. Repeat, meteor-sized. Nature and identity still not known. Blip is cloaked. Request authority to fire upon it." There was a chance, a bare chance, that it was a friendly vehicle, planetoid-sized, arriving under the auspices of and with the permission of the planetary government, and refusal of authorization would be a sign that this was the case.

"Grayfeather, you are authorized to fire."

Oldathan turned toward the void and accelerated. The rapidness with which it grew in his viewport suggested that he was close to it, but he had no good way of determining *how* close. No way before now.

"Arm two bangers. Report their transceiver codes to squadron and Control sensors. Then fire."

Danen's voice, now that he was engaged in acts of war, was cool, professional. "Yes, sir."

A moment later the K-wing shuddered slightly and two glowing lines streaked away from its outer wing hardpoints—emissions from the concussion missiles Danen had launched.

The two lines converged in the distance, and, seconds later, ended in what looked like a single detonation.

Oldathan checked his sensor board. It showed the missile paths as lines and reported a distance to target of 321 kilometers.

He swore, swung the nose of his starfighter out of line with his target, and banked to fall in behind the target's approach path. Now, as he turned back toward the planet, he saw the void as a featureless blackness obscuring the middle of the planet.

"Something's happening." Danen's voice sounded professionally detached. "Sensor readings—"

On Oldathan's sensor board, a shape appeared for a moment, a huge shape, then disappeared again. Moments later, it returned . . . and through the forward canopy he could finally see his target.

It was roughly oval, but very irregular, with a dark, mottled surface. There was activity on its surface, lights igniting. He increased magnification on his visual scanner and could see small craft launching from what looked like a power plant installation on the surface. One vehicle was a shuttle; there were also a dozen or more starfighters and something that looked like a small, highly modified Blockade Runner–style frigate, but with a prow shaped like a balloon instead of a sledgehammer.

Danen no longer sounded matter-of-fact. "Nickel-iron asteroid. Millions of tons."

"We've got to . . . we've got to . . ." Words failed Oldathan. There was nothing they *could* do. It would take hours, maybe days, to mount an operation that could divert or destroy such a target. Commenor had no planet-buster weapons, no Death Star main gun, nothing that could cope with this.

As he watched, the fleeing enemy craft cleared well away from the asteroid . . . and then bright lines appeared on the asteroid's surface, as though a giant child were scribbling on it with a pen filled with glowing ink.

The asteroid separated into dozens of chunks, each massing hundreds or thousands of tons. They drifted apart, moving in a slow, curiously stately fashion away from the center of the explosion that had shattered the asteroid.

"Got to evacuate . . ." Helpless, Oldathan shook his head. He had to do *something*. By an act of will, he got his voice under control again. "Danen, transmit constant sensor feed to Control. Control, here's what's coming at you."

He didn't have enough firepower to affect any shard of that asteroid. But he could, perhaps, prevent the enemy from using the same equipment to employ the same tactic. He reacquired the flight of enemy starfighters on sensor and swung toward them. "Grayfeathers, join me here. Primary target is the vehicle with the balloon-shaped prow, which I'm assuming is the cloaking mechanism. Secondary is the shuttle. All others insignificant."

He heard affirmatives from his squadmates.

He pushed them from his mind. He wasn't likely ever to see them again. But maybe he could delay the enemy's exit from the system long enough for the other Grayfeathers to reach them, to finish the job he was about to start.

He engaged the K-wing's auxiliary thruster, the one used for short bursts of acceleration, and roared toward the enemy formation. "Hey, Danen."

"Yeah."

"Good working with you."

"Yeah. You, too."

chapter ten

CORUSCANT UNDERCITY,
NEAR SENATE BUILDING

Hours after their arrival at their destination, each Jedi was positioned beneath a different plaza-level access cover—except for Seha, who shared Master Katarn's.

Valin studied his hands. His palms were bandaged over the scrapes and cuts he'd picked up both in getting to this spot and then from the hours of training Seha had put them through, tracing and retracing routes from their assigned stations to the exit point where Master Katarn and Seha were now situated.

But he didn't mind. Now he suspected that he could make his way back to the exit point if he were blindfolded, during a quake, with a full orchestra blaring away beside him. The only things likely to thwart a mad scramble to the escape route would be the many crawling, venomous denizens to be found in the undercity, so much more numerous since the Yuuzhan Vong had executed their Vong-forming of Coruscant and introduced thousands of new species as part of their effort to reshape the world.

Valin hung in a vertical shaft similar to the one Seha had pointed out earlier. Suspended from durasteel access rungs by cables and snap-to climbing hooks, sitting on a broad cloth sling that had been comfortable an hour earlier, he was a bare meter below the exit hatch. In addition to the slicksuit and his backpack, he wore a set of optics—not electrobinoculars, but a holocam monitor structured as a set of goggles. Attached to them was a tiny optic cable that ran up and through the locking mechanism of the access hatch, its tiny holocam end protruding through the other side and oriented toward the main Senate Building entrance. Just now it showed little; there was still an hour or more to go until dawn, and there was little pedestrian or speeder traffic at surface level. Overhead, however, the streams of airspeeder traffic remained constant, multicolored glows of movement in hundreds of trails of light. That was Coruscant, in wartime or peacetime—never asleep, always vividly colorful.

The holocam cable was not the only one that ran from him. Another ran from the earbud he wore to the wall, to which it was attached by a lump of greenish glue. It ran down the shaft and off to the station Katarn and Seha shared.

Comlink transmissions might be detected, especially so close to the Senate Building, where security was so high. Exchanges of images or feelings through the Force might be detected by Jacen Solo. That left an antiquated but remarkably reliable standby, the intercom.

Mithric's voice came across it now. "Kolir has got her antenna up and out, and she's receiving HoloNet news."

Valin snorted. "What's new?"

"Elements of the Third Fleet attacked Commenor. In addition to hammering at military forces, they dropped asteroids onto the planet proper. They hit population centers like city-buster bombs."

Valin whistled. "Had to be Colonel Solo's orders, not Admiral Niathal's."

"That's the weird thing. Apparently it was neither. The task force commander did it on his own initiative. He's been brought to Coruscant to face charges."

The next voice Valin heard was Kolir's. "The Commenori are going to retaliate. I mean, beyond just a normal military response. Aren't they?"

"Probably." That was Master Katarn. "Even if it wasn't because of orders from the Chiefs of State, the GA just violated conventions of war. How is Admiral Niathal going to persuade them that it was a rogue commander, that the Commenori should fight fair? I don't think it's going to happen."

Valin's holocam view, a wrenching 360-degree panorama, showed distant lights inbound—a short stream of them at ground level. "Heads up, Jedi. Looks like a convoy approaching my position."

Mithric snorted. "Relax. It won't be Colonel Solo. He only shows up when there are holocams on hand to record the event, the better for Alliance morale."

Valin frowned. "A logical fallacy. The only occasions we know about are his public entrances. We can't conclude that he doesn't make private ones."

Mithric's voice turned baiting. "Do all the Horns delight in their logical faculties?"

Master Katarn's response was mild. "Quiet, please." But it served to shut everyone up.

The convoy, three airspeeders, passed Valin's position. The first one was a black Galactic Alliance Guard vehicle, a small, speedy four-passenger model. The alert lights atop the vehicle were not active. The second was a civilian speeder: long, black, enclosed, and—from the way it bobbed on its repulsors as they crossed uneven patches of plaza duracrete—very heavy, probably armored. The third was a black GAG group carrier. Its slablike sides could lift away to reveal up to a full squadron of armed and armored troopers.

And the one individual whose identity Valin could make out through the second speeder's side viewpoint set off alarm bells in his mind. "Uh, this could be him. It's all GAG and a VIP."

Katarn's voice remained outwardly calm. "Did you see Solo?"

"No, but there's other bad news. The second vehicle is carrying a YVH combat droid."

The Yuuzhan Vong Hunter droids, designed at the height of the Yuuzhan Vong War, were formidable. In a one-on-one match between a Jedi Knight and a YVH droid, the odds were about even. If the Jedi was inexperienced, if the battle dragged on long enough for her to tire, she was likely to be the loser . . . a dead loser.

"Oh, I *hate* those." There was a wealth of dismay and experience in Kolir's tone.

"Ready yourself." Katarn continued to sound calm, almost bored. "They're pulling to a stop near my position."

Valin sat up and out of his sling seat, hanging on to the durasteel rungs, and reached into his backpack for the grenade launcher there. He hooked his elbow through the wall rung so he could more easily use both hands to open out the weapon's folding stock. It clicked reassuringly into place. He did all this by touch, watching through his holo-cam feed as the three vehicles slowed to a simultaneous stop.

First the side slabs of the troop carrier lifted. Six GAG troopers with blaster rifles stepped out from the benches on each side. Six flanked the center vehicle; the other six moved toward the Senate Building and then stopped, arrayed in two lines of three, with three meters of space between the lines.

Valin climbed until his head was just beneath the hatch. This was looking more and more like a go.

The doors of the second vehicle rose, and the first being to emerge was the YVH. The angular droid moved out from the front seat, opened the rear passenger's-side door, and extracted a shipping crate from the backseat. At a meter tall and wide, a meter and a half long, black like most GAG gear, the crate was large enough to be unwieldy. The droid pulled it partway out, then lifted it, demonstrating remarkable care and delicacy.

Valin wanted desperately to reach out through the Force and see if he could divine the crate's contents, but any such action might alert Jacen. He just bit his lip.

Then the rear driver's-side door opened and Jacen Solo, his cape fluttering in a light breeze, stepped out.

Katarn's voice remained maddeningly calm. "Wait until he's a few meters from the vehicle."

Solo himself waited until the combat droid carried its mystery package around to his side of the speeder. Then, side by side, they walked toward the Senate Building entrance.

"Go."

Behind him, from all over the nearly deserted plaza, Caedus heard four metal clanks and knew there was trouble.

He and YVH-908 spun. He heard a faint exclamation of complaint from inside the crate as Allana was whirled. Then, from out in the darkness, came a succession of *poomp-poomp-poomp* noises—familiar to him as the sounds made by a grenade launcher set to sustained automatic fire.

He ignited his lightsaber. "Secure the package." In his peripheral vision, he saw the combat droid whirl again, completing a 360-degree turn—accompanied by another "Whoof!" from Allana—and then begin running toward the doors, its metal heels clanging with each step.

A flare ignited high in the air, and Caedus reached upward, sensing through the Force, feeling the descent of many tumbling metal cylinders—

He raised a hand to sweep them away, but a tingle of alarm caused him to stiffen. This came not through the Force but from a simple mathematical realization. Four metal clangs. Two grenade launchers firing. What were the other two positions doing?

He had a moment before the descending grenades would be close enough to explode and do him harm, so he looked down, out toward the darkened plaza, and extended his perceptions in that direction.

And felt them—more metal cylinders, at least a dozen, rolling toward him rather than flying. Now he could feel the ripples in the Force as they were propelled telekinetically toward him.

Contemptuous, he flicked his hand toward the darkness and felt his own power turn the cylinders around. They began rolling back the way they had come.

The sky above lit up as though noon had come more than six hours early—worse, for the brightness surpassed that of high noon. Troopers all around him cried out, threw their arms over their eyes. The visors of their helmets could not darken fast enough to protect their wearers from these dazzle-grenades.

Caedus cursed. His assumption that the falling missiles were explosives, that he had a second before they reached him, had just cost him his support troops. But he, at least, could see.

Out in the darkness, the rolling grenades exploded with moist *crump* noises. *Gas grenades, then. Coma gas? Stun gas?* The breeze was from behind him. The gas would not reach him or his troops.

Finally he detected more than just telekinetic pushes; he felt presences as his enemies drew on Force abilities. He felt them rush toward him, caught sight of them as they entered the glow of lights from the front of the Senate Building—four Jedi, Master Kyle Katarn foremost among them.

Katarn ignited his lightsaber as he came to a stop a few meters away. "Care to surrender, Colonel Solo?"

"Not to a traitor." Caedus looked at the other three as their Force-augmented sprints came to an end, leaving them in a semicircle before him. Three Jedi Knights: the younger Horn, the Falleen Mithric, the Bothan Hu'lya. He resisted the urge to snort. Separately or collectively, these Jedi Knights were no match for him.

Katarn, though, was a threat. Still, the Jedi had only moments before GA reinforcements would arrive. Their attack was already a failure.

He sensed Katarn's attack, threw up his blade in a block so well practiced that his muscle memory could have performed it while he slept. With his free hand, he gestured at the Bothan Jedi. She was suddenly airborne, hurtling sideways to slam into the Falleen, knocking them both down.

Katarn's blade struck his, rebounded with a *snap-hiss*, and came around from the other side as the Jedi Master executed a lightning-fast spin. Caedus stepped back from it, not engaging the blade. He watched the blade flash harmlessly past him.

He stepped forward again into a side kick, aimed not at Katarn but at the onrushing Valin Horn. His boot heel caught the Jedi Knight on the point of his chin, knocking Horn backward off his feet.

Two seconds had passed since the attack began.

Only Seha's head protruded from the pavement hatch as she watched her four companions assault Colonel Solo.

In one sense, it was a beautiful and brilliant thing to see. The five combatants moved as though they'd been choreographing this event for years and had planned, all along, that the two sides would somehow be even. Each time the lightsabers came together, the resulting flash of light, slightly greater than two glows by themselves, cast the five combatants into relief. Around them, blinded GAG troopers withdrew, finding one another by touch, keeping their blasters up and at the ready, waiting for the moment when their sight would return and allow them to open fire. Above, though at a distance from the Senate Building, the trails of airspeeder lights glimmered in their passage.

And Seha still had one task to perform.

In her free hand she held a patch of black cloth. It was square, five centimeters to a side, and very soft and pliant, despite the fact that its center layer consisted of circuitry embedded in a flexible polymer.

One side was covered by a transparent layer of flimsi. With her teeth, she worried an edge of the flimsi free, then pulled the whole layer off, dropping it into the access hole she occupied. The removal of the flimsi exposed a layer of adhesive.

With her own Force powers, so much less subtle than those of her allies, she sent the cloth patch flying, centimeters above ground level, toward the fight.

But she couldn't send it on to her target, not yet. Master Katarn had been clear about that. She had to wait until things were at their most chaotic, their most distracting.

So she guided the patch ever closer to the fight, but waited, waited . . .

Ten seconds.

Caedus rolled out of Katarn's kick to his head, catching a scrape along his cheek, and swung at the Master's leg, but Kolir's blade intercepted his before it bit into flesh. His strength batted her weapon away, but she had deflected his blow and spared Katarn an amputation.

They're coordinating. Good for them. Bad for me.

Caedus heard a siren—an oncoming GAG vehicle. No, two—maybe three.

He allowed himself a certain satisfaction at their speed of response. He hadn't expected anything of the sort for another half minute.

Then, from the corner of his eye, he saw the first oncoming vehicle, an aging *Sentinel*-class armored shuttle. It was yellow, with spots of rust. He could not make out its markings without looking at it, but he knew it was not in GAG or Alliance colors. Entering airspace above the plaza, it began a dangerously steep and fast repulsorlift descent. Behind it came three GAG airspeeders, one of them firing a top-mounted laser at the shuttle.

Ah. So they were not responding with brilliant speed to an alarm. They were chasing the Jedi escape vehicle. Caedus swung at Horn, a blow meant not to connect but to cause the young Jedi to flinch away into the path of the Falleen, which he did. While they were interfering with each other, Caedus gestured at the Bothan Jedi, hurling her toward Katarn.

Katarn hurled his lightsaber off to the side and caught Hu'lya with both hands, preventing her from falling, prepared to pull her out of harm's way if Caedus followed through.

Caedus did not. He kept his senses on Katarn's light-saber, and, when it vectored to fly toward him from the side, he negligently swatted it away with his own blade.

Fifteen seconds.

Caedus gave Katarn and Hu'lya a little smile. "You could save yourselves a lot of pain by telling me now where Luke has set up the new Jedi headquarters. I swear, when you are in my hands, you *will* answer that question."

The Bothan got her feet back under her and stood at the ready.

Katarn caught his returning lightsaber. "Meaning you will torture us to death. Are you listening to yourself, Jacen? Do you even know who you are anymore?"

"I do. It's *you* who have no idea who I am."

He felt Force energy growing within Mithric and Horn. He gestured, telekinetically yanking the Bothan forward, positioning her between him and them. He felt their Force exertion as it was suddenly cut off.

Katarn advanced, lightsaber at the ready. Caedus withdrew before him. With part of his awareness, he was keeping track of the four inbound vehicles, plotting their trajectories . . .

One of the GAG vehicles was circling ahead and to starboard of the descending shuttle. Its arc, intended to put it toward the bow of the shuttle so it could fire on the cockpit, would bring it near the combatants, just a few meters above them. The pilot's maneuver was smooth, the vehicle clearly under control. Caedus could see the Jedi barely registering its presence, since it did not figure into the combat.

Caedus reached out a hand as if intending to hurl Katarn away from him. The Master raised his own hand, a deflecting gesture. But Caedus exerted himself against the oncoming GAG speeder, yanking it down and toward all of them.

A moment's inattention or focus elsewhere. That's all it

ever took. By the time Katarn felt the speeder coming toward him—spinning, its stern a mere two meters from his back—it was already too late for him to send a command even to Force-augmented nerves and muscles. His face changed with the awareness of danger.

Then the speeder's port quarter hit his back, hurling him forward to slam into Caedus. The speeder, continuing its out-of-control motion, slid through the location of the other Jedi, knocking Hu'lya to the permacrete, causing Horn and Mithric to leap to safety.

Katarn now stood so close to Caedus that every facial feature was visible, every scar and line in his weathered face, every hair on his brow, mustache, and beard.

Caedus felt a rush of satisfaction, enjoyment, as Katarn's expression turned from one of surprise to pain. Katarn looked down to see Caedus's lightsaber buried to its hilt in his chest.

A noise, something halfway between a groan and a death rattle, emerged from Katarn's lips. Smiling, Caedus yanked his lightsaber free and let the stricken Jedi Master fall face-first on the pavement.

chapter eleven

Seha felt all breath leave her body, as though it had been her chest, not Katarn's, that had been pierced. Jacen Solo's exultation washed through the Force and over her like a wave at a beach, almost knocking her free from the rung she held.

No, no, no . . . The words rang in her head and were echoed by Mithric. The Falleen Jedi howled as he charged Solo, his anguish giving him speed and strength as he threw blow after blow at his enemy.

Things were at their most chaotic.

The words sprang up in her mind, incongruous, like golden flowers in a burned field—and her last task, the one Master Katarn had given her, was not accomplished.

She focused herself on the distant black patch. It was now only three meters from where Colonel Solo disinterestedly blocked Mithric's attacks.

Valin Horn was charging toward the combat. Kolir was up, too, but limping badly as she headed toward their enemy. The shuttle was just meters above the plaza, settling precisely into place so that its belly hatch was positioned exactly above the access hole through which Kolir had emerged. Laserfire from the GAG speeders was raking the shuttle's top armor to pieces.

Seha's vision blurred with tears. She dashed them away and flicked a hand at the distant patch. As Colonel Solo twirled, causing his cloak to flare up and away from him, the patch flew to its lower hem and merged with it.

Now the three Jedi Knights assailed Solo all-out, a fight they were doomed to lose. Seha could not save them. Her tasks were accomplished. She should leave before Colonel Solo detected her.

No, she couldn't. Not while a good man, a teacher, lay dead on the duracrete in an enemy capital. She reached out to Kyle Katarn.

His body jerked and he slid a meter toward her.

She poured more of herself, of her concentration, into her effort. Master Katarn's body began sliding again, continuously now, picking up speed as it scraped its way across the plaza.

One of the GAG troopers fired his blaster at Mithric. Kolir, hobbling, managed to get her lightsaber blade up and caught the bolt.

But it meant the troopers' vision was returning.

Seha saw the Jedi exchanging words. Valin spun away from the engagement with Jacen and moved toward the one sighted trooper. That man fired again and Valin deflected the bolt with his lightsaber—deflected it straight toward Jacen. The improvised attack evidently came as a surprise: The bolt grazed Jacen's right leg, sending him to his knee. Mithric redoubled his attack, hammering away at Jacen's defense like a toolsmith on a primitive world battering away at a stubborn harvester droid.

Kolir, bent over from distress more than pain, hesitated, then turned and moved at a fast hobble toward the shuttle.

Seha pulled one last time and Master Katarn, shoulders-first, slid into her grasp.

Katarn's eyes opened. His voice was little more than a wheeze. "Go . . ."

"You're alive!"

"Explosives package . . . give me one . . . other one to block exit . . ."

Seha hauled him into the access hole, lowering him face-down, wincing as the movements made him gasp with pain. "I'll blow up our exit route, yes. We'll all get out."

"Girl, leave me . . ."

She had to rely on her telekinetic power to lower him to the floor. Her skill was not the greatest. She lowered him four meters without incident, rotated him so that for the last portion of the descent he would be supine . . . and then, not meaning to, she dropped him. He fell two meters and slammed down onto duracrete flooring. He grunted and his eyes closed.

Seha yanked the hatch shut. She took a few moments to patch one of her explosives charges into the holocam goggles she would be leaving behind. Then she scrambled down the ladder. "I'm going to get you out alive. Or we can blow up together."

Caedus hadn't felt the blaster bolt coming. His concentration was slipping.

And this madman of a Falleen Jedi was starting to beat down his parries. His strength was slipping.

He wasn't yet recovered from his duel with Luke. And now, as more of his troopers began firing, Horn began deflecting more bolts at him. The imprecise, barely aimed nature of the attacks worked in Horn's favor. The shots were unpredictable and Caedus had to divide his attention between a mad swordsman and a growing number of half-blind snipers.

But he was still the best lightsaber swordsman around—excepting possibly Luke, perhaps the best there ever had been.

Caedus waited until the timing was perfect, waited until an incoming bolt arrived at the same moment as one of Mithric's attacks so he could devote a single maneuver to both. He caught Mithric's blow toward the hilt of his lightsaber. He caught the bolt near the tip, deflecting it up and straight into Mithric's chest.

Mithric staggered back, the center of his chest blackened, as the smell of burned skin and meat filled the air. Caedus leapt up and executed a single, precise lateral blow.

Mithric's head fell from his shoulders. His body toppled down half a second later.

Caedus and Horn spun to face each other. An expression of sadness crossed Horn's face, but his dismay did not distract him. He caught three more blaster bolts with his lightsaber blade without looking at their firers.

Caedus gestured toward his troopers, signaling them to cease fire. They did; now the only ranged fire to be heard came from the speeders, still chewing the shuttle to pieces.

Caedus flexed his injured leg experimentally and decided it was not too bad. It would take his weight and allow him some footwork. He gestured toward Horn. "You going to try this alone?"

Horn shook his head.

Caedus smiled. "You're a fraction of the man your father is."

"Funny. That's what I was going to say to you." Horn seemed to blur as he dashed toward the shuttle, his sprinting speed augmented by the Force.

"Don't be an idiot! That thing will never take off again."

Caedus left off his harangue as Horn ran up the side ramp where the Bothan had disappeared moments before.

No matter. The shuttle would not take off; Horn or Hu'lya, or both, would be captured, and after a lengthy enough interrogation, Caedus would know where Luke and the Jedi were now hiding.

He bent over to pick up Mithric's head by its ponytail. The Falleen's eyes were still open, staring forward, eerily lifelike, but his skin color had gone to gray. Caedus dropped the head and looked around.

Where was Katarn?

The door slid open and Allana saw Jacen filling the doorway. He was sweaty but calm.

She wasn't sure why, but the first thing she said was, "You're hurt."

He nodded, unconcerned, and entered. "A little bit. Nothing important. I put a bandage on it."

"What happened?"

"Well, when Why-Vee was taking you out of the speeder, bad people showed up to try to take you away from me."

Uncomfortable, she fidgeted. "I don't like riding around in the box."

"It helps keep people from seeing you. That way it's harder for them to figure out where you are, harder for them to try to take you. Is it uncomfortable?"

"Not really." In fact, it had a miniature cooling unit that kept the air fresh and clean, and she had her datapad in it. And Why-Vee, though he was dull and didn't know any games—except Shoot the Scarhead, which he wouldn't tell her how to play—carried it in a very smooth ride. But it was cramped. She couldn't stand up or move around in it. "I just don't like it."

"Well, this morning was just a test. Most places, we'll be

able to drive right into a building in the speeder and not worry about the crate. But you'll still have to use it sometimes."

She knew her voice sounded glum. "All right." She looked at him, waiting again for him to say the special words, but he didn't.

He did have other special words, though. "I love you, Allana."

"I love you, too. But I miss Mommy."

"So do I." His voice turned sad. "So do I."

SANCTUARY MOON OF ENDOR, JEDI OUTPOST

The thorns dug deeper into Ben's cheek, pressing against him in the fevered way the creations of the Yuuzhan Vong had when inflicting pain, and he could feel them injecting their venom. His cheek swelled, and kept swelling. He could feel the skin growing taut, the tissues beneath it beginning to rip, his nerves screaming . . .

And so he knew it was a dream. He was gone from the *Anakin Solo,* out of the Embrace of Pain, away from Jacen and his tortures. It was over.

He didn't wake up immediately, but the dream ended there, with his realization. The vine had no more power over him. It went limp and still. His cheek ceased to hurt. A moment later he realized that he was growing impatient, bored, and it was then that he opened his eyes.

Actually, his cheek did hurt, just a little, and was still slightly swollen. He rubbed it as he stared around.

His "room" had once been a walk-in wardrobe belonging to the commander of this outpost, and as such it was large enough for the military cot, small table, and chair that had been brought in as his personal furniture. It wasn't much of a room, but it was better than most of the Jedi here received.

He rose, tossing his blanket aside, and took down his robes from the hanger. Dressed, he moved out into his father's living room. It was still and dark, and Ben assumed at first that he was the only occupant. Then he saw his father sitting cross-legged before the big viewport, staring, as was so often his custom, at the trees of Endor.

Ben watched his father for a minute. Luke sat perfectly still, expressionless, blinking less often than was normal for a man who was awake. He had to be aware of Ben's movements and scrutiny, but he did not react.

Ben knew why. His father had been so solicitous of him in the days since his rescue from the *Anakin Solo* that Ben had begun snapping at him. The realization made Ben wince inside. Pain, self-consciousness, a pervasive feeling of betrayal from Jacen's torture of him, and, for all he knew, the teenage hormones everybody talked about all the time had made him twitchy and angry.

Ben felt he had plenty of reasons to be twitchy and angry, reasons that went beyond the torture he had experienced. He suspected—he knew, deep down—that it had been Jacen, not Alema Rar, who had killed his mother. And in all the universe, he seemed to be the only one who recognized that fact. It was hard to be the one person keeping alive a thought that big.

But his father didn't deserve his anger. Maybe Ben couldn't always stop himself from being that way, but he could at least recognize that it wasn't his father's fault.

Ben spent a few moments juggling words in his head, then moved over to sit beside his father—facing him, but in the same pose. The posture made his joints ache. The medics had said he would ache for weeks after what Jacen had done to him.

He tried to make his voice calm, mature. "I did my homework, you know."

Luke blinked several times in succession. He did not look confused, but Ben knew, and took a little uncharitable delight in the fact, that his words had baffled his father.

Luke turned toward him. "What homework?"

"The assignment you and Mom gave me just before I went off to Almania."

Luke shook his head. "I'm glad you did it. But I don't understand what you're saying."

"It was about my grandfather. Anakin Skywalker. How he got to be Darth Vader. The Emperor did horrible things to him. Made him suspicious of his friends so they wouldn't be friends anymore. Made him kill younglings so no one would ever trust him again. Made him alone. Made it so nobody else in the universe understood him . . . except the Emperor. I bet, just before he became Darth Vader, he probably *hated* the Emperor. But the Emperor had worked it out so that he was the only one Anakin Skywalker had."

Luke considered, then nodded. "I expect you're right."

"So I figured it out. That's what Jacen was doing to me."

Comprehension dawned in Luke's eyes. "That's *exactly* right."

"And if I had killed him that day, I would have turned into Darth Vader."

"Maybe. For a while."

"Maybe forever."

"Maybe." Luke shrugged. "But if you understand that, if you remember it forever, you'll never turn into Darth Vader." He shifted to look out across the forest vista again. "I think you're probably smarter than my father."

"I got my brains from Mom."

Luke snorted, jarred out of his contemplative mood. "As well as your tendency toward verbal abuse."

"You sent Valin Horn off on a mission."

"Yes, I did."

"Even though he's the son of an old friend."

"I have to forget about that sort of thing when deciding who to send off on missions. If I don't, I'll compromise the ethics of the Order, and the trust the Jedi Masters and Jedi Knights have in me. I might even cause the downfall of the Order."

"Would you send me off on a mission where I might be killed?"

"You've been on missions like that. Centerpoint."

"Yeah . . . with Jacen. You were actually sending Jacen, not me. Would you send me, as a Jedi Knight?"

"When you're a Jedi Knight. You've only just been appointed as my apprentice."

Ben took a deep breath. "If you could kill Jacen *or* save Valin from going to the dark side, which would you choose?"

Luke didn't answer.

Ben fell silent. If he started talking again, his father could ignore the question. But Ben very much wanted to hear the answer.

"Ben, I would kill Jacen."

"So you gave me special consideration you wouldn't give Valin."

"Yes." Luke lowered his gaze to his hands, which rested in his lap. "Speaking as the Grand Master . . . I shouldn't have."

"It makes me . . ." Ben choked up and stopped. He spent a few moments regaining control of his voice. "It makes me partly to blame that he's still out there."

"No, it doesn't."

"Yes, it does. And I'm not saying anything except . . . I

don't want any special treatment. Not anymore. Not when there's anything important riding on it."

Luke nodded. "You're right." He gave Ben a sidelong look. "You realize what a concession that is for me to give. How hard it is for me, as your father, to do it."

"Yeah."

"I want a concession from you."

"What is it?"

"If you're ever in the same position you were on the *Anakin Solo,* with Jacen at your mercy, you take your shot only if you can do it without hate. No kidding yourself, no logical gymnastics. Without hate."

"Deal." Ben extended his hand.

Luke shook it. "Kyp's coming." He glanced over his shoulder.

Ben felt a little pulse in the Force and heard a click from the button on the doorjamb. The door slid open, revealing Kyp Durron in the act of reaching for the chime button outside.

Kyp stepped in. "Grand Master. Apprentice Skywalker." He held up the datapad in his other hand. "I have news."

Luke rose. "From Coruscant?"

"Yes."

Luke moved to a table and sat, gesturing for Kyp to take the seat opposite. "Let's hear it."

Kyp paused, glancing at Ben.

Ben stood, too. "I'll go. I need to arrange to be moved into the apprentice dormitory."

Luke shook his head. "You staying here is not special treatment. You're my apprentice until and unless I decide to reassign you. Kyp, he can stay for this. He's full of insights today."

Kyp shrugged and sat. Ben took a stuffed chair next to the table.

Kyp's voice became more sober. "The mission group reports partial success. Colonel Solo remains at large. Master Katarn was badly injured but has been successfully taken to a safe house. Jedi Mithric lost his life. The others are with Katarn. The droid-piloted shuttle did not get off the ground after its landing. The surviving team members did successfully evacuate through it into the undercity, but since it never got airborne, traces of their escape route were detected. We can anticipate that the undercity will not be a viable approach in the future."

Luke took in the news, shaking his head over Mithric's death. "And the package?"

"The package is on Colonel Solo."

Ben frowned, puzzled. "What's the package?"

"A tracer." Luke outlined a square about five centimeters across on the table surface. "About so big. Black cloth. As long as it remains on Jacen, we can accurately plot where he is, get a better sense of his movements."

Ben considered that. "So . . . you were sure that the mission you sent Valin on would fail."

Kyp nodded. "The ambush portion of it, yes. Once I realized that we couldn't mount a successful grab-or-terminate mission against Jacen without being able to control the place and the time, I decided that it should be as realistic as possible . . . but also that it would serve chiefly to set up future operations. Ones that have a chance of succeeding."

"Did the team members know?"

Luke shook his head. "Only Master Katarn. We couldn't risk any of the others being captured and tortured into confessing. I was certain Kyle would be able to escape—or die before being broken."

Kyp caught Ben's eye. "So. Insights?"

"Just that he'll try to punish the Jedi now. He may have

called them cowards and stuff in the holonews before, but he didn't do anything that would make it impossible for you to go crawling back to him. Attacking him like this probably made it clear you're not going back. He'll discredit the Jedi every chance he gets and hunt us with whatever resources he can."

Luke nodded. "We need to improve our resources, too. I think it's time to call Wedge Antilles. Booster Terrik. Talon Karrde. See what kind of surprises we can arrange for Jacen. It's time to come up with some new plans."

Kyp smiled at him. "Welcome back."

But there was a look in Luke's eye, a distant worry, that told Ben his father was not truly back, not truly recovered, not yet.

chapter twelve

KASHYYYK,
MAITELL BASE

The popular conception of the Wookiee world of Kashyyyk
was that it was all forest—pole-to-pole, kilometers deep,
with the forest floor an impossibly thick layer of organic
matter, twisted roots, monsters, and darkness.

And of course, there were huge belts of terrain that could
be described exactly that way. But there were also oceans,
mountains, and regions where the vegetation, growing
atop shelves of rock only a few meters down, was no taller
than on any other world. There, living beings could stand
on the ground and see the sky through the branches.

It was at such a place that Palpatine's occupation forces
had built Maitell Base some six decades before. They had
landed prefabricated buildings, had poured duracrete, had
raised hangars and installed perimeter defenses. From
places like this they had ruled the world. Then, after Palpatine died, the Wookiees had reclaimed their planet, one
base at a time, driving the stormtroopers into flight. The
wildlife of Kashyyyk had overgrown many of the bases,

while others, like Maitell, had been kept in sporadic use as sites where offworlders could be housed and their spacecraft could be landed.

Zekk, panting in the shade of a tree less than thirty meters tall, decided that the years had not blunted the base's utilitarian ugliness. Though green and brown vines snaked across the roofs of many of the buildings, the walls remained a dirty gray-white, shining like bones in the sun. The streets and landing strips were precise, straight lines, intersecting at right angles, all at odds with the flowing, organic nature of the world around them. Though currently employed by the Wookiees as a base to stage firefighting operations, this place still didn't belong here.

"Hey." Jaina's call was curt. "Again."

Zekk looked over at her. She stood in her Jedi robes, perspiring and tense, lightsaber unlit in her hands.

Zekk sighed. "Give me a minute."

"I need to practice."

"I'm not sure you can gain anything from sparring more with me. You've outstripped me with the lightsaber. Practice is all you think about, day and night. I doubt any Jedi Knight can stand against you. You need to practice against a Master."

"Come on." Her tone was not wheedling, but commanding.

Shaking his head, sure it was a bad idea, Zekk approached her again. He thumbed on his lightsaber—

Before he could even bring it into line, Jaina gestured. The hilt popped out of his hand and flew into Jaina's grip. Anticipating her rush, he twisted out of the way as she dashed up to him. He ducked under her attack, grabbed the hilt of her own unlit lightsaber, and yanked.

But she did not release it. Using his own strength to augment her move, she somersaulted over him. Then, as she landed, she kicked out, hammering the side of his knee.

He fell, rolling away from her follow-up blow, and felt a chill of fear. "Hold it! End practice!"

She paused, annoyed, and looked down at him. "What?"

"If I don't have a lightsaber, I can't parry."

"Well, you should hold on to yours." She switched it off and tossed it to him. Then she retreated to her start position and took up her ready stance again. "Come on."

"We're switching to training lightsabers." Scowling at her, Zekk moved to the pack of workout gear they had brought. He dropped his lightsaber on the blanket beside the pack. Then, from inside, he drew out two practice weapons. Made for use by Jedi trainees and apprentices, their energy blades delivered a painful shock, but no accident with one could sever an arm . . . or a head.

"I'm not going to learn anything from facing a shock weapon. Come on, pick up your lightsaber."

Zekk shook his head and approached her, one training weapon in each hand. "You're not going to learn anything from practicing with me unless you switch to shock weapons. Because otherwise I'm not going to be a part of it. Jaina, you're playing too rough. You're a danger to yourself and others."

"Zekk, you know you can trust me."

"I know I used to be able to. Before you turned into . . ." Zekk saw what was approaching them from the direction of the *Millennium Falcon* hangar and his voice trailed off.

Jaina's eyes narrowed, as though she saw through his simple trick and was offended by it. Then, either through the Force or simply by being convinced by his expression that someone was indeed approaching, she turned to look.

Walking toward them was Jacen Solo.

He was clad head-to-foot in a black Guard uniform. He wore thick jackboots and thick gloves. His helmet's full-face visor concealed his features. His cape billowed behind him as he strode.

Zekk felt a chill of almost supernatural dread. In his full regalia, Solo looked so much like Darth Vader that anyone allied with the Jedi, remembering or having studied the by-gone times of the Jedi Purge, would be similarly affected.

Jaina's voice came as a whisper: "Too short."

"Yeah, Vader was much taller."

"Too short even for my brother, idiot." She raised her voice so the intruder could hear her. "Whoever you are, that's not funny."

Reaching the edge of their practice clearing, their visitor pushed up his visor, revealing the features of Jag Fel. "I wasn't trying to be funny. But, Zekk, you should have seen your face."

Zekk blinked at him. "Trying to get a date with an Alliance loyalist?"

"No."

"Because you're not going to find many on Kashyyyk."

Jag gestured at Jaina. "I came to spar with her. You know, lightsabers."

Jaina gave him a scornful look. "Jag, do you even know how to use a lightsaber?"

"I know Lesson One. Don't grab the glowy end."

Jaina paused, obviously uncertain as to how to respond to his curious request. She walked up to face him. "Jag, I don't want to hurt your feelings. I have every respect for you as a pilot, as a tactician, as a soldier. But in hand-to-hand combat, you're nowhere near my equal. And you can't begin to simulate Jacen's abilities. I won't get anything out of a practice session, and you might get hurt."

"I might indeed." He looked around. "Which are the real lightsabers, and which are the fakes?"

Zekk handed him one of the practice weapons. "This is one of the safe ones." He handed Jaina the other. "Show him what you're talking about, Jaina. I could use the rest."

Unwillingly, she handed Zekk her lightsaber. "He knows *exactly* what I'm talking about. He's studied Alema Rar for years. He knows what she's capable of. I'm worse."

"Well, then this won't take too much of your time or energy." Jag looked down at himself, then gave his thigh a slap. "Here, give me a jolt. So I know what I'm in for."

Shaking her head in exasperation, Jaina lit the training weapon. Its violet blade leapt into life with a softer *snap-hiss* than that of a true lightsaber. Then, slowly, she leaned over to strike Jag's leg.

The blade made a crackling noise. Jag's leg jerked, a muscular spasm, and he almost fell.

He put weight on it again, took a few experimental steps around. "Ah. Got it. I bet that teaches the young Jedi the virtues of not getting hit."

Zekk nodded. "It does."

"All right, let's do it. Zekk, you call it." Jag flipped his faceplate down, becoming a believable, if slightly short, simulacrum of Jacen Solo. He thumbed his training lightsaber into life and raised it in a credible two-handed grip.

"Go."

Almost faster than the eye could follow, Jaina lunged. Jag moved his blade laterally to sweep her point out of line, a clumsy maneuver suited to a first-year sword student. Jaina disengaged before their blades met and thrust, popping her blade across the side of Jag's neck.

Jag let out a yell and staggered back, patting at the point of the blow. "Wow."

"Necks aren't too bad." Zekk rubbed his own in sympathetic memory. "Wait until you catch one across your eyelid. Or groin."

Recovered, Jag stood once more in ready position. "Again."

"Go."

This time Jag initiated the attack, a basic vertical slash. He was strong enough to give it a lot of power.

Jaina stepped aside and her lateral blow hit him across the upper arm.

"Ow. Blast it." Jag rubbed the spot of the injury.

Jaina gave him an exasperated look. "Technically, this bout isn't over, because all I did was take your arm off, in theory. A Jedi might be able to continue for a while with a wound like that. But let's call that one a win for me."

"Sounds reasonable. Jaina, you're *fast*."

"I'm going to keep going until I think I'm fast *enough*. Are we done?"

"Oh, I'm not bright enough to be done yet." Jag resumed the ready position. "Again."

Zekk snorted, amused. "Would it be wrong of me to admit that I'm really starting to enjoy this?"

"Yes."

"Go."

Jag tried the same maneuver. Jaina stepped aside again, swung—

Jag took the blow on his left forearm. The glowing blade bounced. Jag's arm didn't twitch, didn't react at all to the electric shock.

He reached out with that arm. Fast as a blaster duelist drawing and firing, he caught the hilt of Jaina's practice weapon just above her hand and squeezed.

The weapon crumpled. The beam cut off.

Jaina, caught off guard for only a fraction of a second,

stepped back, chambered her leg, and kicked Jag in the solar plexus.

His solar plexus went *konk,* a metallic noise.

Jag rapped his training sword against her support leg. It spasmed and she fell. She rolled out of her fall, but Jag was already swinging in the direction of her roll. His blade caught her across the back of the neck. She completed her roll, ending up on her back, looking up at him with a pained expression. "What was *that?*"

Jag shrugged and pushed up his visor again. "I won."

Jaina's face twisted in anger. "Flying's what you're best at. So fly." She gestured as if pushing the air before her.

Jag's feet left the ground. He hurtled backward five meters and crashed into the bole of the glade's shade tree. Then he slid down atop the tangled roots. Leaves rained down on him.

"Jaina!" Zekk ran up to Jag, bent over him. "What do you think you're doing?"

Jag grimaced. "Punishing me. For embarrassing her."

Jaina flipped acrobatically to her feet and stalked toward Jag. "I am not embarrassed. You *tricked* me." She was shouting now, and Zekk saw distant heads turning to look—Wookiees working in the area, humans in the *Falcon* hangar.

"What part of tricking you would be impossible for Alema Rar or Jacen Solo to do?" Stiffly, Jag began to rise, and accepted a hand from Zekk for aid. Jag's gloved hand felt, to Zekk, rigid and metallic.

Once Jag was on his feet, Zekk rapped the man's forearm with his knuckles. "What have you got on under there?" He repeated the experiment on Jag's chest, which also rang metallically.

"The crushgaunts and *beskar* breastplate from the other day."

Jaina came to a stop in front of Jag, almost spitting in her anger. "What are you trying to prove?"

"That you're training yourself to lose. To die."

That stopped her. She stared up at him, her anger vanishing in an instant, replaced by surprise . . . and doubt.

"Jaina, I've watched you for a long time now, preparing yourself for a confrontation with Alema and—and you're not kidding anyone here—your brother. You've trained and trained and sweated and persevered, and as far as I can tell you've done a brilliant job at the wrong task."

"Explain that." Her eyes searched his.

Zekk was surprised not to see more anger in hers. She must have been afraid of exactly what Jag was talking about and, in typically Jaina-ish fashion, not discussed it with anyone, not dealt with it except through avoidance.

"Sword of the Jedi. That's what you are, even though nobody's sure what it means. But I'm sure of this. There are two important words there. *Sword* and *Jedi*. You've been sharpening yourself into an amazing sword, but you've forgotten what it means to be a Jedi."

"You're not qualified to say that—"

"Answer me this. What Jedi do you know who would have thrown me into that tree that hard for winning a practice bout? You didn't know my armor protected my back. You could have broken my spine. The helmet *didn't* protect my neck. You could have broken that. What Jedi would have done that to a friend?"

She shook her head. It was as though Jag's arguments were blaster bolts, and she was batting most of them harmlessly out of the way—but the occasional bolt was getting through, striking her, searing her.

"So. You're a good Sword and a rotten Jedi. But even if you get back to being a good Jedi, you're going to die. You know why? Because you're training in Jedi skills as though

you're going to have a straight-up Jedi duel with your enemies, all lightsabers and light-side Force tricks. But you
need to be thinking like someone who *hunts* Jedi. Like
me." He stepped so close to Jaina that Zekk thought for a
moment he was going to stoop and kiss her. "That's what I
did. And I beat you."

"Once." Her words were soft, uncertain. "The third
time."

"Are you absolutely sure that if I'd tried that tactic on
our first bout, it wouldn't have worked?"

She was silent for a long moment. Then she shook her
head.

Jag unbuckled his helmet and took it off, holding it at his
side. "Jaina, as your commanding officer, I'm ordering you
to take today off. No training, no strategizing, nothing. Report to me first thing in the morning. At that time, if you
think you need another day off, I require you to tell me so.
You'll get it."

"Yes . . . Colonel."

Jag nodded at her and Zekk, then spun and headed back
to the hangar.

Jag maintained his brisk walking pace until he reached the
Falcon's hangar. Then he looked around and, seeing no one
within sight, moved more slowly and heavily to the *Falcon*'s boarding ramp. He sat on its slope, leaning away
from its angle of descent to remain upright. He set his helmet down, then slowly peeled the thin black gloves off the
crushgaunts, staring blankly at the floor as he did so.

"I expected—"

The voice came from the tall, dark figure who seemed to
materialize in front of Jag. Jag jumped up, reaching for a
blaster pistol that was not there, then relaxed as he recognized the speaker.

"—you to be jubilant." Zekk frowned down at him. "Not jumpy. And morose."

Jag sat again and scowled up at the Jedi. Carefully, he used his right hand to pull his left-hand crushgaunt free of his arm. He set it down beside the helmet. "I'm not morose."

"And I'm a Sullustan."

"Yes, the ears tipped me off."

Zekk managed a brief grin. "I just wanted to say congratulations."

"For what?"

"For getting through to her. She looked as shocked as if you'd clobbered her with a force pike. Now she's thinking."

"Good." Jag pulled the other crushgaunt free and set it down. He looked at his palms, which were red and sweaty. "I didn't like shouting at her."

"Well, you don't shout much."

"That's not it." Jag's eyes focused past the floor, to some distant place and time. "Years ago, I thought I could see my future in her eyes. My future, maybe even the future of my line, my name. Since then, she's slipped away from me. I helped that happen. Out of anger. Out of pride." He shook his head and met Zekk's gaze again. "But I can't let her slip away from what it is to be human."

Zekk was silent for a long moment, and when he spoke again, his voice was unusually gentle. "Jag, I'm going to let you in on a secret. You're an irritant, like itching powder in an enviro-suit."

Jag glared at him.

"On top of that, you've got no sense of humor, you're more Force-blind than a rock, you handle a lightsaber like a drunken Hutt, and you're short. But after today, I'm exceedingly proud to have you as a comrade-in-arms." He extended his hand.

Jag looked at it as if expecting a final insult to be written on its palm, then shook it. "Thanks."

"So do I have today off, too?"

Jag's shoulders slumped. "Sure."

"Go have a drink or something, Colonel." Zekk spun and headed out through the hangar's main entrance, walking toward the base crew quarters.

Jag sat where he was for long minutes, then collected his gear and left.

Leia, silent, stepped out from the shadows at the top of the boarding ramp and shook her head. She glanced back over her shoulder. "Han?"

"Yeah, sweetie."

"How do you teach a man not to be a noble, long-suffering, self-sacrificing idiot?"

"I don't know, sweetie. Mostly I shoot them."

"I'll consider that."

chapter thirteen

CORUSCANT

The war raged on.

Back in control of his portions of the Alliance military and no longer distracted by Allana's absence—for, secretly, she accompanied him everywhere, smuggled between GA government buildings and the *Anakin Solo* in shuttles, guarded by only the most trusted officers and YVH-908—Caedus found himself stymied on some fronts, wildly successful on others.

First, there was the Hapes situation. Tenel Ka did not immediately turn over her fleets to his control. Instead she withdrew them to Hapes Consortium space and cut off all communication with the Galactic Alliance . . . and with the Confederation, with the world of Kashyyyk, and, as far as anyone could tell, with the Jedi. Caedus did not know quite what to make of this maneuver. Tenel Ka could have been killed by the explosion that allowed Caedus to escape her palace, or subsequently deposed, her successor choosing to return the Consortium to a neutral position. Or Tenel Ka could be taking what she must see as a terrible chance with the life of her daughter. Either way, Caedus had still been able to turn the situation into a victory. By using his Intelligence resources to suggest to Confederation analysts that Tenel Ka's nonaggression treaty with them was now void, Caedus ensured that the Confederation maintained resources to monitor and safeguard against possible Hapan attack, and that gave Caedus some breathing room. Soon enough, he could determine whether Tenel Ka still ruled the Consortium, get in touch with her . . . and persuade her that Allana's life was forfeit if she did not cooperate fully.

While waiting to reach Tenel Ka, Caedus concentrated on other things.

Such as the Jedi. They had been quite successful at going underground after the battle at Kuat, so much so that the only sign he had seen of their activity had been the futile attack on him a few days before. He dispatched Tahiri in her StealthX to run down her own leads and sources, to find out where the Jedi had headquartered themselves. He had thought she could simply use her association with other Jedi to find out the information, but no, it appeared that Tenel Ka had managed to communicate her suspicions of Tahiri to the other Jedi at Kuat. Tahiri still had no answer for Caedus; it was a big galaxy and she was, in his eyes, a stupid girl—and a needy one, constantly importuning him for new chances to flow-walk into the past and reexperience the wonders of Anakin Solo in the days and hours before his death.

Caedus shook his head over that. He had seen so much of Anakin in recent months that he had come to despise the brat. The reasons why he had ever held the boy in any regard, why he had chosen to name his Star Destroyer for him, were now lost to Caedus.

Meanwhile, the war raged on. With the Hapans back in play, the Alliance no longer had to worry about staging a fighting retreat. The balance of power was now once again slightly in the Alliance's favor. Caedus personally led new fleet operations at Kuat and on the outskirts of the Corellian system, commanding elements of the Fifth and Second fleets, respectively, and his Sith battle meditation ability helped his forces inflict heavy losses in both theaters of operation.

Commenor retaliated for the asteroid bombardment, and in savage fashion. The first sign of it was a statistical spike in the number of head colds among humans who had recently passed through Galactic City Spaceport—civilians and military personnel alike. Within days those head colds developed into raging fevers and dangerous dehydration, and the infection spread like Kashyyyk's forest fires through the ranks of the armed forces and lower social classes. Left untreated, the illness could kill. It was affliceria, caused by an airborne bacterium, the cure for which had been discovered a century before, with the illness pronounced extinct not long after.

There were no stores of affliceria-specific antibiotics; there had been none needed in a hundred years. Quantities were cultured and rapidly distributed . . . to the military. There was not enough to protect the civilian population, and, by the third week of the outbreak, when the first doses began to filter into the civilian distribution network, the illness had reached epidemic proportions, causing massive personnel shortages in critical fabrication industries.

Spies captured and interrogated by the Guard confessed to being Commenori—and to spreading the bacteria. The Alliance-controlled portions of the HoloNet howled with outrage. Civilian space traffic was severely curtailed as quarantine measures were put into effect.

The war raged on.

There were other annoyances. Caedus's subordinates reported that Dr. Seyah, failed spy of Centerpoint Station, had disappeared minutes before they moved in to arrest him. In subsequent days, no sign of him turned up, suggesting strongly that Caedus had been right to suspect him—he was obviously a double agent and had been rushed to safety by his Corellian masters.

Allana was responding with less and less enthusiasm to her time with Caedus. He had to keep his frustration in check and wait for her to get over missing her mother. Perhaps it was time to work on her a bit, to diminish her affection for Tenel Ka by judiciously erasing some of her memories here and there. Some faint misgivings stayed his hand for the time being, but if the situation continued worsening, he would take that step.

And the war raged on.

KASHYYYK,
MAITELL BASE, HANGAR HOUSING
THE MILLENNIUM FALCON

Han eased the *Falcon* off the duracrete roadway and into the shadow of her usual hangar. The ship, he knew, was covered in soot from the firefighting mission they had just concluded—no firebreak mission, this time they had gone in to rescue a unit of Wookiee firefighters who had been cut off by fire moving more rapidly than expected. He was sure the freighter was covered in soot because Leia, in the copilot's seat, certainly was, from head to foot, except for a goggle-shaped patch of pink around her eyes and a breather-mask-shaped oval around her mouth. The Wookiees she had brought aboard were similarly discolored by, and stank of, smoke.

As soon as the *Falcon* entered the hangar and Han's eyes adjusted to the deep shadow there, he and Leia spotted a new visitor. Parked in the bay next to the *Falcon*'s was a long yacht with curved lines and a swirling sky-blue-and-green hull. Its exterior, too, was marred with patches of soot and burn, evidence of its own recent contribution to the firefighting mission.

Han winced. "Do you suppose, when Lando's back is turned, we could get some Wookiee teenagers to vandalize her? Put graffiti all over her hull?"

Leia's tone was more thoughtful. "I thought Lando was stationed halfway across Kashyyyk."

"He was."

Lando was nowhere in sight. Han and Leia had set the *Falcon* down, ushered the Wookiee firefighters off, and called in for routine refueling before Lando made his appearance. The boarding ramp of the *Love Commander* came down and he stood at its top, clad in purple synthsilk and a flowing velvet hip cloak in black.

But it wasn't the same old Lando. His face was fixed, nearly emotionless, his complexion waxy.

Leia didn't wait for him to descend. She started up the ramp toward him. "Lando, what's wrong?"

"I have to go." Lando managed two faltering steps down the ramp before Leia reached him. She held him there, steadied him on his feet, then turned and assisted him down the ramp.

Han tried to keep his own voice steady, unperturbed, but Lando's appearance set off alarm bells in his head. "What's going on, old buddy?"

At the bottom of the ramp, Lando reached into a tunic pocket. He fetched forth a datacard, which he looked at blankly for a moment before handing to Han. "That's everything you need for the *Love Commander*. Registration, annotated schematic, everything. Thought I'd donate her to the cause. Firefighting, side missions . . . You can sell her if you're ever strapped for credits."

"Lando, what's *wrong*?" By this point, Leia could no longer keep a sharp edge of worry out of her voice.

"It's Tendra . . ."

Leia paled, and Han felt a jolt of dread. Tendra had to be dying—or already dead—for Lando to be so affected.

It wasn't fair. Lando had found his perfect match long after he had given up on the thought that he ever would, and so much of his and Tendra's life together had been interrupted by protracted crises, including the Yuuzhan Vong War.

And now this . . .

Lando was clearly struggling to continue. "Tendra's . . . she's . . . going to have a baby."

Leia froze, staring up into his shocked features. "What? *What*?" A smile started to spread across her face.

Han sagged in relief. "Is that all? You had us really scared there."

"All? Is that *all*?" Lando put a hand on the yacht's hull to steady himself. "Fine, you can stop being scared. Not me. I'm too *old* to be a father. Emperor's black bones! I'm not ready."

Leia embraced him. "Lando, there are two types of people in this universe: those who think they're not ready to be parents, and those who are kidding themselves."

Suddenly relieved of a crushing weight of worry, Han sagged. He bent over, putting his hands on his knees. "Buddy, the next time you scare me like that . . ."

"You'll shoot me? Do I have your word on that?"

"Lando, listen." Leia's voice was compelling. "You and Tendra are going to be the parents every child dreams about. Rich, famous, dashing . . . and so scared of fouling up you're going to spoil your child to death. Am I right?"

Lando considered. His expression was starting to return to normal. "How old does he have to be before I start him on sabacc?"

"Two." Han straightened up. "And no wine appreciation training until he's at least four."

Leia corrected him: "She."

"It's just . . . this is something I can't fix with charm or a rigged game or a hold-out blaster."

Leia smiled up at him. "You can't fix it because it's not broken."

"Yeah." Lando took a deep breath, fortifying himself against the future. "I have to go. My transport home lifts off in half an hour. I was worried that I wouldn't get to see you at all before I left."

Han clapped him on the shoulder. "Well, your luck is holding out, old buddy."

Lando gave Leia a final squeeze, grabbed Han for a quick hug. "I want to know where you two are at all times. In case I have to holocomm you for advice."

"Just send your message to wherever the noise is the loudest. It'll be either us or Luke."

"Right." His walk once again jaunty, Lando headed for the main doors out of the hangar. He waved, giving them one last look over his shoulder, and took a final, wistful glance at the *Millennium Falcon*. Then he was gone.

Leia tucked herself under Han's arm, wrapping it around her shoulders. "I am so jealous."

"I'm not. Imagine trying to take care of a baby with this war going on."

"Imagine having one thing, one innocent life, to think about, to the exclusion of everything else, including the war."

"Well . . . yeah. You have a point." He wheeled her

around toward the *Falcon*. "C'mon, let's see if we can trick some big furry guys into washing the ship."

ABOARD THE **ANAKIN SOLO**

It was good to be back home, and it surprised Caedus that he had truly begun to think of his ship that way. All through his life, "home" had been wherever he hung his robes at night, as his parents' missions and then his own missions and goals carried him from one end of the galaxy to the other.

Now he could travel those same distances and still sleep in the same bunk each night. He could keep Allana with him, safe—as safe as she could be anywhere in the galaxy—in the hidden quarters so close to his official cabin. Having a familiar location wherever he went offered comforts that he had never experienced before, offered some small compensation for the loss of friendship he had experienced since embarking on his plan to restore order, and he found himself appreciating that fact.

Of course, he could keep Allana even safer, and have even more comforts, if he traveled in a bigger, more power-ful, more heavily defended vessel, something suited to the Chief of State of the Galactic Alliance. He'd have to go to the drawing board and do a little preliminary designing.

These were his thoughts as he stood on the *Anakin Solo*'s bridge, looking out through the forward viewports in a rare moment of inactivity. Ahead and down, relative to the ship's keel, he could see a Golan III Space Defense Nova-Gun, one of several space stations, packed with shield gen-erators and weapons, guarding space above Coruscant. It was far enough away to be little more than an elongated blue triangle with tiny bumps and knobs all over it, like an odd-shaped blaster pistol aimed out into space. Also visible was the constant, soothing stream of vehicles and vessels entering or leaving Coruscant's atmosphere—troop transports, freighters hauling military supplies, holonews transports, naval interceptors ensuring that everything was as it should be.

"Sir?"

Caedus turned to face the speaker. Captain Kral "Deuce" Nevil, a male Quarren with a distinguished record in starfighter operations, had, like many fellow pilots, made the transfer to naval operations and a command role when his cockpit skills had begun to diminish. Now he wore the blue naval uniform with the same professionalism with which he had worn the garish orange of the X-wing pilot, but Caedus sometimes wondered if he brought the same enthusiasm to his role as the *Anakin Solo*'s new captain.

Caedus nodded, acknowledging that he had heard his captain.

"Admiral Niathal is coming up, sir. On her personal shuttle."

"Really." Caedus considered that. Whatever news she brought had to be important enough that it couldn't wait for their next regularly scheduled meeting; nor could it be committed to the potential insecurity of holocomm transmission. "Make standard preparations for her arrival and have Security do a sweep of my conference room."

"Yes, sir." Nevil saluted and withdrew.

chapter fourteen

Niathal barely waited until her GAG security escort was out of the conference room and the door shut behind them before getting to the point; she did not even bother to sit. "Sadras Koyan, Corellia's Five Worlds Prime Minister, is talking to us about changing sides."

"*Really.*" Caedus sat and leaned back in his chair. "Just betraying the rest of the Confederation and risking retaliation."

"My analysts suspect that the boost of hope he might have received when the Hapans withdrew from the war was lost when they isolated themselves from the Confederation again, and that he would much prefer to be on the winning side." She offered a good simulation of a human shrug. "It's not inappropriate for his psychological profile."

Koyan had been Chief of State of the Corellian world of Tralus, but had been elected, by a majority though not unanimous vote of the other Chiefs of State when Dur Gejjen had been assassinated. A member of the aggressive Centerpoint Party, he had probably been seen by the other chiefs as the lesser of several evils in the succession scramble that followed Gejjen's death.

"What are they offering?"

"They want to negotiate with you—you specifically. We designate a point in space—any point—equidistant between Corellia and Coruscant. The two sides bring an equal number of vessels in equivalent class ratings. You and their negotiator can negotiate either face-to-face or ship-to-ship through tight-beam transmission."

"Who is their negotiator?"

"I do not know."

"Not Koyan?"

Niathal shook her head. "His profile suggests a distinct aversion to being in the company of dangerous people. This is clearly how he has survived so long."

"I don't like it." No longer even pretending to be at ease, Caedus leaned forward. "Even if they give us the opportunity to choose the spot for the meeting, they can communicate that information to a secondary force—"

"As can we."

"—which can then jump to that site and attack."

"As can we. They have no advantage."

"Except in insisting that I be there. If their plan is intended to be an attempt on me, then success on their part, even if military losses are equivalent, disrupts our own coalition government and removes me as a strategic resource for the military."

Niathal cocked her head, a gesture of curiosity. "You are unusually cautious today. Learning from Koyan himself?"

Caedus opened his mouth to hurl back a retaliatory remark, then closed it again.

Niathal was right. He was more cautious—not because of possible danger to himself, but because of danger to Allana. He was not going to let her be more than a few paces from him until the war was resolved. Taking her into the vicinity of what might be a trap was the last thing he wanted to do.

On the other hand, Niathal could not be allowed to learn that Caedus's behavior was changing because of concern for the child. So far as she knew, Allana was a hostage, leverage against the Hapan Queen Mother. For Niathal to suspect that Caedus's feelings were more personal, more heartfelt, could endanger both of them if Niathal ever turned against him.

Caedus relented, shrugging. "Fine. I'll do it. Do you mind if I make an effort not to get killed when this turns out to be a trap?"

"Do what you need to."

"I'll have units of the Second Fleet standing by to jump to the talk site. To deal with whatever forces Koyan decides to bring in."

"As you wish. I'll comm the Corellians with an acceptance."

Caedus nodded, a gesture of agreement that he meant as one of dismissal, as well. Whether she understood that or not, Niathal paused for a moment, looking at him, before turning and leaving.

SANCTUARY MOON OF ENDOR, JEDI OUTPOST

Through the transparisteel of the door separating the waiting room from the infirmary proper, Luke studied Master Katarn's face and listened to the words of Valin and Cilghal.

Katarn was unconscious—whether from drugs, pain, or voluntary immersion in a Jedi healing trance, Luke couldn't say. His face was flushed, sweating, and he looked as though he'd lost weight in the days he'd been on Coruscant.

Cilghal managed to impart considerable worry and sympathy into her gravelly Mon Cal voice. "The attack severed two ribs, penetrated his left lung, and exited through his left shoulder blade. A few centimeters off, and it would have gone clean through his heart. He has also contracted the affliceria bug and some opportunistic infections. He is dehydrated and very weak, and traveling so far to get here could not have helped—except that it was still a better choice than remaining in hiding on Coruscant."

"I patched him up as well as I could, as soon as possible after he was injured." Valin sounded morose. "But we had to drag him through about a kilometer of filthy pipes before we could do even that. Explosives we planted to seal our escape routes kicked dust into the air, dust and germs." He shook his head, pained by his failure. "Basic medical training isn't sufficient for a situation like that."

Luke patted his shoulder. "You did remarkably well. The fact that he's here alive is proof of that, and if anyone can heal him, it's Cilghal." He finally turned away from studying Katarn to look at Valin. The young Jedi Knight was solemn but not showing evidence of protracted stress or guilt, a good sign. "Do you have a full report for me?"

Valin reached into his belt and removed a datacard, which he handed to Luke. "I've flagged one or two points of interest on the report; you may want to pay special attention to them. A YVH combat droid that was programmed to get its cargo out of harm's way rather than help its master defend against four Jedi. Mob violence in response to the affliceria epidemic, against both state medical officials and people of Commenori descent—plus the fact that these reports were suppressed on the holonews broadcast after they were first reported, almost as though the GA government *isn't* whipping the population up into a frenzy about it."

Luke pocketed the card. "I'll look for those details." He was distracted by a stirring in the Force, the imminent arrival of others. There was no sense of menace associated with the presentiment, though. He glanced at the two Jedi. "Anything else?"

But the answer came from behind Luke, accompanying a bustle of several moving bodies. Boots creaked, durable uniform cloth rubbed, equipment clattered, and a new voice rose above it all: "How about some news from Corellia?"

Luke turned around to see a half squadron of pilots headed his way—wearing sweat-stained orange flight suits, their helmets under their arms, they had to have just come from their starfighters. In front, familiar and reassuring, was Wedge Antilles, sharp-featured and graying; behind, a step to the right, was Wes Janson, his alert eyes and broad grin suggesting that he was taking copious mental notes now so that he could engage in a marathon of mockery later.

Luke grinned and stepped forward to embrace his two friends. The other four pilots, two men and two women, he recognized as well. "Thanks for coming, Wedge. Good to see you, Wes. *What* news from Corellia?"

Wedge looked around, noting the presence of Jedi medics and workers in this hallway. "Maybe somewhere more private."

Three minutes later, a ground-level security door slid open before them, revealing shaded sunlight—as well as a pair of Ewoks in leather caps, stone-headed spears in hand, creeping their way a few meters beyond. As the door slid open, the Ewoks jabbered in surprise, turned, and fled back into the tree line twenty meters away.

Wedge snorted. "Good neighbors, if you can stay out of their stew pots."

"C'mon." Luke led him out into the fresh air, heavy with the scents of blooming flowers and forest decay. The door rumbled shut behind them. "How are Iella and the kids?"

"Iella's great. She's spending her time doing holonews analysis and passing her conclusions on to me, to Booster, to Talon Karrde. I'll have her add you to the distribution list if you like."

"Please." Luke gestured, and the two of them headed, in a different direction from that taken by the fleeing Ewoks, into the cover of deep forest.

"I don't hear much from Syal, of course. We're certainly not estranged, but since she's serving with Alliance forces, still on the *Blue Diver*, and I'm an official enemy of the Alliance and an unofficial target of the Confederation, I don't get much news of her. Myri is still on the *Errant Venture*, gathering information to pass along to us . . . and making a *fortune* gambling." He shook his head in mock distress. "She's going to be the first rich Antilles, and not from following an honest career. I don't know what to think of it. How's Ben?"

"Better than I have any right to expect." They were deep enough in the trees to be out of hearing range of anyone at the outpost, though still close enough to see bits of it through the screen of hanging branches and vines. "So."

"So, Corellia. A good friend of mine, a space navy lifer with the Corellian Defense Force—he's ninety, been retired for a few years—was just returned to active duty and assigned a recommissioned *Carrack*-class cruiser."

Luke offered Wedge a dubious expression. "A *Carrack*? What's next? Are the Corellians going to start throwing cans of food at the Alliance fleets?"

"Yes. It sounds like they're shoring up depleted units

with increasing desperation. But there's more to it. My old friend is going to be part of a special diplomatic mission to talk to the GA, a hush-hush negotiation that General Phennir, Supreme Commander of the Confederation military forces, wasn't informed of beforehand. Scuttlebutt has it that when he inquired about it with the Corellians, they told him that it was just a delaying tactic, something to distract Colonel Solo for a few days. Now Phennir's people don't know if that's the truth, or if the Corellians are going to try to spring some sort of trap and kill Solo so they can claim the glory and have a bargaining advantage to give them even more influence within the Confederation . . . or whether they're thinking of switching sides."

Luke frowned. "Where does the scuttlebutt come from, in this case?"

Wedge ticked numbers off on his fingers. "One, the granddaughter of my old friend. She got in touch with me by backdoor means to find out if there was any way I could talk her grandfather out of accepting the reactivation of his commission. Two, a pilot formerly under my command, now on Phennir's staff, querying me about what the Corellian Prime Minister is up to, since I'm obviously a neutral party. Three—"

"So it all amounts to *this guy I know*."

Wedge nodded. "The fate of galactic civilization might someday hang on an intelligence network consisting of *this guy I know*."

"Thanks for scaring me." Luke opened himself to the Force for a moment, but the future remained impossibly distant and unclear. All he could detect was the abundance of life around him, including the two Ewoks creeping in his direction. Their emotions consisted largely of curiosity and nervousness, rather than malice or hunger, so he concluded that attack was not on their minds. "If *this guy I know* could figure out where Jacen is going to be, and when, it could prove very valuable to us. We have a means to track his movements, but that leaves us very reactive—he goes, and if we respond in time, we can follow him. To anticipate his movements would be ideal."

"Two days until the meeting with the Corellians. Two days, at a halfway point between Corellia and Coruscant—but that's still a lot of space to cover." Wedge frowned, calculating. "In two days, if you could have a StealthX shadow the *Anakin Solo* out of the Coruscant system, that might give us the exact coordinates. Her course, plus knowledge that the destination will be identical in distance from there to Corellia, as well."

"Right—if we're lucky and he doesn't send the *Anakin Solo* through an elaborate, multiple-leg course."

"I doubt he will. Whether it is one or not, he has to suspect that it's a trap. Why worry about elaborate routing when you're going directly to the adversary anyway?"

"True." Luke nodded. "I'll send out a StealthX immediately." He turned back toward the outpost and led them in that direction. "Wedge, it's good to have you here."

"Speaking of which—"

"No, you're not being paid."

Wedge laughed. "Just like the Rebellion days. No, I was going to say, you've brought me in for military advice, you're acquiring personnel and matériel, you have a base of operations and an agenda that involves interacting with two major galactic powers—has it occurred to you that you're setting up a third government here?"

"No."

"Well, you are. The Jedi are now a cross-planetary, self-governing body, and you're their Chief of State. You might need to start thinking along those lines."

"Huh. You want the job?"

"No. If it lands on me, I'll give it to Booster Terrik. *He'll* figure out a way to get us paid."

ABOARD THE **ANAKIN SOLO**

Caedus relaxed in his Command Salon, away from the bustle and noise of the bridge, waiting for the exit from Coruscant space and the short hyperspace jump to the rendezvous point with the Corellian task force.

He would have preferred to pass the time in one of two secret rooms near his quarters—Allana's playroom, or his cramped workshop, where, finally, he was finding the time to build his new lightsaber. It would be a proper lightsaber, with a red blade, the better to announce his new role as Lord of the Sith—though when it would be time to make that declaration, he still did not know.

The monitor before him, showing nothing but stars and tiny, fast-moving dots that constituted traffic inbound toward Coruscant, suddenly switched to the face of Lieutenant Tebut. A dark-haired human woman with a quiet, no-nonsense manner and an imposing air of efficiency, she had, like all officers aboard the *Anakin Solo,* survived the most intensive security vetting the Guard could conduct. A candidate for promotion to the position of executive officer, she had, with Captain Nevil's blessing, begun a program of mastering every bridge officer's duty, and today she was at the communications officer's station. Caedus approved of both her ambition and her breadth of skills.

"The pilot reports readiness for hyperspace jump," Tebut reported. "But we're being hailed by a private yacht identifying itself as *Love Commander.*"

Caedus grimaced and briefly considered blowing the vehicle out of space. But no, Lando was only *nearly* useless, and the old gambler's instinct for self-preservation meant that he often had some helpful information at hand.

Caedus pressed a button so that his next words would also go to Captain Nevil. "All stop." He released it and looked at the monitor again. "Put her captain through to me."

He waited just long enough for the picture on his display to change from Tebut's face before he began talking. "Calrissian, give me one good reason—"

But the face that materialized on the display was not that of Lando Calrissian. It was Leia Organa Solo. "Mother."

Leia gave him a slight smile. It seemed to Caedus to be a very sad one. "Oh, I'm not *Mom* anymore?"

"Not really, no. What do you need? I'm in a bit of a hurry."

"I need to speak to you."

"And without Father." Caedus frowned. "Where is the *Falcon*?"

"Back on Kashyyyk, putting out fires. Fires you started."

"Yes. Fires to punish an enemy of the Alliance. As I must point out, you are an enemy of the Alliance. Is there some reason I shouldn't start a fire in that ridiculous yacht of Lando's right now?"

"The same reason as before. I need to talk to you."

"That's your need, not mine."

Leia simply stared at him, silent, implacable.

She had to be up to something. Caedus tried to detect what he could of her through the Force. He could sense her, a bright and distinctive presence, alone on the yacht.

Interesting. So Han wasn't with her; nor were there any strangers present. No assassins who might be targeting him. No Hapans come to retrieve Allana.

Well, he'd simply take her aboard, listen to what she had to say, and then throw her in prison, ending the danger she posed to his administration. Han would come after her, and Caedus could throw Han in prison, too. Suddenly he felt cheered by his mother's unexpected visit.

He sighed as if giving in. "Very well. Come aboard my personal hangar bay. You'll be escorted to the Command Salon."

"Understood."

chapter fifteen

Minutes later, two security guards entered the Command Salon with Leia between them. They presented a ridiculous picture—two tall men in crisp uniforms, their buckles, buttons, visors, and blasters gleaming, flanking a diminutive graying woman in plain Jedi robes.

Still, Caedus didn't think Leia looked diminished enough. She needed to be in restraints, her lightsaber missing from her belt, her expression crestfallen, her eyes defeated. She needed to be suffering for all her misbehavior since the conflict with Corellia began. Well, reality would match his imagination soon enough.

He gestured at the guards; they spun and left the salon. The door shut behind them.

He didn't bother to keep impatience and indifference out of his voice. "Well?"

Leia looked him over. Clearly, the visual image he presented—a tall, dangerous Force-user in all-black garments and cloak—was again reminding her of her father more than her son, and Caedus enjoyed having discomfited her. But she didn't let what she was feeling be reflected in her face or voice. "Jacen, it's time for you to look at yourself."

"I'm well aware of what I look like, Mother. I have to cultivate my image carefully for holonews appearances."

"I'm not talking about your *looks*. I'm talking about your life."

He sighed. "You know, I was actually hoping you had come up with some exciting, imaginative new argument to sway me from my path. Not that it has a chance of succeeding. But it would be more entertaining. Don't you have some new heart-wrenching appeal? Some brilliant metaphor to hurl at me and cause me to double over in the anguish of guilt, to reevaluate my whole ethical structure?"

She shook her head, and there was no missing the sadness in her eyes. "All I have is the truth, and the memory of who you used to be."

He pressed a button on the arm of his chair. The door behind Leia slid open. "You're wasting my time. Leave now."

She glanced at the button, and it clicked down without Caedus's help. The door slid closed again. "You no longer have time for me?"

"*Which* you? The mother you used to be, or the interplanetary criminal you've become? I'm not the only one who's changed."

"History decides who's a criminal, Jacen."

Finally, real irritation began to stir within Caedus, and he rose to the argument. "No, the *law* decides who's a criminal. History just forgives them, and for reasons as stupid as they are varied. Han Solo was a spice smuggler, an unapologetic lawbreaker. *You*, even when you were a teenager, were a traitor to the legitimate galactic government, a conspirator planning war and overthrow. The puppet government you put in place may have forgiven you both, but you'll be criminals for the rest of your lives."

Her expression graduated to scorn. "Have you ever

studied Darth Vader? Clearly, you got your intelligence and your political acumen from your grandfather."

He nodded. "There we are in agreement."

In the private hangar bay set aside for the use of *Anakin Solo*'s commander, a team of security specialists, carrying standard scanning gear, walked down the yacht's boarding ramp. Moments after the last one reached the hangar floor, the ramp rose into place, sealing the yacht.

Jaina Solo, stretched out on her back in an oppressively enclosed space, watched them leave. She did not watch them directly, but through the portable monitor she held in her hands. A shielded data feed led from the device into the metal wall of this smuggling compartment.

Beside her, Han stirred but did not open his eyes. "Are they gone?"

Jaina twisted a dial at the bottom of the screen, flipping its view through all of the *Love Commander*'s exterior holocam feeds. "No, they're walking the yacht perimeter, doing a final scan." Irritated, she checked her chrono. "How long can Mom keep Jacen distracted?"

Han shrugged. "Hard to guess. My estimate is that he's not going to fall for guilt, but he's pretty reactionary these days. If she can push the right argument buttons, he'll be defending his politics and decisions from now until his next birthday."

"How's that going to make Mom feel?"

Han's expression turned sad. "How do you think?"

An ominous scratching sounded from the far end of the compartment.

Jaina looked past her feet to the cage situated there on the compartment floor. A cube one meter in each dimension, it was made of thin, brightly painted durasteel bars.

Within it was a jagged piece of polymer shaped like a stunted tree bole, and holding on to the sculpture was a reptile—a little over a meter long, greenish, with two sets of clawed legs and a long tail. It stared at them as if waiting for a reply to its statement.

Jaina wrinkled her nose at it. "I hate that thing." It was an ysalamir, a lizard from the world of Myrkr—one of a species that had long ago evolved the ability to project an invisible bubble of Force energy in counterbalance to the Force all around it, making everything inside its border undetectable by Force-sensitives outside its range. So long as Jaina and Han, and Zekk and Jag in the next compartment, remained nearby, Jacen could not detect them.

Of course, Force-sensitives *within* the bubble were blind to the Force while they remained there.

Han's voice turned mocking. "Poor little girl. Suddenly has to rely on just her sight, hearing, and wits—"

"It's still like losing one of your senses."

"—just like her old man." He opened an eye and peered down at the reptile. He waved. "Hang on there, little guy. I'll get you back to Karrde when we're all done here."

As if in response, the ysalamir flicked out its tongue for a fraction of a second.

Movement on the monitor drew Jaina's attention. "Sensor crew is leaving. But there are still two guards on the exit, and two just outside."

Han leaned over to peer at the monitor. "Got the hangar holocams picked out?"

Jaina nodded. "Yeah. I don't want to Force-flash them constantly, but we can use blind spots between parked vehicles a lot of the time. And we have one piece of real luck. Jacen's shuttle is right here, in this hangar."

"Let's go." Han exerted himself against the durasteel

panel directly overhead and it swung open, admitting cool air from the *Love Commander*'s atmosphere conditioners.

They executed their plan in several stages, each accomplished very quickly and with the precision that only Jedi and someone like Han Solo could manage.

Silently, the four exited the *Love Commander* through a cargo hatch in the blind spot between her starboard side and the mass of maintenance machinery immediately beside her. Jaina, carrying the electronics package whose construction had been supervised by Iella Antilles—a package now disguised as a mouse droid—reached a wall datajack and plugged the package in.

Its code, optimized not only for this task but for this specific vessel, as well, sampled hangar holocam feeds, looped them, and extracted visual glitches such as glow rod flickers that might alert viewers they were watching a recording. Then the programming subverted security measures—not the ship's main programming, just those pertaining to the holocams—and began sending the looped recordings instead of the live feeds to the bridge.

Next, as Han and Jag covered the door from concealed positions, Jaina and Zekk rushed the guards there. The advantage of surprise allowed them to cross meters of distance before the guards could bring their blaster rifles into line, and a few swift blows put them down. The Jedi dragged them aside, out of sight of the door.

The third stage was just as potentially dangerous, and just as successful. The four of them positioned themselves out of sight of the hangar doors, two to either side, and then opened them. They heard a surprised exchange from the guards there, but no footsteps suggesting additional traffic out in the corridor. Blaster rifles at the ready, the two guards stepped into the hangar.

As the pair caught sight of the intruders in their peripheral vision, Jag hit the button to shut the doors. Jaina and Zekk stepped forward and launched attacks. Jaina's kick took her target clean off his feet, breaking ribs despite his chest armor, sending him into deep unconsciousness. But Zekk's opponent, clearly an experienced hand-to-hand combatant, blocked Zekk's punch with his rifle butt and swung the barrel around to fire.

So Han shot him in the face. His blaster pistol was set on stun, and the guard merely spasmed and fell.

Zekk breathed a relieved sigh—not at the removal of danger, but at his opponent's size. "This one's big enough."

"Get into his armor and get going." Jaina took up her ersatz mouse droid and headed toward Jacen's shuttle. "Despite what Dad says, we can't guess how long Mom's distraction will give us."

"Yes, boss."

Han helped Zekk strip the armor from the tallest guard and don it. He lowered his voice to a whisper so Jaina would not hear. "I'm used to her being intense. But I don't think I've seen her flash a smile in, I don't know, months."

"She hasn't. She's lost a lot since this war began."

"Leia's lost just as much. And Leia can still smile. Leia knows that she has to, from time to time, or go crazy."

"I don't think it's a problem anymore, Han. I think Jag got through to her."

Han glanced over at his daughter, who, having cracked the shuttle's door security, was just entering that vehicle. "I hope you're right."

Zekk stood and swept his long hair up to the top of his head, holding it there while Han put the last piece of armor, his helmet, in place. Zekk pulled the helmet down low and picked up the guard's blaster rifle. "Next stop,

tractor beams . . . and the installation of some very specialized holocomm gear."

Han gave him a lopsided smile. "Jacen's going to get sick
of people improving his ship."

"Good."

"So if you believe that Palpatine's rule as Emperor was legitimate, you have to believe that any government, no matter how destructive, is legitimate." Leia practically spat the
words out. "Why did we bother taking back Coruscant
from the Yuuzhan Vong? By your figuring, they were the legitimate rulers of the galaxy!"

Caedus stirred, irritated, but did not rise. "That's not
what I said, and don't put words in my mouth. Palpatine
worked within the system to gain prominence. That estab-
lishes a continuity of government. That's part of the legiti-
macy. What you did with the Rebels, like what the
Yuuzhan Vong did, was come in like an agricultural plan-
etformer, digging up and destroying everything in its
path—"

A second set of doors, the ones leading forward to the
bridge, opened. Lieutenant Tebut stood there, looking momentarily surprised to have interrupted the heated exchange between two of the most famous people in the
galaxy.

Grateful for the reprieve, Caedus swiveled his chair
toward her. "Yes?"

"We've dropped out of hyperspace, Colonel. We're at
the negotiation site."

"Thank you." Caedus rose. "Come to the bridge,
Mother. In the unlikely event that this is not some sort of
trap by your Confederation friends, you might witness a
successful negotiation for their legitimate return to the
Galactic Alliance."

Leia accompanied him to the door. "I can't root for either result. You don't deserve to negotiate and benefit from a peace. And I don't want to be here if it's a trap."

Behind Tebut, they walked through into the bridge and were assailed by all its usual noise—chatter of officers at their stations in the pits to either side of the main walkway, the hum of computers and other machinery, the distorted and modulated voices of personnel coming across comm frequencies and intercoms.

Caedus marched up the walkway to the vast viewports at the bow end. He could see the hull of the *Anakin Solo* stretching away below and before him, with the domes of its gravity-well generators protruding like habitat shells and the distant, slightly irregular shapes of enemy ships among the unwinking stars. "Report."

The officer in the sensor station, a woman with a Coruscanti accent, called up, "They dropped out of hyperspace thirty seconds after we did. Their numbers match ours, ship for ship. We're running data on the ships themselves. The *Anakin Solo*'s opposite number is the Star Destroyer *Valorum*."

"*Valorum?*" Caedus's surprise was genuine. "Intelligence, best guess: did they name her for one of Palpatine's political opponents to goad me?"

"No, sir." The man at the intelligence station was dark-skinned; though young, he was completely bald, and his accent suggested worlds of the Unknown Regions. "That was her original name upon launch, about sixty years ago. She's *Victory*-class, from the last years of the Old Republic."

Caedus turned to his mother. "Ancient hardware. They're getting desperate."

Leia nodded. "Which affects the chances of this being a

legitimate negotiation and a trap equally. So it's information, but not informative."

"Stop trying to teach me politics, Mother. I've already attained the highest rank you ever did, and I'm not done yet."

"Except that I attained it by being elected to it, not by rewriting the law and jailing my predecessor."

Caedus turned away, shaking his head. Leia was deluded if she thought there was a meaningful difference. "Communications! Has the enemy initiated comm contact?"

Lieutenant Tebut, back at her station, nodded. "Yes, sir. They've sent routine greetings and asked for you."

"Let them wait. Have we established contact with the *Blue Diver*?"

"Yes, sir."

"Put her on holo."

A moment later a hologram swam into resolution before Caedus and Leia. It showed a female of the Duros people, with bluish skin, large red eyes, and a lipless slit for a mouth with no nose above it. She wore a white admiral's uniform. She nodded to Caedus. "Colonel." Recognizing Leia, she nodded again, her voice taking on a slight note of surprise. "Jedi Solo."

"No, Admiral Limpan, sadly, my mother has not seen the light of reason and rejoined the Alliance. Are you on station?"

"We are."

Caedus glanced his mother's way. "I plan no violation of the terms of our meeting today, Mother, but if they spring a trap, I have elements of the Second Fleet standing by to jump in as a little surprise. Speaking of surprises, Admiral, if our holocomm contact is broken for more than fifteen seconds, consider that authorization to jump in. They could always manage some sort of sabotage or jamming to break contact between us."

"Understood, sir."

"*Anakin Solo* standing by."

The hologram of Admiral Limpan vanished.

Caedus's datapad tweetled, indicating that he had received a message, and the intelligence officer called, "That's the breakdown of enemy forces, sir. All old ships. Some of them nearly derelicts. Some are still listed as decommissioned."

Caedus didn't bother to read the listing. "Very good. Communications, put the enemy commander on. Let's get this farce moving."

There was no hologram this time—the *Valorum* was either too old to have a holotransmitter or too strapped for resources to use one. Monitors all over the bridge, including those near the bow viewports, flickered simultaneously to show an aging woman, long-faced, in the uniform of a Corellian Defense Force captain.

Caedus moved up to stand before one of the monitors. Tebut nodded to him to let him know its holocam was now broadcasting. Caedus allowed a little discontent to creep into his voice. "A captain? They sent only a naval captain for this negotiation?"

"Captain Hoclaw." The Corellian woman gave him a nod of mock-friendly greeting. "Technically, you're a colonel, as I recall. But we both have the power and authority to enter into binding negotiatons."

"I suppose. So you're prepared to surrender?"

"I'm prepared to come to the best agreement that is in everyone's interest, involving the Corellian system's return to the Alliance. But if your first words are going to be, *So you're prepared to surrender,* this could take even longer than it has to. I see you're standing. Perhaps you should summon a chair."

Caedus could see that Captain Hoclaw was seated in a comfortably padded officer's chair at the back of her bridge. "Thank you, no. Let's begin."

chapter sixteen

Jag and Han got the panel covering the main motivators for the hangar exterior doors down and to the floor, revealing the machinery beyond.

Jag shook his head. "I do fine with mechanical gear, but I prefer to have manuals and charts on hand. Jaina's better at this sort of thing than I am."

Han smiled in combined pride and self-appreciation. "Don't worry. She got it from me." He pointed a long, callused forefinger at an expansive cluster of chips. "The main security module will be there. We just have to figure out which chip."

"Out of, oh, three hundred or so."

"Sure, no problem." Han took a moment to wave at his daughter, who was visible in the bridge viewpoint of Jacen's shuttle, then bent for his tool kit. "Just stand back and learn something."

Alone, all but forgotten except by a black-clad Guardsman at the door into the Command Salon who watched her every movement, Leia stood listening to the exchange between her son and the Corellian captain. Frowning, she moved to a monitor at the stern end of the bridge and leaned in so close that her right ear was adjacent to the device's main speaker.

She shook her head and returned to the center of the bridge walkway, then stepped clean off of it, dropping nimbly to land beside the bald-headed intelligence officer who had been providing Jacen with data.

Rather than being alarmed, he offered her a sardonic smile. "Is this an attack?"

"If it were, it would be over by now. Can you give me an isolated audio feed of just the Corellian's side of the transmission? So I can hear it without all this ambient noise?"

"I could, of course. But I won't. Technically, you're a prisoner of war."

"You mean I'm the enemy."

"Yes, that's what I mean."

"I'm also Colonel Solo's mother, and this vessel was named for my other son. I don't want to see either one destroyed. Which might happen if my worst-case suspicions turn out to be true and I don't get some cooperation."

The officer looked at her for a long moment, then sighed. Over Leia's shoulder, he called, "Tebut! Isolation helmet, please."

Tebut opened a cabinet drawer beside her station and withdrew a helmet. Not a piece of protective gear for pilots, it was smaller, smoother, with a full-face polarizing visor. She lobbed it to the intelligence officer, who set it beside his monitor, typed a pair of commands on his keyboard, and then handed it to Leia.

She donned it and immediately heard Captain Hoclaw speaking. " . . . asking us to bear a tremendously disproportionate burden of the cost of rebuilding. If I agree to the numbers you suggest, the Corellian system would be reduced to poverty for generations." There was a long pause.

"No, that's not justice. That's vindictiveness, and it presupposes that the entire burden of blame, that every wrong done in the course of these events, should be laid at the feet of the Corellian government."

There was no other noise. No background conversation, no clattering of fingers across keyboards.

Hastily Leia removed the helmet. "Can you send a message, a text message, to Jacen's monitor so he can read it but Captain Hoclaw can't see it?"

"Of course."

"Here's my message."

She told him, and as the words registered, she could see his instant decision to send the message on to his commander.

Impatient, Jaina glanced at her chrono. Leia had to be doing a magnificent job of delaying Jacen, but even so they couldn't stay here forever. Her mouse droid had drunk in much of the raw telemetry data from the shuttle's memory, but there was plenty more to go.

She saw Jag turn away from helping her father and, blaster pistol drawn, trot over to the hangar's internal doors. He keyed a command to open them and stayed to one side, pistol aimed. But it was Zekk, still in Alliance armor, who marched in. As soon as the doors slid shut again, the tall Jedi relaxed. Talking with Jag, he caught sight of Jaina. Fist upraised, he waved to her, a gesture of success.

She nodded. One more task down. But they couldn't relax. Couldn't lose focus. Could never, ever lose focus.

As Caedus continued expressing his very reasonable demands, words appeared at the bottom of his monitor screen.

JEDI SOLO REPORTS NO BRIDGE OR PERSONNEL NOISES IN
ENEMY TRANSMISSION. COMMUNICATIONS HAS ANALYZED
AND CONFIRMS. SUGGESTS ENEMY COMMAND SHIP BEARS
ONLY SKELETON CREW OR IS AUTOMATED.

Despite the distraction, Caedus did not miss the import
of Captain Hoclaw's last words. He adopted a look of mild
confusion. "Step down? Why would I?"

"Because if you do, we might be able to transform this
conversation from a simple negotiation to a genuine peace.
We might bring an end to this war. I could take the fact of
your cooperation to the Confederation as a whole. My
sources tell me that a concession like that would earn a lot
of favor within the Confederation."

Caedus felt a flash of irritation. "That's not on the table,
Captain." He was also growing impatient. Why had the
Confederates not sprung their trap? Perhaps they would
not until it became clear that the negotiations could not,
would not, succeed.

Well, he could make them aware of that right now.
"Captain, you've heard my terms. I will not budge on any
of them. In fact, as I grow annoyed with you, I will make
them harsher. I'll give you ten standard minutes to accept
them as is. If you do not, when we begin talking again,
you'll be in a worse bargaining position." He switched off
the monitor and Tebut, alert, cut the transmission altogether.

Caedus turned. The bridge walkway behind him was
empty. "Where is my—where is Jedi Solo?"

The intelligence officer gestured toward the doors at the
stern end of the bridge. "The guard there accompanied her
back into the Command Salon."

"Ah." Caedus concealed the sudden chill those words
stabbed into his heart. "I'll be back in ten minutes." At a

trot, Darth Caedus headed aft for what he hoped would
not be a confrontation with his mother.

CENTERPOINT STATION,
FIRE-CONTROL CHAMBER

As with every such enterprise—the use of an unbelievably
complicated, incalculably important piece of machinery in
the hands of the military—the involved parties were divided into groups, each of them secretly condescending to
and uncomprehending of the others.

In the control areas of this large chamber, where consoles, keyboards, monitors, readouts, and datajacks pre-
dominated, technicians were hard at work. They analyzed
energy throughputs, calculated damage to systems from
anticipated energy spikes, theorized about side effects, and
discussed recent hypotheses about the physics of gravity.

In one open area, where once a twice-human-height
droid that had believed it was Anakin Solo had lived—and
died—military officers in the uniforms of the Corellian Defense Force now waited. One of them, a woman in white
instead of the lower-ranking browns, irritably consulted
her chrono. Tall and broad-shouldered, she had an intelligent expression and a gaze that moved everywhere in the
chamber, cataloging hundreds of details and events.

The third group, nearest the doors leading out of this
chamber, was made up of government representatives.
Sadras Koyan, a short, burly man with thinning hair and
an aggressive manner, had a gaze as sweeping and restless
as that of the white-uniformed woman, but he seemed less
to be registering details than waiting for some signal to sat-
isfy his impatience. Beside him stood Denjax Teppler—a
younger man, with bland but confidence-inspiring features.
Teppler had worn many occupational hats since the crisis

had begun in Corellia; he was now Minister of Information—a post disparagingly, and accurately, referred to in other offices as Minister of Propaganda.

Around these two men were arrayed aides and advisers, all dressed in expensive, subdued business garments that were so similar in style that they, too, might as well have been uniforms.

Finally Koyan's patience broke. "What's the holdup, Admiral Delpin?"

The woman in the white uniform moved toward him, stopping at the edge of her group as though it were an invisible national border. "Sim firings are suggesting an unacceptable chance of catastrophic failure. We're locking down and locking out the subsystems that are most likely to be damaged by overloads. It's just a matter of a few minutes."

"Solo is going to jump out of there before we can even get the thing online!"

Teppler shook his head. "I don't think so, sir. Captain Hoclaw says they're in a brief break between conversations, but that Colonel Solo is giving Hoclaw so much to work with, she could probably stall him until her next birthday."

"Oh." Mollified, Koyan nodded. "All right, then."

One of the technicians at the control board nodded in response to something he heard over his earpiece. He turned and flashed five fingers at Admiral Delpin. She, in turn, caught Koyan's eye. "Five minutes."

Koyan nodded and mopped sweat from his forehead and cheeks with his sleeve. "Good."

STAR SYSTEM MZX32905, NEAR BIMMIEL

Alema wondered about worshippers. Now that she was a goddess, she should have some.

At the moment, of course, she did not look very goddess-like. She sat in the topmost chamber of Lumiya's former habitat, the chamber with the curved, bookcase-laden walls and transparisteel dome, in a ridiculously comfortable stuffed chair . . . in her old body, the crippled one. In moments, though, she would shed that body again, float free through the galaxy, restore balance to the universe, and please herself.

How stupid Lumiya had been, to use this gift to further some ancient Sith agenda.

Speaking of the Sith, she would have to deal with them soon. Once she had reduced Leia to a tearful, useless wreck, as she imagined Luke now to be, she would turn her attention to Korriban and begin to exterminate the dangerous pest colony the Sith enclave there constituted.

It would take time. Her last projection to Kashyyyk had tired her immensely. She had slept for days afterward. That would probably be true again this time, but Lumiya's notes had made it clear that with practice came stamina.

Alema relaxed, closing her eyes, and invited the immense pool of dark power waiting hundreds of meters below her, in the asteroid proper, to ascend to her, to flow through her. She stiffened as she felt the power grope its way blindly toward where she reclined. As it washed across her, it seemed to be half hot waterfall, half galvanizing electric current, but too full of malicious emotion to be cleansing or refreshing. It imparted to her a sense of greater power and destiny, yes, but it was also an invasion of her self, and that part of it she did not relish.

Now fully intermingled with the dark power, she set her

mind adrift, looking for familiar presences in the Force. She knew where to start looking, at the cluster of presences where long-life patience warred with animalistic strength and rage—the world of the Wookiees.

But Han and Leia were not among those presences. Vexed, Alema broadened her search.

Minutes passed, with each minute taxing her personal energy further, and then she found them: not together, but close by each other, with thousands of lives around them—but only thousands, not millions or billions. That suggested they were on a ship somewhere between worlds. She propelled herself to be near them, then went looking among the other presences, the other glows in the Force, for one that would be suitable.

Some radiated too brightly. They would be too strong for her to merge with. Others were too dim—they would not anchor her as she needed to be anchored.

One stood out. It was bright with power, but very pure, not marked by anger or sophistication. She circled in toward it, charmed by its simplicity, its innocence.

As she touched it, she decided that it was a child—a human girl, asleep. The child stirred as Alema reached her, almost coming awake, but Alema poured out comforting thoughts through the Force—emotions of safety and security, of being in the nest, surrounded by thousands like her, all clicking and whirring on their many legs, all nearly identical.

Her emotions did not so much soothe as stifle the child, but that was enough. Alema wrapped herself around the girl.

Now she was fixed in that place. She had a base from which to go hunting.

She went looking for Han Solo.

ABOARD THE **ANAKIN SOLO**

Caedus strode into his Command Salon. Only officers were there. "Where are Jedi Solo and the guard?"

Captain Nevil pointed toward the stern doors out of the salon. "Princess Leia asked for some privacy. The guard accompanied her to your private office."

The chill in Caedus's heart intensified. Without answering, he dashed toward the doors. Moments later, he entered his private office.

The guard, a muscular man with yellow skin, was there, slumped in Caedus's desk chair, unconscious. A bruise was already beginning to appear on his chin. Leia was nowhere to be seen.

Caedus shoved him and the rolling chair aside, hearing but not looking as the chair toppled and deposited the guard on the floor. Caedus brought up his desk monitor and clicked it over instantly to his secret chambers, where Allana now lived.

There she was, curled up on a little daybed. Nearby, an entertainment monitor flickered, unwatched, its screen displaying an entertainment broadcast in which Ewoks spoke Basic and befriended shipwrecked little girls. Caedus tensed, remembering the deception he had perpetrated in Tenel Ka's palace, but saw her features and relaxed. This was the real Allana.

He thumbed his comlink to life. "Security. Find Jedi Solo and report her location to me."

"At once, sir."

But it wasn't at once. Thirty agonizingly long seconds went by, then the voice returned. "Sir, she's approaching your personal hangar bay."

"Alone?"

"Alone, sir."

"Alert the guards there. Secure both the internal and external bay doors. If she tries to perform a bypass on the internal doors or begins to cut through them with her lightsaber, unsecure the outer doors, open them, and vent the hangar to space. I doubt she'll want to play in hard vacuum."

"Yes, sir." There was a pause. "Doors secured remotely, sir. But the door guards aren't responding. There's no sign of them on holocam."

Thoughts clicked through Caedus's mind like sabacc cards going through an automated shuffler.

She was under observation until moments ago, so she couldn't have gotten rid of the guards herself.

Conclusion: she has allies aboard, or she smuggled in allies on her yacht. Probably the latter.

She doesn't have Allana, so Allana was not the goal of her mission. He pulled out his datapad and used it to transmit a query to YVH-908, the combat droid serving as Allana's bodyguard. The droid sent back an immediate response, indicating no intrusions, no problems.

But to be sure, Caedus moved to the wall panel concealing the secret door that led to those chambers. It opened before him, and he stepped through into one of the best-kept secrets aboard ship. The narrow corridor led aft, to a succession of small rooms that almost no one living knew about. A few steps later, another door opened for him, presenting him with the same happy view of Allana he had seen on his monitor.

She opened her eyes, groggy, and yawned. "No more work?"

"I'm sorry. Lots more work. But I wanted to stop in to look at you."

"I dreamed there was a lady here."

"Well, have another good dream. I'll be back soon." He

smiled, then stepped out again and let the door shut behind him.

No, Allana had not been Leia's objective. *So what is? Sabotage of the long-range turbolasers? Surely she knows that Luke took care of them. They won't be repaired for weeks or months.* "Engineering, commence a tiered diagnostics scan of all the ship's combat and sensor systems."

"Yes, sir."

The security officer's voice crackled across his comlink almost immediately. "Sir, Jedi Solo reached the bay doors. We had them locked down, but they opened right up for her and she walked in. Holocam image inside doesn't show her. The holocams must have been subverted."

Caedus hissed in frustration. "Vent the outer doors *immediately*."

"We did, sir. Issued the command, I mean. The system acknowledged, but exterior holocams show the doors still shut."

"Bring up all weapons, prepare to blast that yacht to plasma the instant it launches."

Remembering the stratagem he'd used on Hapes, Caedus felt a new fear. Perhaps Leia and accomplices had brought a bomb aboard. He never would have suspected it of her, but the idea had a beautiful simplicity to it. A sufficiently large explosion in his private hangar would cripple or destroy the *Anakin Solo*.

Worse, it would harm or kill *Allana*.

He spun, reentered the room he had just left, and smiled down at his daughter. "I was wrong. Work is done for a little while. Let's go for a fun ride."

CENTERPOINT STATION,
FIRE-CONTROL CHAMBER

The chief technician's voice was quiet and somber. "Anakin Solo imprinting lockout bypasses are holding. Energy charge is holding. Targeting system is holding. We read ready."

Admiral Delpin nodded. "Acknowledge ready." She turned Koyan's way. "We await your authorization to launch."

Koyan gulped. "Launch authorized. Admiral Delpin, I also authorize you to fire the weapon. Don't wait for me to authorize. Fire when you think the moment is perfect."

"Acknowledged." Delpin raised her comlink. "Force Yimi, move in. Force Zexx, all squadrons, make your jump and commence your attack." She paused long enough to hear two confirmations, then turned back toward Koyan. "We're committed."

chapter seventeen

ABOARD THE **ANAKIN SOLO**

The little personnel speeder, Caedus at the controls, hurtled down the main passageway of the *Anakin Solo,* causing crew members, uniformed pilots, and civilian observers to leap cursing out of its way. In the passenger's seat, strapped down tight, Allana laughed, a child's throaty chuckle Caedus could hear even over the roar of the repulsorlifts.

Ordinarily he would have been charmed. Now he was simply alarmed. He would remain so until he was off the *Anakin Solo* and away from whatever it was Leia had brought aboard.

Nor could he leave in the vehicles he knew and trusted most, his shuttle and Tahiri's StealthX. They were in the same hangar as Leia's yacht. So he raced toward the main starfighter bay. He'd take out something fast and well defended, and stay far enough away from the *Anakin Solo* that Allana would remain safe if a bomb detonated aboard.

He hadn't forgotten his negotiations with Captain Hoclaw, but they were no longer important.

He sideslipped into a pedestrian down ramp, causing a

half squad of infantry to dive over a railing to avoid him. Allana laughed again.

He glanced at her and forced a smile. "Having fun?"

"Lots of fun. Can I drive?"

"Next time, sweetie."

Finally, there they were—double doors leading into the main starfighter bay. They slid aside at his approach. He roared in, clearing mechanics standing on either side of the door by a hand span. He glanced at the arrayed ranks of starfighters—old and new, trusted and experimental—and veered toward the line of various TIE series.

One in particular—an experimental design he'd flown once—drew his eye. The prototype TIE Reconnaissance Fighter, nicknamed the Blur by GA pilots, resembled the old TIE bomber—it had low-profile, curved solar array wings and two cylindrical fuselages mounted side by side, making the vessel look curiously like a pair of macrobinoculars mounted between a pair of cupped hands. Unlike the situation with the original bomber, the port-side pod on the Blur was an electronics housing, carrying a modern-era hyperdrive, astronavigation computers, a shield generator, life-support systems, and sophisticated electronic countermeasures; it was the closest thing to a StealthX to come out of Sienar, its manufacturer. This Blur was painted in black, undecorated except for small Galactic Alliance symbols on the outer wings.

Caedus slewed to a stop beside the Blur and was unstrapping Allana as a mechanic ran up to him. "Can I help you, sir?"

Caedus lifted Allana out of her seat. "I'm taking the Blur out."

"Uh, yes, sir, but Captain Olavey is doing a test run in fifteen minutes, a sweep near the Confederation task force—"

"Push it back." Not waiting for a boarding ladder, Caedus leapt atop the Blur and lifted the boarding hatch. "You fill out the forms for me."

"Yes, sir."

Caedus's comlink beeped. Carefully, he clambered with Allana down into the cockpit, pulled the hatch shut, and settled into the pilot's couch before answering. "Yes?"

It was his sensor officer. "Sir, sixteen squadrons of starfighters have dropped out of hyperspace. They're heading toward us at full speed. The Confederation capital ships are also moving in."

"Signal Admiral Limpan. Tell her to bring her task force in now. Launch all starfighters from all vessels." As he spoke, Caedus powered up the Blur and glanced his way through an abbreviated preflight checklist. "Move the *Anakin Solo* to the rear of our formation and do not, repeat, do not bring up our shields until the last possible moment, or until the diagnostics that are running pronounce them safe, whichever comes first."

"Yes, sir."

"I'm launching now." Allana in his lap, Caedus finished pulling webbing tight over the two of them, then activated the Blur's repulsors. In his haste, he caused the vehicle nearly to jump up off the hangar floor.

Alarms filled the air and suddenly mechanics were everywhere, running to the squadrons of starfighters in the hangar, prepping them for the imminent arrival of pilots. The glow rods surrounding the main hangar doors in the floor lit up, signifying that the atmosphere containment field had been activated. The doors themselves began to draw aside, revealing starfield below.

Caedus didn't wait for them to finish opening. He banked across and dropped through the half-opened portal, eliciting a squeal of delight from Allana.

And then he was outside, away from the life-threatening explosion he was sure the *Anakin Solo* represented. Caedus breathed easier for a minute. Outside, surrounded by hard vacuum, with enemy starfighters and capital ships racing in his direction, at last he felt safe.

ABOARD THE **ANAKIN SOLO**, JACEN SOLO'S PRIVATE HANGAR

Leia marched through the doors and Jag hit a series of buttons on the keypad beside them, closing and locking them.

Han, visible through the viewport of the *Love Commander* cockpit, waved, then his voice crackled across the comlink. "Sweetheart, get aboard. We've got it, and it's time to fly."

Leia put on a Force-augmented burst of speed and dashed up the yacht's boarding ramp. She heard Jag hurrying in her wake. Zekk was just inside the yacht's main cabin, standing by to seal the exit hatch. Leia moved forward to the cockpit where Han occupied the pilot's seat, Jaina the copilot's.

Leia dropped into the captain's chair, which Lando formerly had occupied. "We're in deep space about halfway between Coruscant and Corellia. Jacen's occupied talking to the Corellians. Now might be the time to go."

Han half turned and cocked his head at her. "Maybe, maybe not. They've already tried to lock you out, lock us in, and depressurize this hangar. They don't want us to leave. The question is, are they tractor beam angry or turbolaser angry?"

"Good question. But Zekk disabled the tractor beam." In the manner of a cantina drink hustler, Leia batted her eyes at her husband. "Surely you can outfly a few little old turbolaser beams? Like last time, on Kashyyyk?"

Han scowled. "In that case, strap in tight."

Jag's boot heels rang on the boarding ramp, followed by the sound of the ramp being raised into place. Leia's ears popped as the hull sealed for space.

And then there were Han's muttered words, barely audible as he started the engines: "Told you we should have been flying the *Falcon*—"

Leia rolled her eyes. "In the *Falcon,* we never would have persuaded them that you weren't aboard."

Han's next words were lost as general-quarters alarms began shrilling in the hangar.

Caedus brought the Blur around and above the *Anakin Solo,* giving him an unimpeded view of the vessel and open space before it. Allana cooed with appreciation at the vista of stars and ships.

Suddenly there were more ships. A bluish streak resolved itself into the curved, graceful lines of the Mon Cal cruiser *Blue Diver,* flagship of the GA Second Fleet, forward and to port of the Blur's position. Other capital ships, a score of them, ended their hyperspace jumps in formation all around the vessels already on station. Starfighters now began to stream out of the *Anakin Solo*'s belly and the starfighter bays of other vessels like piranha-beetles swarming out of a just-damaged nest.

And if the Blur's sensors were to be believed, the enemy starfighter squadrons and capital ships, increasingly outnumbered, continued to race forward. Caedus saw that the enemy capital ships were not assuming any formation he was familiar with; they remained spread out, too far apart to reinforce one another with overlapping fields of fire.

He snorted. He wouldn't need to employ his Sith battle meditation technique to turn this into a gruesome victory for the Galactic Alliance. The Confederation couldn't have mounted a worse approach than the one he was seeing.

A light appeared on his comm board, and he heard Admiral Limpan's voice. "Sir, I'm arraying us in battle-diamond formation, overlapping fields of fire to deal with the starfighter problem, and holding here, since they seem anxious to do all the work. Unless you have other specific orders."

"No, Admiral. I'll monitor from here and maybe assist in defending against the starfighters." *And maybe not.*

"That seems to be an unnecessary risk, sir."

"But an opportunity to test out the capabilities of the Blur."

"Yes, sir." The light faded.

Allana's voice chided him. "You're *working* again."

"Sorry, sweetie. Something came up." He banked to port and climbed well above the *Blue Diver*'s relative altitude, activating the Blur's electronic countermeasures as he did so. In moments he was well outside the GA formation and, he hoped, not registering on enemy sensors.

Below him, the leading edges of Confederation starfighter squadrons came within firing range of their GA counterparts. Lasers, little needles of green and red light, flashed between the two forces. The lines of starfighters wavered and broke, dissolving into dozens of dogfights.

Caedus frowned. Curiously, the Confederation starfighter force was not hammering its way into the GA formation and going after the big ships. They remained skirmishing in a big furball just before the formation. He shook his head. This was the most extraordinarily stupid way to lose a surprise attack that he had ever seen.

Abruptly, his father's voice sounded in his ears, words spoken twenty years before or more. *Jacen, when you're so much smarter than your opponent that you know you don't even have to make an effort to beat him, that's when he smiles and hands you the vibroblade he just cut your heart out with.*

Caedus shook his head to clear the memory away. His father didn't have anything to teach him anymore.

Now would be the time for the bomb to go off. But no wash of fire burst out of the open hangar door in the *Anakin Solo*'s hull. Baffled, Caedus shook his head.

"Somebody went away." Allana's voice was faint.

"What?"

"Somebody went away. And somebody else. They're going away." There was now a world of hurt and dread in Allana's voice. Caedus leaned forward to see what he could of her face and was surprised to witness tears rolling down her cheeks. But what—

Then he knew the answer. She was Force-sensitive. Pilots were dying, and she was feeling the diminishment in the Force that accompanied each death. Inured as he was to death in combat, he paid no more attention to it than he would to a breeze stirring his hair. But Allana was experiencing each event as a little stab of pain.

He hesitated, caught off guard. What could he tell her to make the pain go away? No soothing words would keep her from feeling each distant loss, and he was suddenly helpless.

ABOARD THE **LOVE COMMANDER**

Jaina's commed signal activated the receiver and chip Han and Jag had planted in the outer door machinery. Rows of warning lights flashed around the outer doors, indicating that the atmosphere shield was being activated. Moments later the doors slid aside, revealing a number of capital ships looming in the starfield.

Han eased the yoke forward. The *Love Commander* glided to the entryway, and her prow emerged through the atmosphere shield.

But Han did not increase thrust for a run into space. As the yacht's nose entered vacuum, Han meticulously turned to port, toward *Anakin Solo*'s stern. Leaving the hangar, the yacht maintained a distance of less than two meters from the Star Destroyer's hull—too close for the ship's guns to target him. They could not depress that far, and even if they could, a clean hit would hull the yacht and damage the *Anakin Solo* itself.

Jaina nodded. "Nice. Slow as a teenager taking her first speeder parking test . . . but nice."

Han shot her a dirty look. "Now we just have to find the perfect time to make our run for it."

chapter eighteen

Jag and Zekk were just strapping themselves into couches in the yacht's den—plush, embarrassingly comfortable couches—when Alema Rar emerged from the hatch to the stern refresher. Her smile was all innocence. "Hello, boys. Does Han Solo have a moment for us?"

Zekk was up in an instant, his lightsaber igniting with a *snap-hiss*. Alema raised her own from beneath her black robes and ignited it.

Unbuckling and rising, Jag turned toward the cockpit. "Trouble! Alema!" Facing Alema again, he did not bother drawing his blaster. He knew the futility of that, at least while she had him in sight. Instead he reached for the large travel bag at his feet, rummaged through it, and brought out a helmet. It had a large visored slit over the eyes rather than a full faceplate, and was an undecorated, burnished gray in color.

Swathed as Alema was in her robes, it was hard to tell whether this was the maimed Twi'lek he had followed for years or the miraculously cured one Han, Leia, and Waroo had faced on Kashyyyk, but her face—unblemished, no sign of muscle damage or old breaks to the cheekbone—suggested that it was the latter.

He caught Zekk's eye and shook his head. Then Jag slipped on his helmet, powering up its internal system with a flick of the switch under its collar.

Alema attacked, lunging at Zekk with speed surpassing that which her Jedi training should have allowed her. The tall Jedi parried, trying to bind Alema's blade with his own.

But her attack was not in earnest. Alema's movement carried her past him in a rolling dive that would have sent her over his most likely counterstrike had he thrown one. She hit the compartment's carpeted floor past him, rolled to her feet, and, speed undiminished, charged into the narrow passageway leading to the cockpit.

Jag heard the buzz and crackle of lightsaber striking lightsaber. Alema immediately backed into the compartment again, Leia following her, the two of them exchanging lighting-fast blows with their weapons.

But where Alema was genuinely striking at Leia's neck, waist, and limbs, Leia looked like a stage performer—her blows designed to connect with her opponent's blade and nothing else. Even Jag, no swordsman, could see Leia pass up an opportunity to cut the Twi'lek down.

Jag cycled through the helmet's suite of sensors, looking at Alema for a few seconds with each. Primary sensors showed everyone present as a fuzzy image—flesh did not reflect sensor pings as well as hard surfaces—but Alema was even fuzzier than the others. Under infrared, where Leia was varied shades of green, clothing and different areas of the body showing up as slightly different intensities, Alema was a homogeneous color, the same exact hue from head to foot—except for her lightsaber blade, which radiated far more brightly.

Experimentally, he launched a sonar ping. Registering

higher than the range of hearing of most species, it was not audible, but it returned an image about as crude as that of his radar set. And Alema was nowhere on that image.

Jag smiled.

As she danced before Leia, alternately advancing and retreating, Alema failed to guard her back from possible assaults by Zekk. The tall Jedi stood inert, as though he were not tempted. When Alema's retreat theatened to run her into him, Zekk merely stepped aside, giving the two women room to maneuver.

"How gallant." There was contempt in Alema's words as she left off hammering at Leia to glare at Zekk. "Well, we will simply have to kill you one at a time instead of all together." She looked among them. "Unless Han Solo wishes to come out and save you trouble by dying nobly, of course. Who will be first?"

None of them moved—none but Jag, who gestured toward the stern. "Air lock's that way."

"Fight us!"

Leia shook her head. "I'm sorry, Alema. We're just not that bored."

Alema gaped at her, then realization dawned. "You know. Who told you?"

Jag shrugged. "Lumiya, of course. She hated you, you know." He tried to make the lie sound casual, offhand.

"Liar!" Alema sprang at him, her anger and speed catching Jag flat-footed.

But Leia was there first, interposing her blade, catching Alema's attack and blocking it, a dismissive expression on her face. "If you just want some more sword training, Alema, come back to the Order. Luke will whistle you up a youngling to practice against."

Alema glared at Leia, her expression suggesting that an

entire thesaurus of expletives was flashing through her mind.

Then she wavered. This was not the waver of a person who was tired. It looked instead as though Alema were painted onto a sail that had just caught the first gust of morning wind—she rippled at her waist, and the ripple spread in both directions to her head and her feet.

Then she was gone, as if she had never been there.

Jag took a deep breath. "Thanks, Leia."

She deactivated her lightsaber. "You might think about learning to dodge . . . did you get anything useful?"

He grinned. "Lots."

The StealthXs of Red Sword Flight—Luke, Kyp, Corran, Tyria Tainer, the Rodian Twool, and Sanola Ti of Dathomir—dropped out of hyperspace and were confronted with the vista of the Galactic Alliance task force drawn up in tight formation, the Confederation task force approaching it in some sort of suicidal, spread-out array, and a furious screen of starfighter dogfights raging between them.

Luke frowned, considering. The engagement zone, not yet the sort of chaotic battlefield he was used to with capital ship engagements, was certainly not going to provide the Jedi with much cover for their run on the *Anakin Solo*.

Luke felt a distraction, something drawing his attention away from the engagement zone toward an empty area of space far to the port side of the GA capital ships. It took him a moment to recognize the source of the distraction— Twool, whose StealthX carried fewer armaments but better sensors than the other vehicles of Sword Flight.

Twool, whose job it was to detect Jacen Solo's tracking device with those sensors.

Twool had to be tracking Jacen now, and Jacen had to be

at the point toward which Twool had directed Luke's attention.

Luke felt, and quickly attempted to quell, a sense of excitement, even celebration. If Jacen was out on some sort of joyride, perhaps observing the capital ship engagement from a safe distance, then the Jedi might be able to ignore several levels of Jacen's defenses that they had prepared for. The cargo compartments of their StealthXs were loaded with equipment especially chosen and crafted for this mission—which originally entailed having the squadron creep up close to the *Anakin Solo* as it waited in space, then launching a salvo of engine-crippling proton torpedoes and having most of the Jedi divert retaliatory attacks and starfighters while Luke and Kyp, laden with equipment, secretly boarded and tried to reach Jacen.

If Jacen really was hovering away from the *Anakin Solo*, though, Luke's squadron could conceivably just fly over to him and compel his surrender . . . or shoot him.

But how would Luke convey a complicated revision in orders to the others while they observed comm silence?

He thought about it, then relaxed. He wouldn't have to. The standing orders he had put together for this mission would suffice even in this new situation.

The other Jedi were to follow Luke in toward the *Anakin Solo*. He would initiate the Jedi battle-meld, not used before then so that Jacen would not be forewarned, and all Jedi present were to begin accomplishing their respective assignments.

But with this new situation, Luke merely needed to give the others a sense, in the Force, of his new direction and begin heading toward the spot Twool had pointed out to him. As they all neared Jacen, their own passive sensors, less sensitive than Twool's, would pick up the signal from the tracking device Seha had placed on Jacen's cloak. When they were near enough, Luke would open fire on Jacen's vehicle and simultaneously initiate the battle-meld. No additional communication was necessary.

With the faintest of follow-me nudges to his comrades through the Force, Luke banked toward the distant target.

Each of the three Masters had a Jedi Knight as his wingmate, and Luke's was Sanola. Because she was the youngest Jedi Knight on this mission, she was paired with the most experienced Master, which bothered Luke neither intellectually nor emotionally . . . except that he was reminded, approximately three times per second, that it should have been Mara's StealthX pacing his own.

Though not actively seeking her in the Force, he could feel Sanola trailing behind him, close enough that she could keep tabs on him visually, far enough back that a moment's inattentiveness would not cause her to collide with him. She was a good, studious Jedi and, though young, had inherited the piloting skill that characterized her aunt Kirana. Luke did not need to worry about her.

A glance out the port side of his canopy showed him that the Confederation capital ships were nearing the starfighter engagement zone. Streamers of dueling vessels were now flowing away from the zone; it appeared that the outmatched Confederation starfighters were fleeing, pursued by their vengeful GA counterparts.

Luke frowned. He felt no sense of panic from that direction. But that was not his concern.

A red target blip appeared on Luke's sensor board, identified as the signal from Jacen's tracer. Luke eased off his thruster and coasted the last few kilometers, open to the Force but not expressing himself through it.

The white crosshairs representing his StealthX neared the target zone. Patient, Luke waited for the other Jedi to arrive.

He could feel them, faintly, nearing his location . . .

It was time. Luke reached out for the other Jedi and felt his awareness merge with theirs, combining into the battle-meld that made them so effective in group missions. Simultaneously, not bothering to work with targeting computers, blips, and brackets, he swung his snubfighter's nose a trifle to starboard, located his target by feel, and fired. Four lances of red light leapt from his StealthX and converged on a distant point in space.

Caedus felt the change a moment before he understood what it meant. One instant he was floating in space with a crying little girl, distraught because he could not charm or coax away her tears. The next, he was expectant, hopeful, ready for a fight—

They weren't his emotions. He had been enveloped by a Jedi battle-meld. Even Allana felt it. Her head came up, her distress momentarily forgotten.

With a curse he had not intended to utter in front of his daughter, Caedus grabbed the Blur's control yoke and hit the thrusters.

Not fast enough. The inner surfaces of his solar arrays flashed red and his Blur kicked as it was hit from behind by a full-strength laser shot. The Blur spun from the impact, then the thrusters kicked in and he was hurtling away from that spot in space, executing one more tumble before he could gain complete control over his prototype TIE.

Use shields or continue to use stealth technology? Each choice was equally good, equally bad. He decided on the latter, hoping that his sudden burst of speed had taken him out of direct view of his attackers.

He could begin to make out the identity of his ambushers now. Luke, the shining presence. Kyp Durron. Corran

Horn. Two or three others he didn't know well enough to recognize.

Three Masters this time. They'd learned their lesson at the Senate Building when he'd finished off Kyle Katarn.

Both times they'd attacked when he was in the company of his daughter. His anger grew, ready to fuel his powers.

He felt his enemies seeking him, felt them turning after him. He made himself smaller in the Force, reducing his presence to nothingness. He would give them nothing to work with.

Lasers erupted behind him, missing by meters. He veered to starboard. The laser burst tracked his movement, clipping his port solar array wing before the burst ended.

Caedus growled. They were doing a fine job of tracking him. Either the Blur was not all it was cracked up to be, or they had some other means of determining his location.

Then Allana started crying again, and Caedus knew he had his answer.

They were homing in on Allana's Force presence, they had to be. They were using *her* to target *him*. Hypocritical opportunists—for all their talk of protecting the innocent, they were now going to use a blameless little girl, shredding her life to get to him.

His anger grew, consuming him, casting everything he saw within the cockpit, every star outside the viewpoint, in a haze of redness. So great it was that he could no longer contain his presence in the Force—his anger flowed through him, through Allana, through his pursuers, through everything in tune with him or the Force.

The *Love Commander* waited, clamped by magnetic landing gear to the stern of the *Anakin Solo*, Han and Jaina staying alert for an opportunity to launch when the ship's gunners were likely to be distracted. The opportunity had not yet come. The Star Destroyer's complement of starfighters had launched, joining the engagement between the capital ship fleets, leaving none behind to harass the yacht, but the instant the yacht moved away from the vessel it would come within sight of its turbolasers and ion cannons.

Leia, seated in the captain's chair, grew more restless . . . and then was hit by a wave of hatred. Redness and heat swamped her—hatred for the Jedi, hatred for Luke, for the Confederation, for lasers and explosives and chaos. She gasped, her back spasming from the overload of emotion. In the starboard seat ahead of her, she saw Jaina jerk, but her daughter was less affected than she had been.

"Sweetheart? Leia! What's wrong?" In an instant Han was by her side, gripping her flailing hand, helpless concern on his face.

"It's Jacen. He's out there." She gestured to starboard, well away from the *Anakin Solo*. "He's . . . I don't know. I've never felt him like this." She shook her head to clear it. "Luke's there, too."

Han's expression shifted from concern to grim determination. "All right. We're going now, turbolasers or no turbolasers. Time to prove that I can fly a sand bucket through an ion storm." He returned to his seat, strapped himself in.

Jaina's voice was a rebuke. "That *we* can."

"Right. We'll argue over who's second best when we're out of here."

chapter nineteen

Luke felt the wave of hatred flow through him. It was so strong it felt like a kick in the gut, and he wondered for an instant if Jacen had perfected some new Force attack.

But no, the undercurrent was of frustration, helplessness, even fear. It was no attack. It was like a man in his last seconds of life, recognizing that fact.

And Luke . . . did not hate. He fired again, his laser cannons chipping away at the top of Jacen's fuselage as his target, through brilliant evasive flying, kept his attacks from striking a more vital portion of the starfighter.

Luke remained calm, reactive, ready to defend, ready to kill. He felt the other two StealthX wing pairs approach his position. Soon, they would be in firing range. Soon, this would be over.

Shields, then.

Caedus disengaged the electronic countermeasures and activated his shields. Since he could not evade detection by his enemies, he would have to elude them for a while.

Nor was there any need to maintain comm silence. "Solo to *Anakin Solo*. Am under starfighter attack. Get me some starfighter support here *now*. Bring the *Anakin Solo,* as well."

Tebut's smooth, controlled voice answered him. "At once, sir."

Caedus heeled over to commence a sprint back to the capital ship formation. But he could feel Kyp and Corran vector to place themselves in his path, while Luke remained close behind.

Caedus stifled a curse. Blast, but they were good, herding him away from his safe haven. If anything, his rage grew.

And with each increase in his anger, Allana's sobbing grew louder, her body shaking against his.

He could not comfort her. *To comfort her now would be to die.*

Juking and jinking, his own skills and Force insights making him an unpredictable target, he moved away from the Alliance formation, driven by his pursuers, his maneuvers eating up so much of his speed that he had no chance of outdistancing them. Luke's lasers, sometimes joined by Kyp's or Corran's, came perilously close to him, occasionally brightening his shields and rattling his Blur.

He became lost in time, lost in his rage, existing in the moment. He could not have remembered his name, only that he had to fly, that he had to protect his daughter. Sweat poured from him. His flight suit had ceased absorbing his sweat long ago. Now it pooled in his boots and drenched his pilot's couch.

Then there was . . . intrusion. More presences. Kyp and Corran were suddenly farther away, reducing the number of inbound attacks.

Caedus hazarded a glance at his sensor board. It showed a changed battlefield.

He was now far away from the Alliance formation. In fact, it no longer *was* an Alliance formation. The Alliance and Corellian capital ships had merged into a single formation, one in which the antiquated Corellian vessels were taking a horrible beating but fighting on. Most of the engagement's starfighters were away from that zone, the Corellians leading the Alliance away in the distance.

Closer, there were Alliance-marked starfighters in Jacen's vicinity, trading fire with the StealthXs, tracking them by their laser emissions.

As Caedus watched, the StealthXs ceased laserfire. Now they would rely solely on shadow bombs, launched with use of the Force and therefore undetectable by ordinary sensors.

Not Luke. He stayed on Caedus's tail, still pouring laserfire at the Blur, as did Luke's wingmates. But a trio of Alliance starfighters—two XJ7 X-wings and one of those ungainly round-nosed Aleph starfighters—now harrassed Caedus's pursuers.

Some distance away, a red blip representing an enemy the size of a small transport was inbound. Its transceiver signal showed it to be the *Love Commander*. Beyond that, the *Anakin Solo* was also inbound.

Caedus nodded. He returned his attention to his flying. A moment's distraction now would kill him, but the end of this engagement was in sight. The *Anakin Solo* would arrive, its turbolasers and ion cannons would chase the Jedi away, and he could return to safety.

Luke stayed on Jacen's tail, but the situation was worsening. Sanola Ti had dropped back to engage the enemy X-wings and Aleph, but if their pilots were good, she couldn't hold them. And without the other two Masters to help herd him, Jacen would be able to turn back to the *Anakin Solo*. Luke had to finish this fight now.

He opened himself further to the Force, hoping that it

would give him insight not just into where Jacen was but also where he intended to be in the next second. Jacen was not concealing himself in the Force now. He was . . . he was . . .

He was with a little girl.

Luke started. He took his thumb off the laser trigger and probed again.

There was, in fact, a little girl in the cockpit with Jacen. Her presence had been washed out by the hatred Jacen was pouring into the Force, but now Jacen was calming, and the little girl's distress made her a brighter presence.

Luke's StealthX shook. A quad laser blast from the pursuing Aleph had grazed him during his moment of surprise.

Kill Jacen . . . kill an innocent.

Luke veered away from his target and sent a nonverbal command for the other Jedi to form up on him. He felt their surprise and distress, but he made his intent stronger, insistent.

The StealthXs veered away, toward empty space.

The starfighters they had been dueling continued to chase them, but gave up after perhaps half a minute. They returned to surround Jacen's TIE prototype, acting as his escort.

Caedus sagged as he gave way to exhaustion. He kept one hand on his control yoke, guiding the Blur back toward the *Anakin Solo,* and used the other to hold Allana to him. She looked up at him, red-eyed, her tears unabated, hiccuping in her distress.

"Colonel Solo to starfighter escort. Who's piloting the Twee?"

A woman's voice came back immediately. "Dancer One, sir."

"I mean your name."

"Yes, sir. Lieutenant Syal Antilles, sir. Off *Blue Diver*."

Caedus grimaced. He'd been helped by the oldest daughter of an enemy, yet another traitor to the Alliance.

Still, he had always promised to reward loyalty and merit, and moments ago he had decided to do just that for the Aleph pilot. "It's Captain Antilles now."

"Uh." It wasn't so much a word as an exhalation. Caedus couldn't tell whether she sounded more pleased or pained. Through the Force, she felt only shocked, though the other presence in the cockpit with her, doubtless her gunner, felt elated. Syal's voice was cool, professional: "Thank you, sir."

"And be advised that the StealthX pilot you chased off was a pretty good pilot himself. Antilles, you just sent Luke Skywalker into retreat."

Ahead of him, space far in the distance behind the *Anakin Solo*, back in the vicinity of the capital ships, was suddenly transfixed by a column of light, kilometers wide, that twisted and writhed like something alive.

Space curled and wrenched, as though a vengeful child were playing with the controls of a monitor, stretching and distorting everything in the middle third of the screen. Caedus saw ships, silhouetted within the beam, elongate as though they were being drawn into wire. Turbolaser fire curved impossibly; one blast bent back on itself, slamming into the shields of the cruiser that had fired it. Ships contracted to tiny dots and disappeared entirely.

With the brightness and distortion came a blow in the Force. It hammered at Caedus, a vast, instantaneous loss of life.

Allana's sobs cut off. She slumped in Caedus's lap, mercifully relieved of the burden of consciousness.

Then space darkened and twisted back to its normal

shape. Where once scores of ships had floated and fought, now there was only nothingness—or perhaps twisted wreckage, with no destructive beams or running lights to illuminate it.

On the verge of distributing hyperspace coordinates for their first jump, Luke bent over as the wave of pain and dread hit him. It was far from enough to incapacitate him, but he could feel a resonating shock from the others in his battle-meld.

He put up a rear holocam view on his cockpit monitor. It showed the *Anakin Solo* and tiny flashes of the ever-more-distant main starfighter engagement . . . and emptiness where all the capital ships should be.

Numbed, he considered options. Turn back to help . . . help whom? With six StealthXs? Look for the cause . . . without a corps of scientists or adequate sensory gear?

Jacen was alive. Luke could feel him. He could feel Leia, too, not far away, and Jaina and Zekk. They were safe. Whatever had hit the region seemed to be an all-or-nothing attack, and it was done.

Dry-mouthed, he activated his comm board and transmitted the jump route. "Let's go."

Proximity alarms screamed all across the *Love Commander*'s bridge. Leia felt a yawning emptiness rise up to swallow her. She forced it back, saw Jaina turn toward her, pale-faced.

It was like that day, long ago, when she had seen Alderaan destroyed. She hadn't known then that she was Force-sensitive, hadn't realized that she was feeling the shock of those millions of deaths as well as her own sense of loss and horror.

This blow through the Force was much less severe, but

her sensitivity to such things was much greater. She stood on shaky legs. "What just happened?"

Han glanced between her and Jaina, then returned his attention to his sensors. "Something just appeared in back of us, in back of the—behind Colonel Solo's ship. Something huge, if its gravitic signature is any indication. Then it faded. The proximity alarms thought we were too near a planetary mass." He looked again, gave a grunt of surprise. "The two task forces are gone."

"Gone? Just *gone*?"

"Just gone. Most of the starfighters are still out there. Away from where the capital ships were."

"Centerpoint." Jaina's voice was subdued. "That had to be Centerpoint Station firing."

"Yeah." Han banked sharply to port and accelerated. "Colonel Solo's ship is behind us, starfighters are headed our way from ahead—it's time to go."

Leia cast out with her feelings and picked up a strong presentiment of Luke, a fading presence that was Jacen.

They were alive. In Jacen's case, she felt both relief and dread.

chapter twenty

CENTERPOINT STATION, FIRE-CONTROL CHAMBER

Smoke filled the air, pooling against the ceiling and being battered in various directions by breezes from air vents. Technicians, unused to immediate action, fumbled with fire suppressors. One leapt away from his station as his keyboard suddenly glowed red; flames licked up through it, consuming its keys.

Admiral Delpin moved from station to station, issuing orders, forcing technicians back into seats or shooing them out of chairs too near burning and sparking control boards, as the situation warranted.

And all the while, Prime Minister Koyan stood where he was, bellowing in ever-escalating volume, "What happened? *What happened? WHAT HAPPENED?*"

Denjax Teppler caught his arm. "They don't know yet, sir. You're not helping."

"I don't have to help! I'm the kriffing Five Worlds Prime Minister! I want answers!"

"Answers don't exist yet." Teppler's voice was low, but

there was a trace of durasteel in his words. "You'll get your answers faster if you stop interfering."

Koyan stared at him as if debating whether to bite off the top of his skull, but nodded and shut up.

A moment later Delpin directed one of the technicians over to the knot of politicians. The man—yellow-skinned, bearded, with long hair in a braid and a patch of soot discoloring the left side of his face—offered Koyan an awkward salute. "Sir, the weapon fired."

"Are you sure?"

The man nodded. "But the system overloaded. Getting past the old security interlocks—the way the system imprinted on Anakin Solo all those years ago, so that only he could fire it—has been problematic. So we fired the system and it punished us."

Koyan shook his head. "I don't get it."

The technician paused, struggling for a way to explain it to the politician. "Think of the station as a body. It has a brain. We're a second brain trying to take over the body, and the first brain is resisting. We take over an area, and the brain retaliates by doing something to foul us up. In this case, we assumed control of the trigger finger . . . and when we fired, to retaliate, to mess us up, it stuck its thumb in our eye."

"Oh." Koyan nodded, clearly believing that he understood some of that. "So we fired it. What happened at the other end?"

"No way to know until we get some eyewitness reports. There's a thumb in our eye, remember?"

Admiral Delpin moved toward them. "We've lost all contact with the decoy fleet. Their holocomms are not responding to our queries, not even automated pings. That suggests they were all wiped out. And if they were . . ."

"The Alliance vessels were, too." Koyan nodded, and

mopped his brow again. "Good. I hope you're right. How soon before we can fire again?"

The technician shrugged. "Unknown. Part of that thumb in our eye looks like power system overloads, and the targeting may have to be recalibrated, which means reentering a lot of star data. Days? A few weeks?"

"Get on it." Koyan turned away and marched to the door, escaping through it into the fresher air of the hallway beyond. His retinue followed him.

All but Teppler. He raised his voice to be heard over the chaos. "Ladies, gentlemen, the Office of the Prime Minister thanks you for all your hard work. You've done extremely well." He gave them a raised-fist gesture of support and enthusiasm, then turned to follow Koyan.

Admiral Delpin stood before him. She whispered so only he could hear, "You're an accomplished liar. But I mean that in a good way."

He gave her a half smile. "Thank you. Um, when Phennir finds out . . ."

"He'll roast us with words alone."

"Anything I can do to take some heat off you?"

"Just make it clear to him that I was following orders . . . and I take them from the Corellian government, not from the Confederation Supreme Military Commander." She glanced in the direction Koyan had gone and was not completely able to keep an expression of distaste from crossing her face.

"I'll do that."

"And if we've killed Jacen Solo and crippled the Second Fleet, it was worth every bit of burn."

Teppler nodded in agreement. "Good luck."

"You, too."

ABOARD THE **ANAKIN SOLO**

The *Anakin Solo,* its hangars stuffed with surviving starfighters from not only its complement but also those of several Second Fleet vessels, its hyperdrive damaged by the gravity-wrenching effect of the attack, limped back into Coruscant space.

Caedus paced the bridge, not having slept since the catastrophe. He wanted to spend every moment with Allana, to be there for her when she awakened from the deep sleep that had claimed her, but he could not. To be away from his duties for so long would alert his crew that he had other priorities. He could not have them asking questions—not even as loyal a crew as he commanded.

The enemy had made Centerpoint Station's primary weapon operational, and had used it to try to kill him— him personally.

It was a tribute. They knew he was the most significant individual in the galaxy, the one person who could lead the Alliance to victory. They had panicked. And they had failed to kill him.

But without knowing it, they had tried to kill *Allana.* They would pay for that. Everyone who had supported Corellia during this action would die, or end up stamping out bits of Alliance trooper armor in a prison workshop, or be fed to rancors.

Captain Nevil approached. The Quarren was as upright and formidable looking as ever, but the skin of his face- and mouth-tentacles was paler than usual. "Sir, we're in planetary orbit. I'd like to transmit a request for permission to take a berth at the orbital shipyards. Get repairs under way immediately."

Caedus glanced at him. "Granted."

"Admiral Niathal has sent a request that you meet with her immediately at the Senate Building."

No. I'd be away when Allana wakes. "I can't leave the *Anakin Solo* at a time like this. Reply that we can have a meeting here, or by holocomm."

"Yes, sir."

It occurred to Caedus that there was something he should have asked before now, something he had not. What was it? Oh, yes. "Kral, in the force we lost . . . did you have any family?"

"Yes, sir." Nevil seemed to sag just a centimeter, then straightened. "My son Turl. An ensign. A weapons officer aboard the frigate *Cheesmeer*."

"I'm sorry." Caedus tried to feel sorry, tried to remember that Turl was to Nevil as Allana was to him, but that mathematical equation was as close as he could come. Turl Nevil was a nobody, and now he was a nobody twisted and compressed by unimaginable gravitational forces into a tiny spot in space. Still, Caedus managed to keep an expression of sympathy fixed on his face.

Nevil apparently accepted it as such. "Thank you, sir." He turned away, walking stiffly, to return to his duties.

The meeting took place in Caedus's private office. Again, Admiral Niathal stood and paced while Caedus, imperturbable, sat.

"The Second Fleet is a shambles." Niathal's voice was deeper than usual, its pitch lowered by emotion.

Caedus nodded.

"The flagship, *Blue Diver*, was lost, and Fleet Admiral Limpan with her."

Well, she wasn't all that spectacular an admiral anyway, was she? "I know. It's a disaster. I *told* you it was a trap. We just had no conception of the scope of the trap. Lure me out into open space, send up some derelict warships with skeleton crews to hold me in place for a few moments, and then fire the biggest gun in the universe at us. It had the elegance of simplicity."

"How did you survive?"

Caedus sighed, then mentally trotted out the story he'd spent some time working up. "During my discussions with Captain Hoclaw, I felt a presentiment in the Force. A realization that part of the plan, a sideline to it, was that an elite unit was coming to retrieve the Hapan princess Allana. That's what the Jedi Solo was there for. Once she escaped my security team, I retrieved the girl from her holding area and took her out in a starfighter to lure the retrieval team to me. The team consisted of Jedi in StealthXs. To my surprise, they were willing to kill me and let the little girl die, too, so I admit I underestimated their priorities a bit. Still, I had no problem eluding them until the primary wave of relief arrived, a squadron of starfighters, and drove them off. I'd ordered the *Anakin Solo* to follow the starfighters, which is why it was away from the engagement zone when the Centerpoint weapon fired."

"Ah." Niathal gave him a that-makes-sense nod. "You're lucky."

"Yes."

"We need all our leaders to be lucky."

"I agree."

"We just lost a lot of unlucky commanders and ships we cannot replace. The Corellians traded us a flying junkyard for modern ships of the line. Confederation military strength may exceed ours now. With Centerpoint Station active, it certainly does."

Caedus smiled. "Admiral, we've just *won* this war."

That soft-spoken assertion stopped Niathal in the midst of her pacing. "Say that again?"

"The Corellians just handed us the trillion-credit game prize. The solution to our problems. We've won."

"How?"

"We go to the Corellian system and take Centerpoint Station from them. And then we point it at anyone we choose."

Niathal's skin darkened—a color change Caedus suspected was similar to a blush or a flush of anger. "Ah. I had not realized that it was so simple. Shall I pack a lunch?"

Caedus waved her sarcasm away. "After Ben and I disabled Centerpoint, it wasn't worth the loss we'd sustain if we devoted all our forces to take it, and at the time we wouldn't have been willing to use it immediately.

"But now . . . if we mount a major naval offensive at the moment they think our navy is at its weakest . . . we can take it. And now we have the will to use it. You and I, we *are* that will."

The admiral stood there for long moments, once again studying him, her own face inscrutable. "Do you have a plan?"

"I will by tomorrow."

Niathal nodded. She turned and left.

chapter twenty-one

ABOARD THE **ANAKIN SOLO,**
MAIN HANGAR BAY

Syal Antilles threaded her way through the *Anakin Solo*'s main hangar bay. Ordinarily this would have been no special task, but currently the space was overcrowded with starfighters—not just the vessel's usual complement, but most of the vehicles that had survived the Centerpoint Station attack. Now starfighters were packed in far more tightly than the floor markings indicated was normal, and mechanics had been working twenty-hour days to repair and maintain them.

A diminutive woman with short brown hair and bangs that went awry whenever the faintest breeze crossed her face, Syal searched among the alphanumeric designations painted on walls, ceilings, and floor sections. V17 was her destination, and only after she squeezed between two armored troop carrier shuttles did she spot it—an ordinary *Lambda*-class shuttle, its atmospheric wings locked into the up position, marked with Alliance symbols on bow, sides, and stern.

She approached it from the front and waved at the uniformed pilot, dimly seen through the forward viewport. He waved back, and moments later the vehicle's boarding ramp descended.

She climbed the ramp with quick, nervous steps and pitched her voice to carry throughout the vehicle. "Lieut— uh, Captain Antilles reporting as requested." At the top of the ramp, she turned forward, facing the shuttle's main compartment, which was laid out in a standard VIP profile—only a few seats, all plush and able to swivel, with a small table beside each one.

But the cockpit door was closed, and there was no one in sight. "Hello?"

The boarding ramp rose, locking into place. Suspicious, she put her hand against the small of her back, where her hold-out blaster was holstered under her tunic. Pilots were not supposed to go armed in secure areas aboard ship, but her mother had taught her that, at times, obedience to the letter of the law was an invitation to assassination.

The cockpit door swung open. In the doorway stood a man of average height. In the dress uniform of Galactic Alliance Starfighter Command, he was middle-aged, lean, with hair that had changed over the years from pale blond to white and features that were aristocratic but sympathetic. His eyes were a startling blue.

He offered her a smile. "Welcome back, Syal."

"Uncle Tycho!" She ran to him, wrapped her arms around him, and held him close for a moment. "It's so good to see you."

"You act as though I were the one in danger." He led her back into the main compartment, sat her down in one of the overstuffed chairs, and took a seat in the one opposite. "*Captain* Antilles. I thought that was a glitch when I saw it on the rescuee roster."

Syal shook her head. "A field promotion. I shot at Luke Skywalker and they decided I warranted a raise in grade." Though she tried, she couldn't keep the pain, the bitterness out of her voice. "A consolation prize for losing my entire command. My fiancé."

"*Fiancé?*" Tycho registered shock. "I knew you were seeing someone—"

"Tiom Rordan. Fighter pilot off the frigate *Mawrunner*." Unable to stand the sight of the sympathy on Tycho's face, she looked down at her boots. "It wasn't official. We weren't even going to think about getting married until the war was done." Syal felt tears begin to well up. Tears again, for the thousandth time. She dashed them away and stared at Tycho, daring him to notice them.

He just shook his head. "I'm so sorry."

"Yeah." She fidgeted. Her left knee began vibrating, early warning that nervous energy was going to cause it to start bouncing up and down soon. She pressed down on her knee with her palm. "Is Winter all right?"

Tycho nodded. "She's fine. Syal, as good as it is to see you, I actually sent for you in an official capacity."

"Ah." Syal straightened. "What can I do for you, General?"

For a moment, Tycho looked a touch sadder, as though her sudden reversion to officer's manners was as unwelcome as it was appropriate. "You know that these days I'm serving as an analyst for Admiral Niathal."

Syal nodded. "I wish you were training pilots again. The rookies could really use your experience."

"Thanks. What I need from you is, well, the truth. The truth with no protective coloration, no filtering."

She considered. "Off the record? And have you swept this shuttle for listening devices?"

"Yes, and yes. Remember, like you, I live in a mixed household. Pilots *and* spies."

That almost fetched a smile from her. But she didn't have any smiles left. "Fire away, General."

"I need intelligent observations from a field officer's perspective. About morale. The course of the war. About Colonel Solo."

She had to think about it. "I'm not sure what to say. I don't have a context. Maybe that's the problem. How can you have a perspective if you have nothing to compare things with? I don't. My squadmates don't. I mean, didn't."

"I don't understand."

"I remember the Yuuzhan Vong War. I was only a kid, but it's all still so vivid. Everyone I knew was fighting for the same thing. Survival. It was simple. If we lost, we died, and we died *out*. If we won, we didn't. *This* war, though . . . Those of us who were in uniform when it started trusted that they'd tell us what it meant, and that it would make sense. But they told us, and it didn't."

She took a long, shuddery breath. "It's getting crazier and crazier out there. It's like both sides are starting to see each other as nothing but droids. I keep hearing stories about infantry units who report that they found enemy towns and compounds blown up, part of some Confederation scorch-and-thwart policy. But scuttlebutt has it that *their* ground forces are reporting the same thing about our towns and compounds, and I know *we* don't have a policy like that. And someone at Centerpoint Station pressed a button to wipe out our entire task force the other day. *Pressed a button.* I'm scared to death that they'll do it again . . . but I'm even more scared that next time, *I'd* be willing to push that button." Finally the tears came and she put her head down into her hand. "Since this started, I've shot at one of my heroes, Luke Skywalker, and at my own *father*. The Alliance and the Confederation both say awful things about both of them. Neither one of them deserves it. It doesn't make any *sense*."

Tycho's tone was kind, but his words pressed her on implacably. "And Colonel Solo?"

"Everyone's afraid of him. *Everyone*. Nobody talks about him. Have you ever heard of that? Someone whose own people never talk about him?"

"Once or twice. A long time ago." Tycho sighed. "Syal, do you want out?"

Jolted and angered by his words, she sat upright and glared at him. "I don't want to run. I just want it to make sense."

"I'm not asking you to run, or to dishonor your uniform. I'm asking, all else being equal, do you want out?"

"No. I want to be doing something I think will help bring the war to an end. My captain's insignia . . . it's not worth the metal it's stamped from without that. I'm *not* going to dishonor my uniform . . . but the way things are going, I can't seem to bring honor *to* it. Do you know what I mean?"

"You're talking to a man who used to fly for Emperor Palpatine. Palpatine, whose subordinates never talked about him."

She wiped at her tears. "I'm sorry, Tycho. I forgot."

"Don't apologize. You have nothing to apologize for." He studied her. "You'll get new orders in a day or two. They'll look awful. They'll look like something no commander with any sense would do to an ace like you. Don't protest, don't make waves. Just go where they tell you. I'll be there."

"Yes, General."

"Can you get in touch with your father?"

She nodded. "I haven't. Technically, it would be treason. But I can."

"It's not treason if a commanding officer orders you to do so."

"True."

"I so order."

"Yes, sir. I don't know how much time it will take."

"My means of reaching him are bound to be just as slow and uncertain. That's why I'm doubling my chances by asking for your help." He gave her his gentle smile again, his Uncle Tycho smile. "So. Official talk is over. Is there anywhere around here to get a good cup of caf? Not the paint remover they serve around the hangar?"

"My gunner, Zueb Zan, brews up a good one."

"Lead the way."

CORELLIA, CORONET, COMMAND BUNKER

The hologram at the center of the darkened chamber showed a lean man in a dark officer's uniform, that of a Confederation general. His face was scarred, his body rigid.

And he was only a double hand span over a meter tall, as Prime Minister Koyan had instructed his technical team to keep the hologram to a "manageable size."

The reduction in stature did not affect the general's voice, however. Rich with anger, it resonated, vibrating Koyan's sternum, echoing off the chamber walls. "Centerpoint Station is a Confederation resource. Utilizing it without coordinating with my office constitutes dereliction of duty—and more important, gross incompetence."

"It's a Corellian resource, General Phennir. We chose to use it in an effort to end the war precipitously." Koyan shrugged. "And we don't know that it hasn't had that effect. Jacen Solo, one of their two Chiefs of State, is dead. His partner, Admiral Niathal, is more reasonable than he was."

"Our stealth craft in the Coruscant system report the *Anakin Solo* reaching planetary orbit. How do you conclude that Solo is dead?"

Koyan felt his stomach sink, as though he'd unwittingly stepped onto a turbolift and it had suddenly plummeted forty stories. He tried to keep his dismay from his face. "Our starfighters reported all Alliance capital ships in the engagement zone destroyed."

"The *Anakin Solo* had apparently withdrawn from the engagement zone by the time the weapon was fired. So in your effort to eliminate the forces besieging Corellia, and one, only one, of the Alliance's important strategists, you've given away the secret of the station's functionality, tipped the balance of power by a few percentage points, and otherwise accomplished nothing. Whereas if you'd worked with me and my office, we could have put together a much more telling stroke. One that genuinely would have turned the tide of the war."

Koyan shook his head. "We were lucky to have rooted out all spies who might have gotten the information about the station's repairs to the GA. Add your people to the mix . . . it becomes too complex to keep secrets."

"I don't say this often, Koyan, but I'll say it now. You're an idiot."

"Which makes you an even more exceptional idiot, for saying it to the man with the most destructive weapon ever created."

"As you have the most destructive weapon ever created, you are clearly capable of defending the Corellian system without aid from the rest of the Confederation. No need for synchronized fleet movements. For sharing intelligence with the other worlds. For food, medicines, supplies."

That brought Koyan up short. Until the station was operational again, those resources were incalculably valuable.

Common sense dictated that he take a step back, offer some appeasement, play nice. As an experienced politician, he knew this.

But his next words surprised even him. "Don't threaten me, General. You wouldn't like the results." He gestured to his technicians, invisible outside the glow of the hologram, and the image of Phennir disappeared, plunging the chamber into blackness.

Gulping, Koyan turned toward the chamber exit. He probably shouldn't have done that. On the other hand, it was important to show the Confederation which world held the controls, and which ruler was boss.

The answers were Corellia, and Sadras Koyan.

chapter twenty-two

KASHYYYK,
MAITELL BASE, HANGAR HOUSING THE
MILLENNIUM FALCON

Jaina trotted into the hangar office—a set of improvised rooms, set off from the rest of the building by sheets of corrugated durasteel, that now served as headquarters and workshop for the Alema hunters—and paused just inside the door. The main office was dark. "Jag?"

His voice floated through the curtain separating this chamber from the next. "Workshop."

She moved to and through the curtain. "We have some preliminary results from Talon Karrde on the data from Jacen's shuttle—" Seeing what stood in the center of the workshop, she stopped short, staring.

Surrounded by tables and shelves piled high with metal parts and electronic components was a man—*probably* a man, though he could have been some new variety of battle droid. Most of him was covered in a jumpsuit of crinkled, reflective silver-gray material. Over this were attached a helmet, metal gauntlets, boots, a mechanical rig held against his back by two straps crossing in an X-pattern across his chest, and a broad belt holding pouches and a holster carrying an oversized blaster pistol. All these accoutrements had similar metallic surfaces resembling brushed silver.

The helmet was the one Jag had worn aboard *Love Commander* during the last engagement with Alema Rar, and the gauntlets were the crushgaunts sent by Boba Fett.

Jaina scowled. "Why is it I always catch you playing dress-up?"

"Just assembling my gear—my current kit." Jag pushed up the visor of his helmet, revealing his eyes and the bridge of his nose.

Jaina approached and rapped her knuckles against his chest. It rang, the noise dulled by the cloth covering it. "And the breastplate, too."

"Not exactly the height of fashion, is it?"

"Well, I'll forgive you for wearing too much shiny stuff if it's useful."

"Oh, it's all useful." Jag tapped each item in turn as he explained. "You're familiar with the helmet, the breastplate, and the crushgaunts."

Jaina nodded.

"The backpack is a thruster. It's not much use in Coruscant-level gravity, but in low-grav conditions it will me get around, help make up for the fact that I can't do Jedi leaps. The blaster pistol I designed from the ground up." He drew it and managed a creditable Han Solo spin around his trigger finger, despite the presence of his crushgaunts. "It's oversized, so I can draw and fire it while wearing the gauntlets; it's engineered to function in the temperatures and vacuum of deep space—I can fire it while extravehicular." He holstered it again. "Plus, it has a feature I don't think any blaster has ever had."

"What's that?"

He shook his head and the bridge of his nose crinkled.

Jaina guessed that he was grinning at her. She felt a flash of annoyance but let it pass. "All right, keep your little boy's secret."

He gestured at the material of his flight suit. "Laced with cortosis alloy. Not much—with the Temple and the academy at Ossus both abandoned, Master Luke could supply me with only a little. But a little still means that a graze from a lightsaber could result in minor or no damage instead of an amputation. The belt pouches, full of surprises for Alema. The boots . . ." His voice trailed off.

"Yes?"

"Keep me from stubbing my toes."

She sighed. "Funny. Or not." She looked over his battle array. "How long have you been working on this?"

"I've been carrying pieces of it for years, gradually adding items as I learned more about our quarry." He shrugged; his entire torso rose as one piece. "It doesn't make me a Jedi . . . but we don't need another Jedi. We need something she can't predict. Also, if I take the crushgaunts off, I can pilot a starfighter in this. The suit offers all the usual virtues of a flight suit."

"Well, I have something your suit doesn't have." From her belt, she extracted a piece of flimsi and held it up before Jag's eyes.

He focused on the astronomical coordinates written on it. "Is that what I hope it is?"

"Probable coordinates for Brisha Syo's habitat. Care to go there and have a picnic?"

"Definitely. You tell the tall fellow with half a name. Should I invite your parents?"

Jaina nodded. "I think they have a right to be there."

ABOARD THE ANAKIN SOLO

Allana's breath came in gasps and she rolled over in her bed, her eyes closed, her face flushed.

In his chair beside her, Caedus winced. The nightmares had come again for her. It had been two days since her collapse, and she'd alternated between deep sleep and troubled dreams. The medical droid had said it was a not-unusual reaction to emotional trauma, but those dispassionate words did nothing to ease the pain Caedus felt.

Then Allana's eyes opened. She looked around, confused, trying to make sense of her surroundings, and caught sight of Caedus.

She drew away from him, huddling against the wall. She reached for her thigh, her hand coming up with the injector pen her mother had given her long ago, the self-defense weapon with which she had once subdued a dangerous assassin.

She was brandishing it against *him*, her own father, and Caedus felt a pain as sharp as if she had plunged it straight into his heart.

Emotion made his voice hoarse. "Good morning, Allana. I'm glad you're feeling better."

She lowered the injector but did not return it to its hideaway sheath. "I want to go home."

"This has to be your home for the time being. You're safer here than anywhere."

She shook her head. "I'm safest with Mommy."

"Bad people keep coming for you when you're with your mother. You need to be here."

"They all died, didn't they?"

Caedus nodded. "Many people died. And though I tried to get you far away from them, I couldn't get far enough away."

"You were . . ." Allana struggled for the words. "You were bad. I hate you."

Another stab to his heart. "No, you don't. You can't hate someone who loves you. I love you, Allana."

"No, you don't! You took me away from Mommy. You said you had permission and you lied. You're the same as anyone else who wants to hurt me. *I hate you.*" She raised the injector again.

"No. Allana, you can't. It's not possible, and I'll tell you why." Caedus remained in his chair by force of will. Every instinct made him want to hold the little girl, to comfort her . . . every instinct but the one that told him she needed to be free to decide, free to act. "You're right that I took you without permission. But I don't need permission."

"Yes, you do!"

"No, I don't. I'll tell you why. And you'll believe me, because I can't lie to you about this. You'd know it if I lied. All you have to do is open up your heart and you'll know how I feel. You'll know the truth."

Defiant, she kept her injector at the ready. Her expression dared him to reach for her.

"Allana, Tenel Ka has the right to decide where you go, and what you learn, and how you are to be protected, and she has that right because she's your mommy. She has had that right for all your life so far.

"I have the same right . . . because I'm your daddy."

Allana froze, her expression transforming from defiant to unbelieving. She shook her head.

Caedus waited, pouring his love for her into the Force, trying to send it through his eyes into hers. He nodded. "You always knew you had a daddy. Your mommy had to keep who it was a secret. But now you're old enough to understand it. I'm your daddy."

He felt the fear within her, the lingering pain from the

events of two days earlier, begin to erode. Allana lowered her injector. Through the Force, he offered her nothing but the truth—for the first time in months, perhaps years, there was nothing of Sith training to his thoughts, nothing of the Jedi, no strategy, no planning. There was only what he felt.

She came to him, clambering over the bed and into his lap. She put her arms around his neck. "Daddy."

"Yes. Your daddy, forever and ever." He held her to him, stroked her hair. "And when the war is over and the bad people have been taught how wrong they were, and everyone is happy again, we can tell everyone that I'm your daddy. And you can sit right next to me and help me decide how things are going to be for everyone. Won't that be nice?"

KORRIBAN, WORLD OF THE SITH

On a ruin of a planet, they stood in the ruins of a citadel— themselves the ruins of an ancient organization, the Sith Order.

In a circular meeting chamber, its stone walls darkened by age and weathering, they stood in a circle, dark hooded robes obscuring their identities. It was an unnecessary precaution; there was no one present who was not part of their Order. But legends and records had taught them the merits of caution, of maintaining customs of secrecy and self-preservation even when in their safest havens.

One of them, a dark-skinned human female whose pale geometric-patterned tattoos stood out in sharp relief on the skin of her cheeks, bowed to the assembly. Her voice was surprisingly light and musical, considering her somber appearance, as she answered the question put to her. "Yes, my lord, I have news and even speculation concerning Alema Rar."

"We will hear them, Dician." The words came from the man guiding this conclave, a human whose fully white eyes suggested blindness but whose alert mannerisms said otherwise.

Dician continued. "The ersatz Sith Holocron provided to her traced her path back to her point of origin. It is an asteroid belt in a star system near Bimmiel. When a cloaked ship comes available, I will requisition its use to pinpoint her location exactly."

The white-eyed leader's voice suggested skepticism. "You think her significant enough to devote important resources to such a mission?"

"I do."

"Why?"

Dician took a long breath, a delaying tactic allowing her a few more seconds to compose her argument. "By offering the Jedi aid in their search for this woman—"

A buzz of offended comments from the others brought her up short. She glanced around, assessing the mood of the assembly, and decided that she would lose respect if she yielded to their outrage. Before the white-eyed man could bring them to order, she continued, her voice rising to cut through their complaints: "In one of my assumed identities, of course, as a Confederation Intelligence operative. I would not aid the Jedi, but they must think of me as an ally." The others quieted. "And having proved myself a legitimate intel officer, I received a considerable amount of information on their hunt for Alema Rar . . . which must necessarily include information and speculation about her.

"It seems that among the resources she inherited from Lumiya is a Force technique permitting her the projection of phantoms across space. It appears in every way to match the lost technique of Darth Vectivus."

At those words, the murmur rose again. "Vectivus's history is clear. He was a fraud," someone muttered.

"A fraud with an art that would benefit us all," said someone else.

"I was not here for her visit—could this Alema Rar be turned to our ends?" yet a third questioned.

"I think not. She seemed as insane as a piranha-beetle with a needle through its brain." The voice was barely audible above the other voices.

The white-eyed man cleared his throat, and the others went silent. "We must recapture the woman, extract the secrets of the technique from her, and seize the power source she utilizes."

There was regret in Dician's tone as she replied. "I think not, my lord. The Jedi are now homing in on her location. Knowledge is much easier to obtain than to contain—once they know where her base is, we will never be able to preserve that secret."

The white-eyed man considered. "Very well. You were correct, Dician. This is of highest priority. We will not concern ourselves with a cloaked ship, but assign a fully armed warship to the task. I am recalling the *Poison Moon* and assigning it to you for this mission. It will be equipped with explosives sufficient to destroy an asteroid. You will use it to locate the dark side energy source used to power Vectivus's Force phantom technique and obliterate it. You will obtain any Sith artifacts in Alema Rar's possession. You will also capture Alema Rar, or, if circumstances warrant, kill her."

Dician bowed again. "It will be my pleasure."

SANCTUARY MOON OF ENDOR

They made a curious parade, Luke decided. Not that he hadn't been part of many curious parades in the course of his curious life.

First went the Hapan Security vanguard, four spectacular-looking women. They wore the most stylish body armor imaginable, its graceful lines broken up by green-and-brown camouflage patterns that made the armor difficult to pick out amid Endor's forest vegetation.

Behind the security guard by some ten meters, walking side by side, came Luke and Queen Mother Tenel Ka, dressed completely inappropriately for their surroundings— Luke wearing his black Jedi Grand Master garments, Tenel Ka sporting a flowing gown in shimmering, metallic shades of blue. Luke suspected that beneath it Tenel Ka probably wore traditional Dathomiri battle dress, but he would never know, unless an attack was staged against them and she felt the need to move freely.

Ten meters farther back were the droids C-3PO and R2-D2—the former to deal with any Ewoks who might approach, and the latter, inasmuch as any droid could, representing a comfortable and friendly "face" for Tenel Ka.

The main body of the odd safari walked behind the droids—Jedi Masters Saba Sebatyne and Cilghal, along with half a dozen advisers to the Queen Mother.

At the rear of the party were four more Hapan security specialists.

Luke pitched his voice as a whisper. "Quite a retinue for a little walk in the woods. How many do you have to take with you when you just want to go to the refresher?"

Tenel Ka had not smiled in the brief time since her arrival on Endor, but she almost did now. Almost. To Luke, it seemed that the facial muscles that permitted such an expression no longer knew how to perform. Her whispered answer was matter-of-fact: "In my own palace, none. In foreign palaces, a minimum of four."

"And if you're visiting Dathomir, where the only thing available is a bush?"

"It's the best-defended bush within a dozen parsecs."

"I thought so."

They walked in silence for a little while. Luke could feel the tension within Tenel Ka—it roiled at the surface of her thoughts, like water just beginning to boil—but he did not feel it appropriate to hurry her toward the conversation to come.

Tenel Ka waited until they found a broad clearing. At its center was a wide, nearly flat stone, some four meters across, the only spot of the clearing visited by shafts of sunlight. She raised her voice so that all could hear. "This will do." As she and Luke moved toward the stone, her guards scattered, forming a defensive perimeter around the clearing, while the Jedi Masters, Hapan advisers, and droids stood in a tight knot well away from its center.

Luke sat at one edge of the stone. It was warm under him, even compared with the warmth of the forest air. He extended his senses through the Force to seek out any intelligences that might be close enough to listen and found none—except for Tenel Ka, who was doing just as he was.

She finally sat next to him. "One of the problems with dealing with Jedi Masters is that they're so patient. It's enough to drive you crazy. They just wait you out."

Remembering his own time on Dagobah with Master Yoda, Luke nodded. "You're right. Now I've become exactly what used to make me insane with frustration. I wonder when that happened."

Tenel Ka took a deep breath. "You know that I turned my back on the Alliance, demanding that Jacen be removed from power. Then I withdrew from the war altogether and did not pursue my agenda against Jacen any longer."

"Yes. I assumed you had a good reason." That was the truth. Luke felt no anger or censure. Tenel Ka was the

Queen Mother. She would not have wavered on this matter without cause.

"I don't know if it's a good reason. It's a very personal reason. Jacen kidnapped my daughter, Allana. He threatened to kill her if I did not resume my duties as an Alliance member."

Luke winced. "I wish I could say I was surprised." He almost added, *He kidnapped Ben, too, and tortured him.* But he clamped down on the words before they left him. Tenel Ka did not need to experience mental images of Jacen torturing Allana. She did not need the additional fear and worry his words would cause.

"I thought—I *think*—that he could probably do it. Kill . . . my baby. The situation cut me in two. The Queen Mother arguing one course of action, Allana's mother arguing another. Allana's mother won."

"I understand."

"But after what happened a few days ago . . . the firing of Centerpoint Station . . ." Tenel Ka's voice wavered. Luke could feel her anguish growing within the Force, and, detecting her distress, Saba and Cilghal glanced over at the two of them. "It shows the ends the Confederation is willing to go to. It shows how insane this war has become. The Hapes Consortium has been rebuilding for more than fifteen years from the damage caused the last time the station was fired. The Corellians can use it to destroy whole worlds if they want."

Luke nodded.

"Awhile back, I thought that Allana and I could perhaps run away. They'd hunt us down, of course. The Alliance, or my political opponents from Hapes. Allana and I would die, but we'd die together, in each other's arms. Now it looks like we won't even have that tiny comfort. We're going to die never having seen each other again."

"You don't know that. If you saw something like that as a Force vision, it isn't necessarily the true future—"

"I don't see visions of the future anymore. Not really. I just feel death and failure all around us. Consuming us like a fire." Tenel Ka looked down at her hand, resting palm-up in her lap. It twitched, and Luke sensed she longed for her lightsaber to be there, lit, with enemies in front of her— enemies she could attack personally, physically. "I have to be the Queen Mother, Master Skywalker. I have to decide what's right for my people."

"Yes."

"I have to turn my fleets against the evil Jacen represents. And then I have to watch him kill my baby." An overpowering wave of grief rolled off Tenel Ka. Luke almost reached for her to comfort her, but in the sight of so many others such a gesture would be utterly inappropriate. He saw Cilghal take an involuntary step toward them, but the Mon Cal healer caught herself and stepped back again.

"Has your intelligence service determined where Allana is? To stage a rescue?"

"They don't have to. I can feel her. Sometimes she's on Coruscant, sometimes elsewhere. Her movements match those of the *Anakin Solo*."

The events of just a few days earlier clicked together in Luke's thoughts. The little girl Jacen had been using as a human shield—that had to have been Allana. Luke decided not to mention it. "A grief-stricken Queen Mother is of no more use to the Hapans than a grief-stricken Jedi is to the Order. What if we just go in and retrieve Allana for you?"

She looked at him, a new dread in her eyes—this time, an unwillingness to let herself hope for something so tremendous. "If I thought it could be done, I'd have done it already."

"One former Jedi and limitless wealth can accomplish a

lot of things." Luke's gesture took in all of the Sanctuary Moon, back to his outpost and beyond. "A whole Order of Jedi can accomplish other things."

"I couldn't ask you to."

"And you didn't. But I think it's the right thing to do. The right thing from a personal *and* military point of view. Without Allana, Jacen loses his influence over the Consortium. With the revelation of his threat to kill Allana, Admiral Niathal may reconsider her alliance with Jacen. With the odds shifted away from the Alliance, Jacen and Niathal may have to sue for peace. Rescuing Allana could end this war, Tenel Ka." He offered his hand to her. "The Jedi Order offers."

Slowly, as if not daring to believe her luck, Tenel Ka took it. "The Hapes Consortium accepts. With gratitude."

chapter twenty-three

STAR SYSTEM MZX32905, NEAR BIMMIEL

The *Millennium Falcon* dropped out of hyperspace well outside the asteroid belt of Star System MZX32905, well away from the floating, tumbling hazards to navigation its asteroids constituted. Han and Leia could see the belt on their sensors, though, as a broad line of irregular lumps, demonstrating widely different masses, shapes, and rotations.

A moment later a starfighter appeared nearby, trailing the *Falcon* by a few dozen kilometers—Jag's X-wing. This meant that Jaina and Zekk's StealthXs were there, as well. Han didn't bother searching for them on his sensors. He might pick up traces, but it would be a pointless exercise.

Leia activated the comm board, adjusted the transmission to its lowest power setting, and directed it precisely toward Jag's starfighter. "We've begun the passive sensor scan. And we're running computations on all observable asteroids of the appropriate size, plotting their locations when Jacen and Ben visited." She didn't get a word or click in response, but hadn't expected one. She could feel Jaina and the other two in the Force and knew them to be patient, unalarmed, waiting. They had to be receiving her.

Han watched as data began accumulating on his sensor board. Red shapes, each one designated with an alphanumeric code decided on by the *Falcon*'s navigational computer, indicated where the relevant asteroids were now. Yellowish shapes with corresponding designations began appearing, showing where those asteroids had been many months earlier. Han adjusted the scale of the sensor image to display the system's entire asteroid belt. "I'm going to prioritize these targets so we can figure out what order we visit them in."

Leia gave him a dubious look. "Based on your extensive knowledge of ore yields and mining techniques, I suppose."

"Of course not. Based on my knowledge of how corporate stiffs *think*. For instance, they like big round things. So we'll focus on the biggest, roundest asteroids first."

Leia put her head down in her hands. "That wouldn't hurt so much if I didn't suspect you were right."

LUMIYA'S SATELLITE HABITAT

Alema felt a little ripple in the Force. It was of no more consequence than if a normal person had had a dream in which a menacing shape stood over her bed as she slept.

But Alema had long ago learned to trust incidents that seemed to be of little consequence. She threw off her bedsheet and rose, then dressed hurriedly—as hurriedly as a being could with only one working arm.

The habitat was silent except for the hiss of atmosphere conditioners. Her chambers—rooms that had once been Lumiya's—were dimly lit by night-intensity glow rods and held no terrors for her while she was awake. Casting out in the Force, she could feel nothing but the beautiful, malevolent furnace of power hundreds of meters beneath her, the wellspring of energy with which she would someday be able to balance the galaxy.

There was nothing to cause the ripple she had felt, but she *had* felt it.

She took one of the few working turbolifts up to the habitat's top level, the observatory, with its curved shelves full of artifacts and its transparisteel dome facing the stars.

Reclining on a comfortable sofa, she relaxed into the Force, seeking any hint, any anomaly that would explain what she had felt. It was at times like this that the vast amount of dark side power down below was an impediment instead of a blessing—like a racing thruster engine, it offered many resources but tended to drown out all lesser noises around it.

Then she felt it again, the ripple.

Someone was hunting her. Someone was here to kill her.

She smiled. She had been hunted many times, but this was the first time she had ever been hunted in a place where she made the rules—*all* the rules.

ABOARD THE FRIGATE **POISON MOON**

Dician stared through the bridge's forward viewports, which offered a view of stars—and irregular black patches obscuring expanses of stars. The black patches, she knew, were the largest of the asteroids in this field, receiving little or none of the light from this system's sun.

Navigating an asteroid field in a 150-meter-long frigate using only passive sensors was not the easiest of tasks. Dician did not unnecessarily intrude on the concentration of Wayniss, her chief pilot. A male human, gray-haired and bearded, Wayniss was an aging pirate and smuggler who knew nothing of the Force, and who would have reacted incuriously to the news that his commander was a member of the Sith Order. He gave good value for his pay and remained loyal so long as the credits kept coming, making him reliable and predictable. Dician approved of him.

Now Wayniss tapped a command sequence into his keyboard. The main bridge monitor, just above the forward viewports, darkened into a view of the starfield before them, then began zooming. Moments later, it displayed a view, heavily pixilated at extreme magnification, of a roughly spherical asteroid—visible only as a crescent of faint sunlight.

Wayniss looked up to catch Dician's attention. "Your target, Captain. Confirmed as the source of your tracer transmissions."

"Excellent. Plot a course to the vicinity of that asteroid. Keep other asteroids between it and us as long as possible— I want little or no direct line of sight on us."

"Stealth approach. Understood." Wayniss turned back to his keyboard and began plotting out the complicated approach.

"Sensor reading." That was Ithila, the *Poison Moon*'s sensor officer. A Hapan woman of middle years, she was lean and beautiful—but for the pattern of livid burn scars that crisscrossed the right side of her face, the result of an explosion aboard a Battle Dragon during the Yuuzhan Vong War. An allergy to bacta had prevented her from eliminating the scars, and the Hapan cultural revulsion for anything damaged had sent Ithila into self-imposed exile.

Dician cleared her throat. "Perhaps some more information would be in order."

Ithila glanced at her captain, evidently trying to gauge whether Dician was being polite or sarcastic. "Two targets. Too far away for a visual reading. Neither one has a transponder active. Fuel emission sensor readings suggest one is a starfighter, and the other is in the class of a yacht or light freighter. The starfighter is approaching our target asteroid. The other vehicle is staying on station a hundred kilometers or so from our target."

Dician considered, drumming her fingers on the armrest of her captain's chair. Sneaking up on a rogue Jedi in an antiquated frigate was tricky enough without the complication of additional observers. Still, it had to be done. "Continue as ordered. However, we may have to make a fast run from the final asteroid to our target. I want all crews and asteroid-buster bombs standing by at the shuttles. I want all weapons primed and ready."

Wayniss nodded, unperturbed. "Yes, Captain."

Jag took the lead in his X-wing—it was only fitting, because of the three starfighters, his was the only one not equipped for stealth. Jaina and Zekk hung back in their StealthXs as Jag approached the habitat. Squat and dome-topped, set atop plascrete columns holding it meters above the asteroid surface, archaic of design, and pitted with meteorite strikes sustained across centuries, it exactly matched the habitat described in Ben Skywalker's report of the Brisha Syo encounter.

Jag brought his vehicle in quickly enough that he could accelerate away at a good clip if weapons turrets suddenly sprouted on the habitat's surface, but the habitat remained inert, and he felt a moment of doubt. Was Alema even there? Leia's last tight-beam transmission, minutes earlier, had indicated that she had felt some movement in the Force, something distinct from the pool of dark energy waiting at the asteroid's center, but that didn't mean their quarry was home.

Well, if she wasn't, her hunters could take up residence and wait for her.

His X-wing comm board reported a signal—an automated query from a hangar facility, offering landing instructions. He ignored it.

He decelerated as he neared the habitat. In the dim light from the distant sun, it was revealed to be an unlovely mass of reinforced duracrete, its viewports dark, perhaps covered by durasteel meteorite shutters. He sent his X-wing into a shallow dive, activating repulsorlifts as he came within meters of the stony asteroid surface, and glided in underneath the habitat, between its support pillars.

A column of light emerged from the center of the habitat's underside, illuminating a section of railed track. The track led down to the asteroid surface—and into it, through a broad gash in the stone.

Jag nodded. The light had to come from the chamber described in Ben Skywalker's report, a room that housed the railcar access to the mines below. The hatch into the chamber was open, with the chamber's air probably being contained by atmosphere shielding.

Not that the presence or lack of atmosphere mattered to him, not now.

He set his X-wing down almost directly beneath the chamber opening and powered down. Then, bypassing warning indicators and programming implemented to prevent accidents, he raised his canopy, venting his cockpit atmosphere into space. He pulled his crushgaunts from the webbing that kept them secure at his feet, donned them, then unstrapped and activated his low-grav thruster pack.

This would be a tricky maneuver. He had to fly up into the lit chamber, which was simple enough . . . but if the habitat's artificial gravity was active, and he calculated his angle and rate of travel wrong, he would immediately be dragged back through the hole again, or would hit the chamber ceiling and carom to an inglorious crash somewhere on the chamber floor.

As he reached the circular opening and emerged into light, he cut his thruster and drew his oversized blaster. His momentum carried him a couple of meters into the air.

—curved wall ahead of him, no targets visible—

He came down on his feet on solid flooring and spun, assessing possible threats, possible targets.

—track protruding nearly up to the high ceiling, a control stand, no railcar, doors, no Alema Rar—

Breathing hard, he took another turn around, confirming that there were no threats at hand.

Excellent. He was in. On the other hand, there had been no one there to see his flashy arrival.

He shrugged and holstered his blaster. He'd just have to do it again sometime when he had an audience.

Jaina and Zekk, their StealthXs side by side and mere meters apart, saw the hangar's blast doors begin to slide open, revealing a large, lit chamber beyond—and Jag Fel standing at one door edge, waving them in.

Jaina goosed her thruster and glided forward, Zekk pacing her. As they approached, Jag waved downward, indicating a litter of items on the floor just inside the door. Jaina saw barrels, wires, electronic components.

Jag held up his hands together, then spread them, miming the effects of an explosion. Jaina nodded. So Alema had left them a trap, a bomb—what looked like an *improvised* bomb. If it was improvised, the odds were improved that Alema Rar was still here, or had only recently fled.

The Jedi set their vehicles down in the center of the hangar, slowly spinning them on repulsorlifts so they faced the doors, and came to a full landing.

Jag shut the outer doors and approached as they raised their canopies. His visor was up. "Two bombs so far." He gestured toward the litter on the floor, and toward the edge of the door where it rested on its guiding rail. There Jaina saw more electronic components. "Simple ones, thrown together. But no Sith ship."

Jaina rolled out of her cockpit and dropped to the floor. There was something malevolent about this hangar, something different from the energy that suffused this place—a different flavor. She searched for it in the Force and found it nearby, a loathing mixed with patience, anger mixed with servility.

Whatever its source was, it had recently rested against a nearby wall and had left only minutes before.

Disappointment weighed down on her. "She's fled."

Zekk moved up to join them. He shook his head. "No, she hasn't. Can't you feel it?" With a pointing finger, he traced a path from the corner where that patient loathing had waited, out through the hangar doors, and then down—straight down, into the asteroid.

Now Jaina could feel it, could follow that trail. The vehicle, for it had to be Alema's Sith craft, had been here until recently, then had been flown down through the rift in the asteroid surface. Alema and her craft waited far below.

Jag shrugged. "She knows we're here. Scratch off the element of surprise. We'll just have to show her some other surprises. Problem is, though the habitat is pressurized, and the caverns are, there's about a fifteen-meter gap of hard vacuum between the two."

"Not a problem." Jaina drew her Jedi cloak around her. "We have the equivalent of flight suits on under our robes. With flight helmets, or with our emergency masks, we can survive several minutes' worth of hard vacuum."

Jag flipped his visor shut. His next words, through the

helmet's speaker, were amplified rather than muffled. "Let's go, then. Let's end this."

ABOARD THE **POISON MOON**

"It's a Corellian light freighter. The disk shape is distinctive."

Dician, jolted by Ithila's words, looked at her sensor officer. The *Poison Moon* had crept closer by several asteroids to the habitat location, and now the sensors could pick up the habitat building itself, and details of the other vehicle that waited nearby.

Dician's mouth went dry. "Compare the vehicle's distinctive markings and modifications with known records of the *Millennium Falcon*." Yes, there were hundreds or thousands of Corellian YT-1300 light freighters still in service around the galaxy . . . but one, and only one, had a vastly increased likelihood, a greater statistical probability, of showing up wherever trouble was brewing.

With growing impatience, she waited while Ithila tapped her way through a series of screens. Then Ithila looked up, her expression startled. "It's a match, Captain. Certainty exceeds ninety-eight percent."

Dician took a deep breath. The *Falcon,* especially if it was captained by Han Solo, would be quite a prize, captured or destroyed. The bragging rights alone for having killed Solo, for ridding the galaxy of his interference, would keep Dician warm for decades. And the pleasure would be doubled if Leia Organa Solo, Jedi and traitor to the noble Sith name of Skywalker, was aboard.

Dician struggled to keep her tone normal. "No mistakes now. We have double the *Falcon*'s firepower and the element of surprise, but none of that means anything if we make a mistake. So we will continue our approach, and we will be perfect. We will make our run on the *Falcon*, and we will be perfect. We will launch our crews to raid the habitat and situate the bombs on the asteroid, and we will be—what will we be?"

The bridge crew members offered their answer in unison: "Perfect."

"That's right. Perfect."

"Perfect." Leia rubbed the back of her neck.

Han glanced her way. "What?"

"*What* what?"

"You said *perfect*. As in, something's really perfect, or something's very messed up, I-don't-really-mean-it's-perfect?"

Leia shook her head. "I don't know. The second one, I guess." She returned her attention to the sensor board. Nothing had changed since she'd seen the habitat's hangar door close, nothing would change until her daughter, Zekk, and Jag emerged, but a nagging thought told her she really needed to keep her attention there.

Then she felt it, a pulse in the Force, a distant query from the direction of the asteroid. Flavored with the darkness that inhabited that place, but distinctly the presence of Alema Rar, it reached out for her, brushed over her, went elsewhere.

Leia stiffened. "Alema's found us." She unstrapped and rose from the copilot's seat, taking her lightsaber in hand. "And if we've guessed right about the way she operates now . . ."

Han nodded glumly. "She'll conjure up a Force phantom and send it against us."

Leia turned to face the cockpit entrance, ready.

chapter twenty-four

Jag leapt up, high above the opening in the floor, and dropped through into hard vacuum.

Passing through the area of the habitat's artificial gravity, he slowed in his descent but continued downward, the metal track close by, into the deeper darkness of the large gash in the asteroid surface below. He thought he could feel his feet hit the atmosphere containment field there—whether he could or not, he felt his rate of descent slow further as he encountered the friction of atmosphere. "I'm in."

He cycled through his helmet sensors. The basic sensors showed cavern walls all around, at distances of thirty to a hundred meters. There were a few faint gleams from glow rods on the metal rails; other than that, all was dark. "You're going to need some lights."

A moment later his sensors showed Jaina and Zekk dropping feetfirst after him. They held lit glow rods, so he could see them with his naked eyes, as well. The glow rod light reflected from the irregular surfaces of the transparisteel foil masks they wore for their brief exposure to hard vacuum.

Jaina's voice crackled in his ear. "We just felt her reaching out for us."

Jaina and Zekk vectored in their slow free fall—an act that would be impossible for normal people, but Jag assumed they simply used the Force to shove themselves laterally. The maneuver allowed them to drift to within reach of the metal track. They did not grab it, but occasionally reached out a hand or foot to brush against it, directing them smoothly down its length. Jag touched his thruster pack to slow himself to their descent rate.

There was something on his sensors, something big but indistinct, on the far side of the widest part of this cavern. Jag rotated and pointed in that direction, alerting the others.

It rushed toward them, streaming through the air, growing more distinct as it came.

A flock of mynocks—

ABOARD THE **MILLENNIUM FALCON**

A thump against the *Falcon*'s cockpit viewport prompted Leia to turn forward again.

There was something outside the viewport, resting against it, a gray, fleshy mass with an enormous gaping mouth full of sharp teeth. Han stared back at the thing, unruffled. "Mynocks, sweetheart. Give me a minute, I'll burn 'em off." He began typing in the commands Leia knew would send electric currents through the *Falcon*'s outer hull.

"Wait!" Leia reached out through the Force toward the mynock. As she did so, it looked away from Han, straight at her.

In the Force, it *was* her husband.

Leia gulped. "Burn that and you burn yourself. That mynock is a Force phantom. And it's *you*."

Han looked outraged. "A *mynock*? Kill me, sure, but does she have to insult me?"

"Han . . ."

"Hang on, Princess. If I can't burn it off, I'll shake it off." As Leia grabbed for the back of her chair, Han hit the thrusters. The sudden acceleration nearly took Leia off her feet—then ended abruptly as Han hit the retros, slamming Leia forward into the back of her chair.

The mynock hurtled forward as if catapulted from the *Falcon*'s cockpit. A few dozen meters away it spread its leather arm-wings and banked as if flying in atmosphere, wheeling around back toward them.

ABOARD THE **POISON MOON**

"The *Falcon* is maneuvering."

Dician gave Ithila a nod and returned her attention to the forward monitor. It showed the Corellian freighter whirling in place, then accelerating away from the asteroid— and then, just as abruptly, vectoring to starboard.

Dician cocked her head. It looked as though the *Falcon* were engaged in a dogfight. But no opponent appeared on the sensor board.

This was the second inexplicable event in just a few moments. Less than a minute earlier, Dician had felt something brush against her in the Force. That presence had moved on, seeming to settle elsewhere on the *Poison Moon*—settling everywhere at once, as far as she could tell, but not doing anything. And now this.

Wayniss seemed unperturbed. "Orders, Captain?"

They were now mostly shielded behind the last large asteroid positioned between them and the habitat. It wasn't all that large; if the *Millennium Falcon*'s curious acrobatics took her farther and farther in random directions, she would inevitably detect the frigate.

"Wait until the *Falcon* is oriented away from us on one of her maneuvers. Then begin your run. The instant I determine that the *Falcon* has detected us, I'll issue the command *Go*. This means all weapons open fire on the *Falcon*, all shuttles launch. Instantly."

"Yes, Captain."

"What are we?"

"Perfect, Captain."

"That's right."

The stream of mynocks, twenty at least, flew straight at Jaina and her companions. She reached out in the Force to find them—and felt incongruously complex presences instead.

One of them, the lead mynock, was unmistakably Jag—or at least bore his unique signature in the Force. The rest were unfamiliar to her, but definitely more complex, more alive in the Force than mynocks. "They're all phantoms. One of them is you, Jag."

She got a grunt of confirmation.

The lead mynock flew straight at Jag. He hit his thruster and twisted aside. The digits at the end of its right wing-arm, grasping at him, missed him by a meter. Its lashing tail missed him by centimeters. Jag maintained his lateral thruster burn, carrying him away from the mynocks and the Jedi.

Most of the mynocks followed him. Four veered toward the Jedi, a fly-by attack made with lashing tails. Jaina and Zekk got their hands on the metal track and had no difficulty twisting out of harm's way as the mynocks attacked and passed.

Jag's voice was calm, unrattled. "Keep going. I'll lead these away. We'll divide Alema's concentration, see if we can overload her."

"Be careful." With an exertion in the Force, Jaina pushed herself downward, causing her to slide much faster down the track. Zekk followed. The last four mynocks didn't— they wheeled for a moment, then took off after Jag.

The light from their glow rods showed the track passing through a hole in the cavern floor, leading into another, deeper chamber.

ABOARD THE MILLENNIUM FALCON

Han spun the *Falcon,* a barrel roll that would have made it next to impossible for a real mynock to reattach itself to her hull. But he lost sight of the creature by eye and by sensor and wondered if it had managed to clamp onto the hull despite his maneuvers.

Leia gripped the back of her chair in a ferocious Wookiee-hug and glared at him. "Remind me why I ever unstrap myself while I'm aboard this crate?"

"Because you're still looking for thrills. That's why you're still with *me.* Where's the mynock, sweetheart?"

Leia's face cleared as she searched in the Force. Then her expression began to change to one of alarm. "Incoming fi—"

Han put the *Falcon* into another gymnastic tumble even as he saw Leia's expression alter. Lances of light glared by outside as linked turbolasers fired on them.

"Where'd *she* come from?" On Han's sensor board, closing fast, was a small capital ship—an *Interceptor*-class frigate, to judge from her elongated spar of a body, broadened chisel-shaped bow, and blocky stern. As Han watched, thruster flares lit from the flanks and top hull of the frigate, and shuttles of several different vehicle classes launched, angling away from the frigate—away from the *Falcon,* toward the asteroid.

Interceptors weren't much by capital ship standards, but they carried more turbolasers than the *Falcon,* proton torpedoes instead of concussion missiles, heavier armor, heavier shields . . . The *Falcon* was outclassed. But Han was not going to leave, not with his daughter still prowling around the depths of the asteroid, away from her StealthX.

"I don't know!"

"Where's the mynock?" Han felt a sudden chill. If the mynock phantom linked to him wandered into the path of the frigate's turbolasers, the attack would kill him as dead as any other.

"I don't know. Gone." In a brief moment of straight-line travel, Leia got to the front of her chair and hopped into it, facing backward to forestall any sneak attack from that direction, and resumed her death grip on the seat back. "Oh. Now it's back again."

It was then that Alema Rar's voice floated, sweet and mocking, from deep within the *Falcon.* "Han? Han *Sooooloooo . . .*"

The attack came as Jaina and Zekk shot down through the hole into the next cavern. It was not signaled by any disturbance in the Force. Inert lumps on the rim of the hole into the cavern suddenly erupted into movement, became bipedal figures swinging two-meter clubs—

Reflexively, Jaina lit her lightsaber and parried. Her blow severed the club, revealing it to be a length of durasteel rail three or four centimeters in diameter. Her attacker was a protocol droid—sky blue, of ancient design and manufacture. Jaina hurtled past it.

She heard a pained "Oof" and looked up to see Zekk

meters above her, descending more slowly. His attacker's rail was pinned under his left arm; his attacker, a scarlet protocol droid, still held the other end. They floated in Jaina's wake, slowed by the fact that what had been Zekk's downward kinetic energy was now divided between them.

"Sorry." Zekk twisted, and then he was a meter away from the track, his attacker right next to it. As Jaina watched, the protocol droid's head began banging against every cross-tie on the track, causing the head to bounce back and forth. The additional impacts and friction slowed Zekk still more, causing him to drop farther behind. "Thought it might have been a Force phantom; didn't attack it before it hit me."

"Are you hurt?"

"A couple of ribs cracked, I think. Not too bad." It sounded worse than that; Zekk's breathing was labored.

The red droid's head came off. The rest of its body went limp. Zekk gestured, and both it and the metal rail went flying off into the darkness.

Jaina returned her attention to her surroundings. Things weren't too bad. Alema Rar had enjoyed plenty of time to work up surprises for unwanted visitors, and so far nothing had been too strange or difficult for her hunters.

The theory they'd developed concerning her Force phantoms and their limitations seemed to be proving true. On Kashyyyk and here, none had demonstrated an ability to project damage at range, as with a blaster—the phantoms seemed to be contained, confined to the limits of the bodies they simulated. Some could wield lightsabers, but that made a certain amount of sense, as the Jedi regarded their lightsabers as extensions of themselves.

This might work. This attack might just work.

Then Jaina felt a pulse of malevolence, followed by

something approaching her—something too massive for her to deflect, moving too fast for her to dodge.

The stream of mynocks flitted by Jag, passing within meters, their angry eyes fixed on him. Several flicked their tails at him. Two swooped close enough to be real threats. He raised his left arm, caught a tail end across his crushgaunt. The blow did not scar the metal. With his right hand he missed the other tail. It lashed across his chest, cutting a razor-thin gash in his flight suit but doing no harm to the *beskar* breastplate beneath.

The blows sent him tumbling through the air in the mynocks' wake. As much as he could, he bent toward the gash in his flight suit, clamping an arm across it, as though he were injured. If anyone was watching, he needed to conceal the presence of his armor as much as possible.

The mynocks wheeled in unison. His blaster hand twitched, every instinct telling him to draw and fire . . . but they flew past too quickly.

When they swept by again, he blocked three tail lashes before they were past—and then felt a jerk as a fourth tail, grappling rather than lashing, wrapped around his left ankle and towed him along in the mynock's wake.

The flock dived, heading toward a narrow gap in the cavern floor far away from the rail track.

Jag gritted his teeth. He was doing his job. He was keeping these mynocks off Jaina and Zekk.

If only he didn't hate this task quite so much.

At the lowest level of the cavern complex, Alema Rar sat on the chamber's stone floor. A few meters ahead of her sat the railcar that provided access between this chamber, the habitat, and all caverns in between; it rested at the bottom of the track, angled upward. A few meters to her left was the entrance into Darth Vectivus's private cavern, the one in which he had built his ridiculous mansion so long ago. The stone door that could seal the chamber was open. The artificial gravity in the chamber was active, and even here, outside its main area of effect, Alema could feel it, providing her with what seemed to be about half Coruscant's gravity.

She was already panting, tired by the effort of maintaining so many phantoms at once. She didn't think she could handle much more gravity than that—unless she drew continually on the power of this place, which would have other consequences. How had Lumiya accomplished what she had with the phantoms? With years of practice and tremendous will, Alema decided.

She felt a little better. It was time to return to the war—to begin finishing off her intruders.

chapter twenty-five

Descending in Jaina's wake, Zekk felt the attack the instant Jaina did, felt its power and speed.

And its intent. It was aimed at Jaina. Reflexively, Zekk lashed out with the Force, pushing. Jaina shot downward as if fired from an ancient artillery piece.

Something flashed by a meter over her head, something silver. It severed the track there, leaving a clean break in the metal rails. A fraction of a second later it hit the far wall of the cavern with a dull flash of light and a resounding *boom*.

Zekk turned his attention toward the source of the attack. It was outside the range of his vision, but he could feel it now that it was on the offensive, no longer lying in wait. It had to be a hundred meters or more away, though exact distances were difficult to predict through the Force.

It reeked of dark side energy and intent, a Force presence that was at once unliving but not inert. It had purpose. Zekk could almost see it, reading its self-image: a large ball, webbed wings projecting from it, a weapon spike protruding from the top, a landing spike from its bottom . . .

And hatred for him, for Jaina, in what served it as a heart.

Zekk read its movements and intentions as it acted. Its top spike was aimed toward Jaina. Now it canted upward, aiming at Zekk, and prepared to fire again—

Zekk grabbed the track with his free hand and pushed off, adding energy from the Force to his movement, and hurtled downward. A fraction of a second later, something flashed by over his head and sliced through the track there, then slammed into the far cavern wall. Cut above him and below him, several dozen meters' worth of track floated free, twisting as it slowly began to accelerate downward.

Zekk grimaced. He was fighting a starfighter, or the equivalent of one, and all he had was his lightsaber. At least he could serve as a distraction, keeping this thing off Jaina.

As he reached the top of the remaining portion of track below, the spot where Jaina had almost been hit, he angled himself so that his feet came down on one of its cross-ties. He took the slight shock of impact easily. "Jaina, you go on. I can deal with this."

"How?" Jaina's tone was flat, disbelieving. She knew he was lying.

"Don't distract me with questions. Just go." *By dying, probably.* He hoped that stray thought did not reach Jaina, that it had not crossed the faint remnants of the link they had shared since they had been Joiners together, years before.

He felt Jaina's anger at him, at Alema Rar. But he felt, too, her acceptance. She knew it was the right thing to do. Divide Alema's concentration. Attack her on as many fronts as possible.

The thing out in the darkness, the Sith ship—for so it had to be—drifted laterally, under power, perhaps trying to determine whether Zekk could track it. Zekk continued staring in the direction he had been originally.

Then something occurred to him and he grinned. Abandoning his Jedi detachment, he poured emotion into the Force: contempt for his enemy, disparaging dismissal of the Sith ship's worth.

He felt his enemy's anger grow, and winced as it lashed out at him, grasping in the Force.

But this was no attack. He could feel its thoughts now, primitive but clear, hammering away insistently at his mind like a fist against a door. He could almost understand them—

He *could* understand them, he realized, if he wanted to. There was something familiar about their patterns, their darkness. Techniques he had learned years before, as a student of the Shadow Academy, gave him that insight. Though he had shoved them away, deep into his memory, those techniques were still with him . . . if he chose to remember them.

He wavered on the rung that supported him, and wavered on the question. But he had no time left. If the Sith starfighter killed him, it would go after Jaina next.

He opened himself to the darkness. It flooded into him, engulfing him, gagging him. Abruptly his surroundings were much clearer in his mind. The exact location, the appearance of that Sith meditation sphere—yes, that was what it was—were now clear to him.

As were its thoughts. It hesitated in its movements, aware of the sudden change in Zekk's outlook. *You are Jedi.*

Am I? I have been many things. I was a Jedi a minute ago. What am I now?

Not to be trusted.

Zekk let some amusement creep into his thoughts. *And*

yet you trust her. He pictured Alema Rar in his mind, and let his memories of her as a young Jedi Knight color his vision.

The meditation sphere's reply was tinged with contempt. *Not trust. Obey. Must obey.*

Because she knows a secret or two? Do you obey anything who knows the dark ways? You would obey me, then.

The meditation sphere did not reply.

A presentiment of victory, like adrenaline, flashed through Zekk. *That's it, isn't it? All you need is the right order. From the right dark sider.*

There was no answer.

What are you called?

I am Ship.

Zekk snorted, amused and contemptuous at the same time. *You are stupid and simplistic. But I will do you a favor anyway. I free you.*

He could tell that Ship received his words, but he felt no indication of understanding.

Of course not—this was a vehicle. It was made to serve. It would always serve. The question was, *what* would it serve.

I free you from Alema Rar. I order you to leave her, to leave this place. I order you to find a master better suited to your nature. I command you to go, as fast as you can, ignoring all commands, all cries for help. Into his words he poured his own power of will, and felt it joined, strengthened by the power of this dark place. His own strength swelled, bloating out beyond the confines of his body, growing like an explosion, until its fringes engulfed Ship.

There, within Ship, was a hard knot of resistance, older orders, planted by Alema Rar. Zekk saw them as a mound, like a standing stone. He lashed that stone with his own strength and saw it begin to erode, flaking away, dissolving.

In moments it was gone, reduced to nothingness. Zekk felt a sort of dark joy rise up within Ship, and then the meditation sphere was accelerating upward, toward the exit out of the chamber. An instant later it was gone.

Zekk sagged, relieved. Jaina would live. He would live.

He would descend to where Ship knew Alema to be. Zekk would kill Alema, cutting her until no remaining piece could sustain life.

Then he would kill Jag and be rid of that moralistic, interfering simulation of a man. That, of course, he would have to do in such a way that it did not distress Jaina.

And finally, there would be Jaina. He would reforge the link between them and, through it, pour his thoughts, his love. He would do so until she understood, until she loved and obeyed him. Until she was *his*.

Worry suddenly gnawed at him, like the sharp teeth of some undercity rodent. *That's not right.* Slowly, he lowered himself to sit on the top cross-tie of the track, wrapping his legs around the rail for security.

That's not what he should be thinking. The dark side was flooding him now, pouring its toxins into his thoughts.

He tried to shove it out, to become what he had been just a few minutes before. But it was strong, so very strong, and it laughed at his pathetic efforts.

Over the comlink, Jaina called for Zekk, for Jag. She got no answer. That was not entirely unexpected. These personal comlinks could transmit across many kilometers, but not through stone or thick duracrete, and she had plummeted into yet another cavern chamber through a narrow passageway since parting from Zekk.

A touch of Force exertion brought her alongside the

track again. She put the soles of her boots against it, allowing friction to slow her. Alone, with only one set of eyes, she needed to descend more slowly, to be more alert.

Alert to presences in the Force. She felt them off to her left. Then they were closer, moving into the range of her glow rod: the flock of mynocks. The rearmost of them now towed Jag, who flailed helplessly.

The foremost of them came on, tail lashing, and struck at her as it passed. She dodged the blow with minimal effort. The other mynocks, strung out behind like a parade, wheeled in the first one's wake, preparing for one attack after another.

Jaina snorted. "Jag, stick out a hand as you pass. I'll pull you free."

Jag didn't respond. His helmet comlink was probably out—

That's an assumption. Whenever I make an assumption like that, you two are free to mock me mercilessly. The words were Jag's, but spoken long ago, during one of their many planning sessions.

And they were correct. She'd just made the sort of assumption that Jag himself routinely mocked.

As she dodged the second mynock attack, and the third, she cast out in the Force to sense the figure being towed by the last mynock.

It was Jag, all right.

Jaina worked the vertical rail track as a gymnast would a set of exercise bars, swinging her wide of every tail attack, or interposing the rails between her and an incoming tail, until only the last mynock remained. Jag, in its grip, struggled and waved frantically at her. Jaina extended her hand to catch his—

Then yanked it back, allowing him to be towed past.

As she did, Jag changed in form and dimension, becoming smaller, slighter. His outstretched hand suddenly had a blue-black lightsaber blade in it, and as Jaina pulled away the blade crossed the spot where her torso had been; it cut a gash in the front of her robe, but did not catch the skin beneath.

Abruptly it was Alema Rar being towed, the young, unmaimed Alema, and she stared angrily at Jaina as she and her mynock passed.

Jaina grinned at them. "Predictable, Alema, predictable."

The other mynocks were suddenly gone, fading out of existence like the details of a dream in the moments after awakening.

Alema swung up onto the last mynock's back, riding it as she would a tauntaun. The creature circled, keeping Jaina and Alema safely out of range of each another.

Alema's reply was similarly lighthearted. "We wish to thank you for coming here and making it more convenient for us to kill you."

Jaina shook her head. "That's not what we're here for. We're going to end the threat you pose. You can die. Or you can surrender. The choice is yours."

"You will never leave these chambers alive."

Jaina shrugged. "Neither will you. I'm prepared to die. Are you?"

chapter twenty-six

ABOARD THE MILLENNIUM FALCON

Despite Han's maddening maneuvers with the *Falcon*, despite his frequent swearing and the way the *Falcon* shuddered whenever her shields sustained a hit from the pursuing frigate, Leia kept her attention on the doorway to the access corridor at the rear of the cockpit. And when the walls of the corridor began to glow, illuminated by a blue-black lightsaber blade that had to be just around the corridor, Leia leapt from her seat, moved to stand in the doorway, and lit her own blade.

Alema stepped into view, again young and unmarred. She rushed Leia, throwing all her effort into a savage attack, all fourth-form technique without the added elements of acrobatics.

Leia withdrew half a pace so that the edges of the cockpit door were centimeters ahead of her. She blocked the first attack economically, offering no undue motion, extending her weapon not one centimeter forward more than she needed to, conserving her energy.

She also extended her awareness through the Force—not

to Alema, but to her husband. Attuned to his moods and conceits as she always was, by experience and her nature, she now became almost a second set of eyes just behind him, anticipating his every move on the *Falcon*'s controls. When he began a sudden spiraling dive, Leia knew it was coming a fraction of a second in advance, enough forewarning that she could stabilize herself with a hand on the doorjamb. Alema was not so prescient; when the maneuver began, she was thrown off balance, and her next blow sizzled into the doorjamb.

Neither woman spoke, but their faces told the story of how the duel proceeded. Alema began with a mocking smile; within the time it took to throw a dozen failed blows, it had faded, replaced by anger. Leia had not bothered to hide her worry and determination; but as Alema grew angrier, Leia allowed a sweet, condescending smile to cross her features.

Baffled, Alema stepped back. "We are young. You are old. You will tire. Or the ship firing on you, whoever it is, will hit your ship, and you will watch your husband die."

Leia nodded agreeably. "Yes, I keep hearing that sort of thing. Across forty years now, the same speech. One of the downsides of being 'old.' "

Alema's lip curled and she lunged again.

Alema stared at Jaina as though the rage she felt could somehow burn holes in the Jedi. She drew a deep breath, signal of a tirade to come, and then stopped, looking upward.

Jaina felt it, too, a sudden sense of satisfaction in the dark energy of this place. It was growing, swelling, absorbing, eating . . .

Eating *Zekk* . . .

Jaina gasped. She reached out through the Force to

Zekk, but he was suddenly no longer there, not in any form she could recognize.

Alema laughed. "There, your first loss of the day. With more to come."

Jaina ignored her, continued looking up. Zekk was out there. He *had* to be.

Though he might now be so much a part of this place that his presence in the Force was indistinguishable from the energy here. Inside, Jaina withered at the thought.

As the mynock banked to pass before Jaina again, Alema turned toward the Jedi, smiling. "No answer for us? We—" Then she froze, her eyes going wide.

Jaina felt a sudden sense of freedom.

Something was leaving this place, something dark and wicked, and Alema Rar paled to a lighter shade of blue.

The Twi'lek shook her head. "Ship . . ."

Jaina looked at her. "Problem? Anything I can help with?"

"Ship? *Ship?*" Alema opened her mouth wide, as though to scream—and then vanished from sight, along with the mynock.

The scream did reach Jaina's ears—tiny and distant, from far below.

Leia kept her guard up and her wits about her, but it was clear—Alema was slowing. Tiring. In their last exchange, the Twi'lek's sledgehammerlike blows had grown weaker.

Now Alema disengaged, took a step back, opened her mouth for another jibe—and her eyes snapped open wide as though she'd been stabbed from behind. Her next breath was a gasp. Then she disappeared, fading instantly from sight.

Wary, Leia looked for her opponent within the Force.

But she felt no one else aboard the *Falcon,* just herself and Han.

She glanced back over her shoulder. "How goes the war?"

Han's voice was a growl. "It'd be better if you were up in a laser turret."

"Not until I get the word that Alema's in chains or in a box."

He growled again.

The flight of mynocks, Jag in tow, entered another narrow passage. Jag's captor swung him toward the side, allowing him to scrape along the rocky tunnel.

A protruding stone caught him in the back, not hurting him, but bouncing him up away from the wall. He oriented his sensors forward, trying to anticipate the next blow, to avoid it with the use of his thruster pack. They had dragged him through what seemed like kilometers of tunnels, bouncing him off every available surface, and he had not managed to avoid every impact—his left elbow throbbed as though it were damaged or even broken, and his head rang from repeated impact.

They entered a new chamber. Jag's sensors picked up a wall in the near distance, perhaps thirty meters away. The mynocks angled toward an aperture . . .

And then they were gone, leaving him hurtling toward the vertical stone surface ahead.

He kicked in his thruster pack, slowing himself, but the mynocks had been moving fast. Despite his braking maneuver, he hit the wall hard. He heard and felt a crack from his left leg . . . and vision failed as if his sensors had all suddenly been switched off.

* * *

Alema stood, legs shaking, from where she had fallen. Her senses, back in her own body after too many minutes divided among several phantoms, cast out in the Force, looking for Ship.

Ship was . . . distant. Ship was fleeing. Ship was happy.

"Come back!" She poured her strength of will into her command, but her effort was too late, too distant. Ship sped onward, uncaring.

This was bad. Now, instead of having an escape method close at hand, she would have to ascend to the asteroid's surface, past the Jedi and the idiot soldier who led them, to steal whatever vehicle had brought them. Or lure the *Falcon* in close, kill Han and Leia, and steal it. This would not be easy.

She was already tired. More than tired.

As she clambered into the railcar, she tried to make herself small in the Force, so that it would be more difficult to find her. The railcar, at least, had no droid brain to malfunction, no Sith sympathies to lead it astray. It had a lever with labels that read UP and DOWN.

She pushed it toward UP and the car began gliding up the rails.

ABOARD THE **POISON MOON**

"New contact, Captain." Ithila sent her sensor board display to Dician's monitor. Its image, now far less pixilated but wavering because of the *Poison Moon*'s maneuvers, showed the asteroid habitat. A starfighter-sized craft, emerging from beneath the structure, headed starward.

Dician sat forward. Tiny as it was on the monitor, this was clearly a Sith meditation sphere—the vehicle that had brought Alema Rar to Korriban. Just as clearly, the Twi'lek was making her escape in it. "All weapons, bear on the meditation sphere. At my command—"

"Captain, the vehicle is empty."

Dician blinked. She reached out toward the sphere through the Force and sensed its mind, its desire . . . but no occupant.

So Alema Rar was still on the asteroid. Interesting.

She was having no luck destroying the *Millennium Falcon*. The freighter's pilot was just too good—evidence that Han Solo was indeed at the controls. His death would be a great prize, but worth only bragging rights.

The meditation sphere, on the other hand, was something tangible, something Dician could have, could keep. It would be the envy of every member of her Order.

She looked at Wayniss. "Have the shuttle crews reported in? Are all the explosives charges in place?"

"Yes, Captain. The big one was just activated and delivered. You can begin detonating them anytime you like."

"Follow the new contact." As the *Poison Moon* heeled over on its new course, she added, "Tell the shuttle crews to assemble on— What's our designation for the largest asteroid in this belt?"

"Omega Three Seven Nine."

"On Omega Three Seven Nine. We'll be back for them. Probably." She reached out for the meditation sphere and was gratified to still feel it, a pulse of dark energy precisely attuned to the ways and wishes of her Order. "Where are you going, charming one?"

She expected no answer, but got one, the clear image of a distant world—arctic, forested, a menacing blue-white eye in a sea of darkness.

Ziost, original homeworld of the Sith.

She flicked a finger at Wayniss. "Lay in a course for

Ziost. All speed. We'll see if we can beat the little fellow there and scoop him up as he arrives."

"Yes, Captain."

"And just before we enter hyperspace, begin the bomb triggering sequence."

"Yes, Captain."

Dician smiled. "Congratulations, everyone. On the perfect resolution to a perfect mission."

chapter twenty-seven

ABOARD THE **MILLENNIUM FALCON**

"They're running."

Leia, once again in her rear-facing seat position, turned to stare through the forward viewports. "What?"

"They're running." Han leaned back and stretched, nonchalant. "I chased 'em off."

"Sure you did." But on the sensor board, the frigate was indeed outbound. "I wonder what they wanted in the first place?"

"Me, of course. Us, I mean. You know the mentality."

Leia glared. "Oh, I know the mentality, all right."

"By the way, thanks for not letting our passenger come visit the captain."

"*That's* better."

On the asteroid, far away from the habitat, light flared, a brilliant, piercing white glow. As it faded, Han and Leia could see damage remaining where it had been—a black-and-red hole, tiny at this distance, through which atmosphere began venting in a column that rapidly grew to be kilometers tall.

* * *

Even at the distance of half a kilometer, Jaina saw the rail-car ascending toward her; it had running lights, making it easy to spot in the darkness. A quick touch with the Force confirmed that neither Jag nor Zekk was in control of the vehicle.

With her lightsaber, she cut through both rails of the track, then hauled herself up a few meters and cut through again, slicing away a span of track. Then she hauled herself back up, coming to a stop twenty meters above the gap she'd created.

The railcar hit the gap. It could have come clean off the rails, floating into the void of the cavern, but it instead angled the other way, and its nose hit the far section of track dead-on. It came to a sudden stop, the cars behind it accordioning, piling up like a freight-hauler disaster.

A small figure was ejected from the lead car. Alema rose, hurtling past the gap, and grabbed at a cross-tie, coming to an abrupt stop a handful of meters below Jaina.

Jaina smiled down at her. "Hello again."

Alema's mouth twisted. "This is no longer a game. Get out of our way."

"For me, it was never a game. Say, how are you going to climb the track and swing a lightsaber with only one working arm?"

"We will find a way." Alema ascended another few cross-ties. Now she was only three meters beneath Jaina's feet.

"You could surrender. Throw away your lightsaber. And your blowgun and darts and other toys. Pretty much everything on your person. And I'll take you to safety, and you'll live."

Alema shook her head. Her half-length brain-tail came

free of her hood. "With the universe still out of balance? With the wicked not punished? We think not."

Then it came, a low, rumbling roar from some great distance to Jaina's left. She peered off into the darkness, remaining mindful of Alema's position through her sense of the Force. "Some new trap?"

"We were about to ask you the same thing."

A speaker box aboard the mangled railcar began talking, its voice speaking Basic with a light, lilting accent Jaina had never heard before. "Attention, all workers of Jonex Mine Eight Eleven B. Our sensors indicate a catastrophe-level event. Seek the nearest omega-designated shelter immediately. Activate all emergency beacon comm posts at once. Attention, all workers of Jonex Mine Eight Eleven B . . ." Faintly, she could hear the same message being echoed off distant stone walls.

She glanced down at Alema again. "Sounds bad. Guess we'd better stay here until we find out what's gone wrong."

Alema released her grip on the cross-tie but did not drift away from the track. She climbed a step toward Jaina, manipulation of the Force keeping her steady on the cross-ties, and drew forth her lightsaber, igniting it with a *snap-hiss*. "Get out of our way."

There was another distant rumble, this time from the right. Jaina's ears popped from a change in pressure. She worked her jaw, equalizing the pressure, and her hearing returned to normal. "Sorry. What was that again?" She lit her own lightsaber.

"Idiot." Alema waved, a sweeping gesture, as if slicing with a vibroblade.

Energy—invisible, reeking of the dark side—slammed into Jaina, forcing her back. The track she held on to bent several meters above her head, moving her out of the way.

The blow drove the wind from her lungs and sent a wave of pain through her chest.

In her moment of discomfiture, Alema leapt up past her. She landed on a cross-tie twenty meters above Jaina. She began climbing as though the vertical track were a staircase, using only her feet and the Force.

A blaster bolt from above caught her nearly by surprise. Alema got her blade up in time to absorb some of it, but the impact knocked her back and away from the track. She fell fifty meters or more, and was almost swallowed by darkness before she recovered sufficiently to vector back toward the lower section of track.

Grimacing with pain, Jaina looked up. Descending toward her was Jag, in a free fall allayed by infrequent pulses of his backpack thruster.

Jaina moved hand over hand along the track, reaching the point where Alema's Force attack had bent it, and began climbing from there. If she got high enough fast enough, she could cut free another section, perhaps making the gap too great for Alema to leap past, even in this low gravity.

The track wavered as something hit the angled section she had just left. She glanced back.

Jag was there, standing on one leg. Through his visor, Jaina could see that he was sweating, probably from pain. He glanced down toward Alema. "Did you give her the chance to surrender?"

Jaina nodded. "She said no. Rudely."

"That's it, then." He jerked a thumb upward, signaling for her to climb. "Go."

"I'll stay. We have to deal with Alema."

"I'll deal with Alema. Someone's using explosives, city-busters at least, and they've cracked the shell of this asteroid. The atmosphere's venting. And Zekk—he's one chamber up and he's a mess. I can't get him to leave..He'll die here if you don't help him."

Jaina looked down at the climbing Alema, up at the distant gap into the next chamber, and finally at Jag. "You're going to die."

"Maybe. But my suit can handle hard vacuum for an hour or more. Yours, with your mask, five minutes. Who dies first? Go on. When you get to the next cavern, cut the track free."

Jaina looked at him. The Jaina of a few weeks ago would have seethed, argued. It was her right to stay here until the bitter end—her *right*.

Jag's, too.

"Good luck." Her words emerged as a whisper. She leapt up and began climbing as fast as her strength and boosts from the Force would allow her.

Jag pulled a pouch free of his utility belt and jammed it onto the metal of the track he stood on. Then he fired off his thruster and ascended. He didn't have to worry about overtaking Jaina; she was climbing fast.

Below, Alema leapt across the gap separating the lower track from the upper. She landed exactly where Jag had stood moments ago.

Jag made sure his comlink was active. "Boom One."

He wasn't fast enough. He'd uttered the first word when Alema gestured. The explosives package he'd affixed to the rail sailed free of the track. It exploded a moment later, far enough away that it did no more to Alema than cause the track she stood on to sway.

She stared up at him, murder in her eyes, and began climbing again, almost as fast as Jaina—faster than Jag's poor low-gravity thrusters could carry him.

As she climbed, the bent section of track beneath her

twisted back the other way, and then again toward her, and finally came free entirely, a broken section four meters long. Rapidly, borne by invisible powers of the Force, it rose past Alema, flying straight toward Jag.

He grimaced. "This is going to hurt."

The track came level with Jag, a few meters away—then swung toward him like a club, one end remaining in place, the other end hammering at his midsection.

The *beskar* plate took the force of the blow, but that merely meant it distributed the impact across his entire chest. Jag hurtled to one side like a ball kicked by a rancor, his head and limbs jerking in the opposite direction. His left leg, probably already broken at the thigh, was suddenly engulfed in greater pain, as though his bone marrow had been replaced by a lit lightsaber blade.

He flew perhaps thirty meters. But the flying section of track got ahead of him and swung again, batting him back toward Alema.

Still, the breastplate held. Still he could breathe, could think—barely.

His body a jangled mass of fiery nerve endings, he crashed into the remaining section of vertical track a couple of meters beneath Alema. He managed to clamp his left crushgaunt onto it.

"We are sure you flew your X-wing." Alema's face was now covered by a transparisteel mask—probably the same one she wore when escaping her own trap at Gilatter VIII, Jag guessed. Her voice came across his helmet speakers. "Your companions will not have sabotaged it. They want you to escape. So we will leave in it. Small compensation for Ship. Clearly, we need to punish you more."

It took an effort to make the words emerge in recognizable fashion. "Alema . . . you're never going to leave this asteroid. Your insanity, and the last traces of the Dark Nest, end here and now."

The shock on Alema's features suggested that she had just witnessed an insect reciting poetry. Profane poetry.

Jag felt his stomach lurch just a little. The track they both held had given way and was beginning to fall.

Alema, distracted by the sudden sensation of free fall, glanced upward.

Fast as a striking sand panther, Jag drew his oversized blaster and aimed it at Alema.

He wasn't fast enough. She did not even look down at him. While he was in mid-draw, Alema released her lightsaber and crooked a finger at his blaster. It flew from Jag's grasp into her hand. Her lightsaber floated beside her.

Alema looked down at him and shook her head. "You die because you oppose us, because you insult the nest. But most of all, you die because you refuse to learn."

Oh, but I do learn. The sensor inside that blaster is now informing its processor that it's gone beyond a certain distance from me. Five . . .

"Droids firing lasers—now, that would have been intelligent and dangerous to us."

Four.

"We cannot feel droid intent, and lasers travel faster than the eye can follow."

Three.

"Such an attack, executed from secrecy, might well have hurt or killed us."

Two.

"But now we will simply cut you to pieces." Alema gestured, and her lightsaber began floating its way toward Jag. She watched, her expression cool and detached beneath her faceplate.

One.

And in that last moment, though Jag had tried to concentrate solely on his pain, on his sense of desperation and failure, something of his growing anticipation must have leaked through his emotional barriers. Alema's eyes widened. She looked back and forth for the new danger she was just beginning to sense.

The blaster in her hand exploded.

The detonation was brilliant and noiseless, sure sign of how near vacuum the atmosphere was. Jag's faceplate polarized almost instantly, leaving him dazzled but not quite blind. He ignited his thrusters, hurtling upward—

Alema's face was contorted in shock and pain. Her right arm was gone from just below the elbow. Blood trailed from it, bubbling and evaporating where it left her injury.

As Jag reached her, he grabbed her neck in his right hand.

She looked at him. Her expression changed from pain to a plea.

He shook his head. *It's too late. You refused to surrender. Your last act was an attempted murder. I can't spare you.* He did not speak these words—they would have taken too long, perhaps giving her time to recover.

He could see that there was fear in her eyes, but not fear of death. Her lips moved, forming a single word. "Remember."

Jag knew he was not suddenly sensitive in the Force, that he could not read her thoughts. But there they were, imprinted on his mind. *Remember us. Remember us as we used to be, before the universe turned against us. Young, beautiful, strong, brave, admirable, loved, loving . . .*

He nodded. *I will.*

The pain and fear in her expression eased.

Jag squeezed. He felt the crack of Alema's vertebrae

under his hand as they shattered. Her body went limp. Her eyes became unfocused and distant.

Static erupted across his comlink. Though there was not enough atmosphere to carry the sound of distant explosions to him, he knew that the high yield of those bombs had to be interfering with comm reception.

He hit his thrusters and began rising toward the stone aperture above.

Jaina found Zekk perched atop a section of track, exactly where she had stood when Alema's mysterious weapon had attacked her and severed the rails. Despite the fact that the air pressure was dropping rapidly, Zekk did not have his mask on.

"Zekk, get moving." She fumbled around in his belt pouch, found his foil mask, and slipped it over his head, drawing its cinch tight around his collar.

He shook his head, not looking at her. "Go on. You need to leave."

"*We* need to leave." She tugged at his shoulder, bringing him to his knees.

"It's in me. The evil of this place. I thought I'd be able to keep it at bay forever. No, it doesn't work that way."

She crouched, getting her arms around his waist, and then straightened, propelling them both up toward the next section of track. "Zekk, are you my friend?"

"I'm your friend. I love you." His words emerged almost as a babble, running together and inflectionless.

"I need—I need you to help me. If I'm going to get out of here alive." They crossed the gap, and she grabbed the next section of track. "Now climb. Or I'll carry you, and I'll be slow, and I'll die."

"All right." Mechanically, he turned, got his hands on the cross-ties, and began climbing.

"We'll get you back to where the Masters are, and they'll get the evil out of you."

"Oh. Maybe." Zekk frowned, struggling to remember something. "Where's Jag?"

"He's . . . following." The lie sounded unconvincing, even pathetic, to Jaina's ears.

But Zekk, dazed as he seemed to be, didn't notice. He nodded, satisfied.

The track wobbled under their hands. Something had to be shaking it. Jaina glanced down, seeing nothing below, and then up.

Above them, a giant sphere was rolling down the tracks. It looked like a plant spore—but two meters across instead of microscopic, and made of grayish metal instead of organic material. It did not roll neatly down the track, but adhered to it as if magnetized.

Jaina assumed it was indeed magnetic, something designed to adhere to ship hulls.

She pulled Zekk around to the underside of the track and held on, preparing to leap free if the thing's projections threatened to crush a limb in passing. But the spheroid rolled on past harmlessly, descending into the darkness.

Zekk stared after it, vaguely curious. "What's that?"

"A space mine, I think. Nothing we want to be near when it goes off. C'mon, keep climbing."

They reached the surface and found the track intact up to the habitat above. But the track shook under their fingers, and they could both see the stony ground shaking all around them, kicking up clouds of dust in oddly beautiful streamers.

Jaina saw a distant flash to spinward—sign of another explosion beyond the horizon. She grabbed Zekk and kicked free, leaping toward the hole into the habitat above.

Together they floated through. As the artificial gravity of the habitat hit them, they dropped, landing awkwardly on the lip of the hole.

Jaina breathed a sigh of relief.

Then the shock wave from the last explosion hit. The ground fifteen meters down rippled as though it were cloth laid atop water. Jaina felt her legs shaking, from external vibrations rather than exhaustion.

Jag's X-wing, visible beneath the hole, rose on one wing as if banking, then tumbled out of sight. The vibrations increased.

The habitat suddenly tilted. The chamber was plunged into darkness—relieved only by the circle of lights around the exit hole—and the two Jedi floated free of the floor.

Suddenly the view through the hole showed more ground, then distant horizon, then stars . . .

The habitat was free of the asteroid, kicked loose by successive explosions, and was tumbling.

When the two Jedi forced open the door into the hangar, they found everything beyond in a state of chaos. Dim emergency lighting revealed two StealthXs, dozens of durasteel storage barrels, two refueling pumps, and countless hundreds of hand tools circulating through the large open space, ricocheting—in a slow and stately way, in the case of the snubfighters—off the walls and colliding with other free-floating debris. As Jaina watched, one cylindrical metal barrel collided with a strike foil of Zekk's StealthX and partially crumpled, its lid popping free, the greenish hydraulic fluid it held slowly pouring out into the atmosphere and spreading. In addition to the sounds of clanks, crashes, and other collisions, the R9 astromechs in the two snubfighters were adding screeches and musical tones of dismay to the din.

The control board for the hangar door and its atmosphere shield was dead.

Jaina glanced at Zekk and gestured at the metal storm they faced. "No way to manage a safe launch. Get in your cockpit. I'll get the hangar doors open."

Zekk shook his head. "You'll be sucked right out into the void when you do." He sounded a bit stronger, as though distance from the pool of dark side energy was restoring his spirits.

"I'll use a shadow bomb."

Zekk winced. A shadow bomb detonated at that proximity to the StealthXs was certain to damage them. But Jaina knew she was right—opening the hangar doors with a lightsaber and telekinetic nudges from the Force was certain death for the opener. Zekk gave her a pained look and pushed off from the wall, floating on an intercept course toward his StealthX.

ABOARD THE **MILLENNIUM FALCON**

The *Falcon*'s comm board made a brief crackling noise, then Leia could hear Jaina's voice across it. "No checklist, no time. Arming."

Zekk was next. "Shields up."

"Shields up, copy. Repulsorlifts to max, hold yourself in place."

Leia felt a weight, something like ten tons, drop away from her shoulders. She keyed her comm board. "Jaina?"

"Firing."

One wall of the distant, tumbling habitat blew out, venting atmosphere and a cloud of particulate matter. A moment later one StealthX emerged, then another, trailing more debris.

One after the other, they angled toward the *Falcon*. Jaina's next words were stronger. "Yes, Mom?"

"Are you all right?"

"As well as can be expected." Jaina's tone was joyless.

"What about Alema? And Jag?"

There was a long pause before Jaina's response. "Both dead, I think."

chapter twenty-eight

Han and Leia watched their monitor screens as the *Falcon*'s rear holocams showed them the last few seconds in the existence of the asteroid.

One moment it was there; the next, it was replaced by a bright glow and an expanding pulse of energy.

Glum, Han activated his comm board. "Sensors show an energy yield that says *fission bombs* to me. I don't think anyone has used fission bombs since near the start of the Yuuzhan Vong War."

Leia shook her head. "Somebody was very serious."

No one answered over the comm board, but a noise came from the speakers—labored breathing.

Leia frowned and activated her microphone. "Zekk, is that you?"

"Not me."

"It's me." The voice was Jag's, pained.

"Jag!" Four people spoke his name simultaneously, Jaina loudest of all. She added, "How did you get off the asteroid?"

"Got to the surface. Commed my astromech and it gave me distance and bearing to my X-wing. Fortunately, it was upright, just covered in dust. But it's damaged, and I'm . . . I don't think I can calculate a hyperspace jump right now."

Han heaved a sigh of relief. "Don't worry about it, kid. We'll run the numbers for you. You just catch up to us." He activated his transceiver, giving Jag's X-wing a clear signal to home in on.

"Will do, sir."

"And don't call me sir. I hate that."

"Understood, sir."

SANCTUARY MOON OF ENDOR, JEDI OUTPOST

Luke and Ben, similarly clad in dark Jedi robes, swept into the communications center. At a nod from Luke, the Jedi technician on station there withdrew into the corridor, leaving them alone with the hologram of Han and Leia.

Han's hologram offered Luke a lopsided smile. "Hey, old buddy."

"It's good to see you." Luke's gesture suggested he would prefer to be able to embrace his sister and brother-in-law. "A live holocomm transmission all the way from Bimmiel? This is an extravagance for you, isn't it?"

Leia nodded. "Big news calls for a big show. Luke, Alema Rar is dead."

Luke let out a long breath. *At last.* He looked between them. "She gave you no choice?"

"None." Leia's tone was decisive. "Jag is badly injured. Zekk is a bit . . . perturbed, but coming out of it. Jaina is unhurt. Also, the asteroid was destroyed."

Luke cocked an eyebrow at her. "That seems a little excessive."

Han snorted. "Not our doing, Luke. An unmarked frigate attacked while we were doing our support-role thing. They launched shuttles that planted fission bombs all over the asteroid. Then they left. Alema's weird little Sith ship got away, too, but it was unoccupied."

"And there's no hint as to who blew up the asteroid or why?"

Han shook his head. "A complete mystery. And you know how I feel about complete mysteries."

"You don't care, as long as they don't interfere with you getting paid."

Han grinned. "Something like that."

Leia said, "We're going to transport Jag to you. Jaina and Zekk will escort us in."

Luke nodded. "It'll be good to see you." He glanced at the monitor that displayed data about this communication. "Another few seconds and the odds of this contact being traced go up by an order of magnitude."

"See you in a couple of days, old buddy." Han reached off to the side, his hand disappearing as it extended beyond the range of the holocam at his end, and the hologram winked out.

Luke felt like sitting down, letting gravity just overcome him for a while, but that might worry Ben.

At least it was over, finally over. Mara's killer was no longer a threat to him, to his family. He felt a touch of regret—unlike Jacen, Alema Rar had insanity to blame for the evils she perpetrated. If she had been able to accept help, she might have remained a force for calmness and order.

But that was pointless speculation. Her life had ended. Perhaps Mara could rest easy now.

"Dad?"

"Yes?"

"Are you all right?"

Luke nodded. "Better. Mara's murderer has met justice, and we can put that uncertainty behind us."

"Yes."

Luke turned to face his son. There was something in Ben's reply . . . it was not in the tone of his voice, but there had been a little tug in the Force when Ben spoke. Surely Ben didn't doubt that Alema was truly dead? Leia would not have said she was if there were any doubt.

Luke pushed the question from his mind. Ben would tell him what was bothering him when he was ready. "Why don't you go get in some training? I have some thinking to do."

Ben nodded, dubious. "Let me know if you need anything."

"Sure, Ben."

On the outpost roof, Luke sat cross-legged on the hard surface of the landing pad, his back straight, a meditative posture.

He could feel the permacrete surface beneath him, feel it as though it were a skin, connected to the outpost's permacrete and durasteel "bones"—its beams, its support columns extending down into the soil and all the way to bedrock. He could feel the kilometers-thick mantle of stone beneath the bedrock, stretching down to the core of the moon, its massiveness suggesting eternity.

He opened himself to the Force and could feel the vibrancy of life around him, the energies of all the people in the outpost, the vitality of all the growing things.

Once, such a contact would have brought him serenity; it would have been peace to his spirit. Now it was merely information.

And the Force still offered him no guidance, no visions of his enemies, no glimpses of his future.

He was no longer disturbed by any of this. He needed no reassurances about his future. Perhaps it all meant that there *was* no future to glimpse. Luke found himself to be unworried by the thought.

There was a hum, the distinctive noise of the roof access lift. Luke could feel the Force presence of his son arrive, could hear him approach.

Ben hesitated, then moved into view, settling to the permacrete directly opposite Luke, assuming the same meditative pose.

The boy did not speak, but neither did he relax into proper meditation. Luke could read Ben's emotions as clearly as though they were on the screen of a datapad: restlessness, concern . . . and an unusual degree of mental focus.

Luke let the boy wait. Eventually Ben's restlessness would get the better of him and he would speak his mind. That was the way of the young, of apprentices.

But Ben still did not speak, and Luke could feel him become calmer, more settled . . . although his focus did not waver. Luke waited while breezes carrying the scents of the Endor forest stirred his hair.

"Your feelings betray you, Ben." It was almost a ritual phrase now—the truth, cloaked in and perhaps even disguised by cliché.

Ben studied him, no emotion on his face. "Betray me? Do they stab me in the back, or do they just give me a swift kick in the butt?"

Despite himself, Luke grinned. "It's true, under many circumstances being betrayed by your emotions will do you no harm. But it's still best to remain aware of the fact that you are expressing them so clearly. Transmitting them for anyone sufficiently sensitive to feel."

"All right."

Luke paused. Clearly the boy was not willing to be drawn out. "You think something is wrong. Wrong with me."

"Wrong is one of those kind of relative things. If I think something is wrong and you think it's right, which one of us is correct?"

Luke nodded. It was a good response. "I suspect I would be. It's the whole Master–apprentice, father–son, wise old man–foolish young man thing."

"Right. It's nice that to be older is to be always right. I can't wait to be older."

"So?"

Ben took a moment to compose himself and his thoughts. "I'm trying to figure out why you don't have any energy."

"I have energy. It's waiting, in reserve."

"Yeah . . . maybe. Except your energy used to empower other people, too. Get them moving. Make them enthusiastic. Not anymore. Ever since Mom was killed, you've been like someone with a landspeeder resting on his back. Crushed flat, hardly able to move because of the pain. I mean, me too. But for me, over time, that landspeeder has slipped off, mostly. I kind of expected that when we learned that the one who'd killed her was captured or dead, the landspeeder would be gone from your back, too. That you'd be able to move again."

Luke frowned, puzzled. "I can move."

"I'm not so sure. And I'm trying to figure out why."

"Let's do some lightsaber training. You'll see more of me moving than you want to."

Ben shook his head. "You're still not *you*. People are asking questions. Things like, *When is Luke Skywalker going to find his center and make things better again?* Nobody knows what to tell them."

"Make things better?" Luke tried not to let his surprise show, but it crept into his voice. "You mean snap my fingers, end this war, and cause flower petals to rain down on all civilized worlds?"

"Yeah, just like that." Ben grinned, then sobered. "No, I think they just mean, when are you going to really take charge again? Of the Jedi, our role in the war? Lead, not just direct? Because that *will* make a difference."

Luke felt his spirits sag even lower. "Oh, Ben. They're asking that sort of question out of a misguided sense of what I can accomplish. They've based their impressions of what I can do on things that happened when I was a younger man with blind luck and boundless energy . . . and when you could count all the known Force-users in the galaxy on the fingers of one hand. Other Jedi can do what I do."

"No, they can't. They can't be Luke Skywalker."

Luke studied the landing pad's surface for a moment. It could still serve its primary purpose, but it was scuffed, weathered, more frail than it had been when first installed. It seemed a perfect metaphor for his situation. "You can't turn back time. It's not a landspeeder resting on my back, it's the weight of years and events. I can't cast them off, and even if I could, I'd undo everything I've learned from them. Today I'm more useful as a teacher, a distributor of resources. That's my role. I really ought to be thinking about grooming a viable candidate to become the next Grand Master."

Ben didn't speak for long moments, and Luke felt a growing swell of confusion and concern radiate from the boy.

Then there was a jolt of stronger emotion from Ben: fear. Luke looked up to see Ben suddenly on his feet, staring with an expression of naked alarm on his face.

Luke offered a quizzical look. "What is it?"

"I don't know how to say it. What are the right words?" Ben turned away from his father, looked around as if seeking confirmation from faces that weren't there, and turned back again. He was suddenly as frantic as someone at the crossroads of a maze with stormtroopers coming up behind him—which way of several was best? Which ways led to capture or death?

And then he was pacing, running his fingers through his hair, ruffling it as though the sudden untidiness would help the thoughts escape. "You want to be with Mom."

"Of course I do. Don't you?"

"Yes, but for me it's different. I want her to be here, with us." Ben stopped in midstride and whirled to face his father, a graceful move that Luke could appreciate with the Jedi Master portion of his mind. "You want to be with her where she is."

"What do you mean?"

"You want to be dead. At peace. With her. *Dead*."

"That's ridiculous."

"No, it isn't. When Uncle Han and Aunt Leia told us Alema Rar was dead, you should have said, *Now I can get back to work*. Instead, you're saying *Now I can turn over the Jedi Order to someone who's worthy*. You're getting ready to *die*. Problem is, you don't have an incurable disease or a blaster pressed against your head. So how's it going to happen?" Ben's voice cracked on the final word.

"Ben, that is so, so . . . You're just leaping to the wrong conclusion." Luke struggled for the right argument to make his son see that this was a ridiculous notion.

But the argument just wasn't there.

"That's what attachment is, isn't it?" Ben began pacing again, and words finally poured from him like water running through a shattered dam. "It's not loving somebody.

It's not marrying somebody. It's not having kids. It's being where, if something goes wrong, there's nothing left of you. It's where if she goes away, you start functioning like a droid with a restraining bolt installed. Mom wouldn't want you to be this way. So why are you?"

"*I can't help it.*" Luke was on his feet and the words wrenched out of him before he realized it. He rocked, unbalanced by the sudden violence of his emotions.

Ben spun to stare at him. "You've got to!"

"How?"

"I don't know. You're the Jedi Master, *you* figure it out."

Luke felt real anger stir within him, a fire fanned by the insolence of Ben's tone.

No, that was another lie, Luke lying to himself. The fire was being fanned by the fact that Ben was *right*.

Luke closed his eyes, feeling his way through the insulation of peacefulness he'd constructed for himself across these past months. Beyond it, he tried to find himself. But at first he could feel nothing but the weight of his grief, and the one thing that kept him functioning while carrying that burden—his desire to be reunited with Mara. Reunited when the time came. Reunited in the Force.

Then there was the other weight, the one he had largely slipped from his shoulders, the weight of his responsibility—to the Order, to his family, to the galaxy.

To the living.

Of course he had shrugged it off. No man could carry two such weights for any length of time. He would be crushed beneath them.

But he had to carry the one he had set aside, didn't he?

I'm sorry, Mara. Knowing it to be a betrayal, Luke slowly, carefully stepped out from under his grief.

It didn't leave him entirely—just as Mara was still part of him, the pain of losing her would always be with him, too.

But suddenly it was easier to breathe, to think. He wondered how long it had been since he had truly thought clearly.

And curiously, it didn't feel like a betrayal at all.

Then there was that other weight, the weight of duty. He had carried it throughout his adult life, and at times it had ground him down. But at other times it had sustained him, helped keep him alive.

Perhaps that was why he had been so willing to abandon it: it had been keeping him alive at a time when he did not want to live.

With meticulous care, he picked up and shouldered that other weight.

He opened his eyes. His son stood before him, anxious, but now Ben sighed, a brief exhalation of relief. "Hey, Dad, look in a mirror."

"I don't need to."

"You know what? Your feelings betray you."

Luke suppressed a snort. "Ben, if you ever, *ever* say *I told you so—*"

"I won't."

"—I'll put you through a training session that would make Kyp Durron cry."

"I won't, I won't."

"How did you get so smart, anyway? When I wasn't looking?"

Ben shrugged, once again an adolescent at a loss for words.

Luke put an arm around his son's shoulders and led him toward the lift. "You know, these are unsettled times. Things are too busy for many of our usual formalities. For ceremonies, for rites."

Ben frowned, suspicious. "What are you getting at?"

"I think you should begin building your lightsaber."

Ben skidded to a stop and looked at Luke. "But . . . but I haven't faced my trials."

"What do you call pulling yourself back from the brink that Jacen pushed you to . . . and then pulling the Grand Master back from his own brink?"

"Being obstinate."

"Show me a Jedi Knight who isn't obstinate." Luke stepped onto the lift plate and held his toe over the button inset in the permacrete. "Get to work on your weapon, son." He pressed the button and let the turbolift carry him down, back to his work, back to his responsibility.

chapter twenty-nine

SANCTUARY MOON OF ENDOR,
SHUTTLE **REVEILLE**, ON APPROACH

The forest stretched for countless kilometers in every direction, but below was a clearing broad enough to house several sports complexes . . . and at its center was a huge sheet of durasteel, curved like the roof of a prefabricated building, burned through in places by the violence of uncontrolled atmospheric entry, elsewhere rusted in spots the size of whole freighters. Nearly forty years earlier, it had been cast off the second Death Star when that vessel exploded. It had come to ground here, crushing and igniting all life beneath it, creating a clearing where before there had been tall trees. Now, decades later, grasses, flowers, and vines grew around the relic, but trees were slow in returning to the once-burned spot.

Syal Antilles, at the pilot's controls, banked the shuttle over the site, taking note of objects and living things on the ground—the *Millennium Falcon*, half protruding from the shadow of the giant metal plate, X-wings, shuttles, Jedi, droids, Ewoks. The Ewoks clambered on the vehicles, climbed the curved slopes of the Death Star remnant. Some had constructed sleds of wood planks and leather, and now they rode the sleds down the smoother, unrusted slopes of the metal plate.

Syal whistled. "What a relic. If my sister Myri were here, she'd be cutting three-centimeter squares off that thing and selling them as souvenirs. *Get your own piece of history. Own a part of the second Death Star.*"

General Celchu, relaxing in the copilot's seat, offered a noncommittal "Ah."

Syal glanced at him, remembering, too late as usual, that her words might dredge up bad memories. Tycho's world of Alderaan had been destroyed by the first Death Star—at the precise moment he was in live holocomm contact with his family on that planet. He had been part of the mission to destroy the second Death Star, flying a first-generation A-wing into the gigantic vehicle's superstructure. Had his skills and reflexes been just a touch less brilliant in those days, his A-wing and his bones might now be lying beneath that wreckage.

She winced. "I'm sorry. Was that stupid of me?"

Absently, he shook his head. "No. But your comment about your sister made me think . . ."

"Yes?"

"Maybe we could get a cutting torch and pick up a few square meters of it before the shuttle heads back to Coruscant."

She grinned.

Moments later, following the landing beacon being transmitted to her, she brought the *Reveille* down to a smooth, wings-up landing near the *Millennium Falcon*. A quick postflight checklist later, she, Tycho, and their passenger stood at the top of the boarding ramp.

As the ramp lowered, it revealed the face of the uniformed man standing below.

Tycho leaned over to whisper in her ear, "Antilles, you're off duty."

"Thank you, sir." The ramp touched down and she ran down its length, throwing herself into the arms of the man waiting there. "Daddy."

Luke grinned at, but otherwise ignored, the Antilles reunion and waited for General Celchu to descend.

Tycho came down the ramp accompanied by a man who was decidedly unmilitary—a bit paunchy, black-bearded, dressed in plain black trousers and a shirt printed with the vista of a volcanic world. In fact, it was more than printed; as Luke watched, one of the volcanoes seemed to erupt, silently spewing smoke and lava up from belly level to nearly the height of the man's collar.

Tycho shook Luke's hand. "Grand Master Skywalker, allow me to introduce—"

"Doctor Seyah!" Ben trotted up, a hand extended to the black-haired man. "I'm surprised you're not dead or something."

Seyah smiled. "Good to see you, Ben. You've gotten taller."

"Good!" Ben turned to his father. "Doctor Seyah is the man who briefed me on Centerpoint Station. He's a gravitic physicist and spy."

Seyah shook Luke's hand in turn. "More successful as a physicist than a spy, I suppose. Which is why I'm here."

Tycho nodded. "Doctor Seyah is on Colonel Solo's arrest-interrogate-and-execute list. For presumed treason, which I know to be incorrect. I, uh, picked him up just before the GAG goons came for him. He's been in safe houses since, but it's hard to keep him out of sight of Solo's investigators."

Ben wrinkled his nose. "I can totally see that, considering how he dresses."

Tycho smiled. "Grand Master, I was hoping we could leave him with you."

Luke snorted, amused. "At least you have the courtesy to identify your spies when you try to place them with us."

Deadpan, Tycho nodded. "Galactic Alliance Intelligence. We're the courteous alternative."

Luke stepped aside and gestured for the newcomers to precede him. "Let's get you some food and caf. Then we can talk."

Wedge decided that the group Luke led through the Death Star wreckage was a mob, and it was perhaps the most dangerous mob within five hundred light-years. Following him and Luke were Han and Leia, Jaina and Zekk, Syal, Tycho, Saba Sebatyne and Corran Horn, Ben, and Kyle Katarn, who trailed the pack but otherwise seemed to be moving well.

Luke chose a shady spot beneath an overhang of Death Star hull. He spread out his cloak on the bare dirt there and sat, gesturing for Han and Leia to join him. The others sat on Jedi cloaks or the bare ground.

Without preamble, Luke began. "I've had a brief talk with General Celchu here, and I'm going to go over some points he made and some other details that have come up recently. Together we're going to make some decisions about a course of action." Wedge saw Saba Sebatyne nod approvingly.

Luke gestured at Tycho. "The general came here to make an official request by the GA government that the Jedi

Order return to the Galactic Alliance fold, as is our sworn duty."

Wedge grinned. "Five credits says the invitation came only from Admiral Niathal, and that Colonel Solo had no part in it."

There were no takers.

Wedge continued, "I think I need to put Tycho's presence here in perspective. All this is speculation on my part, but I speculate pretty well. Tycho wouldn't have asked for this meeting on his own initiative, because he doesn't represent the GA in these matters. But he hasn't once suggested that he's here on behalf of his boss, Admiral Niathal. Which means he's here with either her overt or her tacit approval, representing her interests as joint Chief of State of the GA. If anything goes wrong with this mission, he and his career go up in a flash of smoke, but it's something that has to be done. And now he's not going to say anything, because he can offer neither confirmation nor denial of what I've just said." He grinned at his old friend.

Tycho's jaw worked for a moment, then set. He contented himself merely with glaring at Wedge.

Luke grinned. "I said no to General Celchu's request, for the simple reason that any action that puts the Order under the command of, or potentially at the mercy of, Jacen Solo is an unacceptable one, particularly after what happened at Ossus. My position remains that we serve the GA best by determining the course of action that is best for everyone, and then implementing it, at least until such time as the GA Chief of State's office can be considered trustworthy again."

There were nods from all around the assembly.

"Let me make this clear, though." Luke fixed Tycho with his gaze. "*We serve the Galactic Alliance*. When Jacen Solo is no longer a factor, we will return our seat of authority to Coruscant. We retain trust in Admiral Niathal."

Tycho nodded. "I understand and appreciate that. But once I file my report with her . . . there's always the chance that Colonel Solo will gain access to it, and learn that you're now stationed on Endor."

"By the time you get back to Coruscant, we won't *be* on Endor any longer." Luke looked among the others. "Now in the spirit of serving the Alliance—at least what we want the Alliance to be—and of serving the greater good, we're going to sketch out our next operation. Which, in part, will be to rescue Allana, Chume'da of the Hapes Consortium, and daughter of Tenel Ka, from captivity at the hands of Jacen Solo."

Tycho raised a hand.

"Yes, General."

"Let me see if I understand this. You're going to help the Alliance this way." Tycho began counting items off on his fingers. "First, you return the Chume'da to the Queen Mother. Second, the Queen Mother again, who by now must hate Jacen Solo absolutely, turns her fleets against him and the GA. Third, the Confederation, at that point stronger than the Alliance, *conquers* the Alliance. Fourth . . ." He paused as if confused. "There is no fourth."

Luke smiled. "I left out a detail."

"Ah, good. I was worried there."

"The Corellians just used Centerpoint Station to destroy elements of the Second Fleet. They also tried to kill Jacen. Now, thinking the way Jacen does, the way he *must*, it's inconceivable that he would not make an all-out effort to capture the station and have in his possession the most powerful weapon in the galaxy. We're not going to let the Corellians have it, and we're not going to let Jacen have it.

We're going to destroy it . . . probably at the same time Jacen mounts his operation to capture it."

Tycho shook his head. "So you continue to deprive us of the Hapan fleets, *and* you deprive us of Centerpoint Station."

"No, we give the Queen Mother the right—her *right*—to negotiate the terms under which her fleets will be used by the Alliance, and we deprive the Confederation of Centerpoint Station. This will result in a morale blow to the Confederation, and will cost them allies. If the Hapans stay out of it, the two sides remain roughly equal for now. If Admiral Niathal can stuff Jacen into a box, the Hapans return to the Alliance fold, and the Alliance is suddenly the stronger side."

The general continued to look unhappy. "There are a lot of ifs in that plan, Grand Master."

"True."

"How do you intend to do it?"

Luke glanced toward Kyle Katarn for a moment. "It's inevitable that Jacen will command the mission to Centerpoint Station himself. We've managed to plant a tracer beacon on him, and he still apparently hasn't detected it. Sadly, it's very short-range, but if we can keep StealthXs in rotation near the *Anakin Solo*, we can detect when the mission starts. It would be better if we had a longer-range tracer, but we'll use what we have. Then—"

Leia, looking curiously guilty, interrupted. "Actually . . . there's a full-power holocomm beacon on Jacen's ship. Zekk planted it. He also disabled their tractor beam, partly to allow us to escape and partly to give the ship mechanics some sabotage to detect and repair . . . so that they would miss the more subtle addition to their holocomm system."

Luke looked between Leia and Zekk. "When was this?"

Zekk shrugged. "When we raided to get the information on Brisha Syo's asteroid from his shuttle memory."

"It would have been useful to have known this earlier."

Han shifted, uncomfortable. "We've been busy putting out fires."

Luke sighed, then continued. "With our new, fancy holocomm beacon on the *Anakin Solo,* we detect when Jacen begins his operation, and jump to Corellia. General Celchu brought us an expert who can help us figure out how to destroy it."

"That's not what I brought him for."

"Regardless, he was willing to help blow it up once, he'll be willing to help blow it up a second time." Luke shrugged apologetically and moved on. "Meanwhile, we send a unit of Jedi aboard the *Anakin Solo* to distract Jacen . . . and to retrieve the Chume'da."

"How do you plan to get them aboard?" Han sounded dubious. "I kind of doubt the old *Love Commander* trick will work a second time."

Luke looked at Tycho. "General, when you arrived, your shuttle transceiver broadcast what I assume was a false registration and identity. I also assume that it's capable of broadcasting a registration and identity consistent with General Celchu of Starfighter Command."

Tycho nodded. "Of course."

Luke spread his palms. "There you have it. We go in on General Celchu's shuttle."

Slowly, Tycho shook his head. "Much as I personally might want you to succeed in this, I sort of have to say no. Duty and officer's oaths and all that. You understand."

"Oh, that's right." Luke turned to Wedge. "Could I trouble you to set your blaster on stun and point it at the other general?"

"No, not really."

"Please?"

Wedge sighed. "I'm not going to point a blaster at my best friend. Plus, his pilot will be obliged to jump in the way or do something equally noble and foolish. I'm not going to point a blaster at my little girl."

"Thank you, Daddy."

Wedge thought about it. "I do have a solution, though." He pointed his forefinger at Tycho, aligning his thumb straight up. "Imagine that's a blaster. Wait a second." He adjusted an imaginary knob on his thumb. "Had to make sure it was on stun."

Tycho looked at his hand. "I'm imagining that it's a BlasTech DL-Eighteen."

Wedge shrugged. "An adequate choice, under these circumstances."

"Maybe. If we'd all imagined that it was a DL-Forty-four, big and imposing, I might actually be intimidated. A DL-Eighteen is barely worth surrendering to."

Syal shook her head, her expression sad.

Luke began looking from face to face as he spoke. "Wedge, handpick a starfighter squadron. We'll use it to chase the shuttle to safety aboard the *Anakin Solo,* then to support any operation against Centerpoint Station. I'll lead a unit of Jedi to assault Jacen; our job will be to take him out if possible, and to distract him from the rescue operation in any case. Han, Leia, I want you to lead the expedition to rescue the Chume'da. Master Katarn, I want you in reserve for extraction of the assault and rescue teams. Doctor Seyah and our scientific staff will come up with the best ways to destroy Centerpoint Station. Ben, owing to your experience there, I want you on that mission."

Ben shook his head. "I'll be more useful accompanying you aboard the *Anakin Solo.*"

"How do you figure that?"

"Because with both of us boarding, Jacen will conclude that we're there to kill him. It will help keep him from guessing that Allana is the mission's real goal. And he won't be wondering where I am or what I'm up to."

Luke gave his son a close look. "And will diversion be *your* genuine intent? Not revenge?"

"Yes, Grand Master."

"All right, then." Luke rose, prompting the others to do the same. He turned to Tycho. "General, I'm sorry about imprisoning you and your pilot. And stealing your shuttle. And exposing you to Ewoks again. And such."

Tycho shrugged. "I acknowledge that, from your perspective, you have to keep me a prisoner until your operation begins, to keep me from doing my duty and alerting the Alliance . . ."

"Yes?"

"There's no reason why you couldn't take me with you to Colonel Solo's action against Corellia, put me in the cockpit of a starfighter, and let me make my way home from there. After I fly around getting a good look at everything, that is."

"Good point." Luke nodded. "We may do that. And your pilot?"

"Oh, you don't have to imprison her at all." Tycho reached into his tunic pocket.

Wedge's forefinger dug into Tycho's ribs. "No tricks."

Tycho grinned and passed Luke a datacard. "In our ongoing effort to maintain cordial relations with the Jedi Order, and thus effect your rapid return to the Galactic Alliance, I present you with our special envoy, Captain Syal Antilles, who will remain with you and communicate with my office whenever you permit."

Syal's jaw dropped. "Wait. What?"

Tycho fixed her with a stern look. "This assignment is no milk run, Antilles. This is a tricky diplomatic mission with a lot at stake, and just trying to keep up with the Jedi can get you killed. But if you help keep the Alliance and the Jedi in touch, if you keep them talking, you'll be making a big difference in this war."

Wedge looked proud and reflective. "I was years older than you when I became an ambassador for the first time. Remember that, Tycho? How did we get through that assignment, anyway?"

"Pretty much, we opened fire on everyone who disagreed with us."

Wedge nodded and turned to his daughter. "When all else fails, just do that."

chapter thirty

SANCTUARY MOON OF ENDOR,
JEDI OUTPOST

Jag lay on the medical ward bed. He might have been mistaken for a dead man but for the very slow rise and fall of his chest.

Jaina, sitting on a chair near the foot of the bed, had a good sense of how nearly dead Jag had been. He'd had damage to his neck, a fracture to his left elbow, multiple breaks in his left thigh, internal injuries . . . Since he would never have survived a direct jump from the asteroid system to Endor in the cockpit of a starfighter, they had made a short jump to Bimmiel, transferred Jag to the *Falcon,* and left his X-wing covered by camouflage sheets and sand in a chilly tundra valley.

But now, after time in a restorative bacta tank, after medicines and rest, the medics said he was much improved; he would soon recover fully.

Jaina wasn't sure. In the Force, Jag didn't feel like a man struggling back toward health and vitality.

Jag opened his eyes. He didn't move, not even to turn his

head, until he'd seen everything he could from his position—a survival trait, Jaina decided, possibly one he learned while stranded on Tenupe.

Finally he turned his head and saw her. He offered no smile, but he did speak. "Hello."

"Hello yourself. Remember much?"

"Yes." He started to nod, thought the better of it as half-healed injuries pulled. "I remember everything. Except where we are."

"Endor. You were unconscious when we got here."

"Ah. And Zekk?"

"Better. He was kind of a mess coming out of the asteroid. He took the same amount of damage you did . . . but emotional, not physical."

"Too bad. Physical scars are much better conversation starters at parties." He turned his attention to the ceiling and studied it for long moments. "Well. Mission accomplished."

"That's right, mission accomplished. And you've done what you needed to. To help restore your family honor."

"Yes." There was no pleasure in that word, just acknowledgment.

Jaina wished she hadn't brought up the subject of his family. The Fels, though a human family of Corellian ancestry—Jag's mother was Wedge's older sister, the first Syal Antilles—now lived in the Chiss Ascendancy, by the rules of that blue-skinned folk.

And those rules dictated that, because of mistakes and decisions made by other people—Jaina among them—Jag could never go home. Hunting down Alema Rar had been the last task assigned to him by his clan. In accomplishing it, he had severed his last ties with them.

In fact—the realization struck Jaina like a blow in combat practice—the act of ending the threat posed by Alema had perhaps severed his last ties with everyone.

She made her voice gentle, an unaccustomed task for her. "What's next for you?"

He shrugged, wincing as the action pulled at some of his injuries. "There's a war on. I'm sure someone needs a pilot."

"Stay with the Jedi."

"Sure."

Suddenly she was impatient with him. "I don't mean as a civilian employee. I mean as a friend."

He finally looked at her again. "I haven't done a very good job of making friends. I would rate my success at nearly zero."

"Zekk looks on you as a friend."

"Yes. Well, without him, my rate of success would be *exactly* zero. And truth be told, for reasons I'm sure you understand, he would probably prefer that I not be around too much."

"*I'm* your friend."

"Are you?"

She heaved an exasperated sigh. "Oh, we're not having this conversation again."

"No, we're not. This is a new one. I'm not asking you to set aside your focus, to distract yourself from training for your next mission. I'm not asking you to roll the chrono back fifteen years to when we were teenagers." Despite the discomfort, he pulled himself back so that he could sit up against the pillows at the head of his bed. "I'm asking you to tell me if I have a place in your life. Someone you'd turn to if you'd ever just acknowledge that you needed some help. Someone you'd miss more than occasionally if he went away. *Am I your friend?*"

Knowing the answer he wanted to hear, the answer that

would help him get better, Jaina opened her mouth to offer it. Then she shut up again. He deserved better than that. He deserved the truth. She just wasn't sure what the truth was.

It took her long moments to sift out her feelings from the bewildering insulating layer of decisions and codes of conduct she'd fabricated for herself. To find it, she had to look past what she had to do and be; she had to find the place where she kept what she *wanted* to do and be.

But she found her answer. "Yes. I am."

"Good." He held out his hand.

She put hers on it.

He relaxed. "So, what's next for *you?*"

"A mission. Simple stuff. Rescue a princess—a Solo family tradition. Blow up a big space station."

"Also a Solo family tradition."

"You can get in on it, if you can get yourself back in shape in time."

"I will. And if you ever need someone to dress up in a black costume and beat you up—"

Jaina smiled. "Just shut up."

CORELLIA, CORONET, COMMAND BUNKER

This late at night, with no enemy forces in orbit, the command bunker was nearly deserted, and usually the hum of atmosphere conditioners was the only thing to be heard on most floors, in most chambers.

But in the primary communications chamber—not the elegant studio where most transmissions were initiated or received, not the secure Prime Minister's chamber where Sadras Koyan did so much of his talking—the banks of holocomm equipment were alive, adding their own hum to the ambient noise.

Minister of Information Denjax Teppler looked up for the thousandth time, making sure that the door into the chamber was still secure, that there were no warning diodes lit on the devices he had patched in to subvert the holocam over the door. Then he returned his attention to his task at hand. One of the holocomm control banks was open before him, and it was the work of just a few more moments to finish wiring in the bypass card he'd brought— the device that would keep the communication he was about to receive from being copied to the offices of Corellian Security.

For he was about to commit yet another act of treason, and he needed to do it properly.

His task finished, he stepped to the primary control panel, checked his chrono, and activated the device. He moved to stand against the chamber's one blank wall, an auxiliary transmission spot that had not been used in years.

Thirty seconds later, a glow appeared in the air before him and resolved into a holographic shape—General Turr Phennir, scarred and imposing . . . and just a bit over a meter tall. "Good afternoon, Minister Teppler."

"Night, where I am, but I reciprocate." Teppler frowned. "How tall—never mind, there's something wrong at my end. Hold on." He moved back to the control panel, noted that the received-image scale preference was set to 60 percent for this transmission origin, and overrode it temporarily, setting it to 100 percent.

Phennir flickered, then instantly assumed Teppler's own height.

Teppler returned to the wall and now could look the general eye-to-eye at the same altitude. "That's better."

"Another symptom of your leader's mental deficits."

Teppler waved that subject away. "I didn't ask for this communication to discuss the Prime Minister's eccentricities. I asked for it so we could talk about your unofficial embargo of Corellia. You're holding back supplies and matériel we desperately need."

"And I agreed to this exchange because Koyan's incompetence must be our main topic of discussion. Because that incompetence is the reason for the embargo."

Teppler grimaced. "We're an ally, and you've left us dangerously vulnerable."

"Allow me to explain why. Because you're a politician, I will use similes and other conversational aides."

"Not to mention insults."

Phennir paused. "You're right. My anger at the Prime Minister has spilled over to you. I apologize. Still, imagine you're a mighty warrior. You would be less mighty if you lost one of your arms."

"True."

"It would behoove you not to lose one of your arms. Yet you're walking in the jungle and are bitten on the wrist by a venomous animal. The venom will spread from your arm and fatally poison the rest of you in less than a minute. What do you do?"

"Well, if you've prepared properly for this expedition, you break out the antitoxin and inject it."

"Correct. But in this instance, you have no antitoxin. You have only a large vibroblade."

"Then you tie off a tourniquet, cut your own arm off . . . and hope you can inject the painkillers before you black out."

"Also correct. Because to be a mighty warrior, you need one thing more than you need to have both arms."

"Your life."

"Yes."

Teppler thought it through. "You're saying that the Confederation is the warrior, and Corellia is the arm."

"Yes. And Sadras Koyan is the venom. His use of Centerpoint Station struck almost as deadly a blow to us as it did to the enemy, in terms of morale, of ensuring cooperation between our armed forces. And it's clear that if we win this war—and I mean *if*, not when—his first act will be to point the station at one of his allies and begin to dictate the terms of peace and postwar prosperity."

"What are you suggesting?"

"Remove him from power."

"It's not as easy as that. We have a coalition government whose representatives jockey for power endlessly."

"I'm not telling you who to put in power. I'm telling you to remove Koyan, which *is* as easy as that. It can be done with a small group of specialists who spirit him away in the night and return him when the war is done. It can be done with a hold-out blaster pressed to his kidney and fired. It can be done with planted evidence that does nothing more than prove that he's the idiot he is." Phennir leaned close. "I'm not playing kingmaker here. I don't want to decide who governs Corellia. I just need you to *choose a ruler I can work with*. Until you do, Corellia stays outside the comfort of our campfire."

"I'll think about what you're saying."

"Good." Phennir actually fidgeted, and his tone became conspiratorial. "Listen. I'll admit that I don't understand you Corellians. You place the value of freedom so far above that of duty that you're incomprehensible to me. I've flown with and against the best, most disciplined pilots Corellia has offered—Soontir Fel, Wedge Antilles—and I don't even understand *them*. Perhaps that's my failing, but the Confederation will fall apart if Koyan remains in charge. Get me someone who can understand *me*."

Teppler nodded. "Understood."

Phennir gave him a half bow. Then his hologram disappeared.

Moving fast, Teppler pulled out the card he'd meticulously wired into the holocomm. He pressed a button on it, sending an electrical charge through the frail device—burning out its memory and circuits, destroying most of the evidence of his actions here.

Phennir was right. But Teppler, though he had briefly been Five Worlds Prime Minister, didn't know if he'd be better than Koyan in that role in this time of war. Nor did he know if any military officer could cope with the nearly carnivorous needs for attention and status that characterized the Corellian planetary Chiefs of State he'd have to deal with.

He slapped shut the panel on the holocomm and got to work around the chamber, using a chemical-soaked felt cloth to wipe down every surface he had touched. Fingerprints and genetic evidence were simultaneously destroyed with each stroke.

Wait—the Alliance now had a Chief of State office shared by two collaborators, one originally civilian, one originally military. The same structure might work for Corellia.

Admiral Delpin was intelligent, reasonable, and, unlike Koyan, honorable. She could bring the support of Corellian Defense while Teppler wrangled the civilian chiefs.

It could work. If they could be rid of Sadras Koyan, and soon.

Teppler paused at the doorway into the chamber and surveyed his handiwork. There was nothing to see suggesting he had ever been here—nothing but the wires leading from his holocam subversion device to the recording device above the door. He grabbed the device and gave it a yank, pulling its data wire free of the holocam. He put the rig in his pocket with the burned-out card.

Yes, Admiral Delpin. Perhaps, despite her bearing and reputation, she was willing to become as big a traitor as Teppler himself.

chapter thirty-one

CORUSCANT SYSTEM,
ABOARD THE **ANAKIN SOLO**

At peace with himself, Caedus stared through the bridge viewports at the stars, at the trails of running lights indicating the presence of ships arriving at or departing Coruscant.

Allana was no longer afraid of him, and had accepted him—instantly, with boundless affection—as her father. The Hapans were still behaving well enough, now staging raids on critical Confederation sites and resources. Caedus himself felt healthy again, fully healed for the first time since his fight with Luke. And right up to the day of Caedus's operation to capture Centerpoint, Corellia's defenses had been growing weaker, more lax. Caedus was certain this was no ploy on the part of the Corellians—GA Intelligence believed that Confederation supply lines were being taxed past their limits, and Corellia was not being adequately reprovisioned.

In a day, he would own Centerpoint. In a week, the

major allies of the Confederation would have surrendered. This war was almost done.

"Sir?" Lieutenant Tebut approached from the stern end of the bridge. Today, Caedus recalled, her duty station was ship security.

She presented him with the duty datapad for her station. "All ship sections report secure. Anomalies and unresolved incidents are at a record low."

"Excellent work." Caedus took the datapad from her and tapped its screen, activating the hot spot acknowledging receipt of the report. He turned away, looking at the starfield again as he handed the device back to her. In his inattentiveness, he released it a moment too early. Tebut juggled and dropped it. It hit the bridge floor.

Caedus looked at her.

"My apologies, sir." She stooped to pick up the datapad. She glanced at its screen. Caedus could see that it was undamaged. Tebut snapped it shut, saluted, and turned away.

Two steps later, she skidded to a stop and looked back at him.

"Lieutenant?"

Her voice was distant. "New anomaly." She moved toward him again. "Sir, this is perhaps none of my business, but it has been my observation that you get rid of clothes when they become worn or stop being able to hold creases."

Caedus nodded. "Not just clothes."

"Yes, sir. So why are you wearing a patched cloak? If I may ask."

"Patched?" He looked down at himself.

Tebut stooped again, then rose, bringing up the lower hem of his cloak, turning it so Caedus could see the backside. There, placed in a slightly crooked fashion, was a square cloth patch, five centimeters on a side, identical in color and texture to the surrounding cloak material.

Caedus took the hem and stared at it. He tugged at the corner of the patch. Reluctantly, it yielded, coming up from the cloak material, revealing glue and flexible circuitry beneath.

Though his good mood was spoiled, he kept the fact from his face. "We all make mistakes, Lieutenant, and it appears that one of mine was to let someone plant a beacon on me." He undid his cloak clasps, folded the garment, and handed it to her along with the black patch. "Get that to our security technicians. I want to know its range of abilities. Soonest."

"Yes, sir." She saluted again and left.

Once she was through the doors at the stern end of the bridge, Caedus looked around and found Captain Nevil. "Did you see?"

"I did, sir."

"I run a meritocracy, and the lieutenant shows merit. Put this incident on her record."

"Consider it done, sir."

TWO LIGHT-YEARS OUTSIDE THE CORELLIAN SYSTEM, ABOARD THE **ERRANT VENTURE**

The giant pleasure ship—once an Imperial Star Destroyer named *Virulence,* later a haven for gamblers, shoppers, and vacationers of all species and economic brackets—was oddly quiet, Han decided. Its main hangar bay was comparatively empty, devoid of the usual collection of privately owned yachts, shuttles, and transports that crowded the chamber from wall to wall. Now the only vehicles it hosted were one transport, large enough to evacuate the ship's current skeleton crew, plus a couple of starfighter squadrons, two shuttles, and the *Millennium Falcon*.

Han slouched in the *Falcon*'s copilot's seat. There were more comfortable places to be, but none was very interesting at the moment; the *Errant Venture*'s gambling halls were all temporarily closed. The ship was serving as a staging platform for Luke's Centerpoint mission, and until this mission was done, her owner, Booster Terrik, had chosen to limit staff to the minimum number of tight-lipped crew members necessary for basic functions.

Below the *Falcon*'s cockpit were spread the other operation vehicles. Mechanics and some of the other pilots, many of them Jedi, worked among the starfighters. The Antilles and Horn clans sat at a folding table between two StealthXs, playing what looked like a cutthroat game of sabacc. Luke Skywalker walked among all the starfighters, trailed by R2-D2.

Han looked at the man in the pilot's seat. He scowled. He really didn't like seeing anything from this perspective. "Think you've got it, kid?"

Jag straightened up from his latest simulation run. "I've got it."

"You know, there have never been many people I'd let fly this baby. Chewbacca. Leia. Lando. Now you."

"She's Corellian by design. I'm full-blooded Corellian by ancestry. We'll get along just fine."

"Make sure you do." Restless, Han turned away. This was the fifth time they'd had this conversation, or one much like it, in the last few days.

Oh, well. The kid wouldn't resent it too much. Jag had to understand the love of a man for his ship. Didn't he?

A button on the comm board lit, and Booster Terrik's voice, aged and hoarse, came across the speakers. "Jedi

Recon Three reports the *Anakin Solo* leading a formation of ships out of Coruscant orbit. This looks like no drill."

Han stood. "Good luck, kid."

"You, too, s—Han."

"That's better." Moments later, Han trotted down the boarding ramp, wincing at the unaccustomed, unwelcome sensation of leaving his first love in somebody else's hands.

Kyle Katarn, moving easily, with C-3PO behind him, headed toward the *Falcon* and crossed Han's path. Han trotted past, offering the Jedi Master a wave and calling back over his shoulder to the droid: "Don't talk them to death, Goldenrod."

"Oh, no, sir, I would never endanger a mission or my comrades through the employment of excessive verbiage. Though I appreciate your levity on this matter. As I have appreciated it many, many times in the past. They say the soul of humor is repetition . . ."

A few steps farther, and Han could no longer hear the droid over the sounds of engines being fired up and boots clattering across durasteel decks.

More pilots, mechanics, and Jedi were now running into the bay from turbolift access corridors. Myri Antilles and the woman she was named for, Mirax Horn, carrying the now folded table, passed them in the other direction, hurrying toward the distant operations center of the *Errant Venture.*

Han reached the foot of the shuttle *Reveille,* the first member of his crew to do so. He leaned against the hull, affecting a pose of boredom, tapping his foot while he waited.

Luke and Leia, he in black robes and she in brown and tan, were next.

Leia looked him over. "Sorry if we kept you waiting."

"Do Jedi even *carry* chronos?"

She grinned and dashed up the ramp.

"Hey, do the preflight checklist while you're up there."

Luke waited with Han while the others arrived: Ben, wearing a black high-necked tunic that was neither Guard uniform nor dark Jedi garment but somewhere in between; Saba Sebatyne, silent and imposing in her fearsomely reptilian manner; Iella Antilles, in a black jumpsuit draped with matching utility belts, bandoliers, and backpack, her face and graying brown hair the only areas of color on her; and R2-D2, who hit the bottom of the ramp at speed and rolled up into the shuttle's belly as though he were on level ground.

Luke headed up the ramp. "All present and accounted for."

Han followed. "Do you have to talk that military talk?"

"Hey, you're the one who went to the Academy. I thought you'd like it."

Syal settled into her X-wing—borrowed from one of the Jedi, and she hoped she'd be able to return it in perfect shape—and ran through her checklist as the comlink crackled to life on her squadron frequency.

"Rakehell Leader to Squadron." Her father's voice, and it jolted her to realize that she was finally going to fly with her father, in combat. "Count off by number, and indicate readiness. Rakehell Leader ready."

"Rakehell Two, armed and ready." It was a woman's voice, heavily flavored by an exotic accent—Sanola Ti, the Dathomiri Jedi, one of several squadron members Syal had not met before they transferred to the *Errant Venture*.

Tycho was next. "Rakehell Three, all green, optimal." His comm board was slaved to the squadron frequency, as was Syal's, and would be until the mission was well under way—a precaution implemented to keep him from informing Alliance forces of the true purpose of this mission.

Syal cleared her throat. "Rakehell Four, four lit and in the green." Her knee began bouncing. She pressed down on it. Nerves—she had never flown an X-wing in genuine combat, all of her live-fire experience having been with A-wings and Alephs. But she'd flown X-wings before she'd ever handled an airspeeder, starting when she was a child, when her father would take her up in a twin-seat trainer and hand over the controls. She knew the X-wing like a housebound office drone knew the family sofa.

Other members of the squadron counted off, their roll call suggesting a Starfighter Command hall of fame. Five, Corran Horn, leading the second flight. Six, Twool—an unknown quantity, a Rodian Jedi whom Syal had never heard of. Seven, Tyria Tainer, a Jedi who had flown with Wedge long ago, before Syal was born. Eight, Cheriss ke Hanadi, onetime head vibroblade instructor for Starfighter Command.

"Rake Nine, optimal." That was Jaina Solo, leading the third flight. Zekk called in as Ten; Volu Nyth, a Kuati woman who had flown with Rogue Squadron during the Yuuzhan Vong War, was Eleven; Wes Janson, Twelve, asked, "Is it over?"

Nerves. Syal wasn't nervous about the prospect of dying—no more than usual. What terrified her was that she might manage to look like a rookie in front of her father, and her father's friends. Dying would be less painful.

In the belly of the troop carrier shuttle *Broadside*, Kyp Durron snapped his visor shut and turned to Dr. Seyah. "What do you think?"

Seyah looked him over. He was dressed identically—in a good simulation of the all-black Galactic Alliance Guard uniform, though his helmet visor was still up. He nodded. "Not bad. At least you have the build to carry it off." He patted his own, more expansive stomach. "They're going to take one look at me and think, *Rear echelon bantha fodder.*"

Kyp looked back across the personnel bay of the *Broadside,* at the other ersatz Guard troops—Jedi such as Valin Horn and Jaden Korr among them, anonymous behind their visors. He raised his own visor and shouted back across the troops: "What's our motto?"

They responded with a single, well-practiced roar: "Let the enemy do the work!"

Kyp nodded and gave them an appreciative smile. "That's the spirit."

ABOARD THE **ANAKIN SOLO**

Captain Nevil approached Caedus in his usual quiet fashion. "Boarding shuttles and Rogue Squadron are positioned, sir. They report ready to jump."

Caedus nodded, keeping his eyes closed. He could feel them, the specks of life that constituted the famous starfighter squadron and the clusters of life representing the anonymous commandos and Guard troopers who would spearhead the assault on Centerpoint Station. All around them were the greater masses of life force, the crews of the capital ships of this operation.

And from them, probabilities and eventualities began streaming, glimpses of possible futures—some in logical succession, some mutually contradictory or exclusive. Caedus could focus on any one of them to see the likely next few minutes of a subject's life. But he did not—he couldn't afford to fragment his attention now, and he didn't need to know the fate of every insignificant man or woman under his command.

Maintaining his Sith battle meditation through a hyperspace jump would be tricky enough. But he felt he was ready. He opened his eyes and turned to Nevil. "Go."

The Quarren turned and gestured to his communications officer.

The word was given.

A moment later the starfield beyond the viewports seemed to elongate and twist as the task force made the jump to hyperspace.

CORELLIAN SPACE,
NEAR CENTERPOINT STATION

Rakehell Squadron dropped out of hyperspace, the stars snapping back to single unwinking gleams, and directly ahead of Syal was Centerpoint Station in all its majestic homeliness. A round-tipped cylinder 350 kilometers long, with the center third bulging out to a width of 100 kilometers, it was the largest artificial construction she had ever seen, and even at her current distance—hundreds of klicks away—it seemed vast. Alongside it, a Super Star Destroyer would appear as a speck.

And there were specks nearing it. She saw tiny triangles and lozenge shapes hurtling toward the station, and more moving from the station's vicinity to intercept them. Names began popping up on her sensor board: ANAKIN SOLO. VINSOR. PANTHER STAR. SAXAN'S PRIDE.

ROGUE 1, ROGUE 2, ROGUE 3 . . .

Syal's breath caught. Rogue Squadron was here, the fighter unit Luke Skywalker and her father had founded, the elite force whose reputation alone was enough to turn back some enemies.

Well, she wouldn't be fighting them. She flew in the same force they did. Her assignment here was simple—serve as Tycho's wingmate, see that he made it back to the Alliance force as soon as their comm boards were unslaved and would allow direct communication.

"Rakehell Leader to Rakes." Wedge's voice did not suggest that he was rattled by the fact that his former command was ahead in the battle zone. Perhaps he hadn't seen them on his sensors. "*Reveille* reports ready. Her target is the *Anakin Solo*. We'll follow her in, shooting. Do remember to miss. Three, Four, you can follow us in if you like, but I have a feeling that your participation here might be seen as treasonous . . ."

"Leader, Three." Tycho sounded similarly unconcerned. "No, I'll follow . . . holocams blazing away. The recordings could prove interesting later."

"As you wish. Don't get shot. I don't want Winter hunting me down."

"No, you don't."

Tycho's shuttle, Han Solo visible at the controls, moved out ahead of the Rakehells and accelerated toward the distant conflict.

chapter thirty-two

ABOARD THE **ANAKIN SOLO**

So far, so good. Caedus was satisfied for the moment. His task force's arrival in the Corellian system had not caught Centerpoint's defenders entirely unprepared—the Corellians had a defensive screen of capital ships in position to protect the station—but the enemy were apparently unprepared for the speed and ferocity of the attack, and were presenting less forceful resistance than anticipated. The first round of analysis suggested that they were low on proton torpedoes, concussion missiles, and other physical deterrents.

He lent a touch of urgency to the *Panther Star*'s commander, subtly pushing the Sullustan to greater speed, greater confidence. Too much caution would not benefit his task force.

Capital ships were breaking from orbit around Talus and Tralus, heading toward the conflict, which was halfway between the two worlds. Even when they arrived, the Corellian force would have less strength than his. The troop shuttles were nearing the station itself, only two of them lost so far to defensive fire . . .

He could feel more units in play than should have been present, and only detected them because the streamers of possibility predicting their actions did not align them with either the Alliance or the Corellians. He spared them a look. A fighter squadron, on a mission of . . . harrassment, rather than defense or destruction? He shook his head. The squadron commander had to be a coward, determined to keep himself and his subordinates out of the line of fire. Caedus would deal with them, make them an example to others, when time allowed.

CORELLIA, CORONET, COMMAND BUNKER

"What you're talking about is treason." Admiral Delpin's words were straightforward.

With political skills that had served him well all through his professional life—reading character traits, instantly revising plans to accommodate changing circumstances—Denjax Teppler decided to make a slight alteration to the course of this conversation.

Which meant he had to lie, another of his political skills. "I'm not talking about forcibly removing Koyan from office. But I think you've seen as clearly as I have that he's the sort of duelist who'll shoot his own foot off before his blaster clears its holster. Inevitably, he's going to remove himself from office. At that precise instant, what do we do? Sit obediently by while the war-dogs fight among themselves to choose a new Koyan, or take charge and improve things?"

Her expression didn't change, but for the first time in the conversation, she didn't respond instantly or predictably.

Teppler kept his own elation off his face. *She's consider-ing it. Take the violent removal of Koyan out of the equa-tion, and she has no problem with the idea.*

She leaned forward. "Speaking hypothetically . . . I could probably secure myself in the role of Chief of State just with the backing of the military. Why would I then *need* you?"

"Two reasons. First, you don't want to govern all of the Corellian system any more than I do, meaning that as part-ners we can keep each other's decisions in perspective. Sec-ond, half the burden feels like a tenth the burden. I'll manage the tasks you're unwilling or not entirely compe-tent to handle, and you'll do the same for me."

She took in a breath to answer, and then her comlink beeped.

So did Teppler's, a high-pitched urgency signal.

They looked at each other with the misgivings of profes-sional leaders who knew things were bad when comlinks went off simultaneously.

Teppler pulled out his comlink to answer while the admi-ral did the same with hers. "Teppler here."

Moments later, they were in the corridor, trotting toward the bunker's main situation room, Teppler struggling to keep up with Delpin's long military strides.

The admiral tucked her comlink back into her tunic. "Where's the Prime Minister?"

"Up on the station. Under attack." Teppler considered. There had to be some way for him to use this situation to bring about the very change in government he'd just been proposing to the admiral.

"And the station? Is it operational again?"

Teppler almost spoke one of Koyan's favorite conversation-ending phrases, *That's on a need-to-know basis.* But he bit his tongue. Given Delpin's efforts to convince Koyan to cooperate more fully with the Confederation Supreme Military Commander, Koyan had been cutting her out of the line of information flow more and more frequently. But Teppler decided she *did* need to know. This was a combat situation, and Centerpoint Station was a military resource. "Operational as of four hours ago. The techs also think they've overcome the programming that limited the scope of the last beam. If they're right, on its next use the station could eliminate an entire planet or star. That's why Koyan is there. He's composing his surrender-or-die message to Admiral Niathal."

Delpin nodded, her jaw set. "If the Alliance seizes control of the station, Corellia is the system under the gun. We need more forces up there, now. More than we have. I need to talk to General Phennir."

"No, let me. Believe it or not, I speak his language."

She looked at him, dubious, but seemed convinced by his sudden confidence. She nodded.

At the next cross-corridor, she turned left, toward the situation room. Teppler continued on alone toward the Prime Minister's communications chamber.

The *Reveille* raced toward the *Anakin Solo,* arcing to pass well clear of an engagement between a Corellian frigate and an Alliance starfighter squadron. Syal fumed. The *Reveille* was broadcasting its true registration, its correct password, both belonging to Tycho, the information having been sliced out of its computers by Syal's own mother, who was now aboard the shuttle.

"Rakehell Leader. Begin firing."

All around Syal, the other Rakehell pilots opened up on the shuttle—or rather, began firing in its general vicinity. Shots from their lasers passed all around the shuttle, and one—as beautifully placed as any kill, fired by her father—

glanced off the top shields, not endangering the shuttle in the least.

A turbolaser blast, bright columns of light in parallel streams, flashed toward them from the capital ship. At this range, the *Anakin Solo*'s gunners were only likely to hit by accident, but accidents did happen. Suddenly all the Rakehells were on the defense, their approaches as erratic as the flight of piranha-beetles in mating season.

"Rakehell Leader to squadron. Break by wing pairs whenever you feel like it—or when I say *break*. We'll form up off the *Anakin Solo*'s bow, outside the range of its main guns."

Syal heard acknowledgments from the other pilots and added her own.

Then her comlink—her personal comlink, clipped to her tunic under her flight suit—came to life. "Captain Antilles." It was Tycho's voice.

"Yes, General."

"Break when the others do. Do not, I say again, do not stay with me. I'm going to make my run from here."

"But, sir—"

"That was an order. Acknowledge it."

"Acknowledged, sir." A chill settled in Syal's stomach as a notion of what Tycho planned to do occurred to her.

ABOARD THE **ANAKIN SOLO**

A beep, indicating a high-priority query, sounded from Lieutenant Tebut's terminal. She switched from the screen of scrolling security data to the query. The face of one of the *Anakin Solo*'s communications officers, a Rodian, came up on-screen. "Lieutenant—"

"Yes, Ensign."

"We have an emergency transmission from the shuttle

Reveille, inbound, carrying General Celchu. They're being pursued by enemy fighters and request immediate access to our hangar bay."

"Do they check out?"

"All codes and passwords are correct."

"Grant it."

"Thank you, Lieutenant." The screen cleared, and Tebut switched back to her data.

Incoming fire from the *Anakin Solo* increased as the Rakehells neared the capital ship. The *Anakin Solo*'s gunners were good—laser and ion shots missed the *Reveille* by mere hundreds of meters but came increasingly close to the pursuing X-wings.

Pair by pair, the Rakehells peeled away, zooming to comparatively safe distances. Now only two wing pairs were left: Wedge and Sanola, Tycho and Syal.

Another near hit rattled Tycho's cockpit. He ignored it, focusing on the shuttle before him and on the *Anakin Solo,* rapidly getting bigger.

The plan Luke, Wedge, and their committee of advisers had put together was deceptively simple, and based around the phrase *Let the enemy do the work.*

Was it going to be tough to smuggle a team of infiltrators aboard the *Anakin Solo,* especially because security had doubtless been tightened after the *Love Commander*'s recent mission? Of course. So the Jedi would just steal Tycho's shuttle, with its valid authorizations, and chase it to safety aboard the *Anakin Solo.* Equally tough to get saboteurs aboard Centerpoint Station? They'd dress up as Galactic Alliance Guard and board in the wake of the Alliance's genuine boarding action.

And destroying the station itself—Tycho shook his head. As half ambassador to, half captive of the Jedi, he hadn't been told what method they planned to use to eliminate Centerpoint, but he assumed it followed the same philosophy. Let the enemy do the work. Use the enemy's strength against them. Very Jedi-like.

Wedge's voice sounded in his ear: "Break." Wedge and Sanola banked abruptly to port, vanishing from Tycho's vision but not from his sensor board.

Syal stayed behind Tycho.

He thumbed his personal comlink, the one not slaved or monitored by the Rakehells. "*Now*, Antilles."

"Yes, sir." There was pain in Syal's voice. Then her X-wing, too, banked, following her father's outbound course . . . leaving Tycho alone, staring into the scores of turbolaser batteries and ion cannons of the *Anakin Solo*.

He closed in on the *Reveille*'s tail, discouraging the *Anakin Solo*'s gunners from firing on him. It only discouraged the ones who were sensible, or who actually cared if the *Reveille* made it. The hotshots continued firing, their blasts coming ever closer, until Tycho could barely see through his canopy because of the bright flashes just beyond. His cockpit rattled constantly from energy scraping at the periphery of his shields.

But ahead was the *Anakin Solo*'s underside, the belly doors that led to its hangar bay open just wide enough for a shuttle to enter.

Suddenly the incoming fire ceased. He was too close for the gunners to target.

Ahead, the *Reveille* rose toward the hangar entrance and reduced speed. Tycho decelerated as well, but not as much, and overshot the shuttle, his X-wing's underside missing the shuttle's top hull by three meters or less.

Tycho hit the *Anakin Solo*'s atmosphere containment shield fast enough that the sudden return of friction set off heat warning alarms. He could feel the impact decelerate him further, and the atmosphere catching his S-foils nearly spun him out of control. He wrestled with his control yoke and arced over hundreds of meters of bare hangar floor.

At the end of a ballistic arc, he fired his repulsors and came down to a jarring landing that would, under other circumstances, have been mortifying. He popped his canopy and rose, turning to see the *Reveille* rise into the hangar, then descend toward its own landing.

Tycho keyed his personal comlink. "This is General Celchu. Put me through to the bridge."

A high-pitched, musical Rodian's voice answered, "Welcome aboard, General—"

"Be advised, I am not aboard the *Reveille*." A half-squadron of Alliance security agents rushed toward his X-wing. He raised his hands and kept talking. "The *Reveille* is crewed by an intrusion team of Jedi and saboteurs. I'm in the snubfighter, transponder designation Rake Three."

"Um . . . I'll put you through to Lieutenant Tebut."

Tycho gritted his teeth at both the delay and the unpleasantness of the duty he was performing. But that was it— duty. Duty meant he had to alert his chain of command that insurgents, including his best friend's wife, were aboard. Duty meant he had to do his best to prevent the destruction of Centerpoint—destruction that he privately welcomed, as it would remove one of the galaxy's most destructive and ill-used forces from the playing field.

Abruptly smoke began pouring out of the *Reveille*'s thrusters. It was far too thick, too voluminous, to be the result of an engine fire. It flowed rapidly in all directions, engulfing the security team and mechanics moving toward the shuttle.

It reached the rear edge of the security team guarding Tycho before any of them noticed. Then one waved and shouted. All turned to look.

All but one. Overly tense, startled by the shout, the guard fired. The shot hit Tycho in the center of the chest, frying his comlink.

Tycho went down, dropping once more into his pilot's seat.

chapter thirty-three

"Blast it." Over Syal's helmet speakers, Wedge sounded aggrieved. "He's going to get himself . . ." But Syal saw, as Wedge must, Tycho's X-wing threading its way through the barrage of turbolaser fire with the ease of an airspeeder dodging repulsorlift lane markers. A moment later the X-wing and the shuttle were out of sight, swallowed by the Star Destroyer.

"All right. Rakehell Leader to squadron. Form up on me. It's time to annoy another shuttle. Four, you're at your own discretion."

"I'll stick with you, Leader. My Alliance duties are done for the moment."

"Good." Wedge banked toward the distant Centerpoint Station, and the Rakehells followed.

CORELLIA, CORONET,
COMMAND BUNKER,
PRIME MINISTER'S OFFICE

The hologram of General Phennir swam into resolution before Minister Teppler, who adjusted a knob on the desk beside him; Phennir was suddenly of normal height. "General, we don't have time to fence. Centerpoint Station is under attack. The enemy appear to be trying to board and assume control. Where are the nearest Confederation forces you could send to aid us?"

"We have a few ships near Corellian space, mostly doing reconnaissance. Nearest beyond that will be at Commenor." Phennir frowned. "But as I told . . . Prime Minister Koyan, Corellia can fend for herself while he remains obstinate."

Teppler nodded. "I suspect that Koyan will not remain . . . obstinate much longer. Have your forces standing by to jump into our system."

Phennir nodded. "Understood. We will stand by for confirmation that obstinacy is at an end."

Teppler hit a button, and Phennir disappeared. He hit another to transmit to the assistant in the next office. "Get me Koyan, immediately."

ABOARD THE ANAKIN SOLO

"Sir?" This time Nevil's voice carried some urgency. "We have unsubstantiated reports that there are Jedi and saboteurs aboard. We do know that there is a disturbance in the main hangar bay."

Caedus, eyes still closed, raised a hand to forestall further words. He needed to concentrate. His forces were taking the Corellian defenders to pieces, and he could afford no distractions.

On the other hand, he could not afford to ignore the possible presence of Jedi, either. He carefully withdrew from the active influence of his ship commanders, then opened himself up to a different flow of the Force.

Yes, there were Jedi aboard. Luke. Ben. Saba Sebatyne.

His mother.

His eyes snapped open and his connection to his commanders faltered, vanished. "Security!"

Tebut, answering from her station below the bridge walkway, port side, sounded composed as usual. "Sir."

"Confirm Jedi. They'll be coming here for me."

"Yes, sir. Initiate Plan Bastion?"

"That's correct." Caedus took a deep breath. His ships and boarding parties would have to succeed without benefit of his battle meditation. He needed all his focus now. His focus, and the forces he had assembled against this specific eventuality.

Even now, security teams would be assembling at strategic choke points between the hangar bay and the bridge. Space-tight blast doors would be closing and sealing at other critical points. Backup officers would be entering the auxiliary bridge, ready to assume control of the *Anakin Solo* if things became too dangerous or frantic for officers here to do their work.

And Caedus's additional defenders should be arriving—

The bridge doors opened and they marched in, a double column, eight YVH combat droids in all. Two turned to face the stern as the blast doors there shut. Two dropped to the officers' pits, one on either side, their mass causing deck plates to crumple as they hit. The other four marched forward, then, four meters short of Caedus's position, turned toward the stern. More would be stationing themselves elsewhere in the ship.

Caedus didn't think these measures would stop the Jedi. But they might whittle down the *numbers* of Jedi.

They *had* to. Jacen could defeat his mother or Ben without trouble; Saba, with difficulty. Saba *plus* Luke would be impossible odds. One of the Masters had to fall if Caedus was to survive this day.

* * *

Moving so fast that they blurred, the four Jedi, breather masks over their faces, emerged from the edges of the smoke cloud.

The security team at the entrance to the turbolift corridor opened fire—too late; the Jedi were already among them, striking with fists, feet, and, in Saba's case, tail. Six security personnel fell in an instant, their blaster rifles clattering to the deck plates, barely audible over the alarms howling through the hangar bay.

Iella and Han, R2-D2 between them, emerged from the smoke, removing their own masks.

Luke gave them a nod, clapping his hand on Ben's back. "All right, time to move out. Artoo?"

The astromech wheetled his confirmation, then turned and rolled along the hangar wall toward the nearest datajack.

Ben swung toward the doorway into the corridor and launched a kick. A ship's security officer, not visible before Ben began his maneuver, rounded the corner and ran right into it, catching Ben's heel across his jaw, and staggered back into his men. One was alert and nimble enough to jump clear, and aimed his rifle; Han shot him in the gut, the stun beam folding the man over and putting him down.

The other Jedi leapt forward, making quick work of the rest of the squad.

Han holstered his blaster and smiled at his wife. "Nice not to have to do all the work myself for once."

Rakehell Squadron approached the stern of a troop transport shuttle. It looked as though it had already sustained damage in this battle—the bow was blackened all along the starboard side, with a fracture pattern on the viewport suggesting that the transparisteel was on the verge of cracking, of venting its atmosphere into space—but Syal knew it was a sham. The battle damage was nothing but a paint job.

The shuttle accelerated away from the X-wings, toward the station and the battle raging all around it. "Just like before." Wedge's voice was matter-of-fact. "Shoot, but don't hit."

The X-wings closed in, firing.

The shuttle *Broadside* rocked as a Rakehell near hit grazed its shields. Seyah held on to the webbing across his chest with a white-knuckled grip of death.

"Hey, Doctor." The shout came from the cockpit, where, up until a moment before, the pilot had been singing something about a drunken Devaronian spacer and the females he loved in each port. "Which end, Talus or Tralus?"

"Weren't you awake at the briefing? Tralus end!" Seyah stared, aghast, at what little he could see of the pilot's back and neck through the cockpit door.

"Talus?"

"Tralus!"

"That's the end toward Talus, right?"

Seyah took as deep a breath as he could, intending to blow out eardrums with the volume of his reply, and then he caught sight of Kyp Durron. The Jedi Master was grinning, shaking his head. "He's messing with you, Doctor. Pilots do that."

Seyah let out his breath with a whoosh, and glared. "I'll shoot him after we dock."

ABOARD THE ANAKIN SOLO

Caedus kept track of the battle on one monitor and of the progress of the Jedi on another.

The battle was going well enough, even without his help.

Casualties were higher, of course, but they were mounting among the enemy as well, and reports had several shuttles' worth of Guardsmen and commandos now boarding Centerpoint through captured air locks . . . and meeting tough resistance from station defenders.

Luke, Ben, and Saba were occasionally visible on security holocams. They would appear at some hardpoint, spend a few moments to take out the defenders there, and cut their way through the next set of blast doors in turn.

Caedus hadn't spotted his mother, though he had felt her presence, as he had felt Luke, searching in the Force. Luke had found him easily enough—Caedus wasn't hiding. Leia's presence, however, had brushed over him and gone on. Caedus wondered if she might be wounded, which would account both for the fact that she wasn't keeping up with the others and that her ability to detect him seemed to be reduced.

On a new holocam view, a space-tight blast door began glowing. A lightsaber blade emerged through it and began cutting a slow circle into the hardened durasteel.

On the near side of the blast door, four YVH droids—the first the Jedi would encounter here—withdrew several paces and set up in a firing line.

CENTERPOINT STATION
FIRE-CONTROL STATION

Sadras Koyan used a handkerchief to mop away sweat running down his cheeks. He addressed the head technician on duty—the bearded man who called himself Vibro, the arrogant nek who had once lectured him on station programming and thumbs in the eye. "Any response from Admiral Niathal?"

Vibro looked back toward him and shook his head.

•

"How can I—" Koyan cut his words short before asking the technician a question the man could not answer. *How can I compel Niathal to surrender if she won't talk to me?* He couldn't just destroy an uninhabited world of the Coruscant system as a warning shot—Centerpoint's main weapon might fail again, be inoperable for several days. When he fired, it would be on the world of Coruscant herself. But if he fired without first talking to Niathal, while he might win the war, the Alliance forces here wouldn't know to give up, and they might take the station—and kill *him*—before they realized they were defeated. And then they wouldn't *be* defeated.

As if reading his mind, Vibro grinned. "I think you should just do it, sir."

"What?"

"Destroy Coruscant. Show them what this station is made of. We have reconnaissance ships in the Coruscant system, don't we? They'll get excellent recordings." The man raised his arms, forming a circle, then mimed a big sphere suddenly collapsing to nothingness.

Koyan stared at him, aghast . . . aghast at the notion of killing billions for the sake of seeing what it looked like, rather than for real political gain. "Get back to work."

"Yes, sir." The technician faced forward again, then stared down at his board. "Incoming message for you."

"Niathal?"

"Teppler."

"Put it on."

Vibro adjusted controls. A hologram of Teppler appeared in front of Koyan. He looked worried.

Teppler glanced around. "Sir, you need to confine the audio on this."

"Directional audio, right now!"

Vibro nodded, not looking back, then raised a hand, thumb up, to indicate it had been done.

Teppler's next words had the faint, tinny quality of an audio stream that was being confined to the hearing of one listener. "Sir, we've been analyzing the enemy attack. We don't think it's just directed at capturing the station. Where are you now?"

"Fire control, of course."

"We're seeing a pattern of enemy movement through the station's passageways. They're ignoring routes that would allow them to sabotage or capture the station more efficiently. They're headed straight for *you*."

Koyan felt a flutter in his chest. "For me?"

"I suspect that they have war trials in mind, sir."

"Uh . . ."

"I have a shuttle standing by. Air Lock Epsilon Thirty-four G, well away from the intruders. It'll get you back here, safe, in minutes."

Koyan shook his head. "I have to monitor the situation from here. Decide if and when to fire."

"Admiral Delpin and I can monitor from the command bunker until you arrive. Transmit us joint firing and command authorization and we'll stay on top of things until you arrive and resume command."

Options and consequences clicked through Koyan's mind. Actually, that was an ideal solution, especially if the need to fire came while he was in transit. Teppler and Delpin would press the button. History would credit Koyan for effective leadership if all went well, and would blame Teppler and Delpin if there was any significant outrage.

He nodded, decisive. "Done. Make sure that shuttle is there when I arrive."

"It will be." Teppler's image faded.

Koyan turned toward the tech. "Until you hear from me again, you're taking orders from the Minister of Information and Admiral Delpin."

Vibro looked back, hopeful. "But we *will* be able to fire?"

Koyan nodded, projecting confidence. "I'm sure of it."

"Rake Six to squad." Twool's voice was as musical as any Rodian's, but Syal could hear strain in his tone. "Incoming starfighters dead ahead, coming over the curve of the station."

Syal glanced between the heads-up display on the canopy before her and the more informative sensor monitor beneath. They didn't show the incoming units, but Twool's X-wing had better sensors.

"Squad, Leader. Loosen up, by flights." Wedge's starfighter suddenly rose, relative to the shuttle they pretended to pursue, and Sanola and Syal followed. Corran's two wing pairs rolled to starboard and descended; Jaina's drifted to port.

And then the enemy were there, cresting Centerpoint Station, lined up so their angle of approach was directly between the Rakehells and the star Corell. Syal gave the enemy points for effectiveness and tradition—though they weren't attacking in atmosphere, they were still diving on their foes out of the sun.

They were X-wings, and their sensor designation was Rogue.

Wedge and Sanola were juking and jinking just as Syal recognized the designation. She followed suit instantly, just in time for a long-distance salvo of quad-linked lasers to flash through the space her starfighter had just vacated.

The enemy, a full-strength squadron, broke into three flights of four, each turning toward a corresponding unit of

Rakehells. Laserfire crisscrossed between the two forces, passing harmlessly as the starfighters danced out from under one another's aim. Then the opposed squadrons came together, wing pairs whirling away as if, in their flight, they were trying to replicate the intricate spiral patterns of complex proteins.

Two X-wings came after Wedge; one each angled toward Sanola and Syal. Syal dropped back, putting all her X-wing's discretionary power toward her rear shields.

She hadn't yet fired, still didn't fire. She couldn't fire on an ally.

She saw her father riddle one enemy with laserfire, damaging the starfighter but not putting it out of combat. His other enemy chewed at his tail, just as Syal's opponent was hammering away at hers.

She couldn't fire on an ally.

Nor could she do anything less than give her whole effort for her father.

The two absolutes were mutually exclusive. They swelled up inside her like a bomb going off.

She heard the cry of outrage and confusion before she knew it was hers and acted before she fully understood what she'd decided. She decelerated hard—far more sharply than was normal for X-wing pilots, but she was used to being tossed around by the violent maneuvering thrusters of her Aleph—and threw discretionary power into her lasers. Her opponent overshot her, beginning a sudden roll to starboard, but her lasers caught him, stitching away at his thrusters—

He disappeared in a flash. Debris ignited as it hit and bounced off her forward shields. She turned after her father, tracking his second opponent, firing at him.

She didn't try to hit him, not at first. Her salvo missed deliberately to his starboard, causing him to flinch instinctively to port—away from Wedge. She restored her shields to normal fore-and-aft balance and followed, herding her target away from her father.

She saw a tiny flash to starboard—her father's target was still flying, but his R5 unit had just exploded under persistent laserfire.

Her own target wobbled, beginning a climb—then suddenly decelerated. Syal yanked her yoke back, assuming his climb was a fake, and hit her thrusters. Her enemy seemed to fly in reverse, passing beneath her, nose now pointed downward. Her reflex had been correct, and he was oriented away from her, unable to bring his lasers to bear. She continued her climb, looping around in a tight 360-degree curve, and saw her target doing the same, coming back toward her for a face-to-face pass.

chapter thirty-four

The *Broadside*'s captain shouted, "Clear away, clear away! We're coming in hot, half our systems shot out!"

The crew of the shuttle currently docked at the air lock dead ahead apparently believed him. Through the cockpit door and the viewport beyond, Seyah saw the shuttle thrust free of the air lock.

The *Broadside*'s pilot did bring her in hot, beginning deceleration at the last possible moment. The shuttle did not so much dock as slam into the air lock and stick. Seyah was thrown forward, held in his seat by the webbing, and a moment later fake GAG troopers all around him were unbuckling, rising, readying their rifles.

He managed to get unstrapped and rose, snapping his visor down. He fell into line behind Kyp.

The side door slid open. Troopers poured into the air lock. The door closed, and the air lock cycled.

The far door opened. Blasterfire poured in through it, hitting two fake troopers, throwing them back and down, smoke rising from their burns. Seyah slammed himself to one side, crushing someone against the air lock wall, and suddenly his entire universe was made up of black uniforms, blaster bolts, screams, and oaths.

A shove pushed him through the air lock doorway. He sprawled on the deck plates beyond and looked up. His comrades were advancing by twos along the passageway wall, sustaining ferocious fire, responding with ferocious fire. Someone stepped on his back in passing.

A hand on his arm yanked him to his feet and Kyp Durron hauled him against the wall to the left. The Jedi grinned at him, white teeth barely visible through his visor. "I suggest you fire your weapon. Don't hit us."

Seyah glared and did as he was told.

Firing was good. It was something to concentrate on. Something other than throwing up.

Ben finished cutting the circle out of the durasteel blast doors and, sweating, stepped back. The plug of metal stayed in place, its edges glowing. Ben reached toward it and, with an exertion in the Force, pulled it toward him. It swung open like a hatch, then clattered to the deck plates.

A small object, round and metallic, sailed through the hole. When it hit the deck, instead of rolling, it froze in place.

Ben began to turn, crouching to leap, knowing he might not get far enough in time. He'd seen high-yield grenades before, and many had a blast radius sufficient to reach him in midleap.

He was fast, but not as fast as Saba Sebatyne. The Jedi Master simply reached out and the plug Ben had cut from the blast doors flipped over, coming down atop the detonator. Saba's hand flattened as though she were holding something down.

As Ben leapt, the detonator blew, most of its force now directed downward, punching a charred hole in the deck.

The deck was still vibrating and Ben's ears had only just begun to ring when he came down again, a dozen meters away.

The three Jedi turned toward the hole in the blast doors.

Blasterfire began to pour through, its density and angle suggesting three or four different sources. These weren't the narrow bolts of hand weapons, either. To Ben they looked like they had to originate with heavy, squad-level weapons.

Luke, lightsaber lit and up, charged to the hole, batted away a flurry of bolts, and dived through. The barrage became less ferocious.

Saba was next, squeezing through the gap with surprising grace. The noise made by the barrage of fire continued—but no more bolts came through.

Ben gulped, then ran forward and somersaulted through the gap.

He landed on his feet on the far side, warmed but not singed as he passed by the superheated metal of the hole he'd cut.

Beyond, several meters away, four YVH combat droids poured fire at the two Jedi from the blaster cannons in their right arms.

Ben focused on the droids' weapon arms, not their appearance. Tall, gray-black with glowing red eyes, built to look like armored human skeletons, their appearance had been carefully designed by Lando Calrissian to anger Yuuzhan Vong warriors and frighten everyone else. Their deathlike ugliness *was* distracting. Ben elected not to be distracted.

Saba, her sword work brilliant, was parrying full-autofire streams of blaster cannon fire. Luke, more mobile, was avoiding the fire aimed at him—like a dancer, he kept ahead of every stream, but was making no headway, and in fact was being herded back toward the blast doors. A few moments more and the droids might pin him against the doors, denying him maneuverability, and finish him.

But one of Luke's opponents switched targets—it aimed at Ben, sending its stream of blasterfire at him.

He got his lightsaber up, caught the first several bolts—and was staggered, forced back by their power, which was so much greater than any bolt from a blaster pistol or rifle he had ever encountered. He might be able to intercept every bolt, but stopping them all would exhaust him within seconds.

Don't stop them. Just get rid of them. It was his own voice, not his father's, not his mother's, not Jacen's.

He angled his blade and let the incoming fire ricochet off it. The bolts angled up and to the right, pouring into the ceiling and walls—and hammering much less at his arms.

Good. Now he could survive the attack for perhaps half a minute. *Yippee.*

He shook his head. He could be someone his father and Saba needed to protect, in which case he might get them killed. He could take care of himself, just barely, as he was now, in which case he made a lie of his assertion that he would be useful on this mission.

Or he could contribute. But how?

Let the enemy do the work. The operation's catchphrase flashed into his mind and he knew what to do.

He reached out with his free hand, grabbing and wrenching through the Force at the blaster cannon arm of his enemy. Knowing how heavy the YVH droids were with their layers of laminanium armor, he exerted himself—and spun the droid around, aiming its cannon at one of Saba's foes.

The cannon fire took the YVH droid in the side, riddling

it. It jerked in place, the glows fading from its eyes, then went down sideways, cut in half at the pelvis.

Ben kept up the pressure on his opponent, maneuvering its blaster cannon to aim at Saba's second enemy. The droid ceased fire before hitting its other ally. A vent opened on its chest—

Luke gestured, and smoke emerged from the vent . . . but the minirocket designed to fire from that port did not. A moment later it exploded, blowing the top half of the droid off, leaving the legs still standing.

Now there were two, each facing a Master.

Saba pressed forward, able to push her way up the stream of fire from her droid. Her target raised its other arm, an arc of what looked like lightning flashing toward her, but she caught that on her lightsaber as well—then ducked and rolled under both energy attacks, rising just beyond the droid, her lightsaber blade extended backward and up—into the droid's neck and head. The laminanium armor there did not yield easily, but the precision of her blow and the greater-than-human strength she could put behind it drove the point of her blade through what would, in a human, have been thoracic vertebrae, severing its head.

Nor did she stop there, but spun, driving her point down from a high stance into the newly created gap in the droid's neck.

Luke, meanwhile, gestured. His enemy toppled backward and down, rolled by a telekinetic exertion in the Force to lie facedown. It struggled to rise, but Luke pounced, putting the point of his blade against its back. He drove it home, slow going through the armor, and twisted it around until the droid ceased struggling.

Saba pushed her dead foe over, sending it crashing to the deck plates, and eyed Ben. "Good tacticz," she said. "But warn this one next time. The stream of boltz crossed this one when the droid turned."

Ben winced. "Sorry, Master."

"Do not be sorry. Learn." She turned forward and resumed her advance toward the bridge.

Luke grinned at him. "What did she say first?"

"*Good tacticz.*"

"Don't lose track of the praise even in a stream of constructive criticism. Or vice versa." Luke turned to follow the Barabel Jedi.

His feet ringing on the metal deck plates, Koyan sprinted through what seemed like endless corridors of Centerpoint Station, racing toward an air lock that his datapad map said was less than a kilometer away.

Which, he realized as he was forced to jump over the bodies of a GAG trooper and two dead CorSec security guards, meant that the enemy was within a kilometer of the fire-control chamber. Things were bad.

Though the corridors were narrow and unfamiliar here, the glow rods dim and the metal beams and panels of every passageway resembling those of every other, he found his way to Air Lock Epsilon Thirty-four G. He entered it, noted that there was a shuttle interior visible through the opposite viewport, and cycled it.

Moments later he stepped through into safety. But here, in the main cabin of the troop carrier shuttle, there was no one to be seen. "Hello?"

"Yes?" The voice carried back from the cockpit.

"Get me to Coronet *immediately*."

The pilot rose from her seat and stepped out to stare at him. White-haired and almost as pale as an albino human, with a prominent supraorbital ridge and eyes as black as space, she was a Chev . . . and dressed in the blues of a Galactic Alliance officer.

Koyan grunted and reached for his hideaway blaster.

The Chev was faster. She drew from her holster and fired. Her bolt caught Koyan at the sternum, throwing him back and down.

All of a sudden, sounds reaching his ears were oddly watery and distant, and his vision began to close in. All he could see was the ceiling of the shuttle cabin. He couldn't do anything anyway—the pain in his chest was excruciating.

He heard the pilot speak. "Kork. Forgot to set it to stun." His vision closed in more. "*Chinnith* to *Anakin Solo*. You'll never guess who I just shot."

Koyan's vision failed entirely and he drifted through painless void.

Syal's starfighter rocked. Everything outside the canopy glowed in eye-hurting red, and then she was past her opponent, curving around for another exchange.

Wait—her enemy, designated ROGUE 6 on the sensor board, was breaking away. And Rakes One and Two were headed in toward her position.

She continued her maneuver anyway, clear sign to her opponent that she was still in the hunt, that she was not relying on her squadmates to end this fight for her. But her opponent chose not to face three Rakes all at once. It turned back toward a cluster of Rogues, doubtless to return when it had a wingmate.

Wedge and Sanola drew alongside her. Her father's voice came across her helmet speakers. "Four, this is Leader. Report status."

"I'm intact. Minor damage to my thrusters and starboard topside laser." As she continued, pain crept into her voice. "A minute ago, I just vaped a Rogue."

"I did, too. Rogue Leader. A Duros named Lensi. A good man. They've made kills against us: Six is dead, Eight is dead or extravehicular, and Two here is so shot up I'm sending her out of the combat zone."

Sanola's voice came across, a protest laced with pain. "I'm still fit to fly—"

"Then you're fit to obey orders. Get back to our staging vessel."

"Yes, sir." Rakehell Two banked away, and Syal could see a continuous stream of sparks emerging from her starfighter's underside.

"Four, you're my wing."

"Yes, D—sir."

chapter thirty-five

CENTERPOINT STATION

Seyah slid to a stop, looking intently at the surrounding walls and doorways, at the letters and numbers painted by Corellian mappers, at the symbols incised in the walls by ancient builders or scholars. He nodded. "Here."

Kyp, alert for more attackers, came alongside. "Here, what?"

"Here I implement my master plan to destroy Centerpoint Station."

Kyp scowled. "Excuse me, but that's what you said half a kilometer back. When you made me fight all those CorSec personnel in what you said was the spin thrust control chamber."

Seyah nodded. "That was my first master plan to destroy Centerpoint Station. This is my second. Cup your hands."

Kyp slung his GAG blaster rifle and did as requested. "Out of how many?"

"Well, I'm doing three. Plus, there are hopes that if the Alliance successfully takes charge of this facility, the remaining crew will initiate some sort of self-destruct plan installed since I left. I'm actually banking on that being the way to kill this place. Let the enemy do the work." He placed his left boot in Kyp's hands and stood. Kyp held him high enough that he could reach the passageway ceiling. Rapidly, with tools at his belt, he undid a ceiling panel, revealing wiring above. "At the spin thrust control chamber, I spliced in programming telling the station to count down a certain amount of time, then reverse the spin that gives the station its simulated gravity." From another pouch, he drew a datacard and began splicing it into the wires above.

"Which, if it did so rapidly enough, might tear the station to pieces."

"Very good. You're quite bright for a Jedi."

"How hard would you like to be dropped?"

"I'm just messing with you. Scientists do that. Problem is, the station's master programming, which is half ancient stuff, half cobbled together by the best minds Corellia could force to cooperate, and half evolved out of the interfaces between them—"

"That's three halves."

"I *knew* you were bright. Anyway, the programming resists change. It may reject my plan, for all that I worked years setting it up. Just as I worked for years on *this* one."

"What does this one do?"

"I'm tapping into data feeds that supply the auxiliary star map databases used by the targeting system. I'm redefining every star and planet in the galaxy—starting with the near ones, graduating out farther and farther—with the same set of coordinates."

"Which coordinates?"

"Here."

"Right here?"

"Technically, no. They're being defined to the exact center of Hollowtown—the geographic center of this station.

But the effect of the hyperspace beam is broad enough that, even as narrowly as I'm defining the coordinates, the station and everything for kilometers around it will be squashed down to a mass the size of a pan of ryshcate, but not as sweet."

"Uh-huh. And how much time does this approach give us?"

Finished with his splicing, Seyah reaffixed the ceiling panel. "As long as it takes from now until they fire the weapon. A day . . . two seconds. Unless, again, the master programming rejects the data I just submitted, in which case this master plan is also ineffectual. Down."

Kyp dropped him. Seyah landed awkwardly but came upright, unhurt.

"And what's master plan number three?"

"If we can get to the fire-control chamber, we can splice in programming that might cause Glowpoint, at the center of Hollowtown, to overload and explode."

"Radius of the explosion?"

Seyah shrugged. "A few thousand kilometers? I'm guessing here."

Kyp nodded, his expression fatalistic. "Facts, exact numbers, reassurance . . . a Jedi seeks not these things."

"Good! Let's get going."

ABOARD THE ANAKIN SOLO

Leia pulled herself along the rectangular horizontal shaft. It was a meter wide, somewhat less than that tall, and seemingly endless ahead and behind. Bunches of cables, bound to the surface above by flexible ties, were thick enough to graze her back, particularly when they reached a cross-passage, and some of them—unshielded by accident rather than design, she was sure—carried current. Han had howled when his back had brushed against one, half a kilometer back.

Han was behind her, Iella ahead, and Iella was moving comparatively easily, despite the fact that she was broader in most dimensions than Leia.

"You've done this before, Iella."

Leia sensed but could not see her companion nod. "A bunch of times. Since leaving CorSec, I think I've spent a quarter of my life in air passages, wiring accesses, and turbolift shafts." She stopped and twisted so Leia could see her face—dusty, with rivulets of sweat making interesting patterns through the dust, as Leia knew she herself must look. "Location check, please."

Leia stopped crawling and closed her eyes. Luke, back on Endor, had communicated to her the precise presence in the Force she was to look for, and she had found it soon after boarding the *Anakin Solo*. On that first contact, she had brushed across Jacen, too, but had subsequently managed to avoid touching him through the Force.

She couldn't bear to touch her own son.

She shook the thought away. It was a distraction she didn't need right now.

There was Allana, the Chume'da, a bright, pure presence. The girl did not seem to have moved since Leia first detected her. Leia lifted an arm, pointing ahead, up, to the left.

"What's the holdup?" Han, not surprisingly, sounded impatient.

"Just a pause while I make sure we're on the right course, Han," Iella said. "Thanks, Leia." When Leia opened her eyes, Iella was consulting her datapad. "Getting a diagram update from Artoo. Overlaying the original design specs for this class of ship with the plans used by the onboard maintenance division, I'm finding several spots that are just blanks. Not officially there. One is exactly where Master Skywalker says the torture chamber was."

"Is one of them in the direction Leia was pointing?" Han's voice, floating up from past Leia's feet, suggested that he was doing his best to pretend he wasn't irritated . . . and that his best wasn't enough.

Iella nodded.

Han added some mock sweetness to his tone. "I've got a suggestion. Let's go that way."

Iella gave Leia a sympathetic look. "You could have found a *nice* Corellian to marry. *I* did."

"*I'm* nice. I'm just . . . decisive."

Caedus watched on his monitor as Luke, Saba, and Ben approached the bridge doors from the corridor beyond. There were a few guards on duty, not that it mattered. They fired, the Jedi rushed, fists and lightsabers swung, the guards went down.

This was not good. Both Masters remained intact.

All was not lost, though. Caedus had resources still available to him. He was fresh. He had eight YVH droids.

In the monitor view, the Jedi approached the blast doors. Ben began to drive his lightsaber point into the metal.

Caedus made an impatient gesture. "Open."

The blast doors slid aside. The Jedi stood there in triangular battle array, Luke and Saba now in front, Ben behind. Caedus and his YVH droids stared back at them. The bridge officers pretended to ignore the situation; they kept their eyes on their screens, conducting the space battle that raged around Centerpoint Station.

Caedus offered a smile that in no way reflected how he felt. "Uncle Luke. Ben. Master Sabatyne. Care for some caf?"

The Jedi, lightsabers ready, moved in, paying close attention to the two YVH droids flanking them.

Luke shook his head. "Care to surrender?"

"If I did, I'd never be able to have more fun with Ben, like the last time he was here." Caedus fired the taunt like a blaster bolt—a pair of them, one at Luke, one at Ben.

And yet, in the Force, he felt not one flicker of anger from either of them. That was . . . surprising. Distressing. Time away from him appeared to have undone all the good he'd done Ben during their last session.

Caedus sighed. "All right. Kill."

The combat droids snapped into motion, all eight firing simultaneously, their streams of blasterfire converging on the Jedi.

CORELLIA, CORONET, COMMAND BUNKER

Teppler walked into the situation room. There, over a broad triangular table, floated a holographic display of the battle being waged insystem. At the center of the display was the image of Centerpoint Station, surrounded by a large number of red Alliance ships, a shrinking number of Corellian ships.

Admiral Delpin, standing at one point of the table, surrounded by advisers, caught sight of him. "Where have you been?"

"Dealing with allies. Demands of state, you know." He worked his way through the crowd to her side. "We have the authority to fire the station weapon and full control over all insystem resources until Koyan gets here."

"Where is he?"

"I'm not sure. He said he was looking for a fast transport home . . . But I think he may have missed his shuttle."

"And reinforcements?"

"General Phennir is sending them now."

He wasn't quite through saying those words when the hologram updated. Suddenly there were many more green ship images than there had been a moment before. Teppler nodded toward the display. "Friends from Commenor."

The admiral heaved a sigh of relief. "If we can win this one straight up, we may not have to fire the weapon. Not yet, anyway."

"Agreed."

CENTERPOINT STATION, FIRE-CONTROL CHAMBER

The head technician sat, restless, and listened to the intensity of the firefight outside the open chamber door. The noise grew and grew.

It had started with the shouts of CorSec troopers retreating to this location and setting up a choke point in the corridor outside. More had joined them.

The enemy had arrived, from somewhere off to the left. Now the two forces were exchanging fire. Blaster bolts kept flashing by outside. Sometimes there were screams. It was all very annoying.

And the technician had a secret. Several, really. One was that his real name was Rikel, and that he despised it; his nickname, Vibro, suited him far better, especially after his eighth cup of caf of the day. Another was that he had been married, in secret, concealing the news from his family and hers because they didn't approve. Still another was that he had been widowed in secret, his wife picked up on Coruscant on a security sweep early in the war, never to be seen again . . . until the day her body was positively identified.

Hatred was his biggest secret, not the flippant disregard for pain or death with which he concealed it. Hatred for the Alliance. Hatred for the Coruscanti.

And his newest secret was only a few minutes old. He hadn't been able to listen in on the holocomm exchange between Sadras Koyan and Denjax Teppler, but he had been able to use security cams to follow Koyan's rapid flight from this chamber.

Right up to the point that the Alliance shuttle carried Koyan away.

Had Koyan defected or just been monumentally unlucky or stupid? It didn't matter. He was gone. Leaving Vibro in charge of the weapon.

And he could have told Vibro anything before leaving. Anything. Like . . . *Destroy the people who killed your wife. Go ahead, it'll make you feel better.* Vibro could almost hear the words, spoken in Koyan's flat, none-too-intelligent tones.

Idly, he punched up the astronomical coordinates for the world of Coruscant. Idly, he transferred them over to the targeting input of the station's primary weapons system.

A female technician at the next station looked over at him. "Vibro. What are you doing?"

"Obeying orders. From the big guy. Getting things set up for him to push the big button. He'll be back in a minute."

Satisfied that all proprieties were being observed, she nodded and returned her attention to her work.

Now to activate the power source . . .

From the relative cover of a doorway into a darkened office, Kyp and Seyah looked down the corridor toward the fire-control chamber.

Closest to them, thirty meters up, were rows of GAG troopers and Alliance commandos, many of them protected by riot shields, more of them firing blaster rifles over and around the shields, concentrating fire on a distant enemy.

The enemy: lines of CorSec troopers, and two hovering combat droids, their metal skins a bronze color. Seyah jerked a thumb toward them. "A lingering part of Thrackan Sal-Solo's legacy. Not quite a match for the Why-Vee-Aitches, but still formidable. Or so I'm told."

The air began to vibrate, accompanied by a hum, rising and falling, from the direction of the distant fire-control chamber. Seyah frowned, listening.

Kyp looked over the two forces. "This is going to be tricky. To get us there, I have to rush the CorSec troops. I'll have to use my lightsaber. So while I'm dealing with the floating droids, the CorSec troops will be firing at me. When they see I'm a Jedi, the Alliance troops will fire at me. It's going to take awhile to get through them all."

Seyah gave him a dubious look. "How long?"

"Three minutes or so. Why?"

"I'm not sure we have that long."

"Why not?"

"That sound you hear is them powering up the primary weapon."

"Oh." Kyp considered. "How good are the odds that your sabotage is going to destroy this place?"

"Well, clearly, the rotation-for-gravity thing didn't work. That was a programming change, which we know the main program resists. I know far more about the weapon targeting system. I *am* a genius. With the last master plan, I just substituted data, not programming. And although my ex-wives will argue the point, I have to be right sometime. Call it good odds."

"New plan."

"Let's hear it."

"We abandon your third master plan and get out of here."

Seyah nodded. "I like it."

He led the way, sprinting back the way they'd come, and raised his comlink. "Seyah to *Broadside*. We're headed your way. The remainder of the mission is scrubbed. Prepare for immediate liftoff."

chapter thirty-six

ABOARD THE **ANAKIN SOLO**

Leia finished cutting a hole in the metal surface overhead and pushed the resulting plate out of the way, giving it a little boost in the Force so that its glowing edges would not contact her skin. Cool air flowed across her.

No alarms sounded, no blaster shots rained down on her—so far, so good. She stood, finding herself in a small workshop chamber, and leapt up to the floor, taking a look around.

Tables, electronic parts, computer gear, one door out, no other occupants. She gave a quick look to the items on the table. Complex but rugged wiring and circuitry, hardy cylinders of durasteel, a sophisticated and high-yield battery, familiar-looking buttons and brackets—someone was building a lightsaber. It was almost done; it needed only to have a shell chosen and decorated, a gem installed.

It had to be Jacen. Perhaps he was building a weapon for Ben, under the assumption that he would be able to return Ben to his service.

Iella clambered to her feet beside Leia. "How far?"

Absently, Leia pointed toward the side wall. "Just on the other side. We're there."

"I'll activate the comm frequency jammer." Iella set her backpack down on the lightsaber assembly table and opened it.

Han clambered out of the hole in the floor. "Before you activate that . . ." He pulled out his own comlink and spoke into it. "Artoo, extract."

Iella winced and threw a switch on the side of the box within her backpack. "That might have alerted sensors in this area."

Han shrugged. "We can't leave Artoo where he is, to be picked up and wiped by the Alliance."

The wall Leia had gestured toward crashed inward. A YVH combat droid battered its way into the workroom, raising its arm toward Han, and fired.

Luke and Saba flanked Ben, their lightsabers up, and caught the barrages of blaster damage being hurled their way. Caedus waited, patient. They couldn't sustain that amount of fire for very long. Either they'd die, or they'd figure out how to put the combat droids down fast. As blaster bolts began ricocheting all over the bridge, the *Anakin Solo*'s officers dived for cover behind their stations. Caedus merely ignited his lightsaber, ready to fend off any ricochets coming his way.

Curiously, Ben returned his own lightsaber to his belt. The boy gestured out in either direction. Something flew from each hand, down to the YVH droids in the officers' pits, adhering to their chests.

Caedus sighed. Of course. The Jedi had plundered grenades from the droids they'd defeated.

As the thought occurred to him, the detonators went off. The combat droids disappeared—not vaporized, but hurled into and through the bulkhead armor behind them. The shock wave hammered everything at the stern end of the bridge, shredding officers' stations, setting men and women on fire. Screams and alarms filled the air.

Ben repeated the move, planting a grenade on the chests of the two YVH droids flanking the Jedi. Caedus blinked. It seemed a suicide move. The explosions would consume the Jedi as well as the droids. But Luke and Saba lashed out, each kicking a different direction, and the two droids, still firing, toppled over backward into the pits where their comrades had been.

In the moment he had before those detonators went off, Caedus acted to whittle down the enemy numbers as they had been whittling down his. He gestured, exerting himself telekinetically, and Saba Sebatyne slipped laterally into the starboard pit, almost atop the doomed droid there.

Her leap toward safety was almost instantaneous, but almost wasn't good enough. The detonators went off. The blast caught Sebatyne when she was only a meter or two in the air. It propelled her like an old-fashioned munition to the port-side wall, slamming her into that surface five meters above the floor, and she slid, flaming, down into the pit.

Luke and Ben looked Caedus's way. He smiled at them and shrugged. "One down."

The four droids nearest him kept firing.

As the wall crumpled, Han leapt backward, toward the door, hoping it was automated and would open for him. Leia drew and lit her lightsaber. Iella dived for the hole in the floor.

The exchange took place in what seemed like slow motion. Han's shoulders did not hit the door—he staggered back into the corridor. Leia's blade came up and deflected the first three or five thousand bolts from the droid's right arm.

Someone shot the droid three, four, five times in the chest—Han was surprised to see the blaster in his own hand, firing as fast as his finger could pull the trigger, his brain not figuring into the equation—and then his shoulderblades hit the passageway wall behind him, throwing his aim off.

Aim off. He couldn't hurt this thing by shooting it where a human would be hurt. But at a distance of three meters, he could hit anything he could see, including any symbol on a sabacc card.

He traversed his fire, letting muscle memory and reflex do the work. His blaster shots stitched a line acoss the droid's chest, down its arm, to the blaster embedded in its arm—

To the barrel—

Han's shot entered the barrel aperture and the lower portion of the right arm exploded. The laminanium armor of the forearm mostly contained the detonation. Han saw the composite skin split in places, the rents filling with fire, and felt a tear along his cheek as something grazed him.

The droid wasn't down, though. It raised its other arm—

Relieved of the burden of deflecting blaster shots, Leia stepped in and brought her lightsaber blade down on the arm, just above the elbow, where the armatures were thinnest. Her blow didn't cut through the arm, not immediately, but the force of her blow was enough to knock it sideways, and the arc of electricity emerging from it missed her by centimeters, plowing into the passageway wall above Han's head.

Then the left arm did come off at the elbow.

Han continued firing, spraying bolts at the droid's photoreceptors. The droid swung the remains of its right arm at Leia, a potentially deadly attack—it was strong enough to crush her skull, break her back. But she bent at the waist, allowing the blow to sweep harmlessly over her, and straightened, driving her blade up under the droid's riblike chest armor.

The attack sheared through systems, causing sparks to emerge at both the top and bottom of the ribs, and her blade point entered the skull from below. The droid jittered in place for a moment, raised its arm for a second blow— and collapsed. Rather than have her lightsaber be yanked down by its weight, Leia deactivated the weapon, then re-activated it when the droid was clear.

Iella, pale, emerged partway from their access hole. "*That* was interesting."

Han nodded. "Want to do it again?"

"Noooooo."

They found Allana two compartments down, a frightened little girl in a party frock, hiding in the closet of an armory. When Leia opened the closet door she lunged at them, an injector pen in her hand, but Leia caught her wrist, stopping the blow, and as quickly released the girl.

Such a pretty girl. And so familiar-looking.

Leia raised her hand, palm-out, a gesture of peace to forestall another attack. "I bring a message from your mother."

Suspicious, scowling, Allana backed away from her. "Tell me."

"I'll show you instead." She reached into her robe pouch and brought out a device, a hand-sized holoprojector. She set it on a table and activated it.

A hologram of Tenel Ka, doll-sized, swam into resolution. Tenel Ka smiled, her expression hopeful, and spoke. "Allana, time is short. First: bantha excess glow rod."

Allana lowered her injector pen and smiled. Her gaze was fixed on the image of her mother, and her thoughts were so transparent that Leia could hear them as speech carried through the Force: *The words. The real words.*

"These people are going to bring you to me. Go with them, and trust them as you do me. And know that I love you, and I've missed you more than I can say." Tenel Ka raised a finger to her lips and blew a kiss, then faded away.

Allana looked up at her rescuers. "We can go now?"

Leia nodded. "We can go right now."

"Can I leave a note for, for Jacen?"

"I'm afraid not, sweetie. You can comm him once we get to Hapes. You don't have time to pack."

"That's all right. Everything that's mine is still at home."

Impossibly, Saba stood, even got her lightsaber up to deflect the next wave of blaster bolts aimed at her. Smoke rose from her back and legs, and stretches of her skin were charred, bleeding . . . but she was upright, standing on shaky legs.

Luke didn't turn toward Ben, but pitched his voice to make it easier for the boy to hear. "Get her out of here."

"Remember why I'm here, Grand Master."

Vexed, Luke tightened his jaw and nodded. He raised his voice. "Master Sebatyne: extract."

"This one iz still—"

"Leaving." Luke's tone was unyielding. "Remember what we're here for."

Beyond Jacen, the metal shutters were coming down across the viewports. It wasn't surprisng; the explosions had to have weakened the viewport housings, and the ship's diagnostics were sealing everything up before the atmosphere could explosively escape. Besides, all of a sudden there were more ships to see out there, and some of them were approaching the *Anakin Solo,* laser batteries flashing.

Luke gestured toward Jacen. Jacen raised his lightsaber and his left hand, ready to ward off any attack, but Luke's gesture was a diversion. His exertion in the Force picked up one of the YVH droids and hurtled it backward, against the faltering viewport.

The transparisteel buckled and the droid was lost to space. Air, rushing past the Jedi, tugged them forward, and Jacen staggered back toward the viewports, but then the shutters came down, sealing the bridge.

Meanwhile Luke felt a pained exertion in the Force as Saba leapt up to the walkway and walked—limped—off the bridge.

Three YVH droids were left. And Jacen. Against Luke and Ben. Jacen was Luke's match, which meant Ben had to cope with three combat droids. The odds weren't good.

Then the odds changed.

As he batted blasterfire with his lightsaber, Luke felt a surge of emotion in the Force: innocent joy, a little girl's delight at going home.

Jacen visibly paled. "Allana . . ." Suddenly he charged, crossing his own combat droids' streams of blasterfire, forcing them to cease fire for brief moments.

He came at Luke but leapt laterally, flying across empty air to one of the doorways leading aft, utterly ignoring the Jedi.

Luke snapped a command to his son: "Extract! Warn Leia, Jacen's coming!" He got his lightsaber up and deflected new streams of blasterfire, then began backing toward the bridge's blast doors, toward his son.

Keeping his father and the nearly impenetrable blaster shield Luke represented between himself and the YVH

combat droids, Ben backflipped through the blast doors
and darted to the right, getting behind the cover the door
frame represented. He slammed a palm across the SHUT
button and thumbed his comlink. "Aunt Leia, extract!
Jacen's coming."

Her voice came back clear and calm: "Already extract-
ing."

"Go *fast*." Ben glanced over his shoulder and saw that
the corridor was clear of personnel—the only living thing
to be seen was Saba, limping along in the distance. Blaster
bolts from the combat droids, bolts Luke did not even
bother to deflect, poured out into the corridor like rain
blown sideways, but none ventured near Saba.

Luke backed through the blast doors when there was
just enough of a gap to accommodate him. They slammed
shut, cutting off the torrent of blasterfire.

Ben drove his lightsaber into the control panel and kept
shoving, burning a hole clear through to the corresponding
panel on the far side.

Luke glanced over at him. "Time to go."

chapter thirty-seven

Jacen ran through the doors leading to the Command Salon, flashed past nervous, startled officers there, and hurtled to the doors leading into his private office.

His office, with its secret access to the secret quarters—*Allana.*

In his office, he slammed open the panel leading to his hidden corridor and slid to a halt in the midst of debris and the wreckage that had once been YVH-908.

Mechanically, he raised his comlink to his lips. "Bridge, report on all vehicles proximate to the *Anakin Solo.*"

There was no answer but the hiss of static.

He could feel Allana astern, moving away from him, but precise distances and speeds were impossible for him to measure. There was a hole in the floor of his little workshop—that had to be the means by which Allana's kidnappers had entered. But had they left by the same way, or out his office door? He had to follow, but the wrong choice could cost him precious seconds.

Suddenly gasping for air, he raced back toward his office, toward the access to the corridor there.

ABOARD THE MILLENNIUM FALCON

Jag saw the button light up on the comm board. Instantly he banked the *Falcon* toward the *Anakin Solo,* which was at the heart of renewed conflict, its screen of capital ships now beset by Commenori frigates and cruisers.

In the seat behind him, C-3PO made sliding noises as his restraints failed to keep him in place. "I say, sir, I might suggest a more gradual approach."

Jag nodded. "Good idea. I'll pass it along to Han."

"Why, thank you, sir. Though he's always been reluctant to implement my suggestions."

Kyle Katarn unstrapped himself from the copilot's seat. Not inconvenienced by the *Falcon*'s side-to-side maneuvers, he stood easily. "I'll be ready at the docking ring."

Jag nodded absently. "Watch out for lightsabers."

"Watch out for durasteel rails." Kyle left.

Ignoring further protests from the protocol droid, Jag angled in toward the Star Destroyer, picking a route that would bring him near the smallest number of starfighter conflicts or capital ship laser battery exchanges. He knew his target zone by diagram and by sight—an air lock on the forward port side, not far from Jacen Solo's private hangar.

Now all he had to do was navigate through a bewildering field of turbolaser and ion cannon beams to get there alive.

Syal heard the two-tone musical signal over her comm board, followed by her father's words: "Extraction has begun. All free Rakehells, maneuver to the *Anakin Solo*'s port side, amidships to bow, and draw off its fire."

Most of the Rakehells were free. When the Commenori task force had jumped into the conflict, the Rogues and other Alliance starfighter units had largely lost interest in the mystery squadron that seemed to want to fight but had no other evident objective; they broke off and attacked the Commenori capital ships, leaving the Rakehells unencumbered.

Wedge led the remaining starfighters of his squadron into the proximity of the *Anakin Solo*, skirting just within its firing range, drawing turbolaser fire, responding with quad-linked lasers and the occasional proton torpedo aimed at weapons batteries. Mostly they distracted the Star Destroyer's gunners and worked to keep themselves alive.

In the midst of all this, the *Millennium Falcon* flashed by, weaving through a reduced screen of incoming fire, and managed to arrive just above the Destroyer's hull, too close for its guns to target.

"That boy can fly," Syal admitted.

There was a trace of pride in Wedge's reply. "Yes, he can. He should have kept his mother's family name. It'd be good to have another Jagged Antilles in the galaxy."

"Stop being smug, Leader."

"Yes, Four."

Allana in Leia's arms, the rescue party skidded around a corner. Han slowed, leaning back around the corner, firing with his blaster pistol, keeping the pursuers pinned down.

Iella reached the air lock hatch first—or would have, if R2-D2 hadn't already been there. As she approached, the droid tweetled at her and the hatch slid open.

Beyond, the far hatch opened simultaneously, revealing the starboard docking ring of the *Falcon*, Master Katarn waiting there. Iella didn't even have to slow her running pace.

Leia swept aboard. "Master Katarn. Good to see you."

He bowed. "Two-Injured-Men-and-a-Droid Shuttle Service, as requested."

The sound of Han's blasterfire picked up; then his weapon fell silent. Leia's heart seemed to skip a beat until she realized there were more distant weapon sounds now—lightsabers.

R2-D2 rolled aboard, offering Kyle a musical note of greeting, and Han was mere steps behind. "Luke, Ben, and Saba are coming fast."

Leia nodded and carried Allana into the crew quarters, setting her down on one of the bunks. "You need to strap in, sweetie. We may need to do some violent maneuvers."

Allana's bright eyes made a plea of her next question: "Can I be in the cockpit instead?"

"Not this time. But soon."

With the Force lending him speed, Caedus hurtled down the side passage, his leaps carrying him over the bodies—some injured and moaning, some dead—of ship's security personnel and, here and there, their severed arms.

Far ahead, just past a group of at least a dozen injured personnel, he saw Luke turn rightward at a cross-corridor. But by the time Caedus rounded that corridor, the air lock hatch at the far end was closed and he could see a gray-white hull speeding by.

Gasping for breath, he raised his comlink. "This is Solo. Do not fire on the *Millennium Falcon*. Anyone who fires on her *dies*. Use tractor beams only."

He heard, but paid no attention to, the acknowledgment from the bridge. He took no mind of the confusion in the officer's voice as the man reported progress with the tractor beams—which turned into no progress, as the weapons officers' switchover to the tractor system gave the *Falcon* precious moments in which to pull away from the *Anakin Solo*. *Yes, I once fired on the* Falcon *from this very ship. But my daughter was not aboard her then.* He could feel her, Allana's shining presence, growing ever more distant, and each moment of separation felt like another needle being hammered into his heart.

Finally it came, the report he dreaded, the one he could not forestall no matter how strongly, lovingly, hopelessly he reached out to his daughter through the Force. "Sir, I'm sorry to report that the *Millennium Falcon* has entered hyperspace."

His legs failed him and he sank to the deck plates, kneeling in his pain and sudden grief.

CENTERPOINT STATION, FIRE-CONTROL CHAMBER

Vibro looked over the controls before him. Everything was ready. All it took was a finger on the button.

The shouts from outside were more annoying than ever. "We've got relief coming!" "They're making another push. Hold tight, hold tight!" And as ever, there were screams, more numerous now, getting closer.

The Corellians were losing. This chamber would fall to the Coruscanti. The station would fall to them.

But it would be too late. They wouldn't be able to call themselves Coruscanti anymore.

He hissed to get the other technician's attention. She was looking behind them, toward the door, something like fear on her face, but now she glanced Vibro's way.

He smiled at her. "Hey. Watch this."

He hit the button.

The crew and passengers of the *Millennium Falcon,* outbound, with their escort of Rakehell X-wings, felt something hammer the freighter. It was like a laser shot getting through the shields, but no ship was pursuing them, and the *Falcon*'s rear surfaces lit up with light from behind. Proximity alarms in the cockpit howled.

Han, in the copilot's seat, his expression suggesting he would never again in his life allow a situation in which he sat there, flicked the cockpit monitor over to show the rear holocam view.

Centerpoint Station was a glowing ball, a perfect sphere of light perhaps five hundred kilometers in diameter. As Han watched, the sphere contracted almost instantly.

Leaving nothing behind in the volume it had occupied.

Everything that had been there was gone—Corellian ships, Alliance ships, Commenori ships . . . and Centerpoint Station itself.

The *Anakin Solo,* safely beyond the boundary of that momentary sphere, seemed unharmed, as did every ship and starfighter in its vicinity.

Han gulped. "Was that . . . was that . . ."

Kyle, in the rear seat beside C-3PO, offered a pained grunt. "That was a massive loss of life. A cessation in the Force. Whatever was there no longer exists."

"Jaina? Kyp?"

Jag checked his sensor board. "Jaina's on our flank. And the *Broadside* was even farther away than we were. Their transceiver reports them intact."

Han sagged in relief. Maybe it was better that he *didn't* fly right now.

ABOARD THE **ANAKIN SOLO**

Caedus walked onto the bridge.

His cloak should have been swirling around him. It wasn't. Why? Oh, yes. He'd given it away. It had betrayed him.

The bridge had changed. There was extensive damage.

There were bodies everywhere, and medics working on them, carrying them out.

He nodded. He remembered that, too. There had been a fight.

The officers began shooting questions at him the moment he appeared. "Orders, sir." "Sir, the Confederation forces outnumber us. They're stronger than our forces." "Sir, Admiral Niathal is standing by on holocomm. She wants to talk to you at once."

Allana.

He marched forward to his viewports but couldn't see through them. While he stood there wondering at their sudden opacity, he began answering questions. "Recall our squadrons. Set course for home. We're leaving. Tell Admiral Niathal there's been a problem."

Minutes passed. A sound he had been hearing—distant booms that made the bridge shake—gradually became less frequent, finally dying out altogether.

Yet still he could not see the stars, and Allana did not return.

But a question formed in his mind, a question of his own. He turned to face what remained of his bridge crew. "How did they come aboard my ship? Luke Skywalker and those with him?"

The officers looked among themselves, then Lieutenant Tebut, at the security station, stood. The right sleeve of her tunic was scorched and she had a cut across her neck, not deep enough to be dangerous. "Sir, we were approached by General Celchu's shuttle, which was being fired upon by several X-wings. We allowed the shuttle to land. As it turned out, this was a ruse. The Jedi were aboard the shuttle, and General Celchu was in one of the X-wings, trying to destroy the shuttle. General Celchu is in the medical ward, recovering from a stun bolt."

Caedus regarded her. "Who allowed the shuttle to land?"

"I did, sir. It broadcast all correct identification and passwords."

"It was full of assassins, saboteurs, and criminals, and yet you allowed it to land."

She fidgeted under his gaze. "Yes, sir. I was following security protocols."

"Do the protocols say for you to allow assassins, saboteurs, and criminals aboard?"

"No, sir."

"Then you were not following security protocols. You did not follow security protocols, and because of it many people have died, and I could not coordinate our attack on Centerpoint Station, and this mission is a failure. Correct?"

Her next words were quiet and halting, as though she were giving directions in a language she did not speak very well. "Sir, anyone in my position would have done exactly the same. This is what the protocols are for. To define responses and procedures. I believe my actions were correct, under the known circumstances—"

Caedus gestured, raising a hand, and under his exertion of power Tebut floated up in the air, putting her slightly above his level. Her eyes grew wide. "Sir . . ."

Caedus closed his hand into a fist. Now no more words came from her, just pained gasps. She grasped with increasing desperation at a choking hand that just was not there.

He continued, his voice still level, controlled. "Lieutenant, we can't have that. Gross incompetence. Gross insubordination. The deliberate contravention of orders and top-level plans. Nor can we let it go unpunished. Can we?"

Captain Nevil approached. "Sir, this is not the time or the way—"

Not looking at the Quarren, Caedus gestured with his free hand and Nevil was suddenly flying backward, skidding across the raised walkway, fetching up against the blast doors through which the Skywalkers had so recently left.

Amazingly, Tebut was still trying to talk. "Sir . . . can't . . . loyal . . ."

"*Loyal?*" The word exploded out of Caedus, raising his voice a screechy octave. "How dare you use that word? You may not say that word ever again. Loyal officers do not betray their command, their comrades, their oaths!" His outrage turned everything he saw a reddish hue, even Tebut's face.

And there was only one way to restore everything to its proper color. He tightened his grip.

The sound of Tebut's neck breaking was startlingly loud over the hum of the bridge's monitors and computer gear.

Caedus dashed his hand down. Tebut's body slammed to the deck plates below her. More bones snapped. She lay behind her security station, bent at an odd sideways angle at the waist, her eyes fixed open, staring at the ceiling.

Caedus breathed out all his rage. Colors returned to vibrant normalcy.

He turned and walked toward the stern. As he passed Nevil, still lying where Caedus had thrown him, he said, "I'll be in my quarters."

Nevil stared at him with—what? Fear? Anger? Obsequious acceptance? Caedus couldn't tell. The fishy folk were so hard to read, Mon Cals and Quarren alike. He didn't like them anymore.

chapter thirty-eight

REFUELING STATION, GYNDINE SYSTEM

The Rakehells, the *Broadside*, and the *Millennium Falcon* put in at an abandoned repair and refueling satellite. It orbited the world of Gyndine, burned and ruined by the Yuuzhan Vong during the war named for them. Owned by Tendrando—the corporation headed by Lando Calrissian and his wife, Tendra Risant—it had been decommissioned and shut down, but Han and Leia still carried the codes that would open its air locks, reactivate its life-support systems.

There they swapped personnel around, putting everyone bound for Endor on the *Broadside*, giving the X-wing pilots a brief respite.

In the *Millennium Falcon*'s main hold, which had mostly served as a crew lounge for most of the years Han had owned the freighter, Leia and Han sat Allana down on a sofa and bent to face her more at eye level.

"We're going to take you back to Hapes now," Leia said. Seeing Allana up close for so long, it was hard for her to concentrate. The little girl was so familiar, staring up at her with eyes Leia knew so well.

The realization of where she knew Allana from was like rising from a pool after too long underwater. Suddenly Leia could breathe again, could think again. Allana had Tenel Ka's coloration—the fair skin, red hair, gray eyes—but her face, her expressions, her lively intelligence, were so like *his* when he was a child, before Yuuzhan Vong and voxyn and Vergere and who-knows-what twisted all the happiness out of his life. Leia found she could not speak.

But Allana wiggled, happy. "You're Leia Organa Solo."

Leia nodded, mute.

"You're Jacen's mommy."

Leia nodded again.

"He's my daddy."

Finally Leia found her voice again. "I know," she whispered.

She knelt and pulled Allana to her in an embrace. She stood with the little girl in her arms. "I'm your grandmother."

She turned to face Han. His face was frozen in surprise.

Leia saw his mouth work as he tried to find the perfect quip for the situation. But there was none. His expression softened, and he merely patted the little girl's arm, a clumsy gesture of affection. "Hi, sweetie. I'm your grandfather."

SANCTUARY MOON OF ENDOR, DEATH STAR WRECKAGE

Jaina found Jag lying on a blanket near the edge of the wreckage shadow, watching the huge reddish ball of Endor as it began to sink below the horizon of trees. She sat beside him, allowing herself a moment to appreciate the beauty of the view.

"I have to go," she said.

"Now?"

"No, but soon. A few hours, a few days."

"Where?"

"I don't know."

He grinned. "I recommend you figure that out before you leave."

"That's what I'm trying to do." She shook her head. "Alema's dead. Jacen's next."

"Just about everyone I know plans to be the one to confront Jacen Solo. Grand Master Skywalker, Ben Skywalker, half the Jedi Knights, all the Jedi Masters . . . every pilot I know plans to be there in a starfighter the next time he's in one. So I suggest you get in line."

"If it is someone else, I won't complain. But if it has to be me, I want to be ready. *You* showed me I wasn't." She took a moment to consider her words. "I'm his twin. I have as much power as he does . . . potentially. But he's had training I haven't. I need to counter it with training *he* hasn't had. And the sort of ingenuity you showed me."

He watched her in the deepening shadows. "I'll give you whatever help I can. But I think Alema was just about my match. Jacen . . . he's far more dangerous."

"I know. But I wanted you to understand that you have helped me. Helped me get this far. I just have to get farther. And that means going away."

He nodded. "Just remember who you are. That should mean everything to you. And remember that it means nothing to Jacen anymore. He's already shown that he cares nothing for the families of those he tortures and kills."

"Those he tortures and kills." Jaina froze as something occurred to her. "Those he tortures and kills . . ."

"What is it?"

"Oh, no." She shook her head, almost unaware of Jag, as the thought took hold. "I can't."

"You can't *what*?"

She looked at him, hoping that something in his expression or words might tell her why her idea was wrong, bad.

But it wasn't. It was the only answer. It was inevitable.

She rose. "I have to go."

"I know; you said that."

"But now I know where. I need to make some preparations. Don't worry: I'll say good-bye before I leave."

She turned away from his baffled expression and headed back to the outpost. Toward her mission. Toward an act of last resort.

Toward her teacher.

Read on for a preview of Karen Traviss's

REVELATION

The eighth novel in
the thrilling new *Star Wars* epic!

My brother died in the Yuuzhan Vong War.

Not Anakin: Jacen.

It's taken me years to work that out, but I should have seen it from the start. Jacen, the brother I loved, my twin, never came home. It just looked as if he did.

I think the core of Jacen probably died in the Embrace of Pain, at the hands of Vergere and the Yuuzhan Vong. Whatever came back was another person; a total stranger.

It's the only explanation for what he's become.

So that's why I've reached the point of doing something utterly unthinkable, because the unthinkable is the last card we have left to play, the only way I can stop Jacen and his war from swallowing the whole galaxy. It was the Mandalorian crushgaunts that made up my mind. As Jag has proven, they certainly work. They're nasty weapons. Mandalorian iron—*beskar*—is pretty well nearly lightsaber-proof.

I almost expected the things to detonate when Dad

opened the package. Since when did Boba Fett ever send my father gifts?

Since his daughter was tortured to death by my brother, actually. We've been waiting for Fett's revenge ever since, but so far . . . nothing. Just the gift of crushgaunts and armor plate, all made from Mandalorian iron.

So I'm packing for a journey I didn't think I'd ever make. I'll give Jag this much: he never said *I told you so*. He's the one who said I needed to learn from someone who had a track record in bringing down Jedi.

If anyone can stop Jacen, then, it's me. I'm his equal, and I'm the Sword of the Jedi. But I just don't have his . . . training. I've no idea what he learned from Lumiya, let alone what he picked up on his travels during those five years. But he'll make a mistake sooner or later. He's way too cocky not to overestimate himself.

I just hope it's sooner. And if being a Sith made Jacen invincible, he'd have taken over the galaxy by now.

I have a chance, and Fett's going to help me make the most of it.

It can't be that hard to find him. He's a bounty hunter, so I'll hire him like any other client, except I'm not just any other client—I'm Han Solo's daughter, and I'm a Jedi, and Fett has spent a lifetime hunting us.

And now I'm asking him to train me to hunt and capture my own brother.

For all I know, he'll laugh in my face—if he ever laughs, that is—and tell me to get losr. But I have to ask him. Swallow pride, eat humble pie, and beg if need be. Dad seems to have thawed a little toward him; I still despise him.

But if he says yes—I swear I'll be the best pupil he's ever had. Come on, Fett: show me how it's done.

When the nation is in its darkest peril, the great warrior-sailor Darakaer shall be summoned from his eternal sleep by a rhythm beaten on his ancient drum. For his final pledge was that he would come to our aid when the drum sounded, and that we should call him when we sailed to meet the foe.

— Irmenu folk legend

JEDI OUTPOST, ENDOR: TWELVE WEEKS AFTER THE DEATH OF MARA JADE SKYWALKER

Ben Skywalker had thought it would be a simple matter of thumbing his lightsaber to life—screaming vengeance or choked into silent grief, he didn't care which—and slicing Jacen Solo's head from his body.

He sat flicking the blade on and off, staring down the shaft of blue energy and watching it vanish only to snap back into vivid life over and over again. He saw his mother, who couldn't be summoned back again at the flick of a switch, although he would have given the rest of his life for one more chance to tell her how much he loved her.

But the image that he wanted to erase yet couldn't was Jacen Solo's face. So many people said Jacen was a stranger now, but a stranger was someone you never loved or looked up to, and so their brutality or careless cruelty was just repellent detail, the distant stuff of holonews bulletins. Family, though . . . family could hurt you like nobody else, and they didn't even have to torture you like Jacen did to leave scars.

The face of Jacen that Ben would recall until the day he died was the one he saw on Kavan while he sat with his mother's body, the face that promised Ben they'd get whoever did that to her. And that was why it simply would *not* go away; there was something wrong about that face, something missing, or something there that shouldn't have been. Ben picked away at the memory, checking his chrono every few minutes, convinced that he'd been waiting for Aunt Leia for hours.

I had the chance to kill him. Dad stopped me. Maybe . . . maybe I could have killed Jacen without turning dark. Will I ever get another chance?

Jedi had killed Sith before. They said Qui-Gon Jinn killed a Sith on Naboo, but nobody thought it was an instant passport to the dark side, because dirty jobs had to be done. Ben had thought his absolute, all-consuming need to destroy Jacen had passed; but it hadn't, and neither had his grief. It had simply shifted position. It ebbed and flowed, some days worse than others. He would *not* get over it. He would learn to live with loss—somehow—but the galaxy had changed and would never return to normal; it was an alternate universe, nearly familiar enough for him to navigate, but where the most important landmarks were gone forever.

Now he was ready to pour his heart out to Leia. There were some things he wasn't ready to tell his father; Luke

Skywalker might have looked as if he was dealing with his grief, but Ben knew better, and if he told him what he really thought . . . Dad would kill Jacen, he was sure of it. He'd snap. Ben had to be the responsible one now.

But if I'm wrong . . . I'll only hurt Dad more.

Nothing added up.

I don't believe Alema killed Mom, Sith sphere or not. I just don't.

How did Jacen know where to find me on Kavan?

How did he know I was there with my mother's body?

Ben had thought it was odd at the time, even when the shock of finding her body had nearly paralyzed him. But even in shock, he'd had the presence of mind to record evidence at the scene, every bit of data he could grab, just as Captain Shevu had taught him. Jacen had mind-rubbed him once: he wasn't going to let him rewrite history again.

And that was my instinctive reaction. Even when I found Mom dead . . . something inside me said that was important. I'll trust that.

Jedi would have said it was the certainty of the Force; cops like Captain Shevu would have said that Ben's investigative training had kicked in. Either way, Ben had more questions than he had answers. But he was more sure each passing day that Jacen, his own cousin, his own flesh and blood, really had killed his mother.

He waited.

Eventually he heard two sets of footsteps coming down the passage, and had a sinking feeling that Luke might have met Leia in passing and decided to tag along. But when the doors opened, it was Leia and Jaina.

"Ben?" Leia always had that calming tone that said everything was under control, even when it wasn't. "What's wrong?"

"I've got some difficult things to say," he said. "You might not thank me, but I can't sit on it any longer."

The accusation was meant solely for Leia, and for a moment he was reluctant to blurt it out in front of Jaina as well. But she needed to hear it.

"You know you can tell me anything," Leia said. "Do you want Jaina to leave us alone?"

"No, no. As long as you don't rush off and tell Dad, because he thinks I'm over the Jacen thing now, and I don't want to start him worrying again."

Jaina sat down next to him, leaning forward, as if she was ready to hug him if he burst into tears. "It's okay. I won't say a word, and Mom's the diplomat. What's so bad that you can't tell Uncle Luke?"

Cut to the chase. The longer he built up to it, the worse it would be. Ben concentrated on calm, rational language.

"I don't think Alema Rar killed my mother," he said. The words hung in the air as if he could see them. "I still think Jacen did."

Leia just stood there, arms folded, but she didn't react. Jaina shifted a fraction on the seat. If anything, they seemed . . . embarrassed. He waited in the agonizing silence.

"What makes you think that?" Leia asked at last.

"I'm not going to rely on what I feel," Ben said. "Even though I feel it. I'm going by things that don't add up. You know what police look for? Captain Shevu taught me. Motive, means, opportunity. And family doesn't seem to mean much to Jacen. Look at the things he's done to you and Uncle Han." Ben recalled Jaina's sudden exit from the Galactic Alliance military. "And you, Jaina. Look what he tried to do to *you*."

"I know Jacen's doing some terrible things, but let's go through this a step at a time," Leia said. "You've accused him before, but we're all pretty messed up lately. Why is this still eating at you?"

"The way he found me on Kavan."

"He's good at finding people in the Force, Ben."

"I was *hiding*. Doing my shutdown act. He's not the only Jedi who can do that—he taught me to do it, and I taught Mom. I've even shown Dad how to do it, and he'll tell you—once you switch out, even Master Amazing Super-Smart Jacen shouldn't have been able to find me. And he still walked straight up to me in a tunnel on a deserted planet that's the back end of beyond. That's not luck, and it's not finding me in the Force. He *knew*. And then there was the Sith meditation sphere that Lumiya had."

He'd kept it to himself all this time. The longer you kept a secret, the harder it got. If only he'd disobeyed Jacen and told Dad about the thing. If only . . . maybe Mom would have still been alive.

Ben would never know.

"What about the sphere?" said Jaina.

"I found it on Ziost. I handed it over to Jacen when I docked it in the *Anakin Solo*. Next time I see it, Lumiya's driving."

Leia sucked in a little breath. "Lumiya was adept at taking what she wanted."

"The *Anakin Solo* might be slack when it comes to stopping infiltrators, Aunt Leia, but I can't see Lumiya just wandering in and stealing the sphere without someone knowing about it."

"Okay, file all that under unexplained. How about motive?"

Jaina seemed to be holding her breath. Leia looked away for a moment as if she was weighing the evidence. It didn't amount to much—yet.

"How about the fact that Mara was in his way, like any good Jedi?" said Jaina sourly.

"No, let's hear Ben's view."

Ben was theorizing now. "I spent a lot of time telling Mom about all the things Jacen was asking me to do in the Guard, and I could see it made her mad. I'm sure she bawled him out."

"Okay, so that's motive, maybe. Now let's look at means."

"Only a really skilled Jedi could ever take down Mom. Look at all the stuff Jacen can do."

"But poison? That's Alema's trademark."

"So it's obvious to use it to draw suspicion elsewhere, isn't it?"

"Sweetheart, Alema *had the sphere*. She was in league with Lumiya. We *know* that. And I'm sure Captain Shevu would confirm that people stick with one method of killing that they feel confident using. Alema spent the last year trying to kill as many of us as she could."

Ben was off and running down the behavioral path now. "Okay, Alema was crazy, but she didn't have a motive for killing *Mom*. It was always about you and Uncle Han." He shook his head. "I don't buy it, because she'd have bragged about it to Jag if she'd done it. She'd have wanted us to know she got in one good shot, to hurt us all, to hurt *you*. And then there's opportunity. She was in the area, yes, but we also know for sure that Jacen was in the Hapan system around the time it happened."

Leia really looked as if she was taking it seriously. She hadn't rolled her eyes or told him he was being stupid, or even rushed to defend Jacen. That wasn't a surprise given what Jacen had done to her, his own mother.

"Well, it doesn't clear him," she said at last. "But it's not exactly enough to take to a judge, is it? He could have been in the Hapan system planning to kidnap Allana."

It was a good alibi. *Jacen couldn't have committed a murder because he was too busy planning an abduction, Your Honor.* Ben strove for a rational tone. "Aunt Leia, why do you think Mom hung on in corporeal form for so long? Why do you think her body disappeared just as Jacen showed up at her funeral? Don't you think the Force might be saying something to us? I can't stop thinking about it. I've turned it over and over in my head for weeks. I daren't discuss it with Dad. But it's driving me crazy."

Leia took a few steps forward and squatted in front of him to put her hands on his knees. "Ben, you said you recorded everything you could at the scene."

"Yeah, because nobody can mind-rub *that* or tell me I imagined it . . ."

"Have you found anything in the recordings?"

Ben stood his ground. He was sure, more sure every day now. "Not yet."

"Okay."

"I'm going to find out exactly what happened, Aunt Leia. I *have* to, and I'm going to do it by the book, because I need to be certain or I won't be able to live with it."

"What if you find evidence that it's not Jacen?" asked Jaina. "Are you going to accept what the provable facts tell you?"

Ben had committed himself to take the rational, legal path rather than that of intuition and Force senses. "I don't want to get the wrong person. Whatever I feel about Jacen for the other things he did to me, I don't want to pin it on him if that means Mom's real killer is still walking around. And if it really was Alema—well, fine. The result's the same."

Jaina looked into his face for a few long moments and

then smiled sadly. With Leia still squatting in front of him, wearing that same sorrowful expression, Ben felt pinned down by their tolerant doubt. Maybe they were humoring him. Well, it didn't matter. He'd stated his case, and he was going to prove it, because he couldn't carry on with his life until he got answers.

And he *would* carry on with his life. When Jori Lekauf had been killed saving him, and he'd been drowning in guilt, Mara had told him that the best way to honor that sacrifice was to live well, to the maximum, and not waste a gift so dearly bought.

He'd do that for his mother. He'd live for *her.*

STAR WARS®

LEGACY OF THE FORCE

Read each book in the series

Book 1
Betrayal
by Aaron Allston
Hardcover • On sale 5/30/06
Paperback • On sale 5/1/07

Book 2
Bloodlines
by Karen Traviss
Paperback • On sale 8/29/06

Book 3
Tempest
by Troy Denning
Paperback • On sale 11/28/06

Book 4
Exile
by Aaron Allston
Paperback • On sale 2/27/07

Book 5
Sacrifice
by Karen Traviss
Hardcover • On sale 5/29/07
Paperback • On sale 4/29/08

Book 6
Inferno
by Troy Denning
Paperback • On sale 8/28/07

Book 7
Fury
by Aaron Allston
Paperback • On sale 11/27/07

Book 8
Revelation
by Karen Traviss
Paperback • On sale 2/26/08

Book 9
Invincible
by Troy Denning
Hardcover • On sale 5/20/08